THE EYES

A face swam be_____ while he lay strapped to a bench in some dim place, half glimpsed through the pain and agony of his aching head. Out of the familiar face glared the gaze of the Unclean, the eyes gleaming with mockery and triumph.

Hiero writhed frantically against the bonds that held him fast. The movement brought another face into view. From the eyes came the same blaze of pure evil, with something else added—madness mixed with the malign blasphemy which was the essence of the Unclean.

He felt a fresh stab in his arm and saw a hand holding a glass tube capped with a bloody needle.

"We can kill him later," came a harsh whisper. "Not now. The Princess would know. They say this drug kills the mind powers, but they warn us to be wary. He must die, but away—far away."

Then the pain became too great to fight, and Hiero fainted.

❖ ❖ ❖

"...the many and wonderful creatures [Hiero] encounters in this world, and the circumstances in which they're encountered, are endlessly diverting."
—Isaac Asimov's Science Fiction Magazine

By Sterling E. Lanier
Published by Ballantine Books:

HIERO'S JOURNEY

MENACE UNDER MARSWOOD

THE UNFORSAKEN HIERO

To Mr. Worthington who taught the author to look behind History

THE UNFORSAKEN HIERO

❖

STERLING E. LANIER

Sterling Lanier

1988

A DEL REY BOOK

BALLANTINE BOOKS • NEW YORK

A Del Rey Book
Published by Ballantine Books

Copyright © 1983 by Sterling E. Lanier

All rights reserved under International and Pan-American Copyright Conventions. Published in the United States by Ballantine Books, a division of Random House, Inc., New York, and simultaneously in Canada by Random House of Canada Limited, Toronto.

Library of Congress Catalog Card Number: 82-20793

ISBN: 0-345-30228-1

Printed in Canada

First Hardcover Edition: May 1983
First Paperback Edition: April 1984
Third Printing: July 1987

Cover art by Darrell K. Sweet

For Brother Pete, AKA Berwick B. Lanier,
who, for some reason I have never fathomed,
remains my fan.

CONTENTS

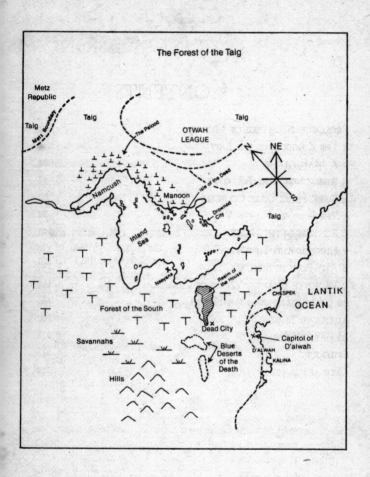

The Forest of the Taig

PROLOGUE:
A CHANGE OF MISSION

IN THE FIVE THOUSAND YEARS THAT HAD PASSED SINCE THE Death, the world had changed. Much of the land was covered with vast forests or desert wastelands. What had once been five lakes now formed a single Inland Sea. The climate was warmer, since the earth was deep in an interglacial period. Some species of plants and animals had died, and others had evolved in strange ways.

In what had once been western Canada, the Metz Republic was struggling to preserve a measure of civilization and to regain lost knowledge, guided by the scholar-priests of the Abbeys. But more and more, they were losing to the Unclean, a Dark Brotherhood of those who sought to destroy normal humanity and subvert natural law to evil purposes. Even the mental powers developed by the Abbeys could not protect them from the latest attacks of the Unclean and their foully mutated beast hordes, the Leemutes.

The Most Reverend Abbot Kulase Demero was sure that a means to defeat the Unclean might be found among all the records and artifacts collected from the past and stored in the Abbey's central files. But the task of gathering and collating all that seemingly random information required time and man-power that he did not have. Once, he knew, such work had been done by something called a computer. Abbot Demero had no computer—but he had evidence that such a device might still exist, buried far to the south.

To find and bring back the computer, however, would be an endeavor fraught with peril. Little was known of the region south of the Inland Sea, and the way there led through lands that were dominated by the Unclean. For this dangerous mission, Abbot Demero chose his former student, Per Hiero Des-

1

teen, a warrior-priest who had proved his ability as Rover and Senior Killman in the Frontier Guards.

Hiero set forth, mounted on his morse Klootz, an evolved moose. The intelligent and loyal animal was controlled telepathically and was an invaluable ally against any foe. They were soon joined by Gorm, a young bear whose Elders had sent him to study human ways. Gorm gave Hiero mental warning that the Unclean had sent an adept to waylay him. The bear helped defeat the adept and later the hordes of loathsome Leemutes the Unclean began mustering against the companions.

Then Hiero rescued a young girl from a tribe that was torturing her. Her name was Luchare, and she claimed to be a princess of D'alwah, a nation on the Lantik Ocean coast. She told of fleeing from an unwelcome marriage, of being caught by slavers, and finally of being sold to the torturers. She was unlike any human Hiero had seen, since her skin was very dark and her hair was tightly curled; his people, the Metz, were straight of hair and had reddish skins, since they were descendants of the *Metis*, crossbreeds of French Canadians and Indians.

Later, Hiero was captured by the Unclean. In their stronghold, his mental powers were nullified by the perverted science of the adepts, but he learned to use a hitherto unknown band of mental power. With it, he seized the mind of an adept and forced the man to help him escape.

Reunited with his companions, Hiero continued to explore his new abilities, while training Luchare in the use of her growing mental powers. They fled eastward, with the Unclean in hot pursuit. But progress became increasingly difficult. Eventually, they were trapped in the half-submerged ruins of an ancient city.

They were saved by the sudden appearance of an Elevener, one of the mysterious wanderers who followed the so-called Eleventh Commandment: "Thou shalt not destroy the Earth nor the life thereon." Brother Aldo used his Elevener power over animals to call up a monster from the depths to destroy the Unclean attackers. Then, joining the companions, he led them to a ship and persuaded Captain Gimp to give them passage across the Inland Sea.

They were pursued and attacked by the Unclean's power-driven destroyers, but were able to reach the southern shore of the sea before their ship was wrecked. Together with Captain Gimp and the sailors, the companions headed into the unknown dangers of the great southern forest—their only route to safety and the probable location of the computer Hiero sought.

After an encounter with a strange race of women who lived in the trees, they approached the area indicated on Hiero's ancient map. There, with the help of Gorm, Hiero finally located an entrance to a vast underground installation, filled with mysterious machinery.

Before he could complete his investigation, the forces of the Unclean began pouring into the underground complex. Hiero had barely time to set a timing device Brother Aldo indicated. Then he and his companions were forced to flee. From a safe distance, they watched as a tremendous explosion destroyed the entire area. If a computer had ever been there, it was now lost forever.

Then Brother Aldo pointed to what Luchare had discovered underground and brought up with her. She was holding a work in three volumes entitled *Principles of a Basic Computer*! With that information, the Abbeys could build their own device. Hiero's mission was accomplished. Now all he had to do was return the books to Abbot Demero in the North.

But Brother Aldo had other plans for him.

There were two fires burning in the night, providing the only lights on the dark plain. A small group was scattered about one. A short distance away, Hiero and Luchare sat by the other, facing Brother Aldo. The old man was staring into the flames, his tightly curled white beard standing out brightly against skin that was as dark as that of Luchare.

"I must go north at once," Brother Aldo said at last. "I must arouse those of my Brotherhood. We have sought peace for many lives, but now there is no peace. Destruction is coming upon us, and we must take action against it. It is no longer enough to watch and study the foe." Sadness deepened the lines on his face, momentarily revealing his great age.

Hiero waited in silence. His skin was lighter and redder in hue than that of his companions, and his black hair was coarse and straight, trimmed just below the ears in a short bob. With his hawk nose and sturdy, lithe frame, he might almost have been one of his remote Amerindian forebears, save for the neat mustache; the facial hair indicated the Caucasoid admixture of his once despised ancestry.

Beside him, Luchare seemed to be drowsing, her head resting against his shoulder. He tightened his arm around her waist, smiling fondly. To his right, he could see that Captain Gimp and the sea rovers were still talking around their fire. Off to his left, the line of the great forest towered in the dark. He wondered what the strange women of the trees and their queen Vilah-ree were doing. Would he ever see one of them again? With an effort, he brought his mind back to the present as Brother Aldo began speaking again.

"We have done well, this far," the old man said. "We've blocked the Unclean, destroyed many of them, and we have this." He pointed to the packet that held the lost volumes of the ancients. "You have accomplished your mission, Per Hiero. But your work is not done. The next danger comes from the South. And it is there that you must go—you and Luchare!"

"What about the books?" Hiero protested. "I am supposed to get them to Abbot Demero as fast as I can. These southern wastes are not my territory. I came here only to get the knowledge we need in the North."

The Elevener smiled faintly. "Don't worry about Demero, my boy. The books will go north with me. Your abbot will approve. I know Demero—have known him longer than you have lived. Who do you think put me on watch for you? Why do you think I was so handy when you were trapped in the drowned city? Think about it for a moment."

Hiero grunted in surprise. But Aldo's words explained many things. It had been no accident, no fortunate coincidence, that had brought the Elevener to aid them so opportunely. How many others had somehow been alerted to watch over this mission? Hiero grinned ruefully. "I should have guessed that Demero would have a few extra tricks he never told me about," he admitted.

Brother Aldo chuckled, then sobered quickly. "I'll leave for the North at dawn. I'll take Gimp and his men with me. We'll get a boat somehow; there are many ways. But I must also take Gorm with me. Call him."

Hiero sent a rapid mind call on the wavelength of the young bear. A moment later, the burly shape of Gorm padded up to them from where he had been curled in apparent sleep. *Does no other ever sleep around here?* came a mental mumble as the bear flopped his bulk down beside them.

Hiero laughed. *You do nothing but sleep while we have to do all the hard thinking and planning.* He eyed Gorm appraisingly. It was fantastic that this strange folk had hardly been noticed by the Abbey students. Their brains were quite as good as human minds, and only their desire for privacy had kept them so long hidden. The Death had caused strange and horrible mutations, but it had also created wonders, and one of those was the race of Gorm, the silent and hidden bear folk, whose Wise Ones had sent Gorm out to gather knowledge.

You want me to go north with the Old One here, came Gorm's thought. He seemed quite placid, and his brain waves were clear and undisturbed.

"I don't want you to go anywhere away from me," Hiero said aloud, then put the idea into thought. He was conscious of how much he would miss this furry friend. *But Brother Aldo thinks it might be best if you went north with him and got back in touch with the Wise Ones of your folk.*

To Hiero's surprise, Brother Aldo had picked up his thoughts, those he meant to be private as well as those to the bear: Now the old man sent a message meant for both Hiero and Gorm.

Listen well, both of you. This is a great struggle between that which is evil and vile and that which we believe to be good and blessed. The high Councils of the Unclean are sealed to us. But my Order has watched them for many years, back beyond the life span of the remotest grandsire of any here. They seek universal domination and they would restore the evils that brought The Death to the world.

We must work together, we of the honest and life-preserving ones of whatever form. We must fight them wherever they appear. There is great evil rising in the South, in D'alwah and its neighbors. I want Hiero to go there with Luchare, to her ancient kingdom, the nation where I was once a native and which I know well. And you, Gorm, I want to go north and make report to your Elders, to tell them of our need. What say you?

There was an instant of mental silence. Then an ursine thought came in answer. *I must go. I understand some of what you think. It must be so, for it is the charge laid upon me by the Wise Ones of my people. Now can I sleep?*

Suiting action to thought, Gorm got up and wandered off into the dark, where they could hear him curling up again.

"Well, Hiero," Brother Aldo said, "we can use speech again. All this thought sending wears one out, eh?" He smiled.

Hiero found little to smile about. "Even if Abbot Demero might agree to let me go, what do you think I can do down in the South? I know little of D'alwah, save for what Luchare has told me. How can I help in a strange country with unknown laws and rules of behavior? What can I do in a foreign land without friends, except for this one?" He bent his cheek to nuzzle the mop of tight black curls that lay on his shoulder.

Luchare looked up at him with eyes that were clear, with no sign of sleep in them. "What can you do? Look, Per Hiero Desteen, have you forgotten who I am? My father is King Danyale of D'alwah, and I'm his only heir. You're my husband. You'll be a prince of the unknown North. Everyone will accept you." She looked over at Brother Aldo. "You have many Eleveners there, don't you? I've seen them helping the village people when there's trouble. That means we have allies there— though not in public. And we'll have Klootz."

She whistled sharply and waved an arm over her head. Hiero smiled as a towering shape paced up to the girl, massive hooves clicking on bits of gravel as it came. A giant head with blubber lips and a drooping snout lowered itself so that the huge, soft nose touched her hair briefly. Then the morse stood quietly waiting to see why he had been summoned.

When humanity began to pick itself up after The Death, the horses were gone, vanished without a trace. In the far North, the reviving structure of the Abbeys and their dependent farms tried many other animals and found these mutated descendants of the moose to be best. Hiero and Klootz had chosen each other at the annual calf-pick years before, and they had never been separated.

I wonder how he'll like the South, Hiero thought to his mate and the older man. *Nothing like him there. Will the people be afraid of him?*

"Not afraid," Luchare answered, stroking a leg of the morse. "He would be admired as a creature no one had ever seen before. He would add to your prestige."

Hiero stood up and began to stroke the enormous, palmate antlers with careful fingers, peeling off the velvet where it came away easily. He could feel the heat underneath where this outer cover of the new antlers was not ready. Klootz lipped his shoulder affectionately.

Aldo resumed his argument. "Consider what you have already done in a land foreign to you and with only the help of friends you found along the way. You've saved a princess, crossed the great Inland Sea, and fought and beaten some of our worst enemies. And you've accomplished a nearly impossible mission."

"You've done what no one else could have done," Luchare added when Aldo stopped. "You have defeated the one who calls himself S'duna, the chief of their horrid Blue Circle. Now you can go on to be a leader of my people."

Hiero looked down at her, and his heart filled with this love that was greater than he had ever known before. Then he thought of Abbot Demero, the grim old warrior who had sent him on this mission. Would the ruler of the Abbey Council approve of his going south with a new wife and a new task? He seemed to see the lined old face in his mind, and it was smiling at him. A sign? Hiero shrugged at the idea and then thought again. Perhaps he was picking up a vague and transient thought from far away. He smiled and looked at Brother Aldo, another wise old man who had gone to war because he had no choice in his own soul.

"Tell Gimp that you'll leave for the North at dawn. Luchare and I will go south on Klootz. I assume that you can communicate with your Eleveners in the South? Then send me word and we'll open a channel of messages." He laughed a little sourly. "You say you know Abbot Demero. Then you can keep him off my back and not let me be cursed and expelled from the church. Now let's get a little sleep."

✤ 1 ✤

THE KINGDOM OF THE EAST

GOLDEN SUNLIGHT STREAMED THROUGH THE NARROW WINdows of the palace, and a great gong boomed, announcing that day had come again to mighty D'alwah. The sound was echoed and re-echoed from far and near as the watch on the walls and the patrols along the bridges and covered ways answered with their smaller strikers of ringing metal. The whole walled city pealed and rang, a vibrant diapason of challenging sound. Hiero sat up in bed with a jerk, covering his ears against the clamor and muttering darkly.

"You do that every morning," Luchare's voice said. "After all the time we've been here, I should think you'd be used to the gong."

He pried his eyes open to see her dressed and seated at her mirror, coloring her lips and her eyelashes with the bluish paste which was currently the height of fashion at court. He pursed his lips and made a light spitting noise.

She looked around and grinned merrily. "Don't be so stiff. I have to look my best when I'm officially entertaining the noble ladies at breakfast. And what kept you up till all hours last night? Talking religion with our high priest again?"

"Umm." He'd found the breakfast she had ordered for him on a tray beside the bed and he began eating. "Old Markama isn't bad for a high priest—for a D'alwah high priest, that is. But, my God, what has happened to the church down here? *Celibate* priests! And all these so-called monasteries where the nobles send their unwanted young of both sexes to paint wooden pictures or sew and pray all day—and to live in silence and *chastity*! It's as if the Unclean were already in control and determined to make people go crazy." His face became suddenly serious. "And I can't be sure that this isn't a hotbed of

8

the Unclean with their minions all wearing mechanical mind shields."

"Hiero!" Her face grew troubled as she stared at him. "I know you really believe that. You may even be right. But you haven't found any proof—just a few people whose minds you can't read. And you told me when you were training me that a lot of people have natural screens, people who are unaware of it themselves."

He sighed and dropped the subject, while she turned the conversation to the Court Ball that was being given in the palace that evening. But after she left for her official duties, he dressed and moved slowly out of the palace and into the maze of the city, still brooding as he exercised his legs.

There was something ugly and dangerous going on in the royal castle. He could feel it, though no clear thoughts came through to him. But there was a deep undercurrent of hatred, impossible to disguise from someone who had been through all he had with the Unclean and their allies.

Yet he had been treated very well. When he and Luchare appeared on Klootz, the guard at the main gate had saluted, let them through, and given her full royal honors. An hour later, he had been closeted with Luchare and her father, Danyale IX, hereditary ruler of the sovereign state of D'alwah.

To Hiero's surprise, he liked the king, and Danyale made it plain that he liked his new son-in-law.

The king was a large, heavy man, still muscular, but inclining a little to fat, now that he had passed the half-century mark. His curly, graying hair was worn short, and his face was handsome and open over his mustache and beard. His kilts and robes were of a magnificent weave and color, and he wore many rings and pendants. But he was never without a long, two-edged sword whose handle was plain and worn. His handgrip was firm and hard.

Was this the brutal tyrant whose only daughter had fled into the wilderness to avoid a marriage foisted upon her by her dynastic-minded father, as Luchare had claimed?

Danyale brought the matter up while he and Hiero sat on the edge of a parapet of the palace. The ever-present guards had been waved out of earshot and lounged some distance away, conversing in low tones and watching both their ruler and their new prince.

"Look, Hiero, I know what Luchare must have told you about that business of marrying her off to Efrem. But all my nobles insisted—the whole council, including the church fathers. What was I to do? God knows, we must have allies. Chespek was all there was. Efrem is afraid of me, and I thought I could control him, see that he didn't harm the girl. I know the bastard's reputation as well as she does. But, damn it, this kind of thing is part of being a king. And with my only son dead . . ." He looked into Hiero's eyes and said nothing further for a moment.

"I understand," the Metz priest said quietly. "The realm has to come first, all the time." He rather admired the older man. It couldn't be easy for the king to apologize for something he saw as a vital, standard matter of politics.

There was no trouble in communication. Hiero was a master linguist, and Luchare had coached him in the speech of D'alwah for weeks as they journeyed toward her home.

"What will Efrem do now?" Hiero's question was only partly idle. The priests, awed by his powers and knowledge of the past, had told him much, and he had learned more by mind search. But, as a matter of honor, he could not probe Luchare's father. And he needed to know what the man thought, how his mind worked, and what his capabilities were. If D'alwah were to be protected from the Unclean and their grim allies—if it were to be enlisted on the side of the Abbeys—then much still had to be learned.

Danyale's answer was a snort of contempt. "He'll fume in private, then do whatever the priests tell him when he goes to confession for half-murdering some slave girl. Forget him." He eyed Hiero, his wariness apparent all at once. "You seem to have pull with the Church Universal, my boy. Do the nobles up your way control the priests? Down here it has been a long, constant struggle to keep the power in my hands and out of theirs—or worse, from some puppet whom they might raise up against me. You seem to know all their priestly secrets and a lot of your own as well. You could be of much help to me," he added. The attempt was regrettable, Hiero thought; Danyale was no intriguer, but a decent, if not-too-bright, soldier, trapped in a decadent court and surrounded by schemers, both civil and ecclesiastic.

"We do things differently," he evaded. "Our nobles and

gentry are so busy fighting the Unclean that we learned long ago to be one pillar of the state and support the church as the other. And," he added, as if in afterthought, "of course we have no actual king, but only a noble, supreme Council with both church and civil members." It was only half a lie, since the Abbey Council was actually that. The fact that there were no nobles could wait until Hiero and the Metz Republic were ready.

"Well," Danyale said heavily, "I suppose you have secrets, too. I find the world harder and harder to understand." He looked up, a smile tugging at the corner of his full lips. "One thing, though. I'm damn glad to have you as a son-in-law, prince or no prince. Oddly enough, I love my daughter and I'm glad to see her happy. But more than that——" He leaned over and tapped Hiero's knee. "I think you're going to be valuable to me, my boy—to me and to D'alwah."

He rose, clapped the Metz on the shoulder, and strode off to his day's duties. He was not an unkingly figure, Hiero reflected, and perhaps somewhat more clever than he appeared.

There were other meetings of a similar nature and meetings with the great men of the kingdom also. Markama, the archpriest, was a decent enough old man and could have exerted great power, had he possessed the basic ability to lead. But he was obsessed with ritual and hieratic obscurantism. But at least he was no enemy, being in awe of Hiero's knowledge, both of church secrets and of the Unclean, whom he truly feared and detested.

Most of the work of the church—the accounts, administration, schools, and such—seemed to be in the hands of one Joseato, a priest just below the archpriest in rank, a thin, colorless bureaucrat who always carried bundles of parchment and had a perpetually distracted air. Hiero found nothing special to dislike about the man. But Joseato had a shielded mind, which was a big factor to consider. Could he have a bluish metal locket under his robes, a mechanical mind screen of the Unclean? Of course, as Luchare had pointed out, the shield could be innate, as many were, or the result of the sketchy mental training which even the southern church had not completely lost. There was no way of telling what power, mental or physical, impelled a good mind shield, and he could hardly ask the priest to strip. Joseato simply had to be watched, as far as that was possible.

He was still pondering as he ceased wandering and turned back toward the palace stables. There were too many shielded minds that needed watching. There was Count Ghiftah Hamili, for instance, a fine soldier as well as a great noble and land-owner. The youngish, quiet man had been a suitor at one time for Luchare's hand and was much at court. Although friendly enough, he had a disconcerting gaze which the Metz priest found fixed on himself far too often for his liking.

But at least Hiero had found one sure friend. A senior lay brother of the Eleveners had approached him, alerted through the agency of Aldo and the underground network of the Brother-hood. The fact that Mitrash was a lieutenant of the palace guard made things even better. Day or night, he could come and go without suspicion within the well-protected precincts of the inner fortress. The balding, middle-aged veteran exuded com-petence. Already, he and Hiero had held several conferences late at night.

The trouble was that Mitrash did not know very much. While eager to be helpful, he was simply a good, honest soldier who had been recruited as an acolyte by the Order and placed in the palace as an observer. He was deeply worried about the inner rot and subversion he saw about him throughout the kingdom, but he was not a mental master like Aldo. He had many contacts and could reach other members of the Order, but this took time. And he was mind-shielded—a good thing in his case. Hiero had requested that Mitrash be assigned as captain of his bodyguard, but the military red tape of D'alwah was no different from that of any other army. Meanwhile, the man was near at hand to guard Luchare if her spouse were called away.

Then the stables were ahead, and it was time to exercise Klootz and Hiero's new mount, a hopper named Segi.

The giant morse was pleased to see Hiero and butted him playfully while being led from his stall by awed grooms. No one in D'alwah had ever seen or heard of a morse, and the great, antlered creature filled everyone with astonished respect, much of which accrued to his rider. Well aware of this, Hiero took every opportunity to display himself on the huge, swart back before the crowd that usually gathered at the exercise grounds to see them.

Behind the morse came Segi, ridden by a groom. At the appearance of the jumper, the mighty barrel of Klootz swelled in rage; had the morse been able to catch Segi alone, he would have made pulp of his rival, since the idea of Hiero on another animal's back was intolerable. Segi seemed well aware of this feeling and gave Klootz a wide berth.

Segi was a hopper, the chosen mount of the cavalry of D'alwah, another mutated replacement mankind had found for the long-extinct horse. Friendly and mild-mannered, Segi towered over his rider by a good six feet. He stood balanced on two giant hind legs and a long, columnar tail. His small forefeet, each no longer than a tall man's arm, were tucked up high on his broad chest. Clothed in smooth, tan fur, with a white blaze on his forehead and great, erect ears cocked first one way and then another, he looked what he was, the prize of the king's stud and a much-valued wedding present to Danyale's new son-in-law.

Hiero knew nothing of the ancestry of the hoppers. But he loved the incredible motion they gave their riders and was determined to learn the complex movements which made mounted drill on hoppers the most fantastic sight that could have been dreamed of by any cavalryman. Segi bore a heavy, almost right-angled saddle high on his back, and its broad girth passed just below his forearms. His jaws carried a snaffle bit, and twin reins led back to the rider. But instead of the conventional stirrups, such as those worn by the morse, a hopper's rider placed his legs in long, stiff sheaths, not unlike expanded versions of the saddle sheath for Hiero's lost thrower. These in turn were secured to the saddle's base and also, by swivels, to a second girth, which was buckled below the first. While difficult to get out of, which was a drawback, these stirrup-boots were absolutely vital. The new prince soon saw why when a guard put a hopper through his paces for the first time. The very high back brace of the saddle also assumed new meaning.

Any ordinary hopper, and Segi was the best, could jump almost fifteen meters from a resting position. Further, the jump could be angled in midair, the mighty tail providing the leverage. At a dead run, or a series of bounds on level terrain, a "full-out" hopper moved at breathtaking speed. Watching a squadron of the household troops drilling at their fastest took Hiero's breath away. Moving in perfect unison, line after line charged, changed direction in the air, and landed in the same matchless formation, never breaking ranks or pausing until the blast of a small brass horn signaled an equally abrupt halt. The long, pennanced lances rose, came to a salute, and were leveled, all in one beautiful fluid motion. Highly trained soldier that he was, Hiero had been enthralled on the spot. With a division of these wonderful creatures and their veteran riders as light cavalry and yet another on the giant morse behind in close support, what an army might one have!

He could have spent the entire day with the hoppers, had he not had a thousand other calls on his time. But he only allowed himself an hour or so, sharing the time exactly with the enraged morse, who paced up and down, snorting with contempt and anger while his master leaped Segi through his exercises under the correction of a time-expired sergeant who now served as royal instructor.

The speed with which their new and exotic prince had mastered his strange mount both amazed and delighted the men of D'alwah. They knew nothing of the mental orders which Hiero used instead of the countless hours they themselves had needed on the drill ground. Segi was by no means as intelligent as Klootz, but he was far from being stupid and took to his new rider at once.

When the exercises were done, Hiero usually took a ride on Klootz, and he always tried to go through the city. D'alwah City was far larger than Kalina, the only other city of the realm, lying many leagues to the south. From his studies and the incessant questions he asked, aided by a fair share of mental eavesdropping, Hiero had managed to acquire a considerable amount of knowledge about his new country. He had taken one all-too-brief trip to the coast and seen for the first time the great, white-topped breakers of the Lantik rolling in to the beach under the high, green dunes. It gave him a strange feeling to think that he was almost certainly the first man of his race ever to have seen both the great ocean of the East and that of the West. Across that foaming sea lay the ultimate in mysteries, Europe, the lost motherland of culture, the home of the original church, long sundered from the children of the western continent. But there was not much time for musings of this nature, on that day or any other.

As he rode through the crowded streets on the great morse, with two hopper-riding guardsmen in front and two behind, the crowds fell back respectfully and caps and helmets were doffed in salute to his rank. Indeed, he looked like a prince, for he was garbed now in purple silk, both the short blouse and the gold-embroidered kilt, while his leather boots were scarlet, as were the supple riding gloves. His beloved short sword hung on his back, but was held now by a cross-belt of gold links. A thin gold coronet supported the purple cap of maintenance. One snow-white osprey plume nodded above his head, secured to his cap by a gemmed brooch of great price. The D'alwahns liked color and what was new and interesting. Their pride was stirred by their new prince and by the bizarre gossip of his adventures and the manner in which he had appeared out of nowhere, bringing their lost princess back to them.

As he acknowledged the salutes by touching his cap, Hiero wondered who in the sea of dark faces did not mean the cheers and the congratulations hurled from every street and balcony. Among those white-toothed smiles and behind some of the shuttered windows lurked enemies, the more dangerous for being unknown. Of that he was certain. Try as he would, he could detect no worse thoughts than the usual leaven of envy from some of the poor and sneers from certain of the nobility who were obsessed with their own ancestry. This was only normal. *Where are the real baddies, boy?* he sent to Klootz, who was preoccupied with picking his way over ancient cobbles slippery with modern refuse. *Where are the Unclean? They're here, Klootz, they're here, that's for certain. How do we find 'em, how do we smoke 'em out, before they come out and get us first?*

A laughing, half-naked girl shouted something funny and coarse about a possible heir. Hiero shrugged helplessly in mock puzzlement, and the crowd screamed with laughter. Yet all the while, he never really relaxed. The enemy was clever, but not perfect. If he watched without ever letting down his guard, and if Luchare did the same, as he had carefully taught her, sooner or later a break might come. Meanwhile, he could only wait and observe.

There was much to observe. Now crossing a plaza before him were men of a religion other than Christianity—something he had not known, except for the Unclean. They worshiped God, but through another prophet, and they revered the crescent moon. They were Mu'amans, dressed in snowy white and with green, flat-topped conical hats. They had a big colony on the southwestern fringe of the kingdom and mostly stayed within it, being great herdsmen and famous breeders of the kaws, the long-horned cattle of the kingdom. For some reason, they despised the hoppers and would have nothing to do with them. But they were mighty runners and made up a fine corps of light infantry, being master bowmen and swordsmen of skill. With their kilts looped up, they could outrun even their own kaws and could keep up the pace for many hours.

Despite their alien rites, their loyalty had never been questioned. Aside from their clothes, they looked like any other D'alwahns, with tight curls and dark faces, sometimes broad of lip and nostril, at other times lean-faced and aquiline. They bowed as Hiero passed, but there was nothing subservient about them, and their sharp eyes carefully appraised him, his weapons and mount, but not his finery.

When they had passed, another company approached, this time a caravan of gaudily clad merchants newly come from the South and stained with travel. Some bore the marks of recent battle, and Hiero knew they would report, as all travelers did, to the court newsmen, whose business it was to know and collate whatever passed throughout the kingdom. Many of these newcomers bore a six-pointed star as a symbol, and Hiero knew them for Davids, the other odd religion of his new country. They seemed identical to all their fellow citizens, being both rich and poor and occupying all places in society. But, though believers in the one God, they had no prophets or saints at all, their priests relying only on certain secret books, never shown to any but coreligionists. Both they and the Mu'amans held high places at court, and some were hereditary nobles; but in private life they kept much to themselves and seldom intermarried with the mainstream of Christianity. Yet Luchare and Danyale trusted them implicitly. "I wish I could be as sure of my fellow churchmen as I am of the Davids and the Mu' amans," the king had said bleakly. And indeed, many of both were in the royal guard and the local militia units which made up the realm's army when assembled.

The street narrowed ahead, and Hiero saw that they were coming to one of the many high-walled bridges which criss-crossed the city. These bridges spanned the numerous canals which ran through the city and far inland as well, linking up a dozen sleepy rivers and also leading to the coastal marshes and estuaries of the Lantik itself. As he approached, Hiero again saw yet a fresh reason for the stone walls of these bridges and the similar ones which lined the canal system. A hideous scaled head, at least two meters long, with fanged jaws still agape in death agony, was thrust on a great iron spike at the bridge's edge, the severed neck dripping scarlet blood into the gutters of the street. As he reined up, Klootz snorted in distaste, stamping his great hooves until the stones rang. One of the rearguard rode his hopper alongside and spoke with the easy familiarity of the long-service man.

"May be a new one to you, Highness. That's a grunter and a damned big one, begging your pardon. I've heard 'em bel-lowing at the moon in the swamps so you'd think you'd go deaf. Funny, but there weren't so many when I was a lad, or so I remember. Must be the bloody things are breeding more. We'll have to build new walls, even in the out-districts, if all I hear be true."

"Have they any use?" the Metz asked. "They look nasty as hell."

"Well, the meat's not bad if you cure it, though it tastes of fish. And the hide makes good shields and such, though it takes a powerful lot of curing. Whether it makes up for the folk and the cattle and hogs the buggers snatch up is something else. If the country folk don't have a well, getting water's a problem. Even a little grunter, not a third that size, can take a kid. I lost a young cousin off a barge some years ago; opened a hatch to look out and the grunter's head come in instead. Hell of a thing, the way they keep swarming into the cities now. Gets worse every year."

Studying the brown, reptilian head and the glassy eyes, Hiero pondered. The guardsman saw no further than effect. But could there be *cause* as well? If the water and boat guards had to be doubled to fight off these deadly vermin—only one of several equally inimical types—would not the kingdom be effectively weakened, with no trace of the directing minds behind the assault? That the Unclean Masters were capable of such a hidden and subtle attack he had no doubt at all. He had seen too much in the North and on his most recent journey not to know better. It was one more factor to ponder over in a complex and chaotic situation.

He crossed the bridge with his little entourage and went on, looping about the city in a lazy arc on his way back to the palace. He was supposed to review the guards in the late afternoon, and there were envoys from the far South to be seen as well. Danyale had been delighted to have his new son-in-law take such an interest in things and was insistent that as many of his subjects as possible both see and hear Hiero. Then there was the great Court Ball to get ready for, the first of the summer ceremonials, with this one being used as well to put the new prince on display.

The thin mouth under Hiero's black mustache curved in a wry smile. To think that he had been forced by Luchare to take dancing lessons! Fortunately, he was not likely to shame her. He had been born with a sense of rhythm, and the dances of the Metz Republic were something he had always excelled at.

Now, as he crossed yet another square, nodding and touching his cap to the continual salutes, a broad smile came to his face. A wildly ridden hopper was bounding toward him from the other side of the plaza. A gaudy figure was waving from its back, maintaining easy but perilous control as the creature leaped over clothing stalls and farmers' wains. The panting animal came to a halt with a thud not an inch from Klootz's disdainful muzzle, and a laughing face under the rider's scarlet turban flashed white teeth in greeting.

"Salutations, most noble prince from the land of ice dragons."

This was Duke Amibale Aeo, Luchare's young cousin, come from his great southern fief only a week ago, but already a favorite of Hiero's, as he was of the whole city's. The son of the king's dead first cousin, only nineteen and still sprouting a first, thin mustache, the boy wore his honors lightly. When not galloping his hopper along the battlements of the castle for a bet, he was hunting the wild river beasts in a one-man canoe. A string of broken hearts lay behind him despite his age, and he could take the strong D'alwahn wine as well as any veteran of the guard. Under the laughter and the bubbling spate of conversation, jest, and gossip, Hiero knew there was a man, if a young one. The slanting black eyes were full of intelligence and wit, and the Metz had noted that when the face was in repose, strong lines etched the narrow, dark features. As he rode along, gossiping gaily, bare to the waist and wearing only a scarlet kilt and boots, Amibale made a fine complement to his companion. The slender, curved sword and dagger at his side proclaimed that he could fight if called upon at a moment's notice.

"All ready for the big ball, Hiero?" he asked. "Wait until you see what I'm wearing. I'll show these stuffy old types around the palace what a Prince of the Blood ought to look like for a change. I hope you and Luchare have something special to knock their eyes out with. Not that I worry about her. But you, you drab northerner, I hear it took the guard to get you out of that leather suit you arrived in."

"We're coming as man and wife in the Metz dress costume," Hiero said, staring straight ahead. "White linen robes with no jewelry. It keeps off evil spirits."

Amibale swerved his hopper neatly to catch a bunch of scarlet orchids a giggling girl had tossed him from a low balcony. He tucked one behind his ear and the others in his mount's harness before turning back to Hiero, his face a blank mask of dismay. At the sight of the broad grin on Hiero's face, the boy exploded in a volley of profanity, ending in more laughter.

"Damn you! That iron face of yours would fool anyone. For all I know—for all any of us knows—you might just do it. Seriously, what are you really wearing? It's a masked ball, you know—an old tradition, they say, from the days when everyone was afraid of being assassinated at parties or afterward. Come on," he wheedled. "I won't tell anyone, honest."

"Well, Luchare said I was to surprise people, but I suppose you don't count, as usual, you scamp. Luchare wouldn't even show me hers. I'm going as one of the Blue Men, but in silk and with a gold border. Be damned if I'd wear anything more elaborate than that. You people have a mania for fancy dress down here in the swamps. I believe most D'alwahns would rather starve than go without pretty clothes, especially on a feast day."

The young duke did not deny the gibe. "It's our warm

southern blood, which you ice people can't understand." He looked thoughtful as they approached the main gates of the palace and the guard began to turn out. "Blue Man, eh? The veiled folk who live on the edges of the western desert. Pretty good disguise, that. They say they took the blue color from the Deserts of The Death, since they were the first to move back into those areas after The Death. It's claimed they can detect the fires of The Death in their own bodies and avoid the places that are still dangerous."

As Hiero returned the guards' salute, reining Klootz to a walk, he reflected that there was no point in telling his companion that he too could avoid such places of peril by the same methods. Idly, he mind-probed Amibale, confirming again that the lad had a mind screen as good as his own. The high nobles were often taught the technique in the monastery schools they attended when young, though the practice was falling into disuse, since the church saw no need for it any longer.

Hiero threw him a farewell, then forgot Amibale as he dismounted and headed for his own quarters, his mind burning with this new thought. No need for mental training? And this at a time when the Unclean were putting forth their greatest effort! The rot was deep in D'alwah, deep indeed. A lot of grubbing and wrenching would be needed to tear it out in the face of ignorance and superstition, especially if the mental masters of evil were actively on the scene, as he and Brother Aldo suspected. The Metz priest was still fuming inwardly as he came into his apartment, his expression as he passed the guard in the corridor making that experienced courtier refrain from greeting him.

"Well," his wife said brightly. "We're alone. I could feel a black cloud coming up the stairs; from your face, I see its origin. What has the mighty master of the marvels and mysteries of Metzland found to annoy him this time?"

Hiero smiled in spite of himself as she kissed him. "Call it the murk and mire of maleficient, monstrous, and malign motivations. Allied," he added, drawing breath, "to the marble-brained moronity and mind-bending muddleheadedness of your—" Here, a small palm covered his lips.

"I know, I don't even have to guess. The stupidity of the local church, the decay of moral fiber among the priesthood and nobility, the unwillingness to face facts and see how the enemy has moved among us. Right on all counts, am I not?"

"On all. And more. But I shouldn't bother you on party night. It's mid-afternoon already. Is that your party dress?" he asked, visibly admiring the semitransparent white shift which appeared to be her sole garment.

"You idiot! This is a house robe! Party dress indeed! Why did I yoke myself to a barbarian peasant who wouldn't notice if I wore rags instead of proper clothes?"

"Well," Hiero said, "you were hardly wearing even that when I first saw you. One look at all that smooth skin, indecent though it was, and I said to Klootz, 'Klootz, old boy,' I said, 'who needs clothes?' Ask him yourself if you don't believe me."

He dropped into a broad chair and she came and plumped herself into his lap. Sometime later, she sat up and looked serious. "Is there something new bothering you? Have you learned anything today?"

"No." He rose and walked to the narrow window, to stare out over the city, whose noise reached their tower suite in a muted hum, before he answered.

"But I saw a fresh head of one of the river monsters on a spike. Old Jabbrah the guard said that the things are much more numerous and more dangerous in recent years. Could be the Unclean are behind it. Nothing there they couldn't handle in some dirty way or other. That's not the real problem, though, at least not at the moment. What bothers me is the increasing *feel* that there is something at work right here, under our noses. I even felt suspicious of that young ape Amibale for a second. But there's something going on and I can't find it, despite all I've learned."

"A lot of it is probably nerves, plus having to wear what you think of as silly costumes and be on display all the time. Though," she added, "if you were a local, you wouldn't jib at being suspicious of Amibale. He's a young brat; but after all, he is also next to me in the royal succession, you know. My father has a lot of plans for him, if we can ever get him to grow up a little. Thank goodness, he doesn't take after his mother. The father was a bit dumb—cousin Karimbale, that is. But Fuala—whew!"

"What was her problem?" Hiero asked idly, still staring

down over the distant streets. "I mean, she's dead, isn't she? And the father, too?"

"Very," was the dry answer. "A lover, one of many, stabbed her while in the ducal bed. He was pulled between two mad hoppers until he came apart. *Lèse majesté* and all that. Frankly, my father was relieved. She never came to court much. Too many eyes. But I remember her well. God knows, she was really beautiful, but there was something purely evil about her. She spent lots of time off alone somewhere in the forest when she was down south, and she used to take Amibale off with her for weeks at a time with almost no attendants except some scary jungle folk who were her family's personal pets. She may have been just a nasty slut, but I never trusted her, nor did Dad. He always felt she had political ambitions. She really ran the duchy, and that fool of a husband did whatever she said. Some of her punishments for slaves were drastic. No, Fuala was not nice. Amibale is far better off with her dead. If she is dead."

"You just said she was very dead indeed. What kind of a remark was that, may I ask?"

It was Luchare's turn to look away, and Hiero realized with some amusement that she was actually embarrassed.

"More than a few people thought she was a witch, and of course they can't be killed, except in special ways." Luchare turned to look him in the eye. "If you must know, she made my skin crawl. I'm not afraid of very much, but I was terrified of her. Of course she's dead, but she radiated such intensity, along with so much nastiness, all as smooth as ice, that she, well, she still makes me nervous, that's all. Karimbale died a month after she did. They said it was disease," she added with seeming inconsequence.

"Well," her husband said soothingly, "we all have a few people who get our backs up. And speaking of getting backs up, I had better see to that inspection of the guard detachment, or the southern traders' delegation will have theirs up when I'm late to receive them in audience with your father. See you back here at dress-up-and-be-a-fool time."

She threw a pillow at him as he went out the door.

* * *

The ball was indeed a thing of splendor and color such as Hiero could never have imagined. The Great Hall was lighted with lanterns and cressets and filled with a thousand fragrances. His azure and gold robes and hood were drab compared with most of the costumes. The king was all in purple and white, with a blaze of great gems. Luchare was sheathed in emerald green, almost without jewels, save for the great bracelet of the tree women flashing on one bare, dark arm; a green half-mask accentuated her lovely face. The priests of the Church Universal attended in their magnificent robes, since this was a state occasion to be blessed. And clad, masked, and jeweled in the colors of the rainbow, the nobility of the realm spun and wheeled to the beat of the drums and horns playing the exotic southern music. The women were no more colorful than the men.

Hiero had little opportunity to do more than gain a general impression. He was leaning against a marble pillar, studying the scene in real wonder, when an upper servant touched his arm.

"Pardon, your Highness, but there is an urgent message. You are wanted in the hall at once. It's from one of your guardsmen, I gather."

Wondering what this might mean, Hiero followed the man, whose face was vaguely familiar. As he left the vast ballroom, he sent a thought to Luchare. She was out in the middle of the floor, apparently being dutifully attentive to some well-connected idiot whose family controlled something important.

A message from some guard, my love, supposed to be urgent. Back soon.

There was a sense of laughter and warm love in her answer. *Take your time, but not too long, love. There are five fat ladies you must dance with before you can really leave—all for the honor of the kingdom!*

He grinned and followed the man through a door into a small side room off the main hall, his mind still on Luchare. He was suddenly conscious of quick movement to his right, but he had no time to turn. Then the blow struck his head, and his consciousness departed.

✤ 2 ✤

A MAN ALONE

FOR A LONG TIME, THERE WAS NO REAL WAKING PERIOD, BUT there were impressions—impressions which Hiero knew were real and not the stuff of nightmares.

Faces swam before his blurred vision. There was the face of Joseato peering down at him, while he lay strapped to a bench in some dim room in the rabbit warren of the palace vaults, a place half-glimpsed through pain and the agony of his aching head. The face was no longer that of the harassed functionary, but something older and colder, the eyes gleaming with mockery and triumph. Hiero realized that he had never really seen Joseato's eyes before and cursed himself in some far corner of his mind. Out of the familiar face glared the gaze of the Unclean!

Hiero writhed frantically against the bonds which held him fast. The movement brought another face into view, and horror stilled his struggles. It was the face of Amibale Aeo, and from the young eyes came the same blaze of pure evil, with something else added to it; Amibale was quite mad, the madness mixed with the malign blasphemy which was the essence of the Unclean. Memory flickered across Hiero's tormented mind. *She was a witch*, the dulled memory said, fighting the constant pain. *She took him on trips to the jungle.*

He felt a fresh stab in his arm and saw that Joseato held a glass tube capped with a bloody needle aloft.

"We can kill him later," came a harsh whisper. "Not now. The chances are that the princess would know and act. They are sure in the North that he can talk to her mind. But if she feels no death, only silence, that gives us time. They say this kills the mind powers, but they warn us to be wary; he is strange and powerful. He must die, but away—far away. Distance lowers the mind touch. Even he cannot reach over long distances—not yet. He must stay drugged. Then he will be silent until he dies. Do you understand?"

"Oh, yes. Quite well." The beardless face grimaced, and the ghastly eyes still shone from the young, unlined face. "I will get him away. Go back to the ball. I will follow shortly. Both of us should not be away. Leave this to me. One of my caravans leaves for the west at dawn and . . ."

Then the pain became too great to fight, and Hiero fainted.

During the following hours, he woke at random intervals, sometimes hot, sometimes chilled with unnatural cold. Tightly bound with dirty cloths, he lay in some strange thing that creaked, swayed, and stank. He wondered idly if he were on a ship, but it did not seem important. He tried weakly to use the mind touch, but nothing happened, and he knew without conscious consideration that he had lost it. Just as he had been robbed of his physical freedom, his mental strength had been despoiled. All sense of time and distance seemed lacking, too, and he had no idea of where or when this was. He dimly remembered being fed some vile broth. He dimly knew it was drugged, but he had no power to resist; he swallowed whatever they gave him, half in a coma. The strange, savage faces he glimpsed at times meant no more to him than any other elements of a seemingly endless nightmare. At times it seemed dark, at others light, but that did not seem important.

Then there was a sudden, hideous chorus of shrieks, followed by a wild discordance of meaningless cries, vibrations, and movements. The thing which carried him lurched violently, and a vast weight fell upon him. Some of his wrappings were torn in the convulsive motions of the weight. For seconds, pain shot through his legs. Instinctively, he kicked as hard as he could, some faint surge of adrenaline coming to his aid, and he found himself almost free of the weight. His eyes were covered, and he could see nothing. His hands were bound, but he could loose them . . .

Don't loose them! Lie quiet, the inmost voice of his being warned. *It is death to move.*

He heard quick, almost furtive movements and the sounds of metal scraping and leather creaking. A voice muttered nearby and was answered by another farther off. There was a thudding as of beasts moving fast, then silence. Still he lay motionless, his tired mind intent only on making no sound. Presently, without knowing he had done so, he fell asleep.

When he awakened, he was hungry and thirsty, but not unreasonably so. His legs seemed free, though not his hands, and some cloth binding still covered his eyes. It was an easy matter to pull away the rag with which his eyes had been shrouded, even with bound hands. He gazed about, blinking in the light of the afternoon sun. He was lying in a hollow, under some low, scrubby bushes. Some large object pressed against his face, looming high over him and obscuring his vision. An already strong smell of decomposition informed him that it had been some animal. He was also tangled in a mesh of what seemed to be canvas and leather.

He lay quiet for a bit and listened. There was a light breeze playing through the bush above him, but the only other sound he could hear was a cackling, gabbling noise which came and went, sometimes rising to a squawk, then dying down again. He had no difficulty in identifying the voices of scavenger birds and he realized he must be lying in a place of death.

His mind was clearing rapidly now. He examined his hands. They were not bound with chains or leather thongs, as he had feared, but only with strips of cotton rag. Evidently his captors had feared no serious effort to escape.

It was no trouble to free himself. Then he pulled himself up over the dead beast whose body had sheltered him.

Five dead, gray kaws, the common beast of burden of D'alwah and the far South, lay about a small clearing. He was peering over the corpse of a sixth, and the broken-off shaft of an arrow an inch from his face was sufficient explanation of its death. Four absolutely naked men, their bodies in contorted attitudes, lay mingled with the dead cattle. Everything had been stripped from the dead, save for the battered harness of his own mount—for such he realized it must have been. He had been carried in some kind of crude canvas and leather litter on its broad back.

A flock of small, black vultures with oily, naked heads were tearing at the dead men. They looked up alertly as his head appeared, then took wing to settle in nearby bushes. Nothing else moved, and the only sound was the muted cackle of the scavengers.

Forcing his mind to throw off its dullness, he tried to reason out what must have happened.

The four men, and perhaps others, were taking him somewhere, walking alongside the kaws. They were ambushed, probably at dusk or even at night. His beast had died instantly, almost, but luckily had not fallen quite on top of him. The attackers' hasty search had missed him, sheltered in the wreckage of his litter and almost covered by the kaw's body. The ambushers had been in a hurry, probably afraid of discovery and pursuit, and they had decamped hastily after stripping the dead of everything they could find and use.

Hiero's legs were as long unused as his head, but he staggered to the middle of the clearing. The croaking of the birds had grown louder, but they did not take wing as he surveyed the scene at closer range.

The dead men were unknown to him. He did not like what he saw of them, particularly since he was now sure they had been his late captors or guards. Even allowing for the agonies of death, they were unprepossessing, being small and of a sallow white color. Their long hair was also pale, and they were clean-shaven, with narrow eyes and protuberant jaws. They somehow did not appear to be creatures of daylight. He wondered who they were and where they had been taking him.

Staring at the landscape of thorn scrub about him in the waning afternoon sun, he forced his dormant training to come back to him, despite his spinning head. Slowly at first, he began to search for anything which might be useful. No weapons lay about, though he was sure there had been plenty of them when the attack came. Indeed, nothing lay about except the corpses. Aside from missing him, the attackers had done a most complete job of plunder. Even the arrows had been retrieved, save for the stub buried in his kaw. There was nothing he could use and no clue to either his captors or those who had slain them.

Other than worn leather shorts and sandals in which he found himself dressed, he had absolutely nothing.

He was just beginning to examine the tracks which littered the clearing, finding only the rough marks of booted feet and some hoofprints of kaws, when the carrion birds fell silent, then lifted from the bushes. From a remote distance to the east, there came the faint note of a questing horn.

Hiero stood frozen. The birds had flown off low over the

thorny scrub, not high in a flock, for which he was grateful. He did not know who had sounded that horn, but as far as he was concerned, this empty waste held nothing but foes. And they might have marked the birds rising.

Again the horn sounded, a solitary call. This time it was answered from the south and the north, though both calls were far off and still well to the east of his position. There had been at least four horns, he estimated, well spaced, signaling position and future movement. Someone had been driving in a long line, looking for something. For what, if not for him?

Hardly thinking, his reflexes taking over, aided by years of training, the Metz stooped and seized a dead branch of thorn-bush that was covered with small leaves. Quickly he erased all traces of his presence from the dry earth. Then he began to run slowly to the west, keeping to gravel where he could; when that was not possible, he brushed the ground gently to blot his tracks.

He ran for what he estimated was half an hour, maintaining constant awareness of where he trod. Behind him, the horns still called. The distance seemed the same as when he had first heard them, indicating that the pursuit was moving at roughly the same speed as he was.

The sun was now sinking fast ahead of him, and it showed him that the scrub was thinning out. There were more patches of sand and pebble underfoot now, and both the bush and the sparse, wiry grass had almost disappeared. The color of the earth itself had changed from a sandy brown to a bluish gray.

Later, the sound of the horns changed. At least two of them pealed out in short, summoning notes. Hiero knew they had come upon the dead and were signaling a rally. He trudged grimly on. It was agonizing to think that they might be friends, perhaps sent by Luchare to rescue him, but the chances were too small; he had no idea where he was or how far he had come since being kidnapped, but it must be a long way. If he were right, the blueness of the ground and the increasing ab-sence of vegetation meant that he was heading into fresh and unknown dangers. He had seen this thinning scrub far to the north and knew that it portended the approach of a desert. In the latitude of D'alwah, there was only one kind of desert marked on the map—one of the Deserts of The Death.

Soon he knew he was right. The last bushes died away;

there before him, glittering with fragments of mica and blue, siliceous sands, stretched the desert, unbroken to the western horizon. Behind him, the horns sounded again with their original, questing notes.

Hiero had no choice of action. Waterless, foodless, and without weapons, he set out into the waste, determined that he would not be taken again. Anything was better than his late captivity.

As night came on, the horns fell silent. But he plodded on and on, his face fixed toward the west. By now, his pace was slow and uneven, and he stumbled at intervals. Once he fell to his knees. Rising took most of his energy.

He limped across a shallow basin and reached a patch of naked rock, where the going was easier than on the soft sand. Here he rested, his breath coming in short gasps. He worked a small pebble over his dry tongue; it was better than nothing, but he needed water badly. His disciplined body could go without food, but he must have water.

He raised his head and surveyed the arid landscape that was revealed by the light of the half-moon. Broad patches of sand stretched south as far as his gaze could reach. To the east, the sands ran to the distant horizon; and the north held more sand, mingled with patches of pebbles and broken rock. But to the west, black spires showed against the stars—perhaps pinnacles of a range or buttresses of a line of low, jagged cliffs.

With a supreme effort, he rose to his feet. If there were any place of safety, those western peaks might hold it. There could be caves or at least crannies in which he could shelter through the heat of the coming day. There might even be sources of water and food, if he were clever enough to find them.

As he braced himself to continue, there came a faint, distant sound out of the south. Hiero listened intently, trying for the hundredth time to focus the powers of his mind for mental search, as he had painstakingly taught himself in the last year. His whole frame tensed with an almost physical effort as he tried to probe the night. At last, he subsided with a silent curse. Whatever had been done to him must have been permanent. He was *blind* in the use of his mental powers. Somehow, his talents had been stolen from him by drugs, and now he was helpless, without either physical or mental weapons on this plain. He cursed himself again, then rebuked himself. He made the sign of the cross on his naked breast and murmured a brief prayer of remorse. He had forgotten he was a priest and that a priest thanked God for his blessings—such as being alive at all!

He set out for the distant hills at a slow, steady trot, trying to ignore his fatigue and the ever-increasing thirst. As he went, he listened intently. No sound broke the silence, save the shuffle and scrape of his sandals, but he was not to be misled. His ability to probe for the minds of other beings might be gone; but, dormant in his brain, some of the synapses that had guarded him for so long still stirred and flickered, if in a dim and half-useless way. There was evil in the night! He knew it as if it were written in letters of fire on the sands. Someone or something hunted, and, since he had no defenses of any kind, he must find shelter or die in the attempt. He forced himself to plod on, concentrating on simply placing one foot in front of the other. He had no illusions about his present predicament. He was in a place of hideous danger, one from which few of the rare travelers who ventured had ever returned, one of the Deserts of The Death.

Thousands of years in the past, the hellfires of the atom had totally blighted many places. The worst of these still shone with the bale-glow of radiation and were utterly lethal. Yet this was not one of those. Like all the Metz of the far North, Hiero had an inbred sensitivity, as well as some tolerance to radiation. He could sense that this was one of the barren patches from which most, if not all, of the killing gamma rays had long since evaporated. That did not mean his peril was less; perhaps it was only longer delayed.

For though no blue witch fires danced upon the sand and broken scree around him, still the area seemed lifeless and waterless. No plants grew, not even lichens, at least not in the stretch he had traversed since the previous dawn. Yet the fading radiation had left its mark in other ways. Strange life had come to be, bred from horrid mutation; all over the world, and in these deserts it was deemed strangest of all. The landscape might appear empty in the wan light but there was life, of a sort. Despite the loss of his mind-search abilities, he could feel it. There was a growing menace which throbbed in his already aching skull. Doggedly, he trudged on, his gaze fixed on the dark towers of rock which rose out of the west to meet him.

Again he paused to catch his breath, but this time went only to one knee, fearful that he would not be able to rise if he squatted. And once more out of the south came the sound. This time it was clearer, a strange, high, wavering noise, as if somehow in the night a monstrous sheep blethered on an impossibly high note. Priest and Killman, soldier and ranger that he was, Hiero felt a finger of ice trace the length of his spine. Whatever made that noise was not something he wanted to meet. Again he crossed himself and then rose and set off once more into the west. He was numb with exhaustion, but he continued on. The cry was surely that of a hunter, and it must be a hunter on his trail. How it had been summoned, whence it had come to place itself on his track, he could not guess. But he *knew* that it was.

Despite his condition, he kept moving steadily along. When he next looked up, he saw that the hills had risen before him and that slopes and ridges of rock were already rising to the left and right from the drifted sand and erg which had been his companions for so many weary hours. He caught a distant glimpse of a spiky thing jutting from a crevice off to his left and recognized it as some sort of plant, though of a strange and unpleasant kind. Perhaps he could find water after all, if he persisted. On and yet on he went, the last moisture in his body coating him in a crackled film of grit and perspiration.

Behind him, the evil cry quavered out under the sky once more, far louder than when last heard, alien and rife with menace, trailing off into that impossibly high note which almost physically hurt the inner fibers of his being. He did not stop this time, but drew on his last stores of energy to lope over the rising ground to his front.

Had the night been dark, he might have been totally helpless, forced to move at a crawl. But the half-moon showed him that a small canyon sloped up into the higher rock ahead of him, black and menacing, yet a haven of refuge to him. If he could only hold out long enough to get into the hills!

He reached the mouth of the ravine and lurched into it, straining at every muscle. The moonlight entered only in patches, but he could see sufficiently for his needs. The floor under his sandals was shale, worn and slippery, but he managed to keep his feet while he sought on either side for the shadow of a cave or other place of refuge. There was no further sound behind him, but he was not deceived. Whatever followed was close upon him. If he found no hiding place in the next few minutes, he was doomed.

For a second a face filled his mind, the face of a lovely woman, dark and mysterious, with masses of tight curls, soft, full lips, and dark, lustrous eyes. Luchare! Was he to perish alone and lost, never to see her smile again? Frantically, clumsily, he clambered up the narrowing gully, his soldier's gaze never ceasing to search for some place that would at least give him a fighting chance to live. Yet no cranny broke the smooth rock walls, which had now closed in until they were no more than the length of his body away on either hand. In desperation, he looked up and then he saw it.

Ahead some small distance, the winding passage bent both upward and to his left. As it did so, a narrow buttress towered up from the southern wall, like a rough and broken turret, narrowing at the top to a tiny platform. But the side of the pinnacle, as it abutted the gorge, was cracked and broken! To a skilled climber, it presented an ascent of no great difficulty. Weary though he was, Hiero felt a thrill of energy course through his veins. In a second he had reached the base of the craglet and had begun his climb, placing his hands and feet swiftly and surely as he swarmed upward.

The spike of crumbling stone was not high, perhaps a little more than five times his own height, and he was soon at the top. With a gasp of effort, he pulled himself up and over the rim and flopped down on the more or less level ledge which crowned it.

But he dared not rest for a second. He did not know what followed, nor its powers, and he knew it was coming hard upon his track. To something which could climb, his new shelter might become a trap of a most terrible kind. His eyes swept the narrow top of the crumbling monolith, and a fierce gleam lit them. At arms' length there lay several massive chunks of broken stone, the products of weather and erosion in the distant past. As quietly as he could, he gathered two of the larger ones close to his chest, trying not to grunt with the effort of his fading strength. Then he sought to relax, while he peered back down the black ravine, watching as steadily as possible for the pursuer he knew to be coming, willing his body to snatch even a few seconds of rest for the ordeal to follow.

And then he heard it. At first it was simply a muffled noise in the silent night, the sound of a heavy movement, then another and another. He was listening to the soft tread of some massive body advancing up the same path he had followed only moments before, a body trying to move as quietly as possible in the hope of coming upon its prey unawares. His eyes narrowed in pure rage. At least he was not taken by surprise. The hunter would learn that a Metz Killman was not to be chivied across the sand like a hunted deer. After days of helplessness, here was something at which he could strike!

Closer and closer came the sounds. Once he heard a faint rattle on the shale, as if a monstrous claw had touched upon a fragment of loose rock. Now he could detect the sounds of breathing, deep and hoarse. And then around a corner below, it came.

Veteran though he was of strange combats, hardened to the monstrous life forms spawned by The Death, Hiero nevertheless drew a deep gulp of air as he stared down at what had been drawn out of the southern wastes to seek his blood.

In the flickering and uncertain moonlight, there appeared a shifting bulk of a strange blue tint, as if the blue poison fires of the great desert had left their awful legacy in the color of this, their spawn. The great tailless trunk, the size of a long-extinct horse, was carried on four massive legs, ending in mighty three-curved hooves which were more like vast talons. The long neck, mottled with the bluish glaze, ended in a head also not unlike that of a horse, but hideous tusks protruded from the blubber lips. And from the great, earless head there rose twin spires of bone, each pointed with a needle spike.

But the most dreadful feature, one which set the monster apart from all normal life, was its *eyes*. Hollow orbs of lambent flame, they were pupilless and ablaze with cold light. And the man, frozen on his ledge, knew at what he looked.

This was the Death Hart, of which he had read in the ancient records of D'alwah. Far in the remote past, these monsters had been common and had preyed on the scattered humans of the South in packs, emerging from their desert lairs to slaughter and pull down any living meat they could find, ravaging the lands which bordered the desert until the few scattered tribes that lived there had fled in anguish and despair. Not for many lives now had the creatures been seen, and they had become only a matter of awful legend, at least in the minds of men.

As he looked at the slavering jaws, Hiero knew that whatever creature had given rise to this abomination in the lost ages, it was now no eater of grass! Of a size scarcely less than Klootz, this thing was yet a carnivore, designed to rend and tear living flesh, to shatter bone and sinew to feed its incredible maw.

As he stared, his mind racing at the embodied sight of the horrific past come to life before him, it looked up and saw him. Once more, that horrid, yammering call rang through the clear night air, this time in a volume of sheer noise that left the senses numb as it resounded and echoed off the rock walls. Hiero closed his eyes for a second as the vibrations of that frightful call pierced through his body to the very marrow of his bones.

As the echoes of that ghastly cry died into silence, he opened his eyes, just in time to see the demon of the desert hurl itself upward at him, the hideous mouth open to expose both the rows of fangs and the massive tusks set at the corners of the colossal gape. Then it sprang.

Braced though he was for the attack, the Metz priest was still taken by surprise. The enormous haunches had a strength he would not have believed, and the leap carried the great body almost to his own level in one incredible bound. For an awful instant, he stared into the oily light of the brute's eyes from no more than a sword's length away, while its filthy breath spume poured over him in a wave of hot loathsomeness. Then it was gone and he heard a colossal thud as it fell back to the base of the rock.

His heart pounding, Hiero peered over the lip of the mono-lith, hoping against hope that the atrocity had done itself some injury in that mighty fall, only to see it crouched below, un-harmed and glaring upward with the same avid lust. Not by any short slip or fall could that strange body be injured. Hiero remembered that the ancient scrolls had emphasized the in-vulnerability of the beasts, claiming they could tear down the heavy timbers of village walls like so many jackstraws. This thing would never fail through any efforts of its own. If he were to survive, he must carry the battle to the enemy, hopeless though that might appear.

As he watched, the monster reared up again, but this time slowly, until the great hoof-claws of the forelimbs were stretched to their fullest limits. As the three great talons of each leg clamped into the rock of the cliff, they bit in, the wirelike sinews contracting, crunching in at almost beyond a believable rate. As Hiero stared, aghast, the rock up which he had clambered ground and crumbled. Below, he could hear the terrible rear limbs crush the eroded stone in the same way. The hideous eyes stared up at him, unwinking. Even as he recoiled, the mighty hindquarters drew *up*. Before his unbelieving stare, the abortion out of vanished memory was actually clinging and grinding its way *into* the rock. It was a feat almost beyond belief, even after his sight of its capabilities in that initial leap. Next, he knew, the great forearms would extend once more, and this time they would be *over* the ledge of his shelter! And a remote, still corner of his mind said that would be all!

The dreadful orbs froze his blood as he crouched on the summit. As in a dream, he saw the talons of the right forepaw begin to extend upward for the last time.

He rose to his feet in one lithe, flowing movement and, high above his head, he balanced the bigger of the two chunks of scree which he had hoarded against such a moment. It was a great, jagged thing, barely within his powers to lift.

The monster gaped, the vast, fang-lined jaws open, as it once more drew breath for that appalling sound. The rock came down with all the strength in Hiero's tired body. Between the foam-flecked lips, past the cruel ranks of fang and tusk, it tore with the weight and speed of an avalanche, deep into the yawning gullet, a projectile of both murderous force and certainty. There was a sound as if some incredible axe had bitten into a vast, half-rotted log. A horrid, choked scream welled up, bubbling through ripped tissue and foul blood. Again came the thump of a tremendous fall, and then a flopping, scrabbling noise, punctuated by the thrashing and beating of giant limbs. Then there was silence, and the exhausted man felt a faint breeze stir his hair and the beat of life in his veins.

Slowly and painfully, Hiero inched his way forward once more and looked down at the base of the crag. His gaze was swimming and he knew he could not hold on to consciousness much longer, but one glance was sufficient.

The great bulk which lay below, limp and awful, could certainly never move again. The long neck writhed outward in the last agony, and a black stream of its life's blood trickled and dripped over the ravine's floor from the shattered skull,

down into darkness. Hiero's crude weapon had driven deep
into the malformed head and had torn into the brain and the
seat of the central nervous system. Unused to any opposition
from its prey, the beast had succumbed to desperation, courage,
and plain gravity.

The man tried to mouth a prayer, but got no further than
the word "God." Then he sank back into a drugged exhaustion.
It was not true sleep, but the reaction of a totally overstrained
mind and body, a sort of trance in which he knew himself to
be alive, but was unable to do more than simply breathe. His
eyes shut and his body slowly curled into a fetal position, while
his brain reeled and spun through emptiness and nullity. Eventually he really slept, his soul adrift in the cosmos.

He awoke suddenly, all senses alert. His body felt as if it
were aflame, and his tongue felt like a dry stick as he tried to
run it over his cracked and broken lips.

Glancing up, he saw the fiery sun at zenith and knew that
he had slept for many long hours. No more than half the night
had gone before his encounter with the unholy Death Hart, and
now it was once again noon. He felt faint and still utterly weary,
but he forced himself to think, though even thought called for
an almost physical effort. Water! Water and some cover. He
could not survive another day in the appalling heat of this empty
waste without liquid and shelter. He had to start at once while
some faint energy remained in his flagging muscles, while he
could still reason, and even search for help.

A quick look and the simultaneous realization of a noisome
stench showed him the bloated carcass of his late enemy sprawled
at the base of his refuge; rot had set in with blinding speed.
Around the huge corpse, he caught small, flickering movements. Light glinted off lithe bodies as a horde of some scav-
enging vermin tore and burrowed into the foul meat of that
huge decay. Focusing as well as he could and squinting in the
desert glare, he could make out pointed heads, glittering green
scales, and short legs, as well as the red glitter of many beady
eyes. The things seemed to be some vile combination of rat
and lizard, well suited to their home and as alien as the dead
monster to the rest of life.

Looking about, the Metz selected yet another loose fragment
of the rock on which he lay, this one a narrow splinter as long

as his forearm, not unlike a crude stalactite. It was not much of a weapon, but it might be enough, should the things below be more than scavengers. In any case, he reminded himself grimly, he had no choice. He had to leave now.

He tucked the crude stone knife in his waist, where a thong supported his ragged leather shorts, and began to climb cautiously down. As he went, he watched the creatures carefully, alert for any signs that they might attack.

He was more than halfway down when they saw him, and then all movement ceased. At least a score of sharp muzzles pointed up, and the red eyes stared unblinkingly, the shimmering bodies frozen, as they watched him descend. Short-legged and no bigger than house cats, there was nevertheless enough of them to menace an exhausted and almost weaponless man. He stared at them for a moment, wondering if the needle claws and fangs he could now see could be poisoned. It would fit with everything else he had seen in this sun-blistered hell. It made no difference. There was still no choice but to go down. He did so, slowly and steadily, one hand ready to snatch the weapon from his side, should it be needed.

For one instant, as his foot touched the rock floor of the gully, he seemed to feel a wave of hate in his mind. Then, like an explosion of greenish light, the creatures were gone, and the stinking, torn bulk of the dead beast was the only other tenant of the place. Hiero leaned against the wall of the spire, limp with reaction. Apparently the things found him as alien as he them, and they had doubts enough about his powers not to challenge them.

Choking in the foetor billowing from the pile of carrion beside him, he set off up the canyon, moving at a walk, which was all he could manage. It was a relief to round the base of the rock at last and move up into cleaner air, but such relief was only momentary. He could die from the terrible sunfire as easily as from the fangs of any beast. The lizard-rats might have the last word in the end.

An hour later, he was again almost at the limit of his strength. He had reached the top of the ravine and found himself on the rim of a low plateau. The top of this mesa ran only a short distance to the north, but its broken, eroded surface stretched as far south as he could see, a brooding emptiness of umber and ebon minerals. Short and weather-worn peaks rose here and there, and now and again shadows betrayed the presence of pits and cratered openings, as well as those of more jagged coulees and ravines, like that from which he had just emerged. The air was still under the blue vault above, and the heat of the sun burned down like a furnace on the grim and empty wastes.

He looked to the west and saw that the plateau, the worn surface of some ancient range of hills, extended for perhaps a kilometer in front of him. Raising his gaze, he noted that even more naked desert swept from the western edge almost to the horizon, but at the very limit of his sight, there to the southwest, was another faint, dark line. Could this be the end of the barrens and the recommencement of the great southern forest? He sighed. It made little difference, really. He would be helpless in a few hours if he could not find water and shelter.

Hiero looked hard at the foreground and presently noted something which caused his spirits to rise. Some distance off to his right front, there ran a low ridge which made him stare in speculation. It was hazy, wavering to a man's height above the heated stones. There was no breeze, so it could not be either blown sand or dust. If his tired eyes were not playing him false, somewhere over there was moisture!

He set off again at the same patient walk, husbanding the last of his strength. He did not allow himself to hope too much. If moisture it were, it could well be some foul pool of reeking poisons, metallic compounds, and mineral salts, of a type whose very vapor could slay him. That such things were common enough in desert regions he knew from his studies, both in D'alwah and, farther back in time, in the northern Abbeys.

There was, of course, no option save to continue, and this he did. Soon he found himself at the base of the ridge over which the strange thickening of the atmosphere had appeared. The slope was neither very high nor difficult, but he moved with great care. His bones felt so brittle and weak that it was hard to believe that they could support him at all, while the thirst in his body was held off from stark madness only by a last effort of will.

Slowly, he drew himself to the top of the ridge and peered over. A faint thrill of hope came to him as he watched, but he still held his weak body under rigid control.

Below lay a large, rounded pit, or crater, with walls which had once been steep, but which were now gashed and scarred with falls of rubble and seamed with numerous cracks and crevices. The floor of the pit was smooth and sand-covered in places, in others broken and tumbled. Here and there around the edges of the place were the irregular mouths of caves and the shadows of overhangs. And there was life.

Growing in patches and sometimes even dense clumps about the bottom were living plants. They resembled nothing Hiero had ever seen or heard of before, but they seemed to come in several types. There was a maroon and purple thing, like a vast barrel, with long, pendulous fronds drooping from its top and trailing about on the ground below. Another type looked somewhat like a huge starfish, set atop a fleshy, brown stalk. This type grew in clumps, as if distorted and ragged umbrellas were somehow grouped in bunches. Smaller growths, as if of some bristling, spiked grasses of yellowish green, waist-high, sprang from patches of sand. Nowhere was there a hint of movement. Nor was there a sign of water. Save for the strange plants, the natural arena appeared as arid as the rock to which he clung.

But it was there! His trained body, sensitive to many influences unknown by his ancestors, could *feel* it. His whole system knew there was water somewhere down below. That it was out of sight meant nothing. It was there and it was close, drinkable, lifesaving water!

Once more he swept the pit with his eyes. Worn though he was, the savage training of the Abbey schools still governed him. If there was water here, and he knew there was, and if there was life, even so strange as these plants, then there was danger. In an oasis, near water holes, there lurked the hunters. He glared over the crater floor again, step by step, trying his best to see into the shadows, past the cave openings, and under the ledges. Nothing moved; the place might have been some strange sculpture, the dream of an unknown artist.

He could wait no longer. He moved over a bit to his right, where one of the broken slides of shale reached almost to the rim, and started slowly down it, never taking his vision from the silent pit. As he drew closer to the bottom, he searched even harder for some sign of life other than the enigmatic plants. Surely there must be insects, even in a place as bizarre as this? Yes, there was something!

Just below him rose a low mound, knee-high, with many small openings into and from which tiny things came and went on incomprehensible errands. The anthill gave him a sense of comfort, the first familiar sight from his own world he had seen since his escape. He watched, entranced, as a column of the little things marched by a few meters distant. He noticed that they seemed to have paths which avoided any of the vegetation by a wide margin, but his wits were now so dazed with tiredness that he simply recorded the fact without drawing any conclusions from it.

Then he drew some conclusions with great rapidity. The edge of the column overran an invisible barrier near one of the solitary purple barrels. The reaction was rapid. The nearest of the trailing fronds whipped up and down like a flail. The intrusive edge of the column was gone. The frond folded itself over, and Hiero saw that an opening had appeared in the top of the barrel plant. The opening *sucked*, as a child licks its fingers. Then the frond, now cleansed, drooped and once more lay idle and seemingly harmless on the white sand.

Hiero stared hard at the barrel. This one was small, not up to his knee; but farther out in the pit, there were some which towered over his head and were as thick around as an Abbey tun of wine. Once again he turned his gaze on the ants that continued on their business, apparently undisturbed. But he saw now that they avoided all the plants, no matter of what variety, not simply the purple barrels. No doubt they had reason.

He put one foot on the floor of the strange pit, then another. No plants were close. He turned around and then surveyed the place from the ground level. Down here, the heat was not so strong, the air ever so slightly damp. *Where is that damned water?*

Even the mild blasphemy was enough to make him correct himself. He fell naturally into a kneeling position, arms outthrust, and let the spirit move him as it had in the past. His splayed arms pointed vaguely to the northeast. Rising slowly and carefully, he set out in that direction, carefully steering clear of any plants along the way.

Hiero limped and tottered on, some inner guide keeping him away from the vegetation. He had now reached the point of no return in terms of response, and his subconscious alone saw the quaver of the various things he came near. If a barrel plant shook as he approached or a clump of the spike grass wavered and leaned toward him, he saw it not. Along a mystic line of safety, he weaved between one danger and another, fell side-

wise in one place, lurched back in another, but always kept to
one direction.

In a moderately short time, he found himself under one of
the overhanging cliffs he had noted from the rim. The heat, to
a stranger, would have still been terrific. To him, fresh from
the glow of the desert sun, it was like stepping out of a furnace
into an ice palace. One moment he was in a place of raging
heat; the next, he was shaded and cool. The light was dimmed
and he found it hard to see. Above him, a great shelf of rock
cut off the sunlight and most of the heat. He strove to peer
ahead through the dimness and found himself on the edge of
a still pool of clear water.

It reached as far as he could see to the left and right and
back into the shadows before him. The smooth rock under his
sandaled feet felt pleasantly cool. Without further ado, he collapsed on his face, falling with a splash across the margin of
the pool.

Some vestige of the training he had spent his life receiving
saved him from death. He took one gulp of the water, then
turned on his back and allowed the coolness to soak into his
skin. A man or woman of less iron will would have died on
the spot, drinking to repletion. His background saved him.
Something told him, even in extremity, that he was close to
death, and he restrained his water-starved body. After a long
while, he took another drink, less in size than the first, and
after a longer period, another, this one less still. All the while
he lay on the rock shelf, barely afloat.

The water tasted slightly acid, but was cool and pure. His
body, trained in the detection and rejection of poisons, would
have told him, had there been something wrong, even in the
last extremity. It was simply water, filtered through strange
rock perhaps, but nothing more. The delight of feeling it come
through, or appearing to come through, his very skin held him
in thrall. He floated in a sea of appreciation, reveling in the
idea of wetness.

Eventually, after about the eighth cautious drink, sanity
began to return. He suddenly saw the damp roof of the shelf
above him and, with a great surge of emotion, realized that he
was alive once more and that further plans could be made.
Also, he felt a new want, one he had not permitted for a long

time. He was hungry. He took another drink, still measured.
He did not want to become waterlogged.

He shot a glance at the roof of the stone above his head and
another down at the pool on whose brink he had been lying.
This must be a catchment basin, where the rare rains were
collected and saved by nature, and where the whole ecosystem
combined to create the oasis of the strange little pocket in which
he found himself. Or into which he had stumbled. Or, said a
side corner of his mind, into which he had been led. He examined this latter idea as calmly as he could and dismissed it.
With the loss of his mental abilities, there had come a con-
comitant reliance on those of the body. He did not believe he
could be led anywhere.

Eventually, he had absorbed all the water he could take and
began to feel the first traces of a chill. This was enough warning, and he got out of the pool at once. Sitting on the bank—
or rather, slope, for it was a very gentle gradient—he stared
out at the rock-rimmed little valley which made up the pocket.
Evening was coming, and he realized bemusedly that he had
been lying in the shallows for most of the afternoon. The
warmth of the sun was still strong, however, and he no longer
felt any chill, despite the lengthening shadows.

As the dark of evening grew upon the landscape, he watched
the strange plants of the crater; and now, refreshed and with
his faculties alert, he saw other things. There was a delicate
movement among the bushes, almost as if a breath of wind
were moving them in the utterly windless air, and he watched
them as they put themselves to sleep. The barrel plants tucked
their long fronds tightly about themselves like ladies' cloaks,
and the spike grasses withdrew into the ground, leaving only
horny sheaths of dull brown on the surface, less than one-third
of the original length. The starfish plants somehow withdrew
into their own stalks, until nothing was left except a thing like
a fat stump, devoid of adornment. The whole appearance of
the little pocket changed, becoming even more still and silent.

As the long shadows crept across the basin floor before him,
he continued watching, utterly motionless. But now from his
belt he drew the narrow fragment of rock, hoarded since his
descent from the crag far down the outer slope. His ears strained
as the swift night of the desert fell like a mantle upon the crater.
Soon he heard what he had been hoping to hear.

There were squeaks and scratching noises in the night. Hiero's eyes, trained to the dark, saw small shadows darting here and there across the sands. Close to the rock on which he crouched stood the cone-stump into which a starfish plant had withdrawn. Now something the size of a small dog, with stumpy legs and a dragging tail, waddled around the base of the plant and sat up on its rump. It began to gnaw the plant-thing, its teeth making a grinding noise. Hiero surmised that it would never have dared to do so in the light of day. At night, the metabolism of the plants forced them to withdraw in nocturnal hibernation. Then they could be made into victims.

The animal was hardly more than arm's length away, and the priest struck like lightning. There was a crunch as the broad skull cracked, and the body fell before him, barely twitching. Holding it close, he gave it a careful examination. Despite the dim light, for the moon had not yet risen, he could see enough for his purposes.

The creature was not all that ill-looking, actually, though not much like anything he had seen before. In some ways, its pale-furred body rather resembled that of a squat rodent, and it had similar chisel teeth. Its round tail appeared overlong for its body, and he wondered if it might not be prehensile. There were no external ears, and its eyes were small and buried deep in the head.

It seemed clearly mammalian, and the blood which stained its fur smelled no more alien than his own. In short, it was food.

What followed would no doubt appall a person used to life under conditions of civilization. Hiero could either take or leave civilized habits; he had been raised on a frontier of strife and savage warfare, under conditions so bitter that only the toughest survived. When you were hungry, in his lexicon, you ate. What you ate and how depended on what was around. If you had no fire, you ate raw meat.

He got enough of the fur off with his stone pick to sink his strong teeth through the tough hide. It was not easy chewing, but he had eaten worse and no doubt would again, he thought to himself. After a dozen rending bites, he stopped long enough to say a rude grace, then went back to hacking and chewing once more. The stringy meat, rank and strong, went down with no particular difficulty. Any alien element, anything like a poison, would have caused him to regurgitate as soon as his body had detected it. There was nothing, though, and after a while his body felt replete. He wrapped the remnant of the carcass in the scraps of hide he had ripped off and looked about for shelter. He had drunk and he had eaten. Now his overtaxed frame needed rest more than anything else.

His eyes swept the sands and the hillocks of dormant vegetation which dotted the moonlit arena, becoming fixed on one spot off to the right. Several round holes, black circles in the paler rock of the wall, showed in the wan light. Small things still moved and rustled out on the floor of the pit. His killing of the hapless plant eater had passed unnoticed. No doubt other predators existed and fed at night also. He would have to be careful of them, as well. He rose quietly, holding the meat in one hand, his crude weapon poised in the other, and moved off toward the openings he had marked down. In forty meters, the water of the pool came to an end; at the same time, the roof of the vault which shielded it tapered back into the inner slope. He passed quietly out under the stars and the half circle of the risen moon. Still the small night sounds continued without a break around him. The oasis pursued the doubtless ancient tenor of its circumscribed life, unconscious that a new killer had come, one far more dangerous than any ever before encountered.

The killer himself felt weary, but also, despite his fatigue, he had a strange sense of peace. For the first time in days— was it only days?—he had lost the feeling of being hunted, of being the helpless prey of powers and enemies with whom he could not contend. Alone he had fought and conquered the demon of the dark; alone he had found water, food, and shelter. Alone he had survived. His God had not turned away His face, and Hiero was grateful and humble. But deep inside, he felt a thrill of pride. The Abbey training could not make a man, but it could find one; and having done so, it could teach him to help himself. That was what God wanted, as did the Church Universal—for men and women to help themselves, to struggle to the end, never to give up. It was a simple lesson and, like so many simple lessons, not really easy to learn.

He paused by the first of the openings and took a careful look at it. Too shallow, no more than a niche in the stone face. The next was barely a scrape, the third too narrow. The fourth opening, however, was something more useful. An entrance barely large enough to permit passage gave onto a rounded chamber, in which he could crouch or lie down, but was no larger than he needed. Further, a pile of rubble partially filled one end—dead sticks and small stones, with some ancient bone fragments. The place had doubtless been the lair of some creature before, but the former owner was long gone, and not even an odor remained. Hiero hastened to block the entrance with as much of the litter as he could sweep up, and soon only a small opening admitted the night air. The floor of the little cave was sand, and he saved some of the softer twigs and bark fragments, as they appeared to be, for a pillow. He dug holes for his hips and shoulders and curled up to get some badly needed rest. If some creature should menace him, he felt his senses were alert enough now to give him the instant's warning which could mean the difference between life and death. He could do no more.

Though his body relaxed and his sinews loosened for the first time in many hours, sleep did not come. He did not try to force it. Any rest, even with open eyes, was still priceless. If his body was exhausted, his mind and his nervous system apparently were not. So be it. If his mind was awake, he could make use of it. He could afford to neglect no assets at this juncture. He would try once again to regain the skills he had somehow lost in the nightmare of the past few days and nights.

He willed his mind to sweep outward, gently at first, trying to build the once mighty powers he had possessed so short a time before. He was very, very cautious now, trying only to shut his ears to the small life forms which scurried about the basin and, instead, to sense them with his brain, to catch their tiny auras, the impulses that distinguished them from not-life, the minute sparks of individuality which made them different each from another.

Supposing he should be able to recapture his vanished ability, or even part of it? Would he also recapture the web of hard-taught defenses? If his unguided thought roamed the night, perhaps partially in use, haltingly effective, could it not lead other minds, other powers, to his present location? And should the Unclean find him once more, the most hated of their foes, how could he protect himself? He had no answer. Yet it must be attempted. He had, once again, no choice.

Eventually, he stopped. The blockage was still intact. He could hear and see, smell and taste, but the years of Abbey training, the genetic ability of the telepath with which he had been endowed at birth, all were gone. So too were the far, far greater powers he had learned on his own during the last year, the strengths which had enabled him to defy and even overthrow certain of the great adepts of the enemy, Masters of the Circles of the Unclean. He could not repress a moan, choking it back in his throat even as it came. Unfair! It was unfair that a man should be reft so, unfair that he could be torn asunder from his greatest weapons, trapped without the force which alone might enable him to go to war! Unfair! Curse the Unclean and their foul science!

With an almost physical effort, he beat back the self-pity. He had lost his mental powers, but not the strength based on moral fiber. Had not Abbot Demero long ago warned of the curse of whining, the sin of believing oneself an object of special care from the Almighty? The thought of the stern old face of his master came into Hiero's mind, and a reluctant smile crossed his sunblackened face. *Yes, Reverend Father*, he thought, *I am a man again.*

True, his hard-won mental powers were gone, but in many ways he had been incredibly lucky. Drugged, bound, and helpless, he had yet escaped his enemies. Though no longer telepathic, his brain was clear and he could think and plan ahead. He could reason, puzzle out what had happened to him, and take action for the future—action and revenge. His black eyes narrowed into burning slits. His enemies would pay for this— pay dearly!

Eventually, Hiero slept, his thoughts still and the memories of recent days mercifully forgotten for the time being.

The little hollow went on about the business of the night. The strange plants were dormant, while the small lives about them pursued their own midget dramas of life and death. Once the stars above were blotted out by something large and dark, passing high and far into the north. But the night shielded the hollow, and the man slumbered on, free of distressing dreams.

✤ 3 ✤

SUMMONED—
AND FOLLOWED

A GLEAM OF LIGHT, REFLECTED OFF A PIECE OF SHINY ROCK, glanced into the tiny cave, striking the worn, unshaven face of the silent human. With a faint sigh, Hiero awoke and peered out of his refuge through the screen of rubble he had built up the night before.

The hollow lay under the morning sun as he had first seen it the day before. The strange plants had unfolded again and were soaking up the warm blaze. A few of them looked gnawed, but none seemed seriously injured. At the moment, however, his own needs were paramount. He inspected the remains of last night's dinner with no great longing, but started to tear at the high-smelling flesh. He must have food, and this was all there was available.

His brief meal over, he wrapped the now scanty remains of the animal in its scrap of hide and walked over to the pool to have a long, filling drink. Then, crouched on his haunches, he looked about.

The first thing he noticed was that the remains of the animal had been stripped of any scrap of meat by the foraging ants. But the skin was intact, as were the white bones. He eyed the surrounding rocks. Sharp flakes of stone lay here and there, and he noted some with the greasy sheen and flaked appearance of some flintlike material. He stirred himself and became busy. Less than an hour later by his inner clock, he prepared to leave the oasis, but in far better guise than when he had stumbled into it.

On his head was an odd hat, contrived from the slender

47

bones of the beast, with leaves of some of the small plants woven over them. From his shoulders hung two crude bags made from the same hide, one filled with water from the pool and leaking only a little, the other containing the remains of the meat, some crude bone needles, and a number of sharp pieces of flint. He was clean and had even managed a rough shave with a bit of fat and some sharp shards of flint. Best of all, his bag held a small, heavy pebble of some massive, iron-bearing mineral which he had tested with the flint to form sparks. Should he find suitable fuel, he now had fire!

On the western rim of the strange little bowl, he paused and looked down the gentle slope. He felt an odd pang. When he was lost and helpless, the oasis had succored him. Again, he bowed his head in prayer, then turned and topped the rise, to set off down the gentle slope of the bowl's western edge. He moved at a steady lope. In his right hand was the stone fragment he had picked up where he slew the Death Hart. Now it had a crudely chipped-away grip and looked not unlike a rude sword, though the thing was all point and no edge.

He found himself back in the full glare of the desert heat once more. The light struck off the blue sand and broken black rock of the surface. But there was an encouraging change now. Tufts of scrubby weed, brown and even greenish in hue, sprouted from shaded crevices. Here and there, barrel-shaped cacti had begun to appear. They contained moisture which could be squeezed from the spiny pulp at need. The land was definitely improving. He jogged on while trying once more to draw a rough idea of his present location.

The stars he had seen the previous evening appeared only a little different from those of D'alwah, so he was probably not very much north or south of the palace. But he had come a long way on that damned kaw litter. Joseato's murmur to Amibale was easy to recall. They wanted Hiero far off and deep in drugs before his throat was to be cut! They had known that the shock of his physical death might well reach one as attuned to him as Luchare. The fact of his disappearance would frighten and wound her, but she would retain hope. So again— where was he now?

West. He must have been brought almost due west, to the very borders of the kingdom or beyond. He recalled the maps he had studied of the realm and its borders, then concentrated once more on his memory of last night's stars. He had come somewhat south, he was sure. Not much, perhaps, but enough to throw his directional sense off a bit. Should he turn north now, he would probably find himself in plains of some length. There he might find men, maybe friendly, maybe not. It was too big a risk to take.

Further, he had to assume that Joseato and Amibale, plus whatever Unclean minds gave them orders or advice, were very careful; their meticulous plot proved they could be just that. Would they assume he was dead when the pallid dwarfs who had conducted him west did not report? Those bodies had not been found by the folk who blew the hunting horns. Even now, the enemy might be issuing new orders to track him down, if they had not already done so.

Where would they look for him? Why, toward the North, from which he had come originally and to which he could be expected to return for aid. Unarmed, he dared not go south or east into the waiting nets of the Unclean. He had to go north!

Well, he would return to the North—but not by the route they might be watching. He must strike even farther west, into the country off the map. Then he could turn north, becoming lost to his foes, to reappear when and where they could not expect him.

He was leaving Luchare behind, and his inner soul winced at the thought. She was not dead, he knew, despite his loss of mental strength; they were linked forever and he would know if she were dead, just as she would know if he were to perish. She had Mitrash of the guard and the hidden help of the Eleveners to protect her. She had Klootz, who would obey her when Hiero was not there. She had her royal father, who had been told enough to alert him. The mad young duke and the cunning priest would not find it easy to outwit her.

Trouble was coming to D'alwah—indeed, was already there. As prince and heir, he had tried to rally the southern kingdom against the Unclean peril. He had been interrupted, his plans broken and set aside, if not destroyed. But he was the sole emissary of the Metz Republic in this strange world of the far South. It was his duty to go on, to find new weapons, to keep up the fight. His lost mental powers might be reborn someday, but if not—so be it. Something else, other weapons, would have to do instead. While life lasted, he must go on, ignoring all personal calls in the interest of the greater task the Abbey Fathers and Brother Aldo had laid on him.

All day, under the burning sky, the bronzed figure trotted patiently along. His sharp eyes missed nothing of his surroundings as he ate up the miles. Small, dun-colored birds appeared, peering at him from rocky outcroppings, and the different types of cacti and desert shrubs increased. Slowly, almost imperceptibly, the bluish tint was fading from the soil. A colony of little striped rodents chattered at him from an assemblage of holes in a sandy bank, but did not seem really concerned at his passing. Looking back, he could see them return to their own affairs while he was still within easy vision. This was an attitude on the part of the locals that he welcomed; it meant that men were little known in this land and hence not feared.

What he wanted at the moment was anonymity. Each league put behind him took him deeper into country where he would be lost to his foes. There would be time enough later to look for allies. This was a time to hide, to vanish utterly from human knowledge.

As the day drew to a close, he began to look for shelter. Food was no longer a problem. In his pouch, along with the rancid meat, he had a dozen cactus fruits, their needled fuzz carefully rubbed off. There were cacti of a different, smaller sort far to the north in the Kandan woods, and he knew them to be highly nutritious. Further, he had found a hollowed-out nest of some fairly large bird or reptile and had cracked the four hen-sized eggs and gulped them down on the spot. Metz Rovers were past masters at living off the country, and he had no fear of starving, especially since the land before him grew more benign with the waning of the desert. He sensed more life all about him. With the coming of night, there would also appear prowlers. It was a time to seek shelter again. Presently, in the red glow of sunset, he thought he saw what he sought.

An hour later, he felt he could relax, at least as much as anyone could relax in an unknown wilderness. He had found a low hillock of rock with one steep side. Halfway up this face was a shallow ledge, shallow but deep enough in the rock for him to lie down under the small overhang. There was also a little hollow in the ledge itself, well back from the lip. In this cavity, protected from most of the rare desert rains, Hiero found the remains of ancient ashes. The sides of the shelf curled around to enclose him as he sat over his tiny fire, made with a bundle of easily gathered twigs from the dry soil below. Only from the south and very near could his small light have been seen. The smear of ash looked incredibly old, made from fires created Heaven only knew how far back in time.

As he stirred his tiny glow with a twig, Hiero could have posed for the figure of some Apache hunter of the immemorial past, only the black mustache testifying to the mixed ancestry of the Metz. He had finished the meat, now charred into something resembling palatability by the fire, and a half dozen of the sweet and fully ripe red cactus fruits. Half his water, foul from its skin container, was untouched. He did not need it, but it would be saved; nasty as it was, it was still water. Beside him on the rock lay several long, dead cactus branches, their dried spines burned off with care. Thrust into the tiny fire, they would become instant torches, a potent weapon should any wild creature try to clamber up to Hiero's perch and use him for its own repast.

Half-turning his body to gather a few more sticks from the pile behind him, he saw something which he had missed on his first exploration of the ledge. Faintly etched into the rock behind and above his head were pictures, revealed by the glow of the fire striking up at them. They were worn, old beyond reckoning, and he could read little of them. There were stick figures of men and four-legged beasts, though what they were was impossible to say. He felt strangely cheered by this fresh proof that men had used this place, however long ago.

He looked out over the flat landscape before him, stretching out under moon and stars until it was lost in the dimness of the South. The stars burned far and bright. The black of scrub and rock made the shadowed country seem a monochrome illusion, a sharply limned mirror image of the bright world he had traversed under the azure sky of the day.

A howl rang out from the middle distance, to be answered by a chorus of similar yells farther off. From the sounds, the Metz judged the makers to be pack hunters of some size. He hoped they were not on his track, though he had protected himself as well as he could. The calls were not unlike those of the wolves of his own Northland, though higher in pitch, and he smiled reminiscently. Whatever the creatures sought, however, it was not he, and he listened with only part of his attention as the hunt swept away south out of earshot. As the sound died, he allowed his minute fire to do the same, leaving only a bed of glowing coals. He would wake, he knew, at frequent enough intervals to renew it.

Not for the first time, he wondered what lay ahead of him. It was useless to speculate, he knew. His Forty Symbols, the precognition markers he had been trained to use since childhood, and the crystal globe that accompanied them were far back with his other belongings in D'alwah City. Even had they not been, his ability to use them was gone, and they would have been so much useless trash. He would have to face the future as most other humans of this day and age did and take what came as God and His Son sent. Presently he fell into a light slumber, knowing his senses would awaken him at need. At first his sleep was dreamless. After a while, his fist clenched and his jaw tightened. His slumber remained unbroken and his breath still came evenly. Nothing moved out in the plain below him, save for the ordinary life of the waste places of the earth. No menacing sound broke the silence of the night.

Yet deep in the mind of the warrior, a faint alert flickered. Perhaps not all of his former powers had quite been silenced and suppressed. Some minute synapse had been started up or impinged upon, some blanketed circuit half-alerted. Into his mind came a thought of hills—smoky, purple hills, with mist rising from folded valleys, their rounded tops a mixture of forest and steep meadow. Strange hills, never seen in life, far lower than the mighty Stonies, the great Shining Mountains of his far-off home, but—hills! He sighed in his sleep and threw one brown arm across his face. In his dream the hills receded, but not altogether. Somewhere deep in his subconscious, their memory lingered. He would see those hills. They were very beautiful.

He awoke before dawn the next day and went hunting. The faint coolness of the desert morning dissipated quickly, and he was warm in a few seconds as he searched for tracks. Soon, under some flat-topped trees, a new sign of better ground, he found a slot, the mark of some dainty, hoofed mammal. The tracks were fresh, and his fine nose could even catch a faint musky warmth where the beast had rubbed itself against a scraggy trunk and left a few brown hairs. He followed cautiously, noting that the animal was not afraid, but lazing along, snatching a mouthful of leaf here and there. The faint breeze blowing came from its direction to him. Soon he saw it moving ahead in the dawn light, a lone antelope of small breed, with lyrate horns and brindle hair.

Now he readied a new weapon, made the day before as he trudged across the scrubland and finished to reasonable perfection before he ate on the ledge he had found. It was a new weapon to him, or rather, for him, one he had only read about in Abbey books. Yet to humanity and throughout history, it was so old that it had no age. Three cords hung from his right hand; at the end of each was a rounded stone, tightly secured to its own cord of leather. The three strips of hide were joined at the base where his hand gripped them.

Suddenly, having stolen as close as he could in safety, he rose from a bush and hurled the device in a whirling motion at the startled animal's legs.

He was amazed at his easy success, but not so much that he did not leap forward and brain the poor brute as it struggled to escape the twisted thongs which held the forelegs fast. His stone spike, reversed, was more than equal to the job. As he began the butchery, he stole more than one respectful glance at the crude bolas which lay beside him on the ground. Nor did he forget to give thanks to God.

Minutes later, he was loping back to his little hill, a full load of meat slung over his shoulder in the beast's own hide. He had buried the remainder to avoid drawing scavengers, though he had little fear of daytime hunters in this remote wilderness.

The Metz priest relighted his small fire and, cutting as much of the meat as he could carry with ease into strips, began to smoke it. Meanwhile, he ate hugely, strength pouring into his wiry frame with each swallow. As he did, he contemplated the two curved, black horns he had dug free from the skull. They weighed little and he had no doubt he would find uses for them as well, though each was no longer than his forearm. Finishing his meal, he packed the meat in a new hide bag, swallowed the last of the murky water, and brushed out traces of his passing as best as he could. He also examined his sandals with care. Though scratched and scuffed, they were still very sound and had no need yet of patching or mending. Soon he was on his way again, threading a path through the bushes and scrub, once more with his face set to the distant West.

For four days the land rolled past him. The bush gave way slowly but surely to denser and taller vegetation, so that, though the terrain was still flat and open, it had now become a prairie interspersed with groves of trees and no longer even semi-desert. Water appeared, first in the form of rare pools, then as shallow, muddy streams, winding here and there in sandy beds. The land was rising too, hardly more than an inch a mile, but steadily and constantly.

Hiero saw no sign whatsoever of any human activity. The camp on the tiny ledge was the only sign that human beings had ever been in the land at all. It was hard to realize the truth of his teachings in the Republic's classrooms and remember that all of this vast country had teemed with people millennia ago—so many people that his whole nation would have been lost and unnoticed among them. Not for the first time, he mused on the mighty past and the awful changes brought by The Death. Whatever its sins thousands of years before, humanity had paid an awful price; the fires of the atom and the scourges of the plagues had exacted a toll beyond conception. And this was what the Unclean wanted restored! He tightened his lips and vowed yet again that he would do whatever was possible to see that they did not succeed.

If human life was absent, animal life was certainly not. The Metz could have eaten at fresh kills three times a day, had he chosen. He could also have served as meat himself, had he not been constantly wary.

Antelope of many kinds now appeared, roaming in vast herds, some so large that he felt it wiser to skirt them. It seemed to be calving time for many varieties, and he had no wish to challenge the forests of horns, either those of the mothers or of the great males who guarded the rim of the herds. There were deer too, and they were in herds as well, though he saw only antlerless bucks at this season.

But there were other beasts totally unfamiliar to him. Some were small, but others were so huge that he gave them the widest berth possible. One gathering of giants recalled the great thing that had blundered through his jungle camp on the journey south, months before. They had great trunks sprouting from their huge brown heads, vast pillarlike legs, and mouths with great, curving, ivory tusks. Along the increasing streams he saw other beasts, smooth-skinned, with heads prolonged into enormous snouts, in bulk no less than the other kind, though with shorter legs. All seemed to be more or less peaceful plant eaters, and he took care to disturb none of them. Once in the distance he saw a group of animals leaping with tremendous bounds of their long hind legs and realized they must be some variety of hopper, perhaps the ancestral type of his lost mount, Segi. He thought sadly of Segi and Klootz, then put the thought behind him. He could not bear to think of Luchare and he needed all his strength of purpose to proceed, knowing that every league took her and her country farther and farther away.

Around and about these thousands of plant eaters, there prowled and lurked the carnivores. Again and again, Hiero had to take to a handy tree and, on one occasion, to fight for his perch on the tree itself. This was when a tawny, catlike beast, as big as he was, followed him into the branches in one flowing bound. A smashing blow with the stone spike, glancing off its flat skull, left it half-stunned and bleeding at the tree's foot. From thence it limped off, snarling, in search of easier prey.

In this encounter he had been lucky, however. Some of the meat eaters were of a bulk far beyond his strength to battle. There was a far larger cat, with a short bobtail and striped spine of black and gold, so huge it could attack all but the most enormous of the herbivores. It had gigantic fangs, protruding well below the lower jaw, and seemed to haunt the watercourses. Hiero grew very wary indeed about drinking and filling his water bag. There were also wolves, big beasts very much like those of the Northland, but lighter and ruddier in color, and a host of smaller, jackallike hunters as well. These and most of the other killers were, fortunately, nocturnal to a degree; though they made the night ring with their wild screams and roars, by then Hiero was careful to be high in a tree fork, selected well in advance by sunset.

It was true that he could have stopped and made himself better weapons than he now carried, but somehow he did not want to stop at all. Some compulsion, very faint at first and growing only by almost imperceptible degrees, made him want to travel as fast as he could, stopping only when absolutely necessary. He killed such small beasts as were on his line of march and lighted fires only to smoke the barest minimum of parched meat. He had commenced moving more to the south than he had planned, but he seemed to brush the thought aside, when it occurred to him, as being somehow unimportant. Ever so faintly, beyond his blurred abilities to recognize, a control had been set on his movements. Yet it never interfered with day-to-day business, and he was in no other way less alert and ready for what came.

On the sixth day after leaving the hillock where he had seen the ash, he topped a ridge somewhat more lofty than any he had observed in the days before. There, far to the southwest, was a distant line of blue. It could only be hills, and the sight sent a thrill through him. These were the hills of his dream a week back, though he did not consciously recall either them or the dream itself. How beautiful they looked and how desirable! He must go there and see them, must walk their slopes and forested heights. This wish, now embedded in his mind, was no bar to his ultimate purpose. The fact that he was, in truth, straying away from the line to the west and north he had planned for himself days earlier simply did not register in his conscious thoughts at all. Lightly and delicately, the fisher had laid the lure, and the fish swam forward, unknowing.

The next thing that came to his notice was far different and an entirely practical and down-to-earth matter. He was being followed!

Several times during the day he had felt that something was on his trail. It was now late afternoon again, with the sun hovering over the far lands before him, yet he knew the thing was still there. Twice during the past hours he had noted birds rising in the distance behind him, and the notice had been filed in his memory. He had not seen or heard any other sign of whatever it was, but he sensed its presence still coming. The powers of his mind, the telepathic networks, might be dead, yet he had no doubt. The skills and feelings of a lifelong hunter had not been dulled, and he knew, as an animal knows, that he was being tracked.

He wondered if it were one of the giant wolves. The members of the cat family were not scent hunters; they never had been, and this faculty had not changed since the beginning of time. But there were many other possibilities. He did not discount the chance of something entirely new, some creature he had never seen before. The wilderness of what had once been called North America was full of strange life, as he had only too-good cause to remember.

Still, he was puzzled. Whatever it was did not seem to be moving on at any great pace; indeed, there were times when the feeling that it was there at all grew very faint in his awareness. It was as if the thing had turned aside or simply stopped. Then the feeling would recur with renewed strength, as if what followed had picked up his marks and was advancing again at an increased speed. This dallying was not the hallmark of the wolf or dog family. Could it be another human? He had seen no smoke of any fires, but the thing or person might have lighted as few and as small ones as he had.

He decided there was nothing he could do at present, save to be even more wary and to see that his march stayed closer to useful trees. Whatever, or whoever, was tracking him down would at some point draw near enough for him to get a look, hopefully from some safe position. He continued on his way toward the southwest and the distant hills, but his eyes roved in search of good ambush locations as he went.

That night, secure in the fork of a lofty oak, he spent a good part of the dark hours awake and listening. But the cacophony of the savanna and the teeming night seemed much the same as ever. The howls and shrieks of the hunters and their prey were no different from what they had been for recent nights past. Once a group of the great, trunked giants meandered near his tree, on their way to some water hole, no doubt, and he stayed very still as the vast bulks drifted by. His tree was tall and sturdy, but he had no wish to see what those titanic shoulders could do if aroused. Presently, with soft squeals from their huge calves, each three times the size of the man, the monsters passed on. Long afterward, Hiero roused to a concerted bellowing of fury which, distant though it was, made the earth tremble. He guessed that some carnivore, possibly a great saberfang, had tried for a calf and that he was hearing the herd in response. Otherwise the night was normal, and he slept at last, undisturbed by any other sounds, however furious.

With dawn, he was on his way again toward the hills, one eye cocked for signs of pursuit, the other scanning the route ahead, so that he was never too far from a tall tree or a great termite mound. The latter, some many times steeper than the surrounding bushes, had begun to appear more and more frequently, and they provided useful places of quick safety and good lookout points.

He took position on one of these at noon, pausing both to rest and to eat his frugal meal of dried meat and berries. Much of the lower scrub was full of the latter, and he had found many of them edible and tasty.

A sudden uprush of a flock of birds, calling and piping in alarm, came suddenly from a few meters off, back on the track by which he had come. Laying down his meat carefully, he crouched just below the far side of the termite hill and watched keenly along the line of his previous march. He had no doubt that his mysterious tracker was close upon him and he was determined to get a look. He had a clump of tall trees at his back, picked out well in advance, should the sunbaked anthill prove inadequate as a defense.

Presently he saw some dense bushes move. Something large was pushing slowly through them. His legs tensed, ready to spring into instant flight. The bulk of whatever was advancing seemed formidable.

Then a glint of something bright and flashing caught his eye, and the next moment the thing moved into the open. A grin of mingled joy and pure amazement broke over Hiero's features, and he could hardly restrain himself from yelling aloud.

Hopping sedately toward the mound, as if wanting to gain the shelter of his comfortable stable, came the shape of a giant hopper. On his back was strapped the owner's saddle, stirrup-boots lashed to their girth so as not to swing loose. Various articles of gear hung on the harness as well, also securely fastened in place. Segi had come to seek his master.

There was no mistaking the great brute. Hiero knew his own harness. If more evidence were needed, the sharp point of his beloved spear, once a part of Klootz's saddle in the North, thrust up along the hopper's withers, tied so as not to catch on branches as the animal moved.

Hiero rose and then slid slowly down the face of the mound, calling to the hopper as he came. Segi put one ear back in mild surprise at the sight of the man but seemed in no way discon-certed or inclined to flee. When Hiero came close, he lowered his great head and sniffed the man thoroughly. Satisfied, he raised himself to his full height again and leaned back on his great tail, looking proudly and haughtily about, as if to say, "Well, I've done *my* job. The rest is up to others."

For a long time, Hiero stood with his face buried in the hopper's great tan shoulder, a prey to raw emotion. That out of the empty wastes such a thing could happen! He had to control himself for a number of minutes. Segi stood patiently, his long ears twitching at flies, but otherwise quite content to wait and see what his owner wanted next.

At length, the man got himself in hand and, patting the great flanks, began to inspect what the hopper had brought him.

First there was the short spear, its broad, steel head and crossbars catching the light, a copy of the medieval boar spears of far-off and forgotten Europe. He freed it from its wrapping and laid it handily by on the ground. Next, also strapped to the saddle, he found something else and again almost whooped with delight. There, leather sheath and all, was the pick of all his weapons, the terrible short sword of the North, the ancient weapon given him at graduation from the Metz Academy. As long as his forearm, curved on one side and straight and edgeless on its back, the bolo of the lost empire gleamed with oily sheen in the sun. The worn badge of the circle with its flaming top and the faded "U.S.A." marks seemed to him a pledge from the past of future victory to come. When he had strapped the shoulder belt on and the heavy weight had settled across his back, hilt ready to his hand over his left shoulder, then indeed did he feel complete.

Spear and sword—yes, here was his dagger, the six-inch, two-edged blade with buckhorn handle—all complete. Next he found a broad leather belt, and then a leather box, heavy though small. His casting pieces and crystal! There were two packs of dried meat, sealed for long journeys. His excitement blazed. He knew who had sent this!

Where was her message? His fingers fumbled as he went over the saddle again like a squirrel going through a pile of nuts. Here was a leather water bottle, a small one, wisely chosen for use on foot and also when mounted. Damn it, where was that message? He knew it was there as well he knew the sender's scent and the feel of her skin!

He forced himself to stop and think finally, while the patient Segi leaned down and snoofed at his black hair. *Use your head, stupid! Suppose Segi had been killed? Would she leave a note*

*pinned to his right ear for anyone, including the enemy, to
read? Think, the way she did for you, you oaf!*

Eventually, he found it by sheer patience. It was wrapped
in a tiny packet of fine, oiled leather, no bigger than his finger
joint and jammed up into the far inside of the saddle horn itself.

With trembling fingers, he unwrapped it and, with the sun
beating down on his head, began to read. Above him, the
hopper's nostrils flared at intervals, picking up the varied smells
eddying past in the light breeze. But none seemed to convey
any danger, and the towering figure stayed relaxed on his great
haunches while his master read and reread the parchment message from his far-off mate.

"My Love," it began, "I know you are not dead. Where
you are, what they have done, I know not. The Unclean have
done something, somehow. If you are not dead and I cannot
reach your mind, they must be the ones. I would have sent this
by Klootz, but he is gone. The stablemen said he went mad in
the night, rearing and bellowing in his stall. When they tried
to calm him, he broke the stall gates as if they were matchwood
and fled through the stable yards into the night. Some guards
say he tore through the northern gate at the hour before dawn,
and he has not been seen since. He may follow you, so be
alert. An assassin tried to kill Danyale at the end of the ball.
The man has not yet spoken. The king is hurt but will live.
My cousin Amibale has vanished also, and none can or will
say where. The priest Joseato is missing too. The high priest
says he knows nothing. The troops seem loyal, and Mitrash is
with me. He says to tell you that he has sent messages. God
help you, my love. Segi has my message planted in his simple
mind. If he can find you, he will. Come back to me." It was
unsigned, save for a single sweeping "L."

Hiero was glad that none but Segi could see him now.
Whoever heard of a Metz Senior Killman, the pick of the
woodsrunners of the North, with two runnels of water flowing
down his sweaty face?

After a while he could see again, and he marveled at the
wonder of his wife. Hardly out of girlhood, but what a woman!
She had never lost her head for a second. Hiero was *not* dead,
so send a message. Klootz was gone, so send the next best
thing, Segi, the pick of hopperdom and a beast who had already
learned to know and love him. He shook his head in admiration.

He would be willing to bet that she had issued all the right orders to the guards as well and that she and Danyale and the kingdom were in as good a state of defense as could be managed. And she had found the sudden departure of Duke Amibale and the priest suspicious, that too was clear. They would not find it easier to surprise her, even with her mate gone.

Mitrash had sent messages, had he? A good man. The messages had gone to the Brotherhood of the Eleventh Commandment, Hiero was sure. Even now, a long way off somewhere, Brother Aldo and his fellow councilors might well know what had happened and be moving in their turn. The Metz felt a tremendous sense of relief. Luchare and her father were safe, as safe as anyone these days, and the kingdom was alerted. He had all the help she could send, and now the rest was up to him. Only Klootz's fate puzzled him. Where could the morse have gotten to?

He patted Segi again and talked soothingly to him. The big hopper had really done wonders. Hampered by his saddle and harness, he had come hundreds upon hundreds of leagues, somehow patiently following his vanished master. He looked fine, too, hardly gaunted at all. Despite all that Hiero had been taught about the hopper's capabilities, he was still amazed. Segi must have crossed the dreadful desert, too, going without water for days; and when through it, he had come unflinchingly on, dodging predators, snatching bits of leaf as he hopped, and never ceasing until Hiero was found. *How many men*, Hiero mused to himself, *would have done as much, would have persevered into an unknown wilderness out of pure affection? Do I, does any man, deserve such devotion?*

In a few seconds, he had run up the termite mound and secured his few possessions. In another, he freed the stirrup-boots and mounted. His head behind but on a level with his steed's, he gently urged the hopper on, south and west, their heads pointed into the sunset and at the distant blue line. The calling hills still held Hiero in their grip; unthinking, he urged his strange mount forward to whatever fate lay hidden in their distant folds.

✤ 4 ✤

DARK PERILS, DARK COUNSELS

IN AN UNDERGROUND PLACE, A LARGE SCREEN COVERED ONE end of a room. Blue bulbs set in the bleak stone walls shed a pallid light upon a great table of polished black marble. Around the table and under the screen were arranged four black chairs with legs carved into contorted shapes and bearing strange arabesques and flourishes along their broad arms and backs. Pulled away from the head of the table was a fifth chair, larger than the others and more ornate. It alone was unoccupied.

In the four chairs in use sat or lounged four gray-robed men. A stranger entering the room might have thought that he had encountered four offspring of a single birth, so alike were the seated men to one another. All were bald, or with heads and faces so shaven that no hair appeared. All had pale ivory skin. At sight of those faces, a child would have screamed in instant horror. The eyes were dead, gray pools of nothingness, in which there yet glowed a baleful fire. The faces were expressionless, carved in a sickly marble, set in grim lines and yet smooth, seeming ageless and yet old beyond memory. Only the flickering of the awful pairs of eyes to the great screen and back toward each other seemed to betray life, together with the writhing and uncoiling of the long white hands when they rested on the smooth surface of the table. The men's attentions were fixed on the screen, but occasionally one would mutter to another or inscribe some notes on one or another small square of writing material laid before him. The Great Council of the Unclean, those who called themselves the Chosen Masters, was in session.

Though the men appeared identical at first glance, a further look would have discerned differences. Each bore upon the gray of his breast an embroidered symbol, worked in threads of metallic, glittering stuff. Each had a different color, one being red, one yellow, one blue, and the last of all green. None of the colors seemed normal somehow, being oily and iridescent, at once too pale and too dark, changing constantly but always sickly and abhorrent. The livid green of the fourth man's mark seemed the worst of all, a ghastly parody of the fresh and limpid hue of spring in the ordinary world. But that world was what these monsters were sworn to destroy or, as they put it, to bring to order. The symbols were spirals and coils worked into mind-bending twists which the eye could not follow, as if they faded in some impossible way into some other and fouler dimension.

The screen itself was covered with a maze of fine metallic wire which, like the symbols of the robed men, was worked into impossible bendings and anglings, back and forth in a weird pattern which changed by the moment. It contorted itself each instant into something new and even more peculiar. Here and there on the wires glowed tiny lights of different colors, like minute bulbs. Yet if they were bulbs, they were as strange as their background, for they also moved, appearing and reappearing at what looked like random, but was not. It was clear that the four could read the board and understand it, as one would read a printed page. None but they and one other could have done so, however. For this was the Great Screen, and all the lore and memory of the Unclean was embedded in it, as were all their plans and contingencies of the future. It would have taken the life of a normal human to learn the basic elements necessary for the interpretation of its easiest and most accessible secrets.

At length, the one who wore the hellish green turned away from the screen and examined his fellows thoughtfully. Just as the one who wore the blue seemed in some indefinable way the youngest, so did the creature of the green seem older than the others, though exactly why, no one could have said.

"I will speak, according to the rules of the Great Council, where no mind can be deemed safe and thoughts cannot be trusted with our deliberations."

It was clear that this was a formula being recited, a formal

opening of the meeting. The voice of the speaker was thin yet
resonant, toneless and yet vibrant. It was also chill, the timbre
gelid and ringing like the slow grinding of ancient glacial ice.

"As the Senior among you, I call on the Lord S'duna, First
among the Brotherhood of the Blue Circle. Upon him mainly
has fallen the brunt of the most recent events. He and his bear
much of the responsibility for them. This is said not in blame,
but only is strict accountability. This is also said," he added
as S'duna stirred and shrugged, "under orders."

As the others looked up in sudden interest, the green-sym-
boled man touched his brow and inclined his head toward the
large and empty chair at the head of the table.

"Yes," he went on, "to me, S'lorn, First of the Green, in
my fortress in the South there came in the night, on the One
Circuit, a message. The Unknown One, That Which Is Not To
Be Named, that which *is* not, but was and will be, sent a
message. Any of us could have received it. Why I was chosen,
save for age, I know not, but can perhaps guess." He paused.
"I think, and I have spent much thought on this matter as I
journeyed, that I received the message to summon the Council
because I am the farthest away in the body. My thought, and
it is no more, reads thus: In many, many lives of the outer
world, we four, or they who taught and preceded us, have
seldom found it necessary to meet in the flesh. Now, I think,
the matter grows urgent, and thus the importance is stressed
that I who live the farthest off should summon us together.
The Nameless One, the Chosen of the Chosen, has many secrets. There may be other explanations, but I think mine will
suffice." He folded the pale hands in the lap of his robe. "Let
the Lord S'duna speak to us and unfold his reading of the recent
past."

The Master of the Blue Circle did not flinch. While he was
not on trial, still the others were watching and judging. All
were equals, the Great Council having been devised to still the
ceaseless internecine warfare which had so long crippled the
Unclean plans in the past. All were equal, but it was not in
the nature of such beings to spare another pain, nor was it the
way they had all been taught since birth. The troubles of the
recent past had involved S'duna far more than the others. So
they would watch, not being hostile, but if there were any sign
of weakness, of indecision . . .

And then there was the Nameless One, their unknown ruler, who had sent instructions. Could those instructions have to do with the failures of this time, and might they also carry orders on dealing with faulty leadership?

If a shudder ran through the Blue Master's frame, it was not detectable. He began. "First, we had warning that all was not well from the death of S'nerg of the Red Circle. For long, his body was not found, though we knew that he must be dead or somehow taken, for his self-seeker was moving away from us. We loosed followers, mere animals, on the track. They too were slain. That was the second warning, though the death of a high Brother was more than that, surely." No one said anything, no features moved, but the point had been taken. The Blue Circle was not the first to be struck.

"Next, the creature or creatures vanished into the Palood, the great marsh where even we do not go. Yet we alerted something which had dwelt there from time out of mind, a thing we feared and scarcely understood, yet thought could be used for our purposes. And it too was slain." The level voice paused. Another point made.

"Now we began somewhat to worry. The thing or things had entered the area I control. It or 'hey had managed to pass through the marsh, no mean feat in itself, as all here know. I estimated the track it might take, for it had discovered and destroyed the self-seeker it bore and we could no longer follow it. And, as all know, I trapped it.

"Surprise upon surprise and wonder upon wonder! What had we caught but one of the despised Abbey priests of the soft religion of the past, the cross worshippers. One of the vagabond pack of woodsrunners, half soldier, half hunter, whom they send about on their stupid errands. For allies, it had two animals and a slave girl, the latter seized from savages on the coast as they were about to eat her. And this motley crew was what had shaken the North and frightened our Councils to their depths!" He stared at each of the others in turn, as if weighing his next words before continuing.

"And there I erred, I freely admit. And if the Great Plan has suffered for it since, I accept *my* full share of responsibility. For I simply could not believe that this very ordinary human, however brave and skilled in the combat of the forests, could be the thing he was. I felt, as did all who studied the matter, that the Abbeys, or perhaps this man alone, had found a secret in a Dead City of the past, something to enhance the mind powers, some machine, perhaps, or even some strange drug. This secret we would extract at leisure on Manoon, the Dead Isle, whence none had ever gone, save at our bidding and direction. We completely ignored the escape of the slave girl and the two animals; let them perish in the wastes, we thought. They meant nothing." His ivory skull wagged slowly as he shook his head.

"Mistake upon mistake, error upon error. The man had inborn or somehow *inbred* powers locked in his skull, some of which, with training, might have brought him here, into this chamber, my Brothers, even as we. That was the sum of our greatest error—not to realize the appalling strength that this seeming woodsrunner, this half priest, masked and kept hidden in the inner part of his mind!" The emphasis, even the passion which had crept into his voice, drew a faint hiss of incredulity from S'lorn, but the older man suppressed it when he saw the expressions of the Masters of the Red and Yellow Circles. For they seemed in total agreement.

"What occurred next, alas, is too well known," S'duna went on. "He escaped. Escaped from the Dead Isle, taking his weapons and slaying still another Brother! A dumb brute, the captain of my Howler pack, sensed the escape on some level we could not and he too was slain, though a doughty fighter trained by me for many years. Now, think on this matter, Brothers, and think hard. We have not yet discovered *how* or by what powers this was done! All of our science, all of our records, which we thought the entire sum of knowledge here today—all of these tell us nothing useful. Oh, yes, the man used his *mind*. He slew the Brother with it. That was obvious. But without weapons or machines and hardly even with them, could *we* do the same? No, you all know we could not.

"What next? More by guesswork than by anything concrete, we traced him again, this stupid priest-assassin, this Per Hiero Desteen, of whom we now know so much. And what occurred this time to the band of ragged wanderers? For he had found the girl and the animals by mind touch, though again we do not know how. What next? This time a whole *shipload*, one of the very few new ships, driven by the powers of The Death itself, ship, crew, and yet another high Brother, S'carn, third under me in rank and no weak foe, all vanished!" This time his pause was both unstudied and longer. Nor was he taking such trouble to conceal his rage and bafflement. The others listened soberly, their own faces now eager as they digested all the meaning of his words. S'lorn of the Green was as attentive as any.

"We did what we could. We issued as many of the hand-wrought, personal mind screens as we had and warned all those that had dealings with us or were under our control on or near the Inland Sea. We alerted our Brothers of the Yellow Circle to the south. And now, too, I went southward myself. For I was convinced at last of our terrible danger from this man who had such strength that he could throw his mental force about like careless bolts of lightning. Oh, yes, by now I had become thoroughly convinced!

"What follows next is not certain, but we have some clues, painfully assembled and collated. The reading seems thus:

"Somehow, the priest crossed the Inland Sea. During this crossing, he again fought, having a ship and crew under his command, found how and where we know not. He fought a pirate long under our control, slew him in personal combat, and with him a Glith, newest and most powerful of what the enemy call Leemutes, the animal slaves we long have bred as our servants. The pirate crew surrendered. Not even fear of us could break their Sea Law, that to the victor goes the spoil. We have interrogated such as we could catch since and have learned a good deal, but gaining information has been slow and tedious.

"This battle," he said, "caused mental storms. Also, there were self-seekers taken. We detected the area, plotted a course, and again sent one of the new ships, this time from a hidden harbor of the sea, near Neeyana on the south coast. It found the enemy and destroyed his ship, homed in on the self-seekers, the mind screens he had captured and forgotten. But we were too late! We gained nothing but the ashes of the paltry boat. All those aboard escaped into the deep forest, a place we go not and know little of. So now, at last, we know, from the sea scum we captured later, much we did not and could not know then.

"Listen well, Brothers!" His voice, never pleasant, had become a susurration, a hissing of pure venom. "Eleveners! Into this comes the so-called Brotherhood of the Eleventh Commandment, our most ancient enemies, the animal and plant lovers, the grubbers in the dirt, the beast minders, the midwives of all that creep and crawl, the adorers of useless life, the pitiers of the weak, the tenders of the helpless and soft! Arrgh! Eleveners!" His rage seemed almost to choke him for a moment, but he mastered himself.

"One of these vermin was on that ship with the priest, his woman, and the two animals. He was seen. An old man, he must have been one of weight in their rotted hierarchy, for he could control the great sea beasts. Mayhap he had something to do with the lost ship in the North.

"I was in Neeyana then and I called upon Brother S'ryath, my fellow and Master of the Yellow Circle here, for aid and counsel. And since I had abandoned direct control to him, I would that he tell of what we devised and what transpired as a result of it." S'duna leaned back, as if glad to be done with his part. His anger had brought unaccustomed beads of sweat to his pallid brow.

S'ryath, on S'duna's left, hesitated for a moment, as if wondering where to begin or, perhaps, how. But he took up the tale readily enough.

"We tried, S'duna and I, something which should have been done far earlier, if only there had been time, which there had *not* been." He looked about, as one would do if perceiving a challenge, but he seemed to see none and went on.

"Our thoughts ran thus: Why had the priest been sent, or why was he going to the South, far beyond the borders of his barbarous land? Indeed, had he been sent at all, or was this all his own venturing? We thought not, we two. S'duna had indeed made it plain to me that this was no false alarm but a grave and sudden danger to us and to all the Great Plan. What did he seek, this priest? Remember, we knew nothing of any Eleveners then. That knowledge came much later.

"We assembled such knowledge as we had. This Rover had S'nerg's maps; that we knew or guessed. On those were the locations of many places of the Great Dead, the masters of the world before The Death. Could this creature be in search of one such, for some purpose of his own? It seemed a good chance, and we had little other information. S'duna's spies were ransacking the North and so were those of Brother S'tarn across from me, the Master of the Red Circle. But spies, even such as we have in the North, take time to gather news, and we were and are stretched to the limit. We had to guess and meanwhile assemble forces for any eventuality. This we did at great speed—men, our animal slaves of all kinds, all we had at hand. It was a powerful force, and there were a half-dozen Brothers in command. And then we had a message, though undesigned by the sender!

"On the eastern edge of the great wood, this priest and his pack used their minds, having some apparent struggle with the strange life of that area. We knew that grim things laired there, bred by the atom and yet not of us. It was an unknown place to us, save for dark rumor. Many had disappeared in that country without trace, both of us and of the ordinary human scum, traders and such.

"We studied our maps, and there was a pre-Death site there, one, moreover, with an entrance marked, one we ourselves could open. It was but one of many marked for future research. We have hundreds of such, some being treasure troves, but most are useless. This is all well known." He looked about again, an expression of defiance on his face, the control slipping as he tried to justify what came next.

"No, S'duna and I did not accompany the army. Perhaps we should have done so, in the light of hindsight. I do not apologize, though. Why do we breed and train servants and inferiors, if not for such tasks? I ask if any here question our courage, before I continue." Seeing no disposition to do as he asked on any of the other faces, he continued, his voice lowered as if in involuntary awe.

"There was a destruction brought upon the army such as we have never seen or dreamed of in our entire history. We received messages from our Brothers of the Robe, mind messages, that they had found the place, just as the maps showed, and that they would enter. Then—nothing! All mind voices ceased, as they went underground, presumably. And there fell a great silence, one still unbroken.

"Many days later, one of our scouts, reconnoitering with all caution, found a vast area of blight and rot, full of foul growth, all of it dying and giving forth a stench which rose to the clouds above. Where the lost cavern of the Mighty Dead had lain was a smoking, tumbled waste, which still gave off heat and reeks of horrid vapor from beneath. Not the atom, not the forces of The Death, for those we can detect, but something else, perhaps older still, some great secret of the ancients, we deem, had been unloosed. And we have learned no more of what befell. My tale ends here." He fell silent and stared at the table.

The silence continued, as if none cared to break it. The sheer magnitude of what they had heard, even though all knew the body of it in advance, seemed to have cast a spell. When a voice finally did speak, the actual sound appeared to have no place there.

"But *I* can add to the tale, Brothers, and in a way that will give us a new strength." S'lorn of the Green was actually smiling, a nasty rictus of no humor but of immense satisfaction. "Take heart, Brothers, while I unfold news from the South, from my own distant lands. Much of it came to hand only today, from my own trusted messengers. But it makes a pretty picture."

He leaned forward as he spoke, and his long white fingers arched and touched each other upon the cold smoothness of the table.

"We all have been told that the priest arrived in D'alwah, throwing years of patient work by our minions and allies into confusion. For lo, as we could never have guessed, the ragged slave woman this woods rat had found in the distant North was the lost princess, daughter of D'alwah's stupid king, one thought by us to be dead in the jungle long ago. The priest knew this, nurtured her, and finally *married* her by their absurd rites. Thus in one incredible stroke, he had himself made the *de facto* ruler of the kingdom.

"I had ascribed much of this creature's past success to sheer luck and, I honestly confess it, to complaisance and bad planning in the North." He looked around, meeting every eye firmly before going on. "I offer my profound apologies to any here who may have thought me somewhat disdainful of their efforts in the past. This stroke of genius, this mating with the seat of power, changed my views of Per Desteen overnight. If he was a mere Abbey servant—and I know little of them, save what is passed to me from your realms—who and what are *they* in turn? Yet if, as I suspected, he was a strange mutant, a spontaneous appearance, as it were, unplanned and unplanning, then some opportunity might present itself.

"I too took counsel and devised a plan. We have powerful allies in that kingdom, even among what they call royal blood, and their strange church is rotted with our servants, who are deep in its secrets. A new drug was under experiment in our hidden centers, a drug which kills the mind powers, even of the most powerful. We have experimented on such." That the experiments probably had involved the death of at least one Brother of the Order who had merited S'lorn's displeasure seemed obvious to all there. It meant nothing to them. Thus was power attained and kept.

"I met with our allies far from their city," S'lorn went on. "For I allowed no mind work near this priest creature at all. I wanted him to find nothing to suspect, and that is what he found—nothing!

"Now listen to this good cheer, Brothers. Today I have the following to tell. Per Hiero Desteen—this prince of D'alwah, this titan who has so shaken our great Order—is dead!"

There was at least one gasp. It did not come from S'duna of the Blue, whose cold face was unchanged.

"This prince-priest, this vagabond ruffian, this mental giant, was simply struck on the head, drugged with the new drug I spoke of, and spirited far away into the wilderness. He was not killed at once, lest his wife, the royal slut, sense his passing and attack our allies before they were ready. But that is the real and inescapable fact. He is *dead*, finally, totally, completely dead. He is gone from the gaming board, Brothers, and we can once again plan as in the past, this random and ruinous factor forever disposed of!"

This time the silence was not brief. The purring voice of S'duna cut in, and there was no pleasure in it, only coldness.

"Before we rejoice, Elder Brother, I, the youngest of you, but nevertheless the one who knows this man best, indeed the only one of us ever to see him and live, have some small questions. Who saw the body? Yes, and also, how and where was he slain? Do your allies have the body in their possession? And if so, what was done with it? When I hear answers to these humble questions, I too shall perhaps rejoice."

A faint hint of red colored the pale cheeks of the Green Master. It was obvious that S'lorn was both angry and unaccustomed to be so taken to task. There was a noticeable rasp as he answered.

"Our chief ally in the kingdom was trained under me as a child. He sent the drugged priest under guard far to the west, by hidden paths known to none but himself. He sent trusted men, childhood servants, in two parties. This proved wise. For the second party found the bodies of the first. All, I repeat, *all* were reported dead and still warm. I see no reason to doubt any of this. Who slew them all is not known, but is thought to be local outlaws who haunt the western marshes. Are you answered?"

"Yes," S'duna said slowly, "I am answered. But I warn all here, with due respect to yourself, Eldest Brother, that this man is very hard to kill. I would a Brother, and a high one at that, had seen the corpse. I shall be honest, if nothing more. I like it not. Yet I may be wrong, and none hopes this more than I. That, at least, you may believe."

"Should it prove in error, then I will answer for it," the other snapped, annoyed by the doubt thrown on his triumph. "But we have wasted far too long on this matter already. The fact that the priest was what he was and did what he did is part of a much larger scheme. We have an organization, Brothers, now plotting against us, moving actively to challenge *us*, who have always been unknown to our enemies. Seldom even has an enemy ever glimpsed a Brother and lived to speak of it in the past. None knew of us, save the Eleveners, curse them, and them we scorned. Their creed of nurturing all life, of harming nothing—that, we thought, was sufficient protection from their lurking and prying. Let them skulk about, we thought, until the Great Plan comes to pass, and then let them be swept away, along with all the other vermin of no use to us!

"But now . . ." His voice hardened. "What do we learn? At least in part, they have abandoned their foolishness at last. They are actively helping our foes. And this is bad, could not be worse. They know much of us, and only the fact that they were passive and stupid held our hand in the past, for they have studied us a long time, longer maybe than we know. Their mere knowledge, imparted to others more prone to violence, could be a deadly weapon against us." He paused, then went on.

"The priest is dead. But what sent him is not. He came from

the North, from your Abbeys that were thought under control, Brothers. Two states of the North, both under Abbey rule or guidance—the Metz Republic to the west and the League of Otwah in the east—are the source of this one deadly trouble-maker. Whence came he and—more to the point—are there more like him? We must plan quickly. This peril must be crushed at its roots—at once! It is for this, I know in my inner being, that I was told to summon this Council."

The other three leaned forward and listened as he began to expound his plan.

In another place, far from the dark and gloomy tunnels of the Unclean, stood a grove of mighty pines or related conifers. Of vast size, their immense boles were stained with lichen and hoary with age. In the heart of the grove lay a ring, bare to the rising moon and padded with many layers of fallen needles. Nothing grew in the ring, though the bed of needles was always fresh and clean.

No sound broke the silence of the night, save for the faraway hooting of a hunting owl and the sough of the soft wind in the lofty branches. Yet the glade was not empty. Here, too, there was a meeting. Shadowy, ursine shapes lay about the ring, only their glowing eyes proclaiming life. Great, furry sides heaved as the bear people kept their attention on the smaller figure of Gorm in the center.

Deep thoughts moved through mental circuits that others in the wild could not follow. Patiently, these Wise Ones of their people studied the new information brought to them. They had long remained hidden from the other sentient races of the world. Now they were not to be hurried in any decision which might affect their future.

The night passed slowly as thoughts moved from one reflective mind to another. The moon waned. After a time, it vanished behind a large drift of cloud. When the white light illumined the clearing once again, the smaller figure of Gorm was gone from the center, but the outer ring of bodies remained, fur-covered sides heaving gently.

A still pool lay deep in the jungle, as far from the tunnels of the Unclean or the grove of the bear people as those places were from each other. Here the trees which arched over the

brown water were of such size as to make the great conifers
look like saplings by comparison. Their incredible branches
did not start to leave the main trunks until they were almost
out of sight from the ground below. Vast cables of liana and
veritable forests of parasitic plants clung to the towering sides
of the giant trees. In the noon warmth, insects buzzed busily
and bird calls rang out.

From down a well-trodden game trail, a great, black beast
came quietly to the pool. He paused and surveyed the surroundings, his wide, flaring nostrils testing the air. Upon one
shining haunch lay the still-bleeding marks of some savage
claw. The mighty palmate antlers which crowned his huge head
were stained and smeared with caked blood. Yet he did not
look fearful in any way, only alert.

Eventually, he decided that the area was safe and slowly
slid into the small pool until only his head protruded, the eyes
always watching, the huge ears and blubber lips twitching at
the slightest sound.

At length, with antlers and hide now clean and glistening,
Klootz heaved his bulk from the far bank of the pool where
the game trail continued on. As silently as he had come, he
vanished down it—going north.

Hiero awoke and looked about him, then stretched and
yawned. Another day had come. From his tree fork, he could
see far over the savanna, his vision obscured only by other
clumps of towering trees like his own. With each day of travel,
the ground rose, and the trees grew thicker, but there were still
wide spaces between them. He could see many drifting herds
of game filtering here and there down the lanes. Most were
antelope and related beasts which would spend the day in the
bush, avoiding both insects and the runners who preyed upon
them in the open. Others were returning to the grasslands after
a visit to a water hole and a night of peril, the prey of grim
hunters who struck them down as they drank.

Hiero leaned down from the branches and gave a low, echoing call. He had scanned the neighborhood and seen no sign
of inimical life.

Presently an inquiring head peered over a tall bush; then the
great hopper bounded into sight, as perky as if he had spent a
night in his straw-filled stall.

The man climbed down and dug the saddle and other gear out of a thicket where he had cached them the evening before. He was always relieved that Segi was still alive when morning came.

"The fact is, my boy," Hiero said, scratching between the long ears as the hopper leaned down and nuzzled him, "you are something of a problem. In fact, I wish you weren't here at all. How's that for gratitude, after all you've done for me, eh?" A long pink tongue swept over his face, and he spluttered and then laughed.

But he was only half-jesting. Segi's safety was something that indeed did worry him, and he could see nothing much that he could do about it. It was all very well for the man to climb into a tree at night, but Segi, bred for the great plains, had no such defense during the dark hours. There was still a good deal of open ground around them, but with each dawn it grew less as they neared the hills. With the encroachment of the forest, it was going to be harder and harder for Segi to look after himself at night, with the wood alive with hungry maws. A hopper's only defense lay in his nose, ears, and huge hind legs. For the last, he needed room, room to leap and dodge, to spring and evade. And this sort of room was becoming increasingly scarce.

All that Hiero could think of was to take off every bit of the harness at evening, so that Segi had at least the total use of his freedom. The Metz hoped with half his mind that each morning would find the animal gone, drawn to his distant home and at least possible safety. Fully girt with saddle and weapons, he had found his way to his master through trackless country alive with predators. He would have had a fair chance, then, with nothing on, of making his way back alive to the distant East.

But Segi would not leave. Whatever Luchare had impressed on his simple mind, allied to plain love for Hiero, was too strong a bond. He had found his man and he proposed to stay with him. No amount of slaps and orders could make him take the trail back. When Hiero crept from the tree one night and, risking his life all the while, tried to steal away, he found the big brute hopping along in his tracks, thereby doubling the risk. It was the last time he tried that maneuver. Had Hiero's mind power been intact, he could have sent the hopper away in an instant. As it was . . . He sighed and patted the warm, brown flank absently. He had come to love the big animal a great deal in the last few days. Before, back in D'alwah, Segi had been a cherished and interesting pet, but nothing beyond that. Now there was much more, a deep, mutual affection. It was not the same as it had been with Klootz, of course. Hiero and the great morse had been raised together, and Klootz's mind, after centuries of Abbey breeding, was far superior to Segi's. Indeed, the Abbey men were uncertain just how clever the morses were becoming. As he ate his simple breakfast, Hiero wondered if Klootz were alive. He stilled the thought for Luchare which came next; he had no time for vain regrets.

Some hours later, he reined in Segi and peered under his hand at the heights in the west. They were in a long ride of the forest, and the trees were very tall. Hiero knew without being told that he was coming to a tip of the great jungle again, the forest of the South. The trees around him now, which would have been considered well grown in his northern home, were but the scrub and the outliers of the incredible growth of the *real* forest, the greatest jungle Earth had ever known. The strange life of the atom fires, spawned by the horrors of The Death, had, among its many effects, the vast increase in bulk of many of the plants. Above all, the great trees of what were now the northern tropics, aided perhaps by what the ancients called the Greenhouse Effect, had reached a size and majesty never known in the planet's past.

And beyond those trees, no more than a good day's march, he thought, there loomed the purple hills. He ached in his bones to be among them, and only his native kindness and good sense restrained him from spurring his mount on at too fast a pace.

Had the Metz even a third of his former powers, he would have known at once that he was being drawn and not acting under his own volition at all, though the thought that had pulled him gently but inexorably to the southwest for days was clever and subtle. But Hiero knew that he had lost all his skills—the thought reading, the shields, the forelooking, and the sheer force of his once mighty mind—weeks in the past. He had tried, over and over again, to reach out, to listen, somehow, somewhere to detect the presence of another intelligence. Every attempt had met with failure. The foul drug of Joseato's administering had done its work only too well. Mentally he was as blind as a newborn baby, and maybe more so if the baby possessed innate powers.

Being this mentally blind himself, he had the feeling that he was a blank to those outside, as well. He was right, but only in part. The drug had been effective, horribly so. To most of the outer world, and certainly to the Unclean, Hiero was a mental nullity, a blank. Not even Luchare could have detected him. The hopper had followed him by scent, his fine-tuned nose able to pick up the man's tracks even after several days. Dogs, some of them, could do as much.

But there were minds other than the Unclean's, also sprung from The Death. Hiero knew this well, none better. But it had never occurred to him that he might still be *reached*, be tapped and beckoned on a hitherto unused level of his brain, one which had lain dormant all his life and which he had not, even in the last year, realized was there at all. Yet so it was.

All day he and Segi moved steadily if slowly into the uplands, using great care to avoid dense clumps of foliage and timber. With each mile, this became harder and harder. The land itself was no longer a help but a hindrance. Folds of ground appeared, at first shallow, but then growing deeper and more precipitous. These ravines were no strong barrier at first, but Hiero knew them to be fingers thrust out from the heights ahead, the channels from which the tropic rains rushed down to the plains below.

Many of the ravines had water in their bottoms, though it was the dry season. At nightfall Hiero made camp on the lip of a sizable gorge, down which sped a small river, flowing fast over boulders and beds of gravel. He found a pocket in the stone, well above the river, and this he blocked, after penning Segi in with him, by dragging all the heavy, fallen timber he could find to barricade the entrance, making it at least partially secure. There were trees in abundance all about, but he could not leave the hopper alone on the ground overnight with no defense in this thick country.

Segi did not care for the small enclosure at first and grew restless, but settled down when Hiero lighted a small fire. There was good herbage, and succulent vines grew down the walls of the place. The big beast finally lay down after feeding, to chew his cud.

The moon was not out, but the stars were bright, and Hiero passed much of the night awake, studying the black outline of the hills, which now actually loomed high above him. They were old mountains, he surmised, worn and rounded, not like his great, sharp Stonies, which towered in white-capped chains in the distant Northwest. Forest reached to the tops wherever the soil was dense enough. He had already seen rock faces, though, bare of trees but hung with matted ranks of moss and fern. He could guess that there would be plenty of cliffs as well, making for hard climbing. As he had done for the last few days, he pondered the problem of the poor hopper. How could he make Segi leave him? As long as they were together in this steep, wooded country, the danger to himself was doubled. He had to care for both his mount and himself at all times, for Segi no longer had space to use his limbs in the colossal bounds which were his only defense.

Twice during the night they were disturbed. Once a sharp, feral reek told them of an intruder, and the hopper snorted and crouched away to the back of the little bay, eyes rolling in fear. He made no effort to flee, relying on his master for defense, thereby showing good sense. Had he bucked or struggled, their shelter would have become a nightmare.

Hiero watched from a crouch, weapons at the ready. Presently, with no sound, a great paw, covered with scarlet fur and ending in huge yellow claws, came gently over the log barrier and felt cautiously about for a hold. This, the man decided, was quite far enough!

Scooping a few red-hot coals from the dormant fire with his broad spear blade, Hiero carefully emptied them over the wide, groping paw. There was a second of silence; then the paw was snatched back, and a hideous roar, almost deafening the Metz, crashed in turn over the barricade. It was followed by equally deafening snarls and growls and the crashing of brush and timber as the paw's owner blundered about in pain and rage. While Hiero grinned hugely and the hopper still froze in panic, the noises died away downhill; the creature, whatever it was, sought distance and possibly the river to quench its burns.

For long afterward there was relative peace, and Hiero dozed, like his mount, crouched on his haunches, stirring only to renew the tiny fire at intervals. That the surrounding foothills were full of life needed no further emphasis. The night about them rang with howls and screams, as hunters and hunted fought through the dark hours. Sometimes the sound of great padded feet came from close by, and the man tensed, coming wide awake automatically. But most of the meat eaters seemed deterred by the fire, the barrier of wood, and perhaps the unfamiliar, mingled scent of man and hopper.

It did not pay to relax completely, and Hiero never did. This was just as well, for the next attack was unfamiliar and might have succeeded by its very strangeness.

The Metz had been conscious of an odd sound for quite a while before he grew alert. It was a soft, fluttering noise, like the flapping of a large fan waved with great speed, and seemed to come from out over the gorge to his left. Sometimes it went away and sometimes came quite near, so that the purling of the small river in the depths of the gorge was almost silenced. He only heard the noise when the chorus of the jungle had momentarily died down; but though it vanished at times, it always returned. Segi, if he noticed it at all, paid no attention, but drowsed, eyes half-shut, staring at the fireglow.

In the dark, just before the first coming of dawn, Hiero heard the soft flutter drifting toward their nook once more, and something impelled him to throw a few more sticks on the dying coals.

The sound grew suddenly louder, and the beat of monster wings forced a blast of wind into the little angle in which Hiero and Segi crouched, causing the fire to flare and the man to start to his feet, his gaze widening in amazement and horror.

Poised in the air before him hung a demon's face, great fangs bared below glowing eyes, wrinkled snout, and ears carved as if in oiled leather. A naked body was held aloft by the roaring beat of the vast, leathery wings. The nightmare head alone was the size of a small wine keg.

As the savage jaws snapped at him, Hiero shrank back, his spear raised in defense. Again the thing wavered in at him, the giant fans of its finger wingers flapping the fire into yet brighter flame. The hopper gave a squeal of utter terror at the sight. But this time, the Metz warrior was ready.

His spear licked out in a short, vicious arc. Despite the ability of the giant bat-thing to change direction, the sharp edge cut deep, not in the face, but in one shoulder, where a great wing joined the hideous body. Screaming on an impossibly high note, the haunter of the night winds fell off and away, down into the misty canyon from whence it had flown in the first place. It was all over in seconds, leaving man and mount staring into the void. Then, even as they stared, Hiero saw the first paling in the east. The long night was over.

Limp with relief, yet not losing his grip on his spear, he slowly sank back to his knees. As the sky gradually brightened around him and the volume of noise shrank with the coming of day, he remained there, eyes shut and giving heartfelt thanks to the Almighty for his delivery from the perils of the dark. Crossbarred spear held before him, the priest prayed for the future, not only of himself but of all mankind and of the world of beasts and the untamed beauty of the land. He asked for strength in future trials and aid for his loved ones. At last, his orisons done, he fell asleep with the sun's first rays just touching the cliff above his head.

Segi, all terrors forgotten with the approach of daylight, flicked his ears and reached for a tender weed. He would keep watch.

✤ 5 ✤

THE SPINNER AND THE WEB

WHEN HIERO AWOKE, HIS HEAD ACHED. HE DID NOT FEEL tired, exactly, but a bit sluggish and stiff. He wondered if it was due to the damp; the day was not cold—indeed it was quite hot—but a thin, light rain was falling. It was this which had finally awakened him, though he had slept in the rain, and heavy rain at that, many times before. Perhaps some miasma had risen from the river spray during the night. He enjoyed superb health as a rule. There was little disease in the old sense abroad in the world these days. Some of the ancient places of The Death still harbored plagues of horrid sorts, so the tales said, and all such were sedulously avoided when known to exist. But other than a cold or two and a broken leg, the hardy Metz had never known a day's illness. Still, his head ached!

He shook it angrily, as if to drive the aching away by sheer force. It was not all that bad, just a dull throb, but he was unused to such things and resented it all the more for that reason. He would have to do something, he supposed, if it persisted. That an ache might come from his subconscious as it battled on his behalf with an outside force never occurred to him. In his state of mental stasis, as far as his innate and taught powers were concerned, there was no way it could.

Meanwhile, he fed himself, thinking gloomily about Segi and the hours before as he did. A few more nights like that would put paid to both of them! Segi was strictly diurnal, and though Hiero could travel in the dark, it was a terribly dangerous thing to do in this unknown land. He thought of the flying horror of the night and whistled to himself. Never before had he been attacked from the air, unless he counted the great birds from whom he had saved Luchare. But that had been an artificial situation, the creatures being lured by human torturers to their prey.

That devil bat was under no one's control but its own, of that he was sure. What a place the world was, with things like that in it, unknown until they struck at one!

He eyed the gorge as he saddled Segi, but nothing flew there save some small birds resembling swallows, seeking insects in the drizzle and fog. The chorus of the night had gone too, only an occasional distant howl or roar attesting to the presence of the hungry bellies of their owners as they slunk back to their lairs. Strange birds sang sweetly or called in mocking echoes from the slopes above, the thin patter of the falling water hardly muffling the sound.

Nevertheless, Hiero was very cautious as he dismantled his barricade and led Segi out. But, save for some torn bushes, no trace remained of the brute which had clawed at the barrier. The man mounted, and the big hopper obediently set off down a narrow alley in the towering trees which gave promise of leading to a gentler slope upward.

A long time later, the two were deep in the folds and ravines of the rising hills. Hiero could not have said where he was going and, indeed, seemed to be proceeding at random. His headache had increased, but he paid it no outward attention. Had an observer been there to note what transpired, there would have seemed a strange look in the man's eyes, one of puzzled concentration, as if some thought were being explained. Or imposed.

It was the beast and not the man who was growing uneasy. Long since, the last bird calls had died away behind them. The thin rain no longer fell, but swirls of increasing fog curled about their bodies now, and visibility had dropped to a few yards in front and to the sides. Great moss-covered stones loomed out of the mist at them and then fell away as they passed. The trees had been largely replaced by monstrous arums and broad-leafed plants like vast rhubarbs. Ferns were everywhere, some with trunks many feet thick and with heads far out of sight in the gray mist overhead. The footing was spongy, and the hopper's pads made a flat squelching sound each time his weight hit the damp soil underfoot. His eyes rolled nervously and his long mule ears flickered constantly as he sought for some sound over the drip and plash of the water, the noise of laden rivulets trickling into their path from the surrounding gullies and heights far above.

Even a normal man without Hiero's skills as a woodsman would have been nervous by now, whether or not he possessed any added powers of the mind. But Hiero seemed caught up in a trance. One part of his brain noted absently that they were in the bottom of a deep ravine or canyon which was leading them upward on a slow incline. Yet the fact was simply recorded as having no relevance of any kind. Segi's snorts and fidgets were firmly but gently controlled, and the big beast, trembling yet obedient, went on at the man's behest. His mingled affection and years of constant training mastered his fears and his animal awareness that all was not well.

For some hours more, they went on in this manner. The ground underfoot, or rather the mixture of moss and mud, began to level off. The upward incline ceased and now took, after a while, an equally shallow downturn. The dribbles of water through which they splashed began to run gently in the way that they themselves were going.

The silence was not oppressive. Save for their own breathing, the creak of leather, and the splash of Segi's feet, nothing stirred in the mist about them. Only the lonely fall of water from heights above and the drip from the leaves surrounded them. It was as if they were lost in some strange world of silent fog, some place where active life never came, but which, since the beginning of time, had been given over to the pearl gray of the mists and the silent, watching plants. It did not seem a place that wanted or would endure movement and the bustle of everyday sounds and stirrings. Here there was only the still life of water and plant, moss and stone. Yet they continued, over marsh and boggy stretches, broken by reaches of smooth, wet rock where even the carpets of omnipresent moss could find no rooting. The mist, light in one place and darker in another, curled in ever-thicker coils around them, deadening even the sounds they made, as if trying to blanket them with its own silence.

Presently, Hiero knew, they were to come to a wider place. The pale fog was no thinner, but his inner knowledge was sure. They were no longer in a narrow ravine, but in some opening, a bowl of some sort in the heart of the hills. Here something waited for them, as it had waited for countless others. Here they had been drawn over vast and empty leagues for some purpose by that which ruled this land of mist. All thinking suspended, all purpose stilled, Hiero reined Segi to a halt and looked about him in idle wonder. The mists lifted slowly as he did so, and he saw the water.

Before them, black and smooth, a tarn stretched out of sight until the fog rolled in upon it and hid its farther shores. They were on a low bank, a sort of reef which projected out into the silent water, its basis something firmer than the moss and ooze through which they had come for so long. It was not rock, but mass upon mass of something white and rounded, with here and there a sharp projection rising above the other rotting matter. Stretching out around them as far as they could see was a shore of bones, moss-covered and old, with a few whiter and newer additions. They had come upon a graveyard of a strange and horrible kind.

How many generations, how many lives of the world outside, must have been spent to create that vast and moldering wrack of skeletons, not even the inhabitant of the lake could have said.

There was no discrimination among the relics of the past. Skulls of the giants, with crumbling tusks many yards in length, were piled in heaps, mingled with the slender crania of the hoofed runners on the grass. Savage fangs, half-buried under the lichen and mildew, showed that meat eaters were not exempt. The femurs and hoofs, the occipitals and astragali of hordes of smaller beasts were inextricably entwined through and over the huge ribs and metacarpals of the greatest brutes. From dead eye sockets, the ghosts of reptiles stared in empty equality at the mammals. All of evolution had met in the common fate of their mortality. The only conquerors were the dampness, the mold, and the swirling mist. The only epitaph was silence.

As quiet now as the dead around them, man and hopper waited. Even Segi had stopped his nervous trembling and had lapsed into a cowed stillness. Hiero simply sat, a copper statue on a bronzed steed. The two heads stared before them at the dark lake, seemingly as patient as the hills which held them captive. The mist dripped unregarded from the leather headband of the Metz. He had discarded his now useless hat days before. His dark eyes looked fixedly forward at the water, never wavering, with no emotion stirring in their depths. He was waiting for a summons. Yet when it came, it came so strangely that his body trembled with the shock. For it came in his mind.

Welcome, Two-Legs! You have been a long time upon your journey, as you and yours count time. That which bears you has helped to bring you to me. Leave the animal now. It has served its purpose, or part of its purpose. It has no further use in our dealings together. Follow the shore around to the right and you will be more comfortable. We have much to discuss, we two.

As the voice entered his mind, Hiero became a changed man. Outwardly, he remained what in fact he had been for a long time, a prisoner of his own body, obedient to the will of that which had summoned him. But the strange voice in his brain had alerted all the long-silenced circuits that had been killed by the drug of the Unclean. They were not operating under his control, but they were activated. He could feel all his emotions again, sense the brain of that which addressed him, plan on the future with his full mentality, review the damage done by the drug, and, above all, feel that he was no longer a prisoner in his own skull. Yet he must obey.

He dismounted as he had been told. The hopper remained squatting on his haunches, as immobile as a statue, his great, gentle eyes fixed in a blank stare, as if he were seeing nothing. The man began to walk along the edge of the dark water, picking his way over the slippery masses of the crumbling bones with care. All the while, his brain was still captive, but racing furiously, considering the voice in his mind and the implications thereof.

It was no human voice, this mental alert. In some ways, it was not unlike the House, that amalgam of fungoid intelligence he had slain in the cavern to the north. The resemblance lay in a sense of coldness and of great age. But there it ended. The House had been all furious malignancy, hating and despising all that was not of its own foul nature, determined to swallow the whole world in its sporate growth. This mind was quite different, being as placid as the mountain tarn before him. It was remote, non-caring. It envied and despised nothing, too aloof and withdrawn from the scheme of things for such pettiness. If it had any deep emotions, it hid them well.

While Hiero was considering the voice and trying to sort

out the burst of galloping thoughts created by the sudden awakening of his mind, he was still clambering over the moss and lichen-strewn bones. Presently, he came to the end and found himself in a little bay on the shore of the black lake. Over the water, the mist still clung to the damp air, wreaths and swathes of it folding and refolding in gauzy tendrils. The light was growing brighter as the sun once more began to make its appearance, and shades of pearly opalescence colored the fog.

Hiero seated himself on a convenient bank of thick, green moss and stared at a narrow ridge of grayish rock which had become revealed some yards from the shore as the mist cleared a little. The voice had been silent for some minutes now, and his brain registered nothing. Yet he was well aware that his summoner was not gone and also that he could make no move save with permission. Far back down the shore, whence he had just come, he heard the sound of a heavy splash. There was no other sound, and he wondered at the noise. While he sat in silent puzzlement, the voice came again to his mind.

So, Two-Legs, you are at rest. I feel in your mind that you do not hunger, nor do you thirst. Good. Very good. We can have speech with each other.

The strange voice was not speaking in words, but rather in instantaneous images. Moreover, the images were halting and somewhat labored, not at all like the clear mind speech Hiero could use with Gorm, the absent bear, his mutant comrade. It was as if the being had developed little or no skill in what it was doing. It had plenty of ability, but the ability was theoretic, not practiced.

You can speak to me, Two-Legs. Not to anyone else, at least not in this manner. And there is no one to speak to with sounds, as you do with your own sort. Here, in my place, there is none other. You must speak with me or with none.

Hiero tensed as he received this, then attempted to use mind speech. As he did so, he tried to throw up a guard as well, so that whatever addressed him could not read his hidden, innermost thoughts.

Who are you? he sent. *What do you want? Why cannot I see you? What is this place?*

He could swear he had felt amusement or at least irony from the voice. But there seemed to be no malice, no feeling of evil, directed toward him. Yet he knew the creature was right. He was sending to it alone. His powers had been restored only on this one "channel." Aside from his unseen interlocutor, he was still cut off from the world of the mind.

Many, many questions, came the reply. *There is no need for so much at once. But I will try to answer. You will see me in due course. I have my own reasons for waiting. You are most impatient—as are, I guess, all those like you?* It ignored its own half question and went on. *This is my place, the only place I have ever known. And perhaps ever will. I have brought you here, as I see you perceive, by pulling on your mind slowly at first and then with more power, increasing the pull by degrees. For I could see that your mind was not such as I have ever encountered before. Many wanings and waxings of the moon have come and gone since one of your two-legged kind was brought here. It has been so long that I have lost count. It did not seem important. Very few ever came, and their minds were blind and foolish, unthinking and so full of terror. In the end, when I could not reach them and their minds, I gave them peace. What passed for their brains was full of blood, full of fear, and yet cruel also, in a way that the simple beasts who come are not. So—like these others, they passed.*

Hiero was made conscious of the sea of mossy bones. He felt a sudden chill. How long had this invisible presence been here, and was this damp charnel house what it meant by "giving them peace" and "passing"?

But the thing which spoke to him detected his fear at once, and he knew that in his present state no mind screen he erected could bar it from any of his thoughts.

Do not be afraid! it said with surprising emphasis. *You are no use to me if you panic like the other things of your species. I mean you no harm. When I felt the strength of your thoughts, which burned in the atmosphere—for even though your mind is bent and silenced, I can still perceive its lost power—I tried to draw you here. You were very far away, Two-Legs, so far I could barely detect you at all. I had to strain my own senses to the uttermost even to reach you. It exhausted me, the first time such a thing ever happened. And then, when I found your brain, I found it blocked, sealed off from all thought outside, even mine.* There was a pause, as if the voice were trying to assemble thought and concepts unused or never used before.

But the ones who shut your mind from the rest of the world—

*for I see that it was done to you, and not for your benefit—
did not know of me.* There was a note of actual pride in the
message, Hiero noted in turn. The voice had accomplished
quite a feat, and it knew it.

*I found a small place that the blockage did not cover, a
hole, you would think. And into this hole I sent my own thought,
calling you to me. It took much energy. I was always hungry.
Even now, after just feeding, I am hungry still. I must summon
more food before we talk again. You also, Two-Legs, are ready
to eat and rest. Go back to where you came from first and get
the food that you have brought with you, then return here to
eat and rest. Later we can have speech together. Fear nothing.
I alone rule here, and no enemy or beast can enter or leave
unless I desire it. None has ever left.*

There was silence in his mind, Hiero realized. The voice
was gone. He thought of the message and shuddered inwardly.
"None has ever left." Was this to be his fate as well, trapped
by some nameless being in the far mountains, to perish alone
and unknown in this lake of fogs, his quest undone, and Luchare
and all who loved him never even to know? He crossed himself.
If he ever needed the Lord's protection, this was the time. It
was not fear or even the loneliness of his plight which unnerved
him. Rather, it was the thought that he had surmounted so
much, only to come to this obscure and hopeless end.

Then, as he thought of the past, both recent and more remote, his spirits began to rise. He recalled the thousands of
leagues he had come from his home in the North, the successes
he had achieved, the foes he had overcome, and, above all,
the woman he had saved and won. It was enough. He was still
a human, and one bred to battle since youth. A warrior knows
when to fight and when to wait upon events. This was a time
to wait. The being whose shape he had not seen had not harmed
him, only withdrawn somewhere. It had bidden him to eat and
rest. Very well, he would do so. Then, refreshed, he would
see what came next.

He began to retrace his steps to where he had left Segi
entranced, as he had been himself a while back, staring out
into the mists. Even with the increase of pallid light and the
cessation of the rain, he had the same trouble picking his way
over the pavement of bones, cracked, broken, and beslimed.

He saw a brown heap on the foreshore in front of him and

decided that Segi was lying down, though the hopper looked curiously foreshortened through the mist. Then, with a thrill of horror, he realized that the animal was not there at all. He broke into a run, careless of his footing, and arrived, panting, at the object he had glimpsed so mistakenly. There at his feet lay the saddle and bridle, all complete, with reins, boots, socketed spear, and saddlebags. But of the brave creature who had followed and carried him for so long, there was no trace. The hopper was totally, completely, gone, as if he had doffed his own well-laced and buckled gear and gone for a cooling swim. Over all the gear was a smear of glutinous slime, clear and odorless!

Hiero drew the great sword-knife from his back and whirled to face the black lake. He remembered now the heavy splash he had heard while seating himself in the mossy bay to which he had been directed. He knew now what had caused it!

Damn you! he raged in his mind, sending the signal as savagely as he could. *Come and get me! Leave off hiding and skulking wherever you are! Here's someone ready to fight, not a poor, dumb animal that did you no harm! Let's see you fight a man, you foul spawn of whatever!* "Come on, I'm waiting for you!"

So enraged was he that he brandished his sword at the lake and shouted the last words aloud. His fury at the sly murder of the helpless Segi—for he was sure that not only was the beast dead but that it had had no chance to defend itself—made him shake with baffled anger.

From the still water there came no reply. No ripples arose on the calm surface; the colored mist, now gray and pearl, now pink and shot with faint golds, swirled as silently as before. The far shore of the tarn remained hidden from view, and nothing moved save for the eternal drip of the trickling droplets from the rocks and leaves, running through the moss channels and lichens until they merged with the substrate and entered the lake far below.

Hiero was trembling with silent rage, though he made a strong effort to master himself. He had been gulled with smooth words to take him off guard, while Segi had been dragged, helpless, to some horrid den to serve as a feast for God knew what atrocity. It made him wild. Soon, however, a new mood of cold anger replaced the hot fury. What was done was done.

They had been lured here by some power which had boasted that it never let go of its prey. His hapless mount had trusted him to the death—and had followed him to that death. His memory working at full throttle now, Hiero had no trouble remembering how Segi had tried to warn him on the long route up the mountain's throat, checking and snorting in a last attempt to make his master see the peril and take action. But, insensate, befooled, his brain under the spell of what laired here, Hiero had simply urged the poor brute on. And this was the result!

Well, then, he would take the being's advice, just as he had done earlier. He took dried meat and some edible roots from the saddlebags and ate, watching the water while he did so. He did not really expect anything to materialize from the silent mere; it was simply that he knew that what had taken Segi came from there. The shore of bones was enough clue to that without any other evidence. Over the centuries, whatever had spoken to him had collected prey, and it was no accident that the lake was the epicenter of its activity. There was no way he could reach it now, but he could at least be ready when it came again. For it would come, he felt sure.

Arriving at the mossy bank, he selected the driest section with care. In the dying light—for he could feel the sun setting through the cloudy reek—he laid himself down. His spear was across his breasts and his sword to hand. Not that, having overcome his first wrath, he felt material weapons were going to be much use to him. They were a symbol of readiness, nothing more. And the crossbar of the spear, forming a cross with the blade, gave him the added security of his faith. He was suddenly drowsy, though not suspiciously so. He remembered, just before full dark fell, to say his prayers and he silently mentioned the good beast who had served to the end and done his master's bidding to the last.

Out in the dark waters of the lake, something listened to the prayer—something both alien and lonely.

When Hiero awoke, it was mid-morning, according to the built-in clock in his head. The mists were far thinner than yesterday, and he could see the lake shore stretching much farther in both directions. Overhead, the sky was still hidden, but the light that came down was golden with the sun, even though strained through the coiling vapors.

He stretched and yawned, then remembered the previous

evening, and once more the anger returned. He drew his knees up, cradling the spear across his arms, and stared malevolently at the water before him, now a silver gray in the glow of the morning. His blast of mental rage received an answer at once.

I have done you a wrong, I perceive, the voice said in his head. *I have seen somewhat of your mind as you rested. This I cannot do with the same ease as when you are awake. Yet when your brain was at rest, I saw in the dark hours great anger against me. That I slew the animal that carried you here is a fact. That I knew that this would anger you is not. Somehow, in some way hidden from me, this creature and you were linked. Yet it was not your mate, not of the same kind at all. It was something that bore you as a burden, a matter which cannot have been agreeable to it, though useful to yourself. It carried you as a larger animal carries a smaller which sucks its blood. Yet you got no sustenance from it, nothing beyond a slight increase in speed and ease.* There was a brief pause, as if the thing were trying to formulate some new thought. At last it said, or sent, *I do not understand the cause of your anger, but I will do what I can to make amends if you will explain.*

A good deal of Hiero's anger evaporated on the instant, for reasons hard for a non-telepath to understand. He *knew* at the very moment that he took the message in that whatever spoke to his mind was telling the truth. His mind had been too well schooled over the years, and particularly in the recent past, for him to be mistaken. The invisible being which addressed him was not lying. Everything that it had stated was true in the context of the creature's understanding. It was honestly puzzled. The relationship between man and mount was a complete mystery to it. The old, cool—why did he think of *that* adjective?—brain which questioned him was quite genuinely baffled. It was seeking an honest answer! He dropped the spear, almost without thinking, and then stood up, his own thoughts all askew.

Then he saw that, by the long rock offshore, the water was moving. The invisible voice had an owner. And, as the voice had promised, the owner was going to reveal itself at last.

A round, shiny surface, dull brown and glistening, broke the surface first. It was the top of an enormous head, several yards across. The eyes came next, large and round, with brown pupils and yellow rims. Above the eyes were two lumps of matter which extended slowly; as they rose, they became long tentacle horns with the same skin as the head. This in turn was smooth and yet grainy, all in mottled shades of brown. There was no nose, and the mouth was only a slit under the chinless head. Ears were also absent.

As the eyes steadily gazed at the fascinated man, the great head rose higher and higher on a smooth, columnar neck. Still the mighty neck rose, and now the head was inclined and looking down at him. The water moved before it as it advanced slowly and majestically. When it reached the rock, the neck lifted farther still, and the thickening of a giant body began to follow. When its body was partly out of the liquid, it stopped and came no farther. Runnels of lake water were pouring from its sides as it finally came to rest.

Now you see me, Two-Legs, with your own eyes and not in fear, as all the others, the countless others of the past, have done.

Hiero stared up at the titan. Whatever its mental powers, which he knew to be great, the colossal thing before him could have smothered a buffer bull like an ant. That its greatest bulk still lay below the surface was obvious. It was simply resting its forepart on the rock so that he could converse with it at ease. There seemed to be no limbs of any sort, unless one counted the two great pseudopods that extended and contracted over the eyes. For a moment there was a pause as the two beings examined each other.

It was the man who sent the next message. It was a somewhat confused one.

Who are you? What are you? The thing you killed was my friend. It trusted me and came here at my bidding, though it did not wish to. Do you know what a friend is? Even as he spoke to the mighty brain before him, he realized that of course he had answered his own last question.

Many, many questions again from the little Two-Legs. Now that Hiero could see the actual possessor of the mental "sound," it seemed to boom and echo in his head, though this was only illusion.

I have never thought of who I am, the giant of the lake went on. *I have always been alone. I perceive that if there are many of one kind, then there must be ways of distinguishing. But there are none like me. Call me what you will. I shall know who is meant.* It seemed to pause.

As to what I am, I cannot be sure. My memory goes back far, Two-Legs, so far that I had not even begun thinking. Back in the time of my beginning, I could not think, I could only feel! I was, I must have been, as one with the dumb beasts, my food of now, whose bones cover the land.

Hiero wondered how long it must have taken to pile up the countless skeletons he had seen and had stumbled over.

The lake creature caught his thought. *Yes, it took long. And longer than you think! For these bones that you have seen are but the latest. The whole shore on which you stand and all around and out of your sight, that too is bone, bone under the moss and the plants. When I began to feed, there was naught here but naked rock!*

Hiero stood, silent and awed. How much time had there been, to have allowed the creation of the very shore of the lake from the detritus of this thing!

So much time, it went on, catching his thought again, *that I, who have never had the skill or the need to measure time, cannot tell how long. But I can dimly recall something. And that something was fear! Even I, the One, I too have known fear. There was a great light in the sky, and lesser lights passed across it. The earth trembled and the mountains fell. And there came a heat and a burning in the air. And the heat was strange and not of the normal kind, which comes from the sky in quickness when there is a storm. That heat I know well. But this other, this heat of long ago, it made the waters hot in turn. I had to leave the lake and burrow deep under hidden rocks. At last, I dared to come above and seek the light again and the cool waters. Now, all this my body remembers, but not my brain. Do you understand, Two-Legs? It was only then that I thought, "I am." And I was not as large as you, not then, and I bore something with me, something which grew from me and which I needed for my own defense. Long, long ago that was. And as I learned to find food, for I suddenly needed much more, I discarded that which I bore. I grew too large to carry it. Yet I saved it, for it was all I had to remember the ancient days, the days of fear, when I too trembled as the mountains shook. I have it yet, for I keep it safe in my body. Perhaps this will tell you in turn of my age and the ages gone before.*

A ripple seemed to pass down the giant neck. Then there came another and another, almost as if the vast body were somehow stretching. As the Metz watched closely, a bulge appeared—not large, but projecting upward from the mottled brown of the smooth, slimy hide. From the place where the body merged with the water, the bulge traveled upward until it was at a level with Hiero's eyes. Then the skin simply split, and that which had caused the bulge was extruded to the surface. It lay on the great body, gleaming in the soft light filtered down through the mist, a lovely golden snail shell, no bigger than a small melon.

As the priest watched, the skin opened again, and the thing was gone. He could almost have smiled, had he not been struck with such wonder. A snail! This deity of the hills, this titan older than memory, was a snail!

He sobered quickly. Whatever the thing was, whatever it had been, it was certainly not to be despised now. And what had it not seen! Why, it was itself an actual, living child of The Death! For what were the fires and the heat, the passing lights and the shaken mountains, but a living memory of what had destroyed the Earth countless years in the past? Ever since that time, this creature had stayed here in the hills, growing and growing, accumulating wisdom as it grew in size, teaching itself by experience, wondering, studying, groping for knowledge. And always it was alone! What must it have been, that life of millennia, always alone? Hiero's pity was stirred, even as he considered that incredible existence. Here was living proof of the thesis of Brother Aldo and those of his fellow Eleveners that all life had purpose. But yet what purpose was there to this?

All the while he thought, the great amber eyes, lidless and lashless, stared down, considering him in turn. And the brain of the giant was still logical, its memory of recent events still functioning.

I have tried, Two-Legs, to tell of what I am. I see that you have understood, as I had hoped you might. But there is yet the matter of the animal which bore you on its back. I took it for food. I removed the things it carried, for those I deemed to be of you and necessary to you. Then I drew it into the water. It felt no pain, but fell asleep. And I fed. Thus have I done since I first knew that I was. I meant you no harm, nor do I now. If I could restore the animal to life, I would do so gladly. I wish you contented, Two-Legs, for I did not bring you here to do you harm. I wish speech, the first speech I have ever had with a fellow mind, and that is my sole purpose in trapping you, as in ages past I learned to lure my food hither.

Not without an ache for Segi, Hiero dismissed all thoughts of vengeance. The tragedy of the hopper's death was no one's fault. The mind of the giant mollusc could not lie to him on this, if indeed on any matter. It had no training in lying, anyway. Why should it mask its purposes? The ages it had lived were enough evidence of its statements in themselves. Emotions had been foreign to this being that had lived without companionship for many thousands of years. In all that stretch of lonely time, it had possessed only one thing to keep it from going mad with boredom. This was its desire to gain knowledge of the world outside, to know what else there was to existence besides its lonely mere, lost and forgotten in the far reaches of the hills. A seeker after knowledge all his life, Hiero could not but sympathize with the desire of the titan for new learning. It had not meant harm, but only to bring to itself the brain it sensed for the first time in its history.

He thought rapidly, *You tell me that without knowing you slew my beast, who was dear to me in a way that you cannot know. I think I believe you. But in addition to this deed, and I will admit that you were ignorant, you spoke also of repairing the harm that you have done. You may have done more harm than you know, even now. For I am on a mission, a journey. There is great need for haste so that my enemies, the enemies of all that is good, will not achieve what they plan. From this path you have diverted me, for you have drawn me countless leagues from my true path, which lies in the far North. Both this and the death of my hopper stand against you, if your mind is honest.*

The reply was instantaneous. *I have told you the truth, if truth is what I believe. I have no way of measuring the truth, as you call it, though I perceive that you have and that so do others. Attend, then.* The creature paused once more, in what Hiero now knew to be its way of marshaling its thoughts in order. It did not like disorder, this solitary mind! And as he thought this, a name came to his lips almost involuntarily. "Solitaire."

The great, cool voice again reverberated in the endless corridors of his mind. *So—you have given me a name in your sounds! I, who have never had or needed a name, accept it. Solitaire!* To the man's continued amazement, the actual letters of the word were formed, in good Metz writing, in his brain! The titan was still sending a message, however.

I have learned much, so much from your mind already! I took such knowledge as your brain would release easily while you slept. I feel—and that is new in itself—that you understand what this means to me. I have new thoughts, new concepts, thousands of them!

The burst of enthusiasm was almost like the shout of a giant in the man's head.

Now listen to what I have found out while you lay in sleep, Hiero. Again, the actual name floated in formed letters in the astonished human head. But the thought went on, unheeding his marvel. *There is a risk, but I think a small one. With much to gain for you, if you are willing to make the attempt. If you have the strength and will continue to trust me, to believe I mean no harm but only that which is to your benefit, then perhaps, but not certainly, for I do not know all that I should, I can help your mind.*

The Metz was seated again, comfortably lounging back on a mound of deep moss while he stared up into the soup-bowl eyes looming over him. But his brain was racing as soon as the last statement registered.

Help my mind? His black eyes flickered away, out over the vapors of the lake and then back again. *My mind, if you mean my powers of thought, my ability to see far off, to communicate with others, is dead. My enemies killed the power with a drug. This is the main reason I am a fugitive in this wilderness and not leading my people in more open battle. And, Solitaire, you yourself have told me that you found only one small gap, with much effort, by which you could reach my thoughts. What, exactly, do you mean?*

The great, calm voice was reassuring. *I mean this, my—* There was an almost shy hesitation—*friend. In the endless time since what you call The Death, the terrible fires that your folk once loosed—for I know now that it was you, small and feeble though you seem—I have had much time to learn. I did not simply draw the lower animals to me for food, though at first*

*that was the only reason. I did other things with them, as I did
also with the plants. Your name for what I did is—study!* And
once more the fiery letters formed.

*With your bones inside and your hot blood, your furry coat
and your quick movements, you are not so unlike the beast
which carried you. Yes, and the hordes of others which have
come before. I have looked into their minds, Hiero, and I have
learned much. I can do things you have not seen as yet, things
with my own body, things I have taught myself. For when I
began to grow in size, my mind was not so strong. When the
fires stopped and life returned to the hills, there came many
great beasts as well, some no doubt quickened to new life,
even as I. I was not alone in the heart of the hills then! There
came things then which hungered also for food, even as when
I was small and bore my only defense upon my back. I had to
hide often then, so far back in time! But I studied my own body
and I learned a great truth concerning that body. I learned
that such as I can mold the basic units of life, what you call
cells! Yes! Even as the smallest and lowest of the tiny things
that swarm in the waters about me, so too can I!*

Riveted to his seat, Hiero watched what followed in new
wonder. That such things were possible was beyond his dreams.

From the mighty neck, if Solitaire possessed a true neck,
there began yet another bulge, such as had heralded the shell.
But this one was much larger. It continued to grow and reach,
as thick at the base as a great tree. Soon the huge tentacle or
pseudopod was as long as the trunk of such a tree. It waved
in the air above the man's head, its end a tapered point no
bigger than his hand, dripping cool water on him as it did so.
Then, with a movement that took his literal breath away, it
swept down.

He felt a cold circle about his waist, and the next moment
he was high in the air, suspended in front of the great, round
head and only inches away from it. Before he had time to draw
in fresh air, he had been lowered with the same lightning speed
and replaced on his moss bed, while again the colossal limb
waved back and forth overhead. The pressure had been as gentle
as a lover's embrace.

Next the incredible "arm" shot off down the shore whence
he had come, so short a time before. In a split second, it was
back, but now in its serpent grasp was the yellowed skull of

some long-dead beast, three times Hiero's size. With a casual flick, it released the thing as if from some enormous catapult. Moments later, from far beyond the range of Hiero's vision, there came back the echo of a great splash. The voice of Solitaire rumbled in the man's mind, and this time there was no doubt about it—there *was* humor in it, and satisfaction, too.

Even if the great beasts could resist my mind now, Hiero, I have a few other ways of keeping myself from being eaten! Now pay yet more attention to what I show you.

The mighty, brown pseudopod came gently down. It stopped no more than a foot from the bronzed, aquiline nose. Then slowly the tip began to narrow and grow smaller and smaller, even more slender and pointed. Soon it was needle-tipped, finer than the smallest surgeon's probe the Metz had ever seen. This was not the end of its marvels, however.

When it had become so thin that Hiero could barely define it with his eyes, it moved closer to his face, so close that his quickened breath could have warmed the end. From the bare tip now sprouted wirelike tendrils, so fine in texture that the man had to squint to focus on them. They waved before his eyes, so ethereal it was hard to be sure he was seeing them at all. Each one had independent movement, though; each one was under the control of its colossal owner, as much as the sensitive horns or any other part of the titanic mollusc body. A wild idea began to form in Hiero's mind, an idea so impossible that he tried to dismiss it before it could take full shape. The mighty message in his brain told him that he was wrong to do so.

Yes. You have grasped what I propose. Far back over the lost years, I made these from my own body. I, who have no hands, no limbs such as yours, must perforce grow my own! It took many of your lives, Hiero, so many that I will not weary you with the account. Bit by bit, effort by effort, I learned to use these tools, fashioned from my own flesh. Look again, now!

The threadlike tendrils seemed to vanish. But where they had danced, there was still a faint haze, something the eye could not quite catch, a flicker almost at the bare edge of visibility.

You cannot see them now, or perhaps you can just do so. But they are still there, still under my command, made so small that there is almost nothing, save the very smoothest and hardest of stones, that they cannot pass into.

Hiero waited for what he now knew was coming.

Through the small, ever-so-small openings in your body, those of what you call your skin, through the bone underneath as well, these can easily go. With your consent, Hiero, my first friend, my first mind partner, I will go into your mind with these! I will study what has been done to you by your enemies. And perhaps, though I cannot be sure, I can do something to right this terrible desecration.

Hiero sensed something new in the mind of this strange ally, something he had not noted before. It was anger, pure and simple. The calm, vast brain of the great mutant was infuriated that anyone could tamper with the mind! This was the ultimate outrage! In all the countless centuries it had devoted to pure thought, waiting and hoping for another mentality to contact, it had never imagined such a thing as possible. Why should it? But now it knew such things not only were possible but were done. It was as close to fury as it could be, and the Metz warmed to his newfound friend.

You make an extraordinary offer, Solitaire, he sent. *Had I not seen what you are capable of, I should never have dreamed such abilities could exist in the world. But,* he added cautiously, *I have a few questions to ask. I do not any longer doubt your good will toward me. But can you be sure that what you do will not harm me further? Better, far better to be blind as I am, with at least the physical senses of an animal, than to endure a fate of mindless, total idiocy!*

The response was encouraging. *I can be sure. Even with my long practice, I may not be able to repair the hurt. But you will be no less than you are at this moment. That I—promise!* Solitaire wrote the word in Hiero's mind, seemingly intrigued by its implications. *What are your other doubts? You had questions.*

Have you no conditions of your own? the man replied. *You brought me here, after all, to gain knowledge. Surely you have other demands?*

The mind speech was now innocently eager, if such a word could be used about any of Solitaire's mental processes. *I have no demands, no conditions. Some requests I have, but only if you choose. I too have a few questions. If you would answer those, I would be more than repaid!*

I certainly can answer a few questions, Hiero thought. *If that's all, go ahead and ask them. I'll do my best to give you honest answers, although I hope the questions are not too hard. What are they?*

I would know all about your human affections, came the reply. *Also, the complete history of your race, its physical and mental accomplishments and, above all, its past. I would know of your own mental abilities and how they came upon you. I would learn of the other minds with which you have spoken, both of your kind and others, those that have grown like my own since the coming of The Death. Then there is The Death itself and its workings and how it came. Next there are the wars of your people and the one in which you are engaged now. I would learn also of your enemies, those you call the Unclean, and of your allies in those places whence you came. What else you can think of that I have not mentioned, I should like to learn as well. And then, too, I must learn whatever you know of the most important question of all.*

The stunned human rallied at this last point, long enough to interject a question of his own. *What on earth is that question?*

It is not on Earth, the answer came. *At least, from what I sensed in your mind when you—prayed—before you slept, I don't think it is. I want to know the nature and meaning of God.*

"Oh, well," Hiero said aloud to himself, "I guess I asked for that!"

Then, when I am finished with your mind, we shall talk, Solitaire sent. *And after that, you must be gone on your urgent journey.*

✤ 6 ✤

RUNNERS IN THE NIGHT

A WEEK'S JOURNEY NORTHWARD FROM SOLITAIRE'S LAKE,
Hiero leaned on his spear and looked back up the long
pass down which he had just come. He rested and relaxed as
much as anyone could and still stay alive in the wilds. A few
small birds twittered in the dense green scrub, and a hawk
almost the size of an eagle peered suspiciously down from its
nest in a cranny of the rock wall to his left. Small rodents and
lizards skipped among the undergrowth. But there were no
dangerous animals near him.

Hiero *knew*. He was no longer mentally blind. His stolen
powers were back and he could once more see with his mind!
He could penetrate the small, wild minds around him and actually see, with some effort, through the eyes of the scurrying
wildlife.

He polished his shield absently on his arm as he stood in
the sunlight of the morning. He had much to be thankful for,
and the shield was further evidence of the gratitude he owed,
for it was a present from a very new friend—but one whom
he had been sorry to leave.

I give you this, Hiero, Solitaire had said at their parting.
*You have pictured your battles for me in your mind. In them,
you have used things such as this. Long ago, perhaps when
your kind ruled the world, a large chunk of this matter fell
deep into my lake. I found it, also long ago, and kept it because
I knew not what it was. But now you may need it, so during
the dark when you rested, I shaped it for you. Carry it and
may it guard you, as my own shield once did for me when the
world was younger and the fires had not come.*

The Metz eyed the small shield fondly. It was round and
very light, only about two feet and a bit across. Its color was

a dull hue, between gray and brown, and it reflected little light. He knew what it was, and he tried to explain it to the great mollusc, who was deeply interested. Bits of plastic were always turning up when ground was broken, mostly brittle and useless, but sometimes in good shape. Hiero's dead mother had once owned such a plate, with a strange creature, a flat-billed bird in human costume, figured upon it.

Even in the vanished past, however, few would have seen plastic this hard and dense. An experimental piece from some lost forgotten laboratory, it had now been put to a new and unforeseen use. The giant brain had even remembered to shape holes in arches on the back for the leather arm straps Hiero needed. And in the center of the boss, Solitaire had somehow set a sharp stone of dull, glinting black. *This is the hardest, densest thing I have ever found*, he told the man. *Had your head been made of this material, we would have had no success in bringing back the lost strength to your mind!*

Hiero had seen a few diamonds, always sparkling in women's hair or on their hands or wrists. This big piece of industrial bort was something unknown to him. But he did not care. He would have happily taken anything that the great master of the lake cared to give him. For the greatest gift of all had been to have most of his mind power and senses back.

Not all, regretfully. When he had awakened the morning after the operation, he found that Solitaire felt it had been done badly. The giant persistently interrupted Hiero's thanks with apologetic remarks. *I failed to understand all of the connections, the purposes of each and every one. Those which I could not understand I dared not meddle with. I am deeply aware that I did less than I should or than I promised*. Nothing the man could tell him made the great creature feel better, though what had been accomplished was well-nigh incredible.

Solitaire had put the man into a deep sleep, using the hypnotic power of his great eyes, with Hiero unresisting and doing his best to relax. Through the whole night, starting at sunset and going well into the following day, the strange surgeon labored, his microtools the minute extensions of his huge body. Knitting, splicing, mending, and operating only by memory and tactile sensation, Solitaire had labored on and on. At last, convinced that all possible had been done and daring no more, the titan aroused his patient.

In growing delight, Hiero found that his lost powers were restored. The mental blindness was gone and his awareness of other life was again intact. When Solitaire lured a young buck from far down the slope, the Metz was first able to sense it and then to feel inside its mind as it drew nearer. After that, he could not let the giant eat it. When Solitaire mentioned with some illness of ease that he was hungry and must eat *something*, Hiero went out of sight down the lake shore. What came in answer to the giant's call, the priest never knew, but he hoped that it was both large and foul-tempered.

When Hiero returned, Solitaire still seemed to be worrying over the fact that there was one power that he had been unable to restore to the man. This was the newest of the skills Hiero had won, the ability to seize another mind and compel it to his will. He could "see" and communicate as well as in the past, or perhaps even better. But he could not do mental battle. The medicine of the Unclean had damaged that ability beyond even Solitaire's skill to repair it.

Then it was question-and-answer time, and Hiero found himself hard-pressed to satisfy the giant's need to know. His Abbey school training was put to undreamed-of tests. *What was everything and how did it get there?* That, in essence, was what the mutant snail wanted to know. Hiero writhed inwardly at what his preceptors in the church would have said about his statements on the nature of the Almighty. Still, he did his honest best, beyond which no one could do more.

It was not as hard as he had thought it might be, either. Solitaire could pick up a clue from any of a dozen angles. That incredible brain, stuffed with five thousand years of memory and thought, needed few aids in following an explanation.

It was while they were discussing some of the nature of the Unclean that Hiero learned of what Solitaire called "the Other Mind."

It comes rarely, this sending, Solitaire said. *It is not as old as I, or at least I never detected it until recently.* By the last word, Hiero gathered, Solitaire might mean a thousand years or so; the mutant snail had little idea of lapsed time.

It seems to change somewhat, this power, at long intervals— at least, by what you and your kind would think of as long. It stays the same, this force, and yet changes as well. What exactly was meant, Solitaire could not explain, but about other aspects of the strange force, he was very emphatic.

Whenever I felt its presence, I hid my own mind. For it had something I feared about it. Now that you have taught me what rage and evil are, I know what I feared. For I have never felt its presence free of anger. It has black anger against all and everything. And it is strong! You have given me much knowledge of your enemies, the Unclean. This is like them, I feel, but far, far more powerful. It may be of them, for what you tell me makes them seem one and the same. I felt it last not long ago, shortly before you came to my calling. It was very quick, like the bolt of fire from the sky in a storm. I regret that my skill could not have given you back the power to kill with your mind. You will need it. The worry in the great brain was very real.

Solitaire was quite amazing. Hiero had discovered that the giant, like most snails, was bisexual, capable of producing both eggs and sperm. On learning this fact, the man had suggested that an obvious thing to do was to raise some young, for company if not for anything else. This was surely not beyond its amazing biological powers, was it?

The reaction to this idea both surprised and amused Hiero. *It was not right, not a pleasant thought. It was not—proper!* The colossus of the hills was a prude! The more one learned about life, Hiero decided, the more one was amazed.

The last message from Solitaire came when Hiero was already far from the lake into which the giant had again retired.

Farewell for now, Hiero, new friend. Remember the direction of the men which I placed in your mind. I cannot reach them, but I know they are there. I can sense them at intervals, though they are not skilled with their minds as you are. Be careful!

And do not forget the Other Mind, the message went on, *the one I have felt over the greatest distance from somewhere far to the south. What it is I cannot tell. But you have taught me well, and I know now that it is a great mind, even greater than mine, I think. Yet it is utterly, horribly wrong. It is evil. It means evil. Beware of it!*

Farewell, once more. I have much to think about. We may meet again, sooner than either of us plans or imagines. I feel it!

Then the link was dissolved and the final contact was broken. Again, Hiero was alone. But now his mind was alert, and he was well armed, ready for any eventuality, as this last week of travel had proved.

Now fully rested, Hiero set off northward again at a steady lope, his gear swinging as he ran. The new shield was hooked firmly over the sword scabbard on his back. In addition to the spear in his hand and his belt knife, he bore the small canteen of leather. The bag slung over his shoulder held firestones, his seeing crystal, and the Forty Symbols, all wrapped in oiled leather. It also held a small supply of freshly dried meat and some roots, but they were for emergencies. In this game-filled country, he should feed well. Leather breeches, sandals, and a headband completed his possessions.

He sped along, his broad chest rising and falling easily. As the miles were eaten up by his steady pace, he rethought what little he had learned about this northward road he was following. He was rapidly leaving all trace of the heights behind, coming down the last gradients to another of the wide savannas once more. Dense clumps of heavy jungle broke the rolling waves of high grasses. Livid scars of green in the distance betrayed patches of marsh—or he had never seen their like before. He knew that he would find lazy rivers trailing here and there across the land as well. He hoped none would be too difficult to cross if one barred his path. The heat was bringing the sweat to his brow, used to the cool of the hills.

If possible, the animals were even thicker here than in the eastward country he had traversed weeks before. There were great red wolves and spotted cats of various sizes. The stripe-backed saberfang was here, its thunders drowning out all lesser feline noises. The mighty-trunked herbivores were also present in quantity, and the kinds and sheer numbers of antelope and grazing varieties of deer simply defied any coherent description. Hiero saw new things often, his active mind doing its best to catalogue each and every one.

There were herds, for want of a better word, of monstrous *shelled* creatures, their armored backs higher than his head. But they had ears and three-toed hooves and were warm-blooded. He entered their dull minds as they grazed and found them mere mountains of sluggish flesh. They saw nothing his size as even a menace. Once for pure fun, he ran up and down over the backs of a whole group of them. They hardly noticed.

Thousands of birds fluttered and sang. Many kinds followed the herds, feasting on stirred-up insects, while yet others perched on the animals' backs, searching for ticks and lice. But not all avian life was so harmless.

His first encounter with another kind of bird nearly ended in disaster. It must have been watching him for some time; when it burst from a clump of tall bushes, it caught him almost off guard. It was twice his height, with a savage, hook-beaked head surmounted by a fan of lurid purple plumes. Its tiny, useless wings beat furiously as its clawed feet pounded down upon him. He parried one furious slash of the beak with his hastily whipped-off shield and then, dodging like a hare, fled for the nearest stand of tall trees. Behind him, overtaking fast, came the bird, now screaming raucously.

Fortunately for him, the closest tree had a mat of trailing vines, and he swarmed up them like one of his simian ancestors, the last stroke of the awful beak missing his sandaled heels by a hairsbreadth.

Breathing hard, he looked down at the angry monster, which was still screeching and venting its anger by tearing up large chunks of ground at the base of his refuge. He realized what must have happened and firmly resolved that lack of caution would not occur again. The great bird thought on another wavelength from that of the mammalian predators he had been guarding against. As a result, he had almost been betrayed by carelessness. He decided to monitor not only the mammals in the future but the birds and reptiles as well. In a world filled with mutant life, some of it unrelated to anything coherent or recognizable, all precautions were in order. He remembered that dead horror, the Dweller in the Mist, only too well, and the way it too had stolen on him unperceived.

After a long while, during which he composed himself in the tree with all the patience he could, the bird wandered away. When he could see, with his mind, that its presence was far off, he descended and resumed his journey. There were no more ambushes during that day. He stayed close to the trees, or to the tall termite mounds, which had also reappeared. This plan had its own hazards, since many of the carnivores lay up in the tree borders, but with his mind alert, he could usually make wide enough arcs to avoid any such. And he always selected a good crotch in some wide-limbed giant well before sunset loosed the main packs of night prowlers on the land. Still, he spent a lot of time in hiding. Without his mental alerts, crossing this land on foot might have been impossible, except for an army.

As the days passed, sunny and clear with occasional violent thunderstorms, he fixed his mind on the area to the north. There, if Solitaire could be trusted, were human beings of some sort, though of what kind the titan had not known, beyond a vague feeling that they were not like Hiero. Each evening, then, the Metz first said his prayers and next tried to reach out with his mind, seeking contact. He was very, very careful. He had no real idea what he was searching for, and the last thing that he wanted was an unlooked-for encounter with the Unclean.

Hiero had deliberately not tried to use the crystal, which would perhaps enable him to see far ahead in a purely physical sense. By staring into it and concentrating, he often could enter the brain of some bird, miles aloft in the blue heavens. Using that creature's own vision, it was possible to spy out the land beneath. But in this strange country, he simply dared not. The process was too random and sweeping. Who knew what other mind he might encounter? Once before, in the distant North, he had tried this kind of viewing and had ended up in the brain of an Unclean adept, aloft in a winged craft in the sky! Once was enough. It was simply too risky at this time.

There were the Forty Symbols, though, each carved with a different sign. Although he had not used them for many months, and though they were not one of his own special talents, they had been some help in the past. The workings of the tiny precognition markers were not entirely understood, even by the Abbey servants, since their origin was lost in the past. Using them with any certitude was a highly individual skill, and it was not something that Hiero had ever excelled in. Still, there was no harm in an attempt.

One evening, therefore, a week after quitting the southern foothills, he arranged the little things in a loose pile on a slab of bark in his lap. He had previously strapped himself high in the branches of a forest lord, so that he could not fall, even if disturbed in a trance state. He had not seen his priest's stole for months, but that was merely an external and not a vital element in what followed. He prayed for guidance and for help in discerning the future. Then he threw himself into a self-induced cataleptic state, now oblivious to all externals. His mental guard still protected him and, in this condition, no one could either read or control his mind. Before blanking himself out, he laid his open left hand on the pile of wooden markers.

It was fully dark when he awoke, stiff and cramped. The moon shone down on the savannas below, and the night was hideous with the sounds of both hunters and prey.

As he had expected and hoped, his left fist was clenched tight around a number of the little symbols. He freed himself from the thongs which held his body to the branch and, putting the remainder away, moved out into the full moonlight on an open limb. Only there did he open his palm and examine the three tiny pieces of ebon wood.

The Spear he knew well. It meant battle or hunting, sometimes both. Nothing new there. The next was another old friend, the tiny, stylized Boots. This too was familiar to him from the past. It meant a *long* journey ahead, another thing he had no trouble anticipating without aid. The last one was a bit of a puzzle, though. It was a leaf, and across it was superimposed a sword! Moreover, as he looked closely, he saw that the sword actually pierced the leaf, in and out again, as a pin does a robe.

He put the little things away and sat for a long time, trying to remember the possible meanings of the last marker. They each had several alternates and, when taken in conjunction with others, each could assume still newer meanings. What a pity he was not better at this! He had once had a classmate who could draw as many as twelve and get really complicated predictions from them.

Peace and war! That was it. But since the two signs were interwoven, it seemed there must be a choice. Peace or war, journeys and battles, or maybe hunts. He laughed quietly. When had his life contained much else? At least it seemed that things would go on as usual. In some distant future, perhaps he would awaken from the trance to discover signs which meant only peace and quiet. What a hope! He laughed again and then made his preparations for slumber, still chuckling. The nightly uproar all about and below he simply shut out of his mind, and he fell happily asleep, eager for what tomorrow would bring.

* * *

In a lamplit chamber, somewhere in Sask City, capital of the Metz Republic, two old men sat on oak benches and eyed each other alertly across a narrow wooden table. Each held a large foaming mug in his gnarled fist and each was robed and bearded. There the outer resemblance ended.

Abbot Demero's aged face was the color of burnished copper, and the white beard and mustache under the hawk nose were straight and wiry. Over his angular frame, he wore a snowy robe, and on his chest was a heavy cross of hammered silver, suspended from a chain of massive silver links. On his left ring finger, he wore a great ring of plain gold. His dark eyes, over high cheekbones, were lit with intelligence and an air of command.

Brother Aldo had a longer beard; it and the mustache which flowed into it were curled, rippling and waving down over his plain brown robe. He wore no jewelry or mark of any kind. His nose, though not snub, was rounded at the tip, and his skin was far darker, almost the color of the oak slab on which his elbows rested. Wisdom and a dancing humor sparkled in his every glance.

Both men had the lines of many strenuous years engraved on their brows, but their strength had not been sapped, and the vigor of their movements, while not that of youth, was neither that of senescence.

Now the Most Reverend Father Demero spoke, a smile lifting the corners of his mouth. "A health, your Majesty, and welcome once again to the North. I only wish this meeting didn't have to be held in secret. I'm tired of this damned skulking around."

"Demero, you old fool, I curse the sorry day I ever told you what I once had been. So they lost a king in D'alwah a few generations back. They long ago forgot the crazy creature. Quit calling me that, will you, Most Reverend Abbot?"

"As you wish, Brother Aldo. Perhaps a republic always likes kings, having got rid of its own. We had a king here once, you know, before The Death. I don't remember who he was, or even if he lived here. I have a feeling that he lived far away and only visited now and again. The Abbey archivists could probably tell you."

The sage in the brown robe laughed. "That's the way kings,

or queens for that matter, ought to be, frequently absent." His face sobered at another thought, and he straightened on his backless bench.

"We should be talking about a prince, not a king, Demero. We have a lot to go through. I have to be on my way tomorrow, you know. So let's get to present business. I have bad news from the South, and you won't be happy."

Abbot Kulase Demero, Senior Priest of the Abbeys of the Metz Republic, Hierarch, First Gonfalonier of the Church Universal, and leader of the Republic's Upper House, bent a piercing gaze on his friend. "It's Hiero, isn't it? I've been uneasy all week. He's so far away and so alone. What's the news? Out with it, man!"

"He's gone. Maybe missing, maybe—worse!" Brother Aldo, who had once borne a very different name and title, had lost all the humor in his voice. "The Order sent me the news only this morning, filtered through many strange routes from the South. I gather there has been a rebellion, led by a young hellion of a duke with a fair claim to the throne, if Luchare and her father were dead. That sounds like old D'alwahn history so far. But there's more. The pretender has Unclean help. Danyale is badly wounded, but alive. Luchare is running things, and her husband has simply disappeared from the face of the earth!"

There was nothing slow about the Father Abbot. "If he were dead, she would know, right?"

"Ye-es," Aldo said slowly. "She swears he isn't. That's our best hope, as far as he is concerned. I pray to God she is right. I'm fond of him. But we have other things to think about. I trust Luchare. She'll hold D'alwah, if it's humanly possible. Danyale can help, if he gets better in a hurry. He's not so dumb that he can't see through a blanket. But the Order says the Unclean are moving fast, too. And they seem to be heading in your direction, toward the Republic. We, the Council of the Order, think you need help fast. How is the work coming on what we brought you from the underground place?" Despite himself, he glanced at one corner, where a small, ivory pendulum hung motionless from wooden crossbars.

Demero followed his glance. "That warding device hasn't failed us yet, and I trust it. Any Unclean mental probe would set it off, so we can talk in confidence. As for the computer, it is showing progress. At first, when we studied the books you brought, it seemed impossible to create the tiny devices—chips, they're called—on which it is based." For a moment, a smile came to his face. "Then one of our brighter young men realized that many of the pieces in our archives, recovered from the sites of the ancients, were really parts of the thing described in the books. We think now there must have been millions of computers around before The Death. But even with the books and the parts, it takes time. We have to re-create a whole new way of thinking. And when finished, the computer is going to need what is called programming. My young men say they can do the job—but again, it takes time. The same old story."

He leaned across the rough table. "How many years ago was it, Aldo, when we first met and determined, even as young men—or youngish men, I should say—that the church and the Order ought to be allies? And even then, we knew that time was working always in every way against us. Well, it hasn't changed. Here you are, high in the Council of the Eleventh Brotherhood, and you know where I am. But it's still time, with them ahead and us behind. Nevertheless, we must get ready, as well as we can. That bear creature, now, the one you call Gorm. Is he really going to be of any use?"

"Very great use—I hope," was the prompt answer. "But he has to get the backing of his people. I gather they have rulers, too, these new bear people. We know of them, though they have never contacted us directly. And before you ask, let me read your mind, dear fellow. Yes, they are as intelligent as we, though also different. On *how* different hangs their willingness to help. And that will, as you have already guessed, take more time."

"Red tape with bears!" the old Metz snorted. "That's all we need! And I've had no reply from the Dam People either, speaking of odd allies. But they never budge without months of fumbling around. The bears will be fast by comparison."

"I hate to bring this up, since you must be sensitive," Brother Aldo said, "but what about your personal problem on the Council? The two—ugh!" He hesitated.

"Don't mind my nicer feelings," Demero snapped. "The two *traitors*. Well, I have almost enough evidence to hang them. A week or so should do it. And meanwhile, they don't blow their snotty noses without my knowledge."

"I suppose they can't just, well, disappear?"

"No, they can't, you peace-loving Elevener! This is not your barbarous ex-kingdom in the swamps of the South! We'll get them, but they have to be tried. Fairly!"

"Too bad. The rough old days had their points, I find in retrospect. A symptom of advanced age, no doubt. Well, what next? How many regiments can you field and in what order? And the new ships you have been building? And, above all, what of the Otwah League? They have traitors, too, you know."

The discussion continued, growing both acrimonious and technical. And when, in the small hours of the morning, two old men said their separate prayers, Hiero would have been comforted to know how largely he figured in both sets.

The prince-priest, the exile from everywhere, as it sometimes seemed to him, had other things to think about. He was currently atop the tallest tree he could find, studying the distant prospect and trying to figure out exactly what he was seeing. The scene in the distance before him was in some ways an odd one, and he wanted to study it carefully before venturing closer.

He had sent out his cautious probes the night before as usual. This time, he had very quickly picked up a human response, the aura of an awake man. Then, widening his search, he had found many others. There were the minds of women and children too, and he sensed as well the massed presence of domestic animals, probably some variety of kaw, such as he had known in D'alwah. There must be villages ahead, or some sort of settlements. He resolved to probe yet further and to see what, if anything, he could learn from one individual mind.

He picked one at random, that of a man who seemed to be slightly closer than others. He settled down and very carefully inserted his thoughts into the brain of his specimen, watching with all his trained ability at the same time in case the man was somehow alerted. The mind was one of a very stupid fellow, indeed. Moreover, it was so full of fear that there was almost no room for anything else. Intrigued, Hiero sought for the source of the fear, which was so overpowering that it seemed a constant condition.

At first he thought that it was a simple fear of the dark. In this savage land, the night with its terrible beasts would be a logical thing to fear. But following the traces through the peasant mind, he found that the situation was more complex. The man knew of the beasts, of course, and was well aware of their danger to himself. But he equated them with other natural terrors, such as lightning, floods, and forest fires. They were to be guarded against, but only that. What he really feared, to the point of acute psychosis, was—ghosts!

Searching the simpleton's memories, the Metz tried to learn about the ghosts, but he was largely unsuccessful. The fear was most deeply ingrained in the man's system but also suppressed to a degree. The fellow couldn't bear to think consciously about his fears. On the surface, he simply feared the night. All would be well for those who lived until dawn. Night was an evil to be endured. The good would survive until another day brought safety. This was the sum of his surface thought.

Hiero dug deeper. There were clues, but ones hard to find. Real though the terror was, the man actually knew very little in the way of fact to bolster his nighttime state of constant panic. He had never seen a ghost. No one he knew had, either. Ghosts came in the dark. No walls, no huts, could exclude them. They took what they wanted. If they were annoyed for any reason, the person who annoyed them disappeared. They were wandering ghosts, for they were not always around. The priest of the community knew much more about them, and the priest said they were not always bad to have as neighbors, these ghosts. They kept away dangerous animals, if they were treated properly. Thus it made sense for the man and his fellows to sacrifice an animal of the herds once in a while when the ghosts wanted one. There was a smoldering resentment in the mind, Hiero noted, at this particular thought. One of the man's own animals had been taken recently. This made the ghosts seem even worse!

The Metz withdrew, puzzled and rather annoyed. A crowd of superstitious cowherds was going to be no help to him at all. He had learned other and perhaps more useful facts from the dull mind, however. The southern fringes of the great jungle, the incredible forest of the South, lay no more than two days' march to the north. Hiero had no idea how far to the west of D'alwah he had come in the last weeks. But north of the jungle, at some distance, of course, must lie the Inland Sea. The brain he had examined had never heard of it, but the lummox had never heard of anything beyond his horizon. Apparently traders never called in this remote area at all. Maybe, Hiero thought, they had heard of the ghosts! He smiled ironically as he fell asleep.

He did not sleep as well as usual and, when he awoke, he felt strained and stiff. His dreams had been full of running and leaping, wild dreams full of excitement. Through his mind ran the thought of a hunt, for some reason. It must be the memory of his cast of the symbols and the little Spear. He stretched himself vigorously and did a few simple exercises to limber up before descending to start a hearty breakfast of yesterday's kill.

At noon, he was staring at what must be the village of his mind search on the previous night. He could see for at least three miles, barring the blanks caused by other tall groves of timber. Then the heat haze closed in. But the sight before him was not half a mile away.

There was a stockade, a good, strong one, with sharpened timbers planted facing out as a *chevaux-de-frise*. Even the great, tusked beasts would have found that hard to penetrate. Inside the stockade rose the smoke of small fires, and he could see the shapes of rounded huts, seemingly thatched. There were corrals for the kaws, and several small herds of these grazed not far from the village, watched by the tiny figures of men. One great tree grew in the heart of the village, but there were no others near at all. A small river lazed over the plain only a short distance on the far side of the village, and he guessed that this would provide all the water they needed, save for times of extreme drought, which was a rare occurrence in the well-watered land. The last one in D'alwah had been over a hundred years in the past.

It was a peaceful scene and one that he had no desire to interrupt. But he needed information badly. This priest of whom his unwitting informant of the night had thought might be able to provide it. Hiero sent out his mind probe again, but soon learned that the man he wanted was away on some errand to another village just over the edge of sight on his left.

He brooded for a while and then decided that he had little to risk by showing himself. He could see some small but well-tended fields on the outskirts of the village, and his keen nose had long since detected the smell of baking. He had not tasted bread for a long time and he needed salt as well. These simple folk with their fear of the night would find little to affright them in the appearance of one man alone in the heat of the day. They would be able to see quite clearly that he was not a ghost! In this supposition he was one hundred percent correct.

Long before he was anywhere near the village, he saw men swarming out of the one great gate. Now that he was closer, he could see a small platform high in the big tree in the village and he realized that these people were not as unprepared as he had thought. They had seen him and taken action accordingly, and now a line of the men was slowly advancing on him.

As they drew near, he laid his spear carefully down so that they could see it. Then he raised both empty arms, in the oldest gesture of amity. At the same time, he searched their minds for any trace of hostility. He found wariness and surprise at his appearance, but no anger. They were, as he had assumed, not afraid of one man.

They were a short, swarthy people, heavy rather than graceful, but sturdy and not ill-looking. They wore simple leather kilts and sandals not unlike his own and also carried spears, though they seemed to have no shields. The spears were mostly stone-tipped, but here and there he saw the light catch a metal point. They had lowered them now and seemed to be waiting for him to make the first overture.

He selected an older, gray-bearded man and addressed him in *batwah*, the trade language used over thousands of leagues. The man jabbered an answer, though in a different tongue. But Hiero had noted a look of surprise in his eyes and caught the fact from the fellow's brain that *batwah* had been heard before. He listened carefully as the man spoke again and this time he heard a few words that sounded familiar. While on the deck of the *Foam Girl*, a year back on the Inland Sea, he had spoken with her mongrel crew, culled by her owner, Captain Gimp, from all over the known world. Later, in the forest, he had gotten to know them all even better. This speech recalled a dialect he had picked up from an escaped slave who had become one of his especial admirers. In a few minutes, using the enhanced ability of his mind to read the fellow's thoughts, he was chattering away with enough skill to make himself easily understood.

They were perfectly friendly and more than willing to give him any information that they possessed. Yes, they had bread, and he was welcome to take all he could carry. But he had better hurry. It was past noon now, and he didn't have much time.

"Time for what?" Hiero asked. "I planned to get some sleep in your village tonight. I'm not in that big a hurry."

The elder, whose name was something like Grilparzer, with a grunt in the middle, looked first baffled, then sad, and finally thoughtful.

"I was afraid of this," he said. "You're like the others, the ones who came when I was a child. Come along and walk to the village. You cannot stay with us. I'm sorry, but it is not permitted. Only those born to us may live inside our walls. I'll send one of the boys along to get the bread, and it will be waiting when we get there. Then, Hiero, you have to go. For your sake, I hope you're a good runner." Several of the others, trudging along close by, shook their shaggy heads in agreement.

"Why?" the Metz asked. "Is there some danger? Why can't I stay in your village? I don't eat babies." He was tempted to add that he certainly bathed more frequently than most of his new acquaintances, but decided against it.

"No, no," Gril-grunt-parzer said. "You don't understand. We won't hurt you. But you have to go. You can't stay in the village. That is the law. And if you're found outside when it's dark . . . !" He shuddered, and Hiero caught the very real fear in the simple mind.

"I can climb pretty well." He pointed with his spear to a distant herd of game. "Nothing that kills those things has been able to catch me yet. If you have some taboo about strangers, why don't I camp under your walls or in a tall tree over there in one of those groves? Then I can come and have a talk with your priest in the morning."

This time, those walking close by suddenly picked up their feet and went on ahead at a faster pace. It was obvious that the conversation was one they chose to avoid.

Grilparzer was made of sterner material. He was unhappy, but he felt he had a duty to this pleasant-spoken foreigner and he was going to do his best. He halted and put his hand on Hiero's chest, to make the Metz halt.

"When I was a little lad, other men came. Not like you, but they spoke the way you did at first. They wanted to trade things with us. For hides and fur, they had metal and cloth such as we almost never see. When we do, well, we get it the way we got theirs." He was obviously wrestling with a concept of utter horror to him, and again Hiero felt the sweat of mental fear. In fact, the man was sweating physically! But he persevered.

"We tried in every way we could to get them to leave. They were well armed and laughed at us. They camped by the gate and lighted many fires. They put out guards and we locked and barred the gate." He paused again. "In the morning they were gone. All of them, as we knew they would be. A great company, two tens of strong men and all their beasts of burden. Most of their gear was left. After a while, we went out and took it and covered the ashes of their burned-out fires." He tapped the bronze hilt of a dagger thrust into his belt. "I got this knife then when we shared their goods among us."

Hiero was silent as he thought. Whatever drove these people, there was no doubt of their sincerity. That could not be concealed. Ghosts! He still stood poised in thought, however. The ugly story he had heard must have had some basis in fact. Whatever had happened to the unfortunate traders of long ago, it appeared to have something besides irrational fright behind it.

"All right," he said at length. "I see that you fear the night and what may come in the dark hours." Some stray thought stirred in his subconscious and he added, not quite sure why, "I do not fear that which runs in the night."

The man who stood before him shrank back as if lashed over the face. Spinning on his heel, he ran for the village gate, bawling something as he went. An approaching youth hastily deposited some burden he carried on the earth and also turned and fled. All the other men were running full out, too, as if Hiero were some demon who would devour them on the instant.

The gate, which was only a few hundred yards away, began to close as the last of the running men passed through it. Hiero heard it thud heavily shut behind them. He walked slowly forward and stooped to examine the parcel that the youngster had dropped so quickly. As he had thought, it was two loaves of the promised bread, still hot from some crude oven and wrapped in a piece of hide.

He stood up and looked about him. The distant herdsmen also were gone, and so were their herds. The westering sun was now slanting down with the light of late afternoon. Hiero looked curiously at the palisade and the sharpened stakes of the village. Neither there nor on the platform in the great tree was any head visible. Some distant antelope raised a small cloud of dust far off in the path of the red sun. Aside from these, nothing moved, save for a few vultures, black dots in the high sky.

His mind went out and he sought to probe the village. All he could get was an amorphous mass of stark terror, even for him almost impossible to penetrate and pick out individual minds. The strength of the fear amazed him. *Why, it's as if it were ingrained, hereditary or something*, he thought.

Picking up the bundle of bread, he shouldered his spear and set off at a walk for the nearest trees, perhaps half a mile away. *Be damned if I'll run*, was his last thought.

✤ 7 ✤

HUNTERS AND THEIR PREY

Hiero lay stretched along a great fork, far up on the outer limb of the tree. In the distance, the roar of a saberfang rumbled, to be followed by silence. It was a cloudy night, and the moon came and went fitfully from gaps in the racing clouds. He was staring in the direction of the distant village, but he could see only its outline, a black and lightless mound in the intermittent moon gleams. No sound had come from it since he had found his present perch, save for the occasional restless mooing of a kaw somewhere in a pen.

He lay at seeming ease, but his spear was firmly held in his right fist, and his shield was strapped on the other arm. In need, he could drop the haft of the spear and draw the ancient short sword from over his shoulder in a second. There was no way he could get into a better position for defense. Now he could only wait and see what the night brought.

The tree had been reached and his site selected well before the last light faded in the west. He had eaten, and the coarse bread tasted fine, after many weeks deprived of grain. With the coming of dark, he had cautiously begun to probe with his mind, sending out his thoughts on an ever-widening sweep. And it was then that the surprises had commenced. Almost instantly he had touch with another mind!

As soon as his own feather caress struck it, the strange mind withdrew, flinching away and out of reach like a snake whipping back into a coil. There was no communication, only the instant retreat. He felt that it had neither known what had touched it nor sought to know. It had simply used a trigger reflex, one as good as his own, an automatic cutoff, so to speak. Whatever the mind was, it had a built-in safety factor, which snapped it out of any contact almost before the contact

had been established. This gave one to think. His own abilities
along those lines had been patiently learned under pressure,
the pressure of the Unclean. But he had a feeling that this mind
needed no such training, but was born the way it was.

In the coolness of the night, with a fine, fresh breeze rustling
the leaves all about him, he set about trying to find the mind
again. And this time he received a fresh surprise. His muscles
tensed in reaction as he felt the new contacts. There was a
whole group of similar minds, perhaps as many as a dozen!

Again came the trigger reaction as they evaded him, hiding
behind mental shields so tight he could gain no opening. This
time, though, he felt that at least one of the strangers had sensed
him, but only fleetingly. He caught the shadow of awareness
as it vanished. It might not know what had touched it, but it
knew something had done so. He decided to lie quiet for a bit
and try nothing further. Perhaps he could learn something by
different methods. His mind stayed open, receptive to any
outside thoughts at all. If he waited thus, the elusive creatures
he had detected might come to him, hunting for contacts in
their own way.

For a long time thereafter, nothing happened. When something finally did, it seemed to have nothing to do with him.
His first notice of it was a physical one. Far out on the savanna,
to the northeast of both the Metz and the silent walls of the
village, he heard the squeal of a frightened animal. Hiero had
idly wondered earlier at the absence of the larger animals from
the vicinity of the village. Earlier, there had been plenty of
them about, but only in the middle distance. Now in the dark
hours, there seemed to be none at all of either predators or
those they hunted. All the life about him was small in size.
There were snakes and lizards, rodents and weasels, plus a few
foxlike beasts. The cry from far out in the dark was that of
something large, something hunted and terrified. He felt for it
with his mind and also listened with his ears. Presently, he
detected it with both. He could hear, though only faintly, the
drum of racing hoofbeats, and in his brain came the panic of
a big herbivore of some kind, running at its hardest, running
until its heart was bursting. He could feel the direction and
knew the animal was coming closer rapidly.

The moon broke through the flying clouds and he now
actually saw the chase, etched in black and grays. The figure

of a big buck with tall lyrate horns was galloping for its life. Behind it, the hunters came—and they were an amazing sight.

They were bipedal and they were running at a speed the man would not have believed possible. The fastest Mu'aman racer of Luchare's kingdom would have been left far behind such runners. Hiero knew well what a pace one of the big antelopes could set, and these things were hauling it down!

Straining his eyes, he could see that there were perhaps a half dozen of the pursuers and that they were very thin and tall. Whatever they were, he decided not to try to probe their minds at this time. The hunt was rapidly drawing close to his clump of trees. If they were the elusive minds he had tried to track earlier, and he was quite certain that they were, this did not seem the time to call their attention to him. Then he realized that he was to have little choice in the matter. He saw suddenly that the hunted beast was not trying to reach his area at all! Being a creature of the open, it was attempting to flee to the outer savannas. It was coming toward his trees because it had no choice. The incredible runners were driving it there.

As he watched, Hiero saw the big antelope try repeatedly to check and break away. Each time, one of the tall bipeds increased its own already fantastic speed and closed the gap, forcing the prey back on the track they had chosen for it. Moreover, it was not being herded to the clump of trees, the Metz realized in a hurry. It was being chased specifically to *his* tree!

Still as a stone, he watched the end. The buck turned at bay, its back to the trunk of his own refuge. He could have dropped a stick on the heaving sides or the lowered horns.

The end came very quickly. One of the shadowy hunters charged straight at the horns and then, with a movement so rapid that the man could hardly follow it, darted away at right angles, no more than the thickness of a knife blade from being impaled on the points. This was all the opportunity needed by the others. At the same incredible pace, another one darted in from the side and merged with the neck of the buck. There was a flash of light, glittering under the moon, and the second killer sped on, hardly seeming to pause.

The antelope shook its head and tried to brace its forelegs. A dark stream was pouring from its throat. With one final shudder, it collapsed, kicked once or twice, and then was still.

Hiero thought he had never seen a neater, quicker kill. He looked quickly away from the body to see what the alien bipeds would do next and got another surprise. They had vanished.

One moment there were six tall, lean shapes in a semicircle around his tree; the next, the night was empty. It was as if they had never been. Were it not for the corpse of the antelope, Hiero might have thought he was dreaming.

He waited warily. It hardly seemed likely that a mere accident had caused the strange chase to be led so unerringly to his hiding place. No, something else was coming, and he had better be ready for it.

What came was nothing physical. He simply began to feel a sensation of fear growing in his mind. It was not a thought of any kind, nothing so clear and identifiable. Rather, it was more like a feeling of oppression, a sensation produced when the barometer was dropping and the air was hushed and heavy with the presence of an oncoming storm. Only in this case, he felt afraid!

Something was coming, something was stalking him, and he was helpless to defend himself. The shadows were full of yellow or orange eyes, all piercing the dark and all concentrated on him alone. A whiff of a curious odor came to him on the night wind, musky, fetid, and also vaguely familiar. The scent seemed to heighten the fear, and his hand even loosened the grip on his spear for an instant.

The movement of his hand served as a bracer. His brain cleared, and he realized that he was falling under a spell of a kind he had never before encountered. He, who had hunted all his life, was now being hunted. Worse, he was being treated as if he were already a helpless victim! He rallied himself and began to trace the strange glamour which was falling over him.

It was not his mind that was under attack. That type of assault he could easily guard against, and no warnings of such a thing had occurred. What, then? His body? Save for the acrid and feral odor, he had detected nothing physical at all. Yet he knew beyond the shadow of any doubt that he was the focusing point of a planned attack. The sensation of great fear was still there, but now he had mastered it, and it no longer had the power to make him do anything he did not choose.

The eyes were an illusion, created by fear. He could not actually see them. The bile rising in his mouth and the sweat starting on his skin were also products of fear, the irrational fear which his brain could control, but which seemed to have nothing to do with any ratiocination. Incredible as it appeared, he was under attack on his will by *chemical* methods aided by a mental assault on his emotions. His eyes narrowed in thought as he began to break down the course of this biological onslaught. At the same time, he mentally apologized to the villagers whom he had thought so stupid. If this was a sample of what they had to live with, he had much maligned them in his previous views on the subject!

Somehow, these runners in the night could take aim at the deep animal levels of the psyche. The scent, probably a natural weapon, was the second weapon, used to enhance the fear started by concentrated will. Intellectual ability was no defense at all against such an animal barrage. It totally bypassed the brain and struck at the root of feelings, the same basic emotions that made a child cry or a dog salivate. By the time these creatures had got a good hold on the emotional centers of their prey's inner self, he was doomed. He was literally frightened to death, long before the actual kill took place. The dead buck could probably have been reduced to utter helplessness, had the hunters chosen, so that it would have been able to make no defense at all.

Now, why had they not so chosen? Hiero thought he knew the answer. For the first time since he had felt their presence directed at his own, a grim smile crossed his lips.

The hunters were growing impatient now. He could feel the irritation coming to him almost as a palpable wave. Why did he not come down from his perch and offer his naked throat? The irritation was growing into anger, and Hiero could feel the heat of the frustrated rage rising from below. There would be some action soon. These beings were not patient at all when thwarted. So be it. He had the fear under perfect control now, holding it in easy check even while he examined the effects on his nerves and body chemistry. He was angry himself now, but in a cold state of anger. Somebody was going to get a sharp lesson in very short order.

He slid down the branch and climbed carefully to a lower fork, the breeze ruffling his hair as he did so. This was far enough. He had not forgotten the unbelievable speed he had witnessed. Yet if his guesses were correct, he would only have to deal with one adversary at a time, at least to begin with.

A rack of clouds began to cover the moon again, and he braced himself. He had mentally measured all the distances to every branch. His sword was drawn and the spear leaned on the main trunk at his back. This ought to be close work. That was what the attackers liked, if he were not mistaken.

As the moon vanished, the faint scrape of claws gave the alert. The dark figure swarmed up the tree like a flitting shadow, scarcely a whit slower than its pace on the ground, but he was quite ready for it. With great care, he used the flat of his sword on the round skull, even as it whipped up to his own level. The dull noise of the impact was followed by a long, slithering, scrambling fall as the half-stunned thing tried to catch itself on the way to ground at the bottom. He heard the thump as it hit, and this time he laughed aloud, deliberately and contemptuously. He knew that this gesture would reach attentive and enraged ears and got ready for the next rush. The fury from around the base of the tree beat up on his senses almost as if it were something tangible.

The next foe came more slowly, though still at a very fast rate of climb. This one was really hopeful; as Hiero struck with the blade's flat again, he saw that in one arm there was a rope or leather lasso of some sort. They wanted him alive, did they? The same crashing, scrabbling fall followed, but there was a cry as well, a high, squalling sound. The fall sounded heavier this time, too. Hiero laughed again, the derisory sound calculated to induce a mad outburst of insane rage in those who were meant to hear it. The reaction was as prompt as he had thought it might be. They had swallowed their pride a little, though, because this time their attack was doubled.

Lightning-fast they might be on the plain; but, with his feet firmly set in the broad tree crotch, Hiero could move his arms and body with equal speed. The first one got the shield in its face and fell back, half-stunned, as had the others. The second, coming up the opposite side of the bole, managed to gain the crotch before getting the flat of the sword behind one ear. A knife tinkled on wood as the hand which held it opened and fell limp. This particular hunter was going to stay in the tree for a bit!

At the same time, the moon burst from behind the clouds,

and the warrior-priest was able for the first time to see what lay at his feet. In the light filtering through the tossing branches and leaves, she was a lovely thing.

As tall or taller than Hiero, she was covered with a fine, close fur, a mixture of small spots and blotches on a lighter background. The tips of her small breasts were bare skin, and so was the nose, which was very blunt, with wide nostrils flaring back and sideways. The forehead was broad and shallow, with a black bar of darker pelage running across it; the chin was slightly receding and also shallow. The closed eyes were large under the heavy brow ridges, and the delicately pointed ears were set higher on the skull than a human's. The narrow skull had plenty of occipital room for brains.

Listening intently for any new movements below, Hiero examined the long, slender limbs. The feet and hands were very human, save for the fur, but no human had sharp, retractile claws rather than nails! She was quite nude, save for a broad leather belt which held a small pouch and an empty dagger sheath. Hiero stood up, his suspicions confirmed.

Cats! Since the first faint reek of the hunting odor and the elusive mind touches, all his reflexes, all his memories, all his knowledge of the world of animal life, studied since birth, had screamed one thing at him—cats! This was a mutation he had never before encountered or even guessed at. He was sure there was no record of it in the Abbey files. These night runners were something new to most human experience. Probably only the lost villages out on the plain had ever encountered them and lived to tell of it! Hiero remembered the elder's tale of the traders who had so silently disappeared. He could easily imagine the scene around the fires as the fear and the musk wafted down on the unsuspecting men. This, then, was the source of the herder's inbred night fear. Eyes in the dark, growing terror, and finally—death!

Now, from the foot of the tree, he could hear very faint movements. If enough of them attacked when the moon was next hidden, they could almost certainly overwhelm him. A lot of them would die, but the end would be an inevitable one. It was time to try something new and quickly.

He reached out with his mind, one foot resting on the body of his captive, feeling the faint rise and fall of her breath through his sandal. This time, on their odd wavelength, he got a mind which did not flinch, a very angry and aroused mind. It was already reaching out, not for him, but for the she, who had so suddenly disappeared. This was the leader, a male mind that had not been challenged so in all its life. Hiero could almost see the blazing amber eyes and the ruff on the back of the neck, the bared carnassials and the flattened ears.

The reaction to Hiero's sudden appearance on the private mental band that the cat people used was first startled, then furious. But—there was a brain there, down below. The link was not broken.

Where is the young she? Come down from that monkey's perch or we will kill you slowly! The message was quite clear to one with Hiero's training. These beings were used to mental speech among themselves, and their images were fast and well formed. The contempt in the words "monkey's perch" was also plain.

Killing me is not so easy, the man sent. *Some of your folk have sore limbs and heads to prove it. I could have killed them very easily. Yet I sheathed my claws.* Why not use their own images? *Think about that. And remember this. I have your she up here in my power. Beyond another sore head, she is unharmed, but only as long as I choose!* He made his defiance flat and unequivocal. These creatures had had things their own way for far too long!

The mental link snapped off, in the way he had come to associate with these cats. But he could hear a purring murmur far below. They were not stupid. He could hardly eavesdrop in their spoken language, and they had no idea what else he could do. So they were being careful with a new discovery. This mouse had teeth! Best to wait and consider for a while.

Meanwhile, Hiero could feel the first stirring of awareness in the body under his heel. Bending swiftly, he unhooked the catch on his belt and tied her arms behind her back at the elbows. With a short length of thong from his pouch, he lashed her feet together at the ankles. If an attack came, he wanted no interference from an enraged wildcat of this frantic race.

After a time, the ruling mind below suddenly sent another message. *Send the young she down. If no harm is done her, we will think again. If not, we will come and kill you.*

In the wan light of the cloud-flecked moon, the Metz considered. Was this simply an arrogant bluff? The creature below had promised nothing. With the young female back in their hands, they could still attack and would have gained rather than lost. He, on the other hand, would have lost a hostage whom they obviously valued. His mind raced, balancing what he knew and had guessed about these folk, above all considering their ancestry and the probable way they would react to any new situation. There had been a merciless confidence in the mind of his menacer, but something else as well, or rather, two somethings. One was a feeling of integrity, as if the mind had never needed to lie. The other, and perhaps the more reliable, was something the man had been hoping for all along. Curiosity, that was it. It might not kill these cats, but it could help. Not for the first time in his turbulent life, Hiero decided to take a chance.

His captive was awake now, and the oval eyes, a third again as large as his own, glared defiantly up at him, the slitted pupils contracting in fury.

The wide, almost lipless mouth bared its sharp-looking teeth in a mute threat of what she would do to him, given the chance. Absently, he noted the fine whiskers on the upper lip and along the slender muzzle. It really was more that than a nose, he decided.

Peace, little sister. I mean no harm. I release you to those down on the ground. Your leader— He sent a picture of the dominant male mind—*has asked for you back safely.* He slowly unfastened her feet, next the elbows, and all the time kept his reflexes tense for any sudden moves. He had no real fear of being caught in unarmed combat by this slender thing, but those teeth and claws were no mere ornaments.

She rose equally carefully, watching him all the while. The wide eyes were now baffled rather than enraged. When he handed her the long knife he had earlier picked up from the tree crotch, the eyes widened further. But she thrust it into the sheath at the refastened belt and slid out of the fork and down in one easy motion. He settled back on his haunches and waited. He had a feeling that it might be a long wait.

The night waned and the moon sank until it disappeared. A few jackals barked in the distance, and a large owl flitted into Hiero's tree, noted the silent man, and flew away, hooting mournfully in disgust. But Hiero knew that he was not alone. He had no intention of leaving his so-called monkey's perch to see how many eyes glared up into the dark. The individual minds were closed to him, but he could feel a group aura growing as more and more of the night people arrived and went into conclave. The ground below must be thick with them by now. He wondered if he were going to die bloodily this night and said his prayers with especial emphasis on the virtues of charity and forgiveness. He was not thinking of his own efforts along those lines, but of others who might possess them!

The summons came as abruptly as all the other reactions he had observed from the catfolk. *If you don't want to be harmed, come down at once*, came the leader's message. *We are leaving and will take you with us*. Grudgingly, it added, *You may keep your weapons. Do not try to use them*.

As he clambered thoughtfully down the tree, Hiero exulted deep inside. It had worked! So far, at least, his guesses were paying off. The next few moments would see whether his throat would gape. He had no illusions about being able to handle a swarm of these extraordinary mutants on the ground. He said a last prayer and touched earth with his feet.

It was dark at the base of the tree, but not so dark that he could not see the ring of tall figures around him and the open anger blazing from the fiery eyes. He wondered how many humans in the past had seen such a group as their last sight, before dying as they knelt paralyzed with terror and incapable of defense. His hand tightened on his spear. He was not kneeling, at least, nor was he in any way paralyzed.

Come! It was the mind of the ruling male who gave orders. *You can go at your own speed. We will go slowly, as slowly as your kind of plodding thing out there*. The contemptuous thought was directed at the silent village.

I am not from out there, Hiero sent, *as perhaps you have learned tonight*. He felt the renewed anger at his open defiance. These people were totally unused to being countered in any way, and certainly not by mere humans.

The tall chieftain kept his temper, however. He was leaning over Hiero now, at least seven feet of him, if the estimate in the poor light were correct. *No, you are certainly not as they. You can speak the way only the* (Hiero translated the strange vocal image as "Eer'owear"; he could get no closer) *can do. This is unheard of. You resist our killing thoughts and even the Wind of Death.* This was obviously the terrible scent, the pheromone, which sapped the will to resist.

No, the catman continued, *you are not of those out there. You may be of another kind altogether. Perhaps you are something much worse! We have certain legends of the past of such as you may be. Our elder folk, some of them, remember these as I do only dimly. If you are what I think you may be, you had better have died in your tree!*

They were moving off now, over the tall grass of the open plain, headed east under the dark clouds. Hiero was in the center of a loose ring, and they moved at a gentle lope that in no way stretched his running ability. He decided not to mention this. It might just come in handy.

The leader spoke again in the man's mind, and Hiero could feel the doubt.

Personally, I hope that you are not what we all suspect. There was a pause, almost a reluctant one. *You have courage. You came down on my word alone. Also, even those you struck with that big knife admit that you could have easily killed them and did not.* Another pause. *The young she likes you, even though her head is sore. She is a Keeper of the Wind.* Hiero gathered the title or honorific was important.

Young shes, even Keepers, will play with anything. They steal the cubs of those apes back in the wooden wall and try to make pets of them! They always die, though. Hiero said a silent prayer for God knew how many lost babies of the unfortunate villagers.

Say your name aloud, in your own speech, he suddenly shot at the chief. The answer was a rumbling, purring, grunting sound that no human could really hope to approximate. Hiero tried, nevertheless, and finally achieved something like "B'uorgh." He could feel the amusement at his attempt in the other's mind. Any small gain of that sort might pay off in a handsome way later on.

A mile or so farther on, B'uorgh's thoughts came again. *You are a hunter, like us, stranger.* The term really meant "oddity/enigma." *Those creatures back in the wall, they hunt with traps and covered pits. Can you hunt, as we do, in the dark?*

Yes, Hiero thought. *I hunt more slowly, though. I cannot*

*see at night as your people do. Nor can I run thus. I have
never seen such running,* he added quite honestly.

None can match us, B'uorgh's thought ran, full of pride.
We are the Children of the Night Wind. Still, he added, *there
are good hunters among the lesser folk, some of whom lie in
wait. At times we hunt them! And at such times, some of us
may not return.*

Hiero realized that the catman was rationalizing an attempt
to accept a mere human, however odd, as a kind of equal or
at least something only slightly inferior. This was a necessity
to the arrogant chief. There was another factor as well, and
this was one the Metz had been counting on all along, one he
had figured out long before. The chief was curious. He found
the new puzzle most intriguing and wanted it to continue. The
kitten had found a new ball of string! Not only the young shes
liked to play with new objects, it seemed. Hiero stifled a smile
in the dark at the thought of the lean giant padding beside him
ever having been a kitten.

*We do not like the apes in the walls, living off plants and
their tame beasts. Though the milk of the beasts is good, and
we take what we want of it. You have met a young she, the
one whose head you almost cracked. Soon you will meet another
kind of she. Perhaps you will learn why we do not like the
creatures which are far more like you than like us. I am beginning to remember bad things, things of long ago. We will
speak no more until we come to the home place/lair.* The last
thought tones were not at all encouraging.

A darker shadow had been rising to meet them for some
time. They were approaching another grove, such as the one
Hiero had taken shelter in. It was larger, though, and the Metz
could feel that it was not empty. The catfolk could silence their
individual minds to him; but in a group, they gave off a sort
of cloudy miasma, a mental mist which he was finding easy
to recognize. This, then, was the home place. He hoped firmly
that it would not be his final place!

In a few moments they were in the shadow of the great
boughs and plunged into a narrow path through the undergrowth
at the edge of the wood. It twisted and turned like a demented
corkscrew but, after a short while, emerged into a densely
shaded clearing. Hiero's night sight was good enough to see

narrow ladders leading up into the trees. Toward one of these, he was gently but firmly urged.

The ladder was quite steep and led a long way up. Eventually, he found that he and B'uorgh were alone at the outer edge of a large platform made, from the feel of it, of woven vines and slender withes. Alone? No. There was another watching, brooding presence there, crouched under a mat of branches at the far side. From the gloom, orange gleams studied them, then an arm was waved. *Sit!*

Side by side, the catman and the human squatted, while the being in front of them stared in silence. There was no attempt to touch his mind, Hiero knew, or to communicate in any way with the chief. He had the feeling that the person before him was simply ruminating, remembering and estimating, considering and rejecting. She took her time. Finally, she rose from her mat of branches and moved forward into the dim light until she could crouch only a small distance from them.

She was old, the Metz saw, old and worn. But she was vibrant with life, her mind and spirit burning, even as her body slackened and her sinews loosened. B'uorgh was no doubt a fine fighter and the capable leader of a hunting or war band. But this was the real ruler!

I have no name, even in our own tongue, Strange One. Her mental voice was fine-timbred and steely, with no age in it. Her great eyes were lighted with an inner fire, but there was no loss of control and no impatience, such as he had noted even with B'uorgh. *I am the Speaker and the One Who Remembers. Since the vanished time when we became free, such a one as I must force the Folk to recall that which was past. They must never forget the Bad Time, which was in another place far away and happened before my mother many times away saw the sun rise and the moon set. Now you come, mayhap for the first time since a Speaker was trained and named, and you may be, in your single body, the sole reason that I and all those other Speakers who are now gone into the Wind ever existed.* She reseated herself in one fluid motion even closer before them. Hiero felt that it was incumbent on him to answer. A vague idea of this race's past was coming to him, but he concealed it and sent a bland concept.

At least I am no enemy of your people. I have told the chief here that I am not of the people out on the plains, the village dwellers. I think he believes me.

The response was quick and cold. *It is not what he believes, Furless One! It is what I believe! That is why I am here.* Her mental pitch lowered and calmed, the challenge having been met. She changed her tack.

We are not, as you seem to think, the foes of those creatures who herd together out in their sties, less alive than the beasts that feed them. No! We use them! And they have another purpose, which directly concerns you, for you are far closer to them than you are to us. Can you guess that other purpose?

The priest thought both rapidly and privately. This was a loaded and horribly dangerous question. He was standing on the edge of a figurative precipice. He might be dead in seconds if he gave the wrong response! Yet he had to do something fast. He chose to gamble.

Those people out in the open land, who are of my kind, though simple and harmless in themselves, they serve as an— example. They help us to remember times long ago. Times when others, who looked like them in the body, at least, were not harmless! He held his breath, his eyes locked on the vertical pupils of the Speaker.

She drew in her own breath with a faint hiss, a sound of mingled appreciation and recognition. *You know, then? And if you know, how much do you know? And, most of all, if you do indeed know, whence does your knowledge come?*

Hiero framed the concepts in his mind with exquisite care. He was still balanced on a knife edge. One wrong move and the big chief, so silent beside him, would attempt to rend him limb from limb before he could move. All the aged female would have to do was nod.

Believe that I know nothing, he sent. *Still, I have traveled far in my life. I have fought and journeyed in many lands, with stranger allies than you could begin to imagine. Against us have been pitted even stranger foes, some like me in appearance, some not. The worst of these evil beings, my greatest and most terrible enemies, are outwardly of my race.* He paused for effect. *Only outwardly. And even then, they have no trace of hair, being truly furless, on their heads and bodies.* Was there a momentary contraction of the barred pupils? He continued. *In secret places, usually far from the light of the sun, they breed slaves, many of them of other races, whom they would warp and change into servants of evil. Such as these:* He formed an image of one of the Hairy Howlers, the monkey Leemutes, and when she had had time to absorb it, another of a scowling Man-rat, one of the giant, intelligent rodents. Ever so slightly, the Speaker relaxed, her posture slumping a little. But her eyes never left his.

Her next thought had something of supplication in it. The anger was gone, at least from his direction. *So—if you do not know, then you can guess at least at the shame that we, the freest of the free, still bear?*

I hold it no shame to be kept captive and tortured against my will by the servants of all that is bad. I have been so held and tortured. And I escaped! Indeed, I am fleeing even now, to join my own folk far to the north. As once, long and far in the distant past, the Children of the Wind fled also, seeking the open sky and the fresh air of freedom. Hiero was now fairly relaxed. His shrewd postulates, buoyed by hints dropped all evening, were being proved correct. The Speaker's next thought confirmed him in his assurance.

Show me an enemy in your mind! One of those who command the others!

This was easy for the man. The hated face of S'duna, the Unclean Master, his inveterate and deadly foe, was often in his head. The pale, hairless face, the almost pupilless eyes, burning with a dead fire, the whole aura of malign purpose, were displayed for the catwoman's view.

She hissed again, and the chief beside him did also, a susurration of venomous rage, an anger that many generations of freedom could not kill, the hatred of the proudest and most independent of the mammalian breeds for those who had once presumed to chain them!

It is they! May they burn in the fires of the lightning! Death to them in their caves, death to them who brought the pain, who slew the cubs and the old, who worked with their cunning tools and their sharp knives! For they held us helpless with their minds, frozen in place, and they laughed as we suffered! They would make us useful, they said. We would be good servants when our wills were broken to their taste. Listen, Strange One, you who hate them also. I, the Remembrancer, the Speaker of the Eastern Pride, will tell you of that time, as

*my mother told me, having learned it from hers in turn! Learn
the tale, as all our cubs must. For if you hate them, and I
sense that you do not lie, then you are our friend and I offer
you the help of the Pride!*

Now, at last, Hiero could lounge back and allow all tension
to leave his body. The Unclean, who would have writhed at
the very idea, had found him new allies!

As the night finally faded and the dawn came in the east,
he heard of the capture of the cat people in another land, many
hundreds of leagues away in the southwest somewhere. He
guessed, but did not say, that the Unclean had bred them for
enhanced brain power as well as for physical stamina, feeling
that they had acquired a splendid race of warriors.

What a mistake! With the increased brain power had come
increased self-will. The catfolk learned that they were slaves,
mere chattels, considered no more than tools of the Great Plan.
From their enforced captivity, they learned cooperation. From
their pain and loss, they learned patience. From their captors'
lies and cunning, they learned deception. They organized.

There was a night of blood. They broke from the caverns
and buried laboratories, suffering and inflicting much loss.
They had so taken their overlords by surprise that those who
survived were hardly pursued. And they ran, the proud ones,
the free, ran until their hearts almost broke, ran with their shes
carrying the cubs. At last they were beyond the mental reach,
the invisible chains, of their former masters, but still they went
on, until one day they reached a new land. Here they stayed,
but never forgot what had passed. They would never be taken
so again. Their grim history was taught to every young one
until it became a permanent scar on his racial memory.

When a wandering group of human settlers appeared in the
area with their cattle, slitted eyes watched in the shadows. The
only men the cat people had ever known were the Unclean.
Almost, the decision was taken to kill them all out of hand.
Wiser counsels prevailed. They studied the loathed creatures
and decided that these men were in essence harmless. The milk
and, when wanted, the flesh of their beasts were useful. Let
the settlers stay in their villages. They would be taxed—and
ruled.

The rule was not onerous, but it had a few strict laws. Any
human being who saw one of the Children of the Wind, except

at very long range, died. There were no exceptions. Among
the ruling elders of the cat people, the thought was that the
humans would serve a variety of purposes. Aside from the food
easily taken, they would be a living reminder of the past. Also,
if the Unclean or their allies should ever reappear, the villagers
would mask the presence of the catfolk, thus allowing them
time to plan. And so affairs had continued for what Hiero
estimated was perhaps some two hundred years of his time.

The villagers were invariably inside their stockade by dusk.
Then the People of the Dark, naturally nocturnal, emerged and
took over the land. Their skilled hunting kept the area largely
free of dangerous animals, thus benefiting the three villages.
And the catfolk separated into three packs, or Prides, one for
each village. It was cruel in a way, but the villagers did not
live too badly. They soon learned the rules. One lived with the
ghosts and put out food and milk at certain hours and in certain
ways. Any who simply disappeared or vanished after dark had
seen a ghost. Their fear kept them in their villages and dis-
couraged exploration. Once in a while, a man trapped by night
in a tree would see the hunt sweeping far away over the savanna
and know that the racing figures he had seen were the gods of
his tribe, thus reinforcing both awe and the observation of the
law.

Hiero philosophically reflected that he had seen plenty of
people who lived worse, in what they called freedom. One day
in the future perhaps, he or others would be able to take thought
to this odd, disparate set of cultures and attempt to modify
things and bring some changes.

Eventually, her tale done, the Speaker allowed the man to
be led away to a branch-shaded platform to sleep with the
coming of day. This was their own sleep time, though they
needed less sleep than humans and interrupted their drowsing
with minor tasks, such as leather work and the making of rude
pottery and baskets.

The next afternoon, B'uorgh awakened the man. All of the
Pride were assembled in an open space, and Hiero was formally
introduced to all of them, down to the smallest cubs. A mes-
senger was sent to the other two Prides, telling them what had
been done and why. After this, Hiero had the freedom of the
land and began to enjoy himself hugely.

They were a simple folk in terms of physical culture, at

about the level of the ancient aborigines of far Australia. They used no weapons save for long knives, of metal when they could obtain them, but otherwise of sharpened flint. These they took from the villages. In truth, as the Metz had witnessed, they needed nothing else. Their incredible agility plus the Wind of Death made hunting almost too easy! Everything they needed was at hand, and they lived very well, wanting no more than they had. They used fire, but only for warmth and light, preferring their flesh raw. They ate certain tubers and berries when they felt they needed them, and they knew which plants were useful in their rude pharmacopeia.

Two cubs were the normal birth, and Hiero found them enchanting. They decided the new, furless person was a fine toy; as he strolled through the encampment of an evening, he usually had a bouncing, wiggling, furry ball in the crook of each arm. Behind tagged a trail of older children and shy adolescents, racking him with so many questions at once that his head ached from trying to sort out the thoughts and answer them. He was welcome at every hearth and tried to eat at different places every day.

In the evenings, he always paid a formal call—for the catpeople were very formal—on the Speaker, where he chatted for an hour or so with her, B'uorgh, and the young Speaker-to-be, she whom he had clubbed on his first encounter. Her name, as close as he could form it, was M'reen, and she bade fair, in his opinion, to being as smart as her teacher.

The personal relations of the catfolk were subtle and often hard to understand. There were pair bonds and also deep affection between couples, but sex seemed to be indiscriminate. Any mother's cubs were hers, but some shes stayed always with the same male and others changed mates. He gathered there were festivals when all rules were abrogated for brief periods. At such times they burned the leaves of a certain herb and grew wildly excited, if not actually intoxicated.

The Speakership was selective and took long training; but, as Hiero might have guessed, B'uorgh had fought his way to his position as hunting and war chief and would someday be challenged again by one of the younger males. Should he survive all such combat, as sometimes occurred, he would become one of an honored circle of elder males who advised the Speaker and helped to preserve tradition.

On certain nights, the Pride held group sings, for want of a better word. These were mixtures of poetry, chanting, and, Hiero thought privately, just plain yowling. Sometimes the massed rumbling and purring was soothing and at others made his ears ache, though he always gravely expressed vast appreciation. During the week he spent with the Pride, they held several in honor of his arrival and alliance.

Hiero found the catfolk delightful. He was even able to help with a problem that had been concerning the elders, that of a slowly declining birth rate. He discovered that the Pride, being so group-minded, had more or less stopped intermating with the other two Prides. There were obvious results in terms of inbreeding. He politely told the Speaker and her council of old males that this simply had to stop and that the younger folk of the three Prides should be made to meet more often. Outmating should be strongly encouraged, and the reasons for it should be thoroughly gone into and explained to all the folk. He was solemnly thanked for the advice and told it would be adhered to in the fullest way possible with personal independence! He wondered about this, but M'reen told him privately that it would happen, though probably slowly. One did not give Pride members orders, only veiled and delicate suggestions. This would result in the ideas seeming to be of their own origination.

Every other night or so, those able to do so hunted. Of course, the new friend had to be taken along, not that he needed any urging. He could not run at their pace, so the game came to him. The Wind of Death was not used, since the adults of both sexes preferred not to utilize it unless they were in a hurry or at war. Hiero never found out what it was made from, but he strongly suspected a natural secretion of the glands, enhanced by the juices of a rare plant. It was a secret held by certain of the females, who alone could release it. It had been discovered long ago and had been used to help them escape from the horror of the Unclean.

Their favorite game was becoming scarce in the neighborhood, but they located a specimen and took the Metz out one night under a bright moon to see how he felt about it. He was positioned in a certain place, not too far from the trees, which he thought tactful, and told to get ready. He understood that the honor of the kill was to be his and wondered what it might be and if, indeed, he were capable of holding up his end. The catfolk would not tell him what it was. Knowing their whimsical humor, he wondered if one of the trunked giants were being herded in his direction.

He was therefore considerably relieved when he heard the drumming of hooves and the angry snorts of a fast-running herbivore. However, when the moon gleams showed him the prey, he was not so sure.

From the head down, the form was that of a giant buck. Over the deep-socketed eyes grew two long, straight horns, mighty enough weapons in themselves. But on the broad muzzle rose another, a straight stem which forked into two more evil-looking points. As the enraged animal twisted and darted at the tormentors who were herding it in his direction, the man wondered how they escaped, even with their speed, from the vicious and lethal lunges. When at length it sighted him, a solitary and fixed target, he had no more time to think. Meeting those terrible horns head-on would obviously be insane. As the brute charged, he hurled the heavy spear straight at the broad chest and then dodged, whipping out his long dagger and poising it.

The broad spear sank to the socket, for a brief moment bringing the great beast up standing. In that moment, he aimed and threw the knife from no more than ten feet away, not at the body, but at the nearest bulging, bloodshot eye. The blade sank to the hilt. With a final bellow, the animal fell over, its brain pierced instantaneously. The other hunters let out a wild, squalling cry of triumph, and Hiero felt that his knees were somewhat weak.

On examining the kill while they cut it up to carry back, Hiero thought his knees felt even weaker. The animal's eyes were surrounded by rings of heavy bone, and a very slight miss would have proved useless! He thanked his Creator silently for the good shot.

You did very well with old Four-Horns, came B'uorgh's jovial thought. *We could not have helped, not at that range. One reason we like him so much is that he frequently gets the hunter. Always good sport when we meet him.*

Hiero formally thanked all the hunters for the wonderful opportunity they had provided. They did not need to know his private feelings, which was just as well!

✤ 8 ✤

ANY PORT IN A STORM

THE HOPPERS, EVEN THE PICKED BEASTS OF THE ROYAL GUARD, were very tired. All the interminable day, they had sped from one end of the battle line to the other as the guard followed its royal mistress. The princess had been everywhere, her gilded mail and bright plumes shining like an oriflamme of war as she rallied lagging spearmen here and sent fresh lancers there. Each threatened point had seen her, cheered her to the marrow, and then fought the harder as a result.

But the day was lost, nonetheless. The royal army, outnumbered and with its flanks turned, had been forced to withdraw. The rebel duke, or one of his advisors, had planned shrewdly and moved far more quickly than either Luchare or the king had believed possible. Also, the cunning Amibale had used several unexpected tricks, either through his own sharp wits or through Unclean guidance. Joseato was in it somewhere, but Amibale, Luchare reflected glumly, was quite clever enough on his own. A revolt of the beggars and thieves, allied with disgruntled petty shopkeepers, had erupted in the city as the army was setting out. It had been put down quickly and the ringleaders promptly hanged, but this cost both time and lives. As a result, when the two armies finally met, twenty miles south of D'alwah City, the royal troops were already tired from street fighting and had sustained losses.

Amibale, who to do him justice was brave, had brought not only the troops of his dukedom but also hordes of savages, some of unknown races, to assist. A particular menace was the swarm of small, pallid men used as skirmishers, who fired clouds of poisoned arrows from both bows and blowguns. And there was worse. The Unclean wizards were coming out into the open at last. A regiment of the ape mutants, the Hairy

Howlers, stormed against one wing, while a mob of shrieking, chattering Man-rats assaulted the other.

Moreover, so quickly had Amibale moved that the full resources available to the royal army simply had not been there on time. The Mu'aman infantry, summoned from their western plains, had not arrived. Would they come late or not at all? Had they, too, been rotted with treason? The village militia and the frontier guards had not had time to draw back, either, nor had most of the hardy boatmen of the bays on the Lantik, stern fighters and badly needed.

So the battle had been fought and lost with the household troops, plus the personal armies of the loyal nobility who lived near the capital. Indeed, at one point the center had almost broken under a heavy onslaught, and only the unexpected arrival of Count Ghiftah Hamili, charging in person at the head of his two lancer squadrons, had saved the stricken field. Any doubts that Luchare might have had about the silent count were cleared on the spot as, fighting like a demon at the front of his hoppers, he drove back Amibale's infantry.

But it was not enough. Sullenly, unbroken but unable to maintain the fight, the royal army fell back, covering its flanks and snapping at the enemy as it did so. There was no choice. By nightfall, Luchare was conferring with her commanders while the battered troops were being entrenched on the outskirts of D'alwah City itself. There was still no word from the outlying districts, and rumors of a new and dreadful attack from within had started in the city. There was little talk and no laughter at all in the tired ranks that night.

Around a tiny fire, four silent figures crouched. The fire was burning in the mammoth crotch of a tree so vast it could have shaded a small town unaided. A fifth person, posted as a sentinel, peered from a branch a little higher up. Far below, out of sight even in the daylight, hidden by innumerable leaves, vines, and limbs, lay the nighted swamp from which the tree had sprung, ages in the past.

Hiero was conferring with M'reen, B'uorgh, and Za'reekh, a powerful young warrior. On watch above them, Ch'uirsh, the other youngster, could join in the mingled thoughts when he chose. Usually the two young males were silent when their elders spoke, but they sometimes disagreed and they had the right to be heard. There was a mental silence now, for they were all listening to the sounds of the morass many hundreds of feet below.

A hideous bellow erupted upward, croaking and guttural, but so enormous in sheer volume as to make the very perfumed air of the trees seem to shiver. All the myriad forest noises appeared to hush at the terrible cry.

What is it, Hiero? B'uorgh had learned as had the others, that their new friend could tap the minds of many other beings, while the catfolk were restricted to those of their own species. Above the man's head a great, scented blossom waved, giving off a wonderful aroma as he concentrated. Once more the monstrous, raging grunt reverberated up through the foliage. At length, the Metz relaxed again and smiled.

I don't know. An Elevener, one of our friends whom I have told you of, well, one of them might be able to find out. They specialize in all life, everything that breathes, you know. I can't distinguish between lots of the lower types, the ones with little or no brain. This may be a reptile, like a snake or lizard. But I rather think it's an amphibian, something like a frog or a salamander. They have even less brain than the reptiles. I get a feeling of blind, fumbling anger on a very low level. I met something like that once before, up in the Palood, the great marshes of the North. Their intelligence is so sluggish you can't detect them at all. At least, I can't.

A frog! If that's a frog, it could jump up here. The thought came down from Ch'uirsh.

Nothing that makes that much noise could jump anywhere, M'reen retorted. *It might just push the tree over, though.* She shuddered appreciatively, the firelight catching the smooth muscles under her dappled coat. *I'm glad we can travel up here and not in that muck down there.*

Hiero decided not to mention that some of the incredible frog monsters of the Palood could jump very well. Anyway, he felt that it was not one of them making the night hideous, but some vast, crawling thing that lurked in the mud and water at the bases of the great trees.

The little party had been on its way north for over two weeks now, and the past two days had been spent traversing the swamp. The jungle at the foot of the giant tree boles was quite dangerous enough, so much so that they had always to be on the alert, by day or night. But when they encountered the beginnings of this huge bog, it was an obvious impossibility to continue. They had seen tracks on its edge which made any such idea unthinkable. The catfolk were runners of the open plains, and they knew nothing of this shrouded murk and its inhabitants. The trees went on as if the dark water at their feet were simply a new form of soil, so the travelers simply did the logical thing. They went aloft. They lost time, of course. Sometimes the vined highways and the mighty limbs came to a dead end, and they all had to backtrack. But Hiero always knew where his home lay, his built-in compass never ceasing to function. He could get a rude sighting on the sun through the leaves as well, and thus their course, to the north, stayed pretty constant.

There were other advantages. The cat people and Hiero were good climbers. Then, too, the really monstrous things, such as whatever wallowed far below at the moment, were not apt to be climbers at all. The air was cool and fresh, and there was plenty of game, in the form of unwary birds and mammals. Only that afternoon, B'uorgh had scurried up a nearby trunk and neatly cut the throat of a large nesting bird. It and its half-grown young had made an excellent dinner, with plenty left over for the morrow.

Nothing in this life was completely safe, of course. Once they had been forced to scamper for their lives when a nest of tree vipers had all leaped or slithered at them. At another point a colony of malignant-looking apes, far too much like the Hairy Howlers for Hiero's liking, had followed them a long way, obviously nerving themselves up to an open attack. They were big, stump-tailed brutes, glossy black and with savage, naked, green faces and horrendous fangs. But just as Hiero had been about to kill one and risk losing his spear, the whole gibbering crew reached the end of some obscure and invisible boundary.

Hiero's group hastened away, leaving behind the barking and chattering mob in the sea of verdant leaves. The two young males were furious at being chivied along in this manner and pleaded to be allowed to go back and wipe out the horde, but B'uorgh's coughed orders put an end to that nonsense at once, and they subsided.

The man realized how lucky he was. He certainly had not been looking forward to his lonely but inevitable journey through the incredibly dangerous southern wood. For one thing, he had to sleep at times; for another, he had been there before, though in another part, and had some idea of the perils which lay hidden in the depths of the giant trees. He had been taken wholly by surprise, therefore, when the old Speaker called him to a sudden meeting and blandly informed him that four of her people would go with him. The war chief, the young Speaker-to-be, and the two younger warriors were all volunteers, but also came with her full consent and approval.

You go into great peril, as great as any you have been through, we think. Hiero had informed the tribe, through necessity, of some of his recent adventures and had not even been sure that they believed him. The art of telling tall tales was well developed among this strange people.

The soft-furred hand laid its naked palm on his as the Speaker continued. *Hiero, you go to fight the ancient enemy of us all. Your she fights for you far away, and so do others. You are our friend. If the defilers, the cub-killers, the naked-faced mind-warpers, if they should be the victors, how long would we be safe, we whom they have forgotten, perhaps? Not long, we all think. We are few in number, and none outside knows of us as yet, save only you. But how long would that last if the enemy with the terrible machines you tell of were to conquer all who now oppose them? No, we must help, for your errand, even though we do not fully comprehend it, is of the utmost importance. It must be so, for you do not lie and you have shown us how they hate you and have tried to kill you, not once but many times. You must be one of their chiefest foes, if not the most important. Friends are for help, and you shall have ours. This chewed-up, old scar-fur of a B'uorgh can be replaced easily enough.* The doughty individual in question simply purred; he knew what condition he was in and, moreover, looked it.

The Speaker sighed mentally. *I would come myself, to see new things and learn much of the outer world I will never know. But I can send M'reen. She will be my eyes and ears. I can train another, should she be lost, though she is a good mind. The two young males are idiots, like all males, both the young and the older. Still, they are among the best hunters in the pack. They can help guard you. And M'reen has the secret of the Wind of Death!*

It had been hard to thank them all, especially since he alone knew, or at least had some idea, of what they were getting into. And they had done another thing without being asked, which made him feel even more warmly about them. They had sworn, quite simply, to leave the humans out in the villages alone and, while remaining secret, to kill no more of them for any reason. No more babies would be removed as pets, nor would solitary hunters be hounded to a terrified doom. This was a great concession.

Now here they were, Hiero mused, watching the blunt faces with their brows black-barred and lively, lambent eyes, the rippling muscles, and the ivory claws stretching as their owners eased their limbs. Who would have thought this only two weeks ago? For indeed they had been a fantastic help. It was very hard to winnow out thoughts in this life-infested jungle; though he did his best, not all inimical creatures were detectable in time. The great ape-things were very intelligent, and he, concentrating on lower carnivores and other predacious forms of existence, had missed them completely. It was the young Za'reekh who had heard the rustle of branches, unswayed by treetop breezes, and thus had warned them in time to turn from the ambush. The catfolk had no noses worth speaking of; indeed, Hiero's was far better. But their eyes and ears were fantastic and, in the often dim light, invaluable. It was M'reen who had heard the whispering rush of the oncoming brood of vipers and thus had turned them back, fortunately to a series of broad, flat limbs.

Their aid was well worth having, and they were good company too, though Ch'uirsh was going to get nailed one of these days for his practical jokes! Finding a giant worm from a bromeliad growth on one's chest in the small hours of the night was a bit much. The priest-warrior grinned to himself. He had flung the supposed serpent off with a yelp of horror before even getting a good look at it. B'uorgh, also wakened, had wanted to scalp the young hunter, but M'reen had given him a good talking-to instead. A Speaker-to-be, even a young one, in a female rage, had made Ch'uirsh's ears go back in instant regret for his folly. Hiero contented himself with a very brief lecture on the idiocy of frightening people who had a lot of real dangers on their minds. And that was that. It *had* been funny, though.

I wonder where we are, B'uorgh sent, after a companionable silence, while they listened to the monster in the slime below, now retreating noisily. *Can this sea, this mighty water, be far off, do you think, Hiero? I have viewed it in your mind, but frankly, I find it hard to believe, even so. So much water in one place!*

Oh, it's there, the man answered. *We have to cross it somehow. I simply have to get back to the real war, to find out what my own people are doing, to say nothing of the Unclean. I don't know if the weapon that I found, the machine that thinks for all*—this was as close to describing the computer idea as he could get—*ever arrived in my country. I don't know if my country is even still defending itself. I don't know if any messages have come from the South, from my she and her country. The only thing I do know is that going all the way around the edge of the Inland Sea would take many months, assuming that we ever got there at all. We have to cross it and cross it fast.*

There was a silence again as the cat minds considered yet once more all the marvelous new ideas. The great waters alone were wild enough in conception for folk who only knew the lazy little rivers of the savannas. But the idea of going on things that floated, like sticks on a rivulet! It was frightening, yes, but also wonderful.

These boats, these ships, I understand, I think, M'reen sent. *But the way they move! I can understand that if many people put sticks in the water that push, the boat-thing moves forward. But that the wind itself can make the boat move, that is almost beyond any belief.*

For perhaps the fiftieth time, Hiero tried to explain what sails were and what it was that they did. The real joke, which he could not share, was that he was sure that the cat people would make marvelous sailors! They had no fear at all of heights and moved up and down smooth branches, well—like cats. He felt sure that a crew of trained catmen would rival the finest human sailors in existence. Probably they would need little or no training, either, once the principles were understood. Of course, there was a possible problem of seasickness, but he doubted that such a small thing would stop his friends for very long. As they fell into a drowsy slumber, he was still chuckling to himself at the thought of a great barque, such as *The Ravished Bride*, her rigging full of flitting, dancing figures, like spotted sprites.

* * *

The following day brought Hiero to a sudden halt. It was mid-afternoon and they were moving rapidly along a highway of the world aloft, a series of interlaced branches of great size, almost as easy to run on as a town street. The man suddenly held up one hand, and the others stopped in their tracks as the message penetrated.

Hiero's mind had gone roving ahead in its usual manner, but he had been pushing it a bit harder and farther than he normally did. Then he realized they were already near the Inland Sea. There could be no other explanation for the void in the life auras he was accustomed to gathering into his head. The vast, teeming mass of sheer life which made up the collective biota of the titanic forest suddenly halted. There was a clear limit beyond which, with sharp finality, all surface life ceased. All *normal* surface life, that was!

Motioning the others to stillness, he crouched on the branch and listened with all his mental ability, for he was operating his power at extreme range. He was sensing men, men of so-called civilization, for the first time in months. And they were very much the wrong kind of men!

He was detecting the crew of an Unclean ship! No other explanation made any sense. They were closely grouped physically; that he could tell with ease. And they were out in the emptiness that he knew from the past, which could only mean the sea. The sea had many forms of life, but they did not as a rule operate on its surface, certainly not on bands of mental energy used by humans. And none of the natural forms of the great freshwater ocean would be likely to own an Unclean mind shield! One assortment of people, of whatever stock he could not tell, had such. He had learned in his flight from the North to detect these things when they were being used to send messages. In their closed or defensive condition, they revealed nothing. But the creature of the enemy was using this one to send. This left him open to detection by Hiero and, more than that, enabled the Metz to read the message. What was being sent was most interesting.

None of our ships have been sighted. Not even a trader of the common scum. It is as if the coast west of Neeyana had been swept clean somehow. I have received messages only from yourself. Suggest that a Brother be sent in one of the secret ships to investigate. We are two days' sail from Neeyana, but we are hampered by bad winds. There is a strong feeling among both the officers and the crew that something very funny is going on. We should have sighted the front-runners of the spring trade by now, but have seen nothing. We return to port unless I receive further orders. Message ends. Sulkas.

Hiero listened intently with every fiber of his senses, but could detect no answer. If there were one, it must be coming on some wavelength too attenuated, possibly by distance, for him to reach. But he rather thought not. Whoever Sulkas was, he was no member of the Unclean Brotherhood. The mind, though intelligent, was not of the same caliber, nor was it of the same "feel." This was some trusted servant, a pirate, perhaps, like the late Bald Roke, whom Hiero and Gimp had killed. While the catfolk chatted quietly among themselves, the priest settled down to try to analyze what he had heard.

The message had probably been sent at a fixed time. No reply was thought necessary for the present. Clearly, the Unclean, whom he knew controlled the port of Neeyana on the southern coast of the sea, were uneasy about something. This vessel, which had a crew of no more than a dozen, was sent out as a scout. The crew had found nothing save an empty ocean, and this made them in turn uneasy, for it should not have been so, not at this time of the year. The report had gone to home base, to Neeyana, for further action. A suggestion had been made that one of the Brothers, a robed wizard of the Unclean, should be sent on one of the "secret ships."

Hiero had no trouble guessing what was meant. He had been a prisoner on one of those secret ships, powered by some force he did not as yet understand, but of which he had many suspicions. He was reasonably sure, as was Brother Aldo of the Eleventh Brotherhood, that the Unclean had atomics! Both men felt that the metal vessels they had encountered were driven by the powers of the atom, the shunned, the abhorred, the unspeakable! In their hidden laboratories, the scientists of the Unclean had wrought many horrors. They had bred mutated animals as slaves, as they had tried to do with the cat people. But this was the Ultimate Crime. This was the final horror of The Death, something so awful that normal humanity shrank from even contemplating it.

Hiero remembered their group thrill of nausea when he,

Luchare, Aldo, and the bear Gorm had first glimpsed the buried cavern of the past, where the great, plastic-shrouded machines had lain, the dispatchers of the ancient terror throughout the world. Aldo, the lover of all life, had almost fainted.

As Hiero sat now, brooding over what he had learned, his determination hardened. The Unclean were going to perish, root and branch, down to the last serf, the merest acolyte in the most minor degree. This was his mission, and he would not fail.

At length, he turned to his fellow venturers. He knew what he wanted to do, but it might prove a trifle hard to explain. Yet he must make the attempt.

We must be just south of the main road from the west to a city held by our enemies. One old road runs from the southeast to the northwest, springing from many other roads far away in the South. We must have been moving roughly parallel to it, though a goodish way off. It is the only way from the east to the port of Neeyana, at least through the forest. West of Neeyana there are other roads and eventually, I think, also more open country, at least in part, but I have never been there or examined detailed maps of that region, except in the most casual way. The shores are very dangerous, and most traffic goes by ship.

He explained further what he had just been doing. There was an enemy vessel present out on the waters, and they must all be very, very careful from now on. If the Unclean ship were no more than two days' sail from the harbor of the foe, then there would soon be contact with someone, probably a someone they had no wish to meet unawares.

We must guard our minds, he went on. *Use your speech aloud to one another and talk with me only if urgent. You people use an odd mental band and not one likely to be constantly watched, which is good. But the Unclean have many servants who are not human and with whom they must speak, so be careful! Also, the nonhumans watch and listen, as well as send messages on their own account. We must go like shadows from here on. Something strange out on the sea seems to have disturbed our enemies. I have no idea what it is, but anything that bothers them is likely to be in our favor.*

The catfolk had no trouble understanding him, though they grew wildly excited at the thought of actually coming into

contact with the legendary wizard lords, whose crimes had been
instilled into each of them in their youth. When Hiero explained
that he had no real plans other than somehow to steal a small
vessel and escape with it, they seemed to feel that this would
prove easy—a simple matter of overpowering whoever stood
in their way.

*I will loose the Wind of Death on them. Then we will cut
their throats!* This was M'reen, tapping the pouch which hung
at her belt. It took a while for Hiero to quiet them down, to
explain the numbers of the Unclean and their servants, and to
make sure they would do nothing rash, but would follow his
orders. After a while, he felt sure of them. The first rush of
hatred would not make them behave in an irresponsible way.

They continued on for the remainder of the day with redoubled caution, using hand signals when they wanted to tell
Hiero something and conversing in their own purring murmur
among themselves.

That night they camped on another natural platform. After
Hiero had grilled his share of the meat, they put out the fire,
remote though the chance was that it might be observed. Water
had never been a problem to date; not only did the tree crotches
often hold it in quantity, but many of the large, epiphytic plants
contained small pools as well.

As the catfolk dozed through the dark hours, the man continued to reach out with his thoughts into the night, not only
in the direction they were moving but on either side as well.
He was beginning, if his senses were operating in a correct
manner, to feel what he thought was the town of Neeyana, a
way off to the north and east of their present position. He could
not read any individual minds, but the sensation of grouped
humanity gave off a feeling almost of heat in his head. He was
fairly sure he was right.

It was not in his original plans to approach the place at all,
at least not closely. There was far too much danger of Unclean
detection. He now realized that it might prove to be the only
sensible course, especially if they were to steal a small boat.
He knew of no other towns to the east; Captain Gimp, on the
previous voyage, had mentioned none, though they must exist
somewhere along the coast. But he knew nothing at all of the
western and southwestern coasts, either. There was a port,
known to and used on occasion by the Abbeys, but it lay a

thousand leagues to the northwest. He had been warned to avoid it by his superiors when he had set out a year before, for it was full of spies, and only a few of the traders could be really trusted. This was the brawling port of Namcush. A river led down to it from far up near the borders of the territories of the Republic, a river along which trade ran in both directions, though uncertain and often interrupted. In any case, it was of no present use to him, though it might prove a place to steer for in an emergency.

Eventually he slept, but the guard on his mind never relaxed. In the morning he felt there would be much to do.

They had not been on the march for more than a few hours when the road he had been seeking appeared below them. On Hiero's orders, the group had been traveling through the lowest level of the arboreal highway, though even that was far above the ground. The bog had come to an unheralded end sometime during the day before, and firm ground now lay at the base of the mighty trees.

It was M'reen, taking a turn to scout ahead, who signaled the break in the trees. The others joined her to peer down at what lay below.

The trade route was well trampled and wide, though circuitous, for the tremendous task of felling the forest giants had never been attempted, at least not in these parts. The track simply wound about among their bases, back and forth, but always holding a rough course from east to west. Hiero had never before seen it, since he had left it leagues off to his right on his previous venture south. He knew, however, that it connected after Neeyana through a maze of other paths and roads with distant D'alwah, and that goods passed along it of every sort, ranging from fabrics and furs to dried fruit and spices, and not excluding slaves. It was most probably along the eastern part of this route that his wife had been taken as a slave to Neeyana. At least, from her description, it had sounded like this way.

The trail lay empty and silent under the green shadows of the giant trees, with dappled sunbeams illuminating patches of it here and there. While the others waited patiently, the Metz scanned the immediate surroundings with his mind, using the utmost care. The Unclean would be sure to have a watch on this route, a main artery of trade to both east and west, and the last thing the little party needed now was to stumble on some outpost or other. He could detect nothing, however, in either direction, and this puzzled him. The distant mass of mental activity which he felt sure was Neeyana had grown increasingly stronger throughout the morning, but why was there nothing nearer? Surely some traders or one of the Unclean patrols ought to be within detection range.

He considered. The mental shields that the Unclean had begun to issue when last he was in the North might account for the silence all about. This seemed implausible, though. He knew the shields were rare and probably very costly in both time and skilled workmanship. He felt sure such shields would be issued to only key personnel—commanders, members of the Unclean Brotherhood, and others in high authority. A simple unit of watchers on the trails would be most unlikely to have one; or, if the captain possessed one, then Hiero ought to be able to pick up the thoughts of the other, humbler members of the group. It was most perplexing.

Keeping his thoughts to the catfolk on the lowest energy level, undetectable save at close range, he issued his orders. They would scout along on either side of the path, moving east and going very slowly and with the utmost care. His allies would signal in their own speech, which was highly unlikely to be sorted out from the myriad forest noises around them, if they found anything worthy of reporting. Meanwhile, he would bring up to the rear and screen everything in a circle with his own mental nets. M'reen would stay close to him on the left side of the trail with B'uorgh, while the other two would take the right. So it was decided and they set out, descending a mighty tangle of lianas and interwoven aerial roots until within a few feet of the earth. Then they dropped and separated.

Their progress was slow, but they covered the ground nonetheless. Every cluster of the widespread roots and great base flanges of the colossal trees had to be scouted and then circled after investigation. Since many of them were enormous in circumference, making the redwoods of the past look like saplings by comparison, this took time. They tried never to lose sight of the trail, while remaining invisible from any eyes that they might somehow have overlooked. Hiero had warned them to be especially wary of any attack from overhead, and he was soon proved right, even though they were not attacked.

A faint yowling call from Ch'uirsh on the far side of the trail brought them up short. Following B'uorgh's hand signals, the three crept closer, until they were on the edge of the broad path and could see the spotted forms of the two young warriors on the other side. Ch'uirsh and Za'reekh were pointing upward along the route, to something in the fork of a great tree, overgrown with cable-sized vines and even bushes. Straining his eyes, Hiero finally picked out something alien in the mass of tangled foliage, some darker and more structured shape.

They spent five more minutes scouting the neighborhood before climbing cautiously upward. In another minute, they were in the neatly concealed watchtower of the enemy. It was a roofed platform of logs, cleverly bound about with living plants of all kinds and providing a clear view of the path below in both directions—and it was completely empty. That it had not been empty long was obvious. There was a pile of ripe but not yet rotten fruit in one corner; a rude cabinet in another held dried meat and even some hard biscuit. A perfectly good belt of heavy leather, with a brass buckle and studs, had been dropped under a half-full wineskin near the leaf-covered entrance. Smelling the wine, Hiero found it perfectly drinkable.

Over all the place hung a faint, sour odor, and it was one the man had no trouble identifying. *Man-rats*, he sent, using the lowest energy level of brain waves. *The enemy has had a garrison of the foul things they bred here. There was at least one human as well, since they do not drink this stuff in the leather bag. They have been called away suddenly, and I would badly like to know why.* He thought hard and came to a decision.

The other four crouched on their haunches, and, very carefully, Hiero sent a probe out in the direction of the Inland Sea. It could not lie more than a few miles to the north of their present position, and he wanted to know what was going on off their flank as they continued. Presently, he found a thing of interest, although exactly what he had found, he was not sure. There was something out there or a number of somethings, maybe, but the whole embodiment of whatever it was lay under a mental blanket, a cover concealing the nature and identity of what was hidden therein. All Hiero could detect was a mass like a huge mental cloud, an inchoate something which he could not pierce. Beyond all shadow of a doubt, the thing was moving; and it was moving, though not fast, in his direction.

He had felt nothing like this in his mind since the year before, when the Unclean ship with the lightning gun mounted forward had caught them all in the drowned city of the northern shore. After a while, he gave up on the area. He could do nothing more, and the mysterious, cloaked patch of energy could not be penetrated. He switched his attention instead, if possible using even more care, to the direciton of what he felt sure was Neeyana. This was a real change!

Neeyana was boiling, in the sense of turbulent mental energy. It was as if an ants' nest had been stirred with a stick, so violent and numerous were the thoughts he detected. His group must be even closer than he had thought, no more than a few miles out of the town boundaries. Now the empty trails and the missing guards made sense. From the various minds that he tapped, Hiero quickly learned that the place was under or about to come under attack! Everyone who could be mustered was being sent to the sea, to man defenses along the waterfront. The threat which had so galvanized the Unclean was coming from the water, and it took little deduction to identify it with the strange mass of sealed-off minds that he had just been searching out. What on earth could all this mean?

He managed to isolate one mind at length, that of a man, a thoroughly nasty man at that, who seemed to be some kind of under-officer of the town garrison. The man was directing a group of underlings who were putting up barricades of logs and sandbags on a street near the water's edge, and they were working frantically. From the fellow's brain, the Metz picked up the image of a great fleet, as many as thirty ships, coming from the North. Further, he learned that the Unclean wizards had not been able either to detect or to penetrate in any way the minds of the people on board those ships. This fact had become generally known pretty quickly, and the ordinary soldiers didn't like it one bit! They were used to having things all their own way, casually killing anyone who disagreed, protected by their Dark Masters' corrupted science and weapons, both mental and physical. Something had gone wrong, and the Unclean Lords had let the fact that they were taken by surprise become public knowledge a little too fast. Hiero probed further, his excitement growing as he did so.

The man whose skull he was ransacking had not lost all confidence, despite his evident worry. Two of the secret ships were coming. The strange fleet would see what would happen then, when the lightning guns began to speak.

Sitting back and closing his mind to all externals, Hiero made his head stop aching with the effort he had been using and simply tried to reason out what he and the others should be doing next. It was not easy. Yet with all this excitement and the attack coming from those who must somehow be his friends, a better opportunity to escape to the North might never reoccur. If his group could not get to the strange fleet, they might at least be able to steal a decent boat and flee during the confusion of battle. It had to be risked.

Quickly he informed the others of what was taking place ahead of them. *We have to get into the town, near the great water somehow, while they are all concentrating on the sea. They must have had a bad scare, because I'm sure that they have pulled out all the landward patrols and guards to reinforce the town defenses. They may have left some small body of troops on this side, but there can't be many of them. Kill if you have to—quietly. Don't hurt shes or young; stun them or silence them only.*

They now moved off at a much faster pace, with Hiero leading on one side of the trail, while B'uorgh took the point on the other.

As they passed along like shadows, in and out of the tree gloom and through the patches of mottled sunlight, Hiero concentrated on the road immediately ahead. He wanted no encounters with anyone and he was desperately afraid of running into someone or something protected by one of the Unclean mind shields, the lockets of bluish metal he remembered from the past. At his strongest, when he had possessed the power of mental compulsion and even the ability to kill with his mind alone, he had not been able to penetrate one of these mechanisms; he was sure he could not do so now. At the same time, in the back of his mind some half-remembered thing, also from the past, was stirring. He had forgotten something, and it was something he needed right now, this instant. What the devil was it? He shrugged mentally. It would not come, whatever it was, and he would have to wait until it surfaced of its own accord.

They loped along for a mile or so. Then B'uorgh suddenly raised one long, spotted arm and signaled a halt. The catman turned and sped across the trail and took Hiero urgently by the arm, at the same time holding his other hand to a furry ear. They all stopped, and Hiero listened for the sound that the catman's better hearing had detected. Presently he caught it also, a distant surge and roar, with an occasional higher, more piercing note at intervals. It was the sound of a battle, or he had never heard one. Occasionally there came a heavy crash through the other noises, as if a building or a great tree had fallen. All animal sounds around them seemed hushed now, as if the forest were stilling itself in fright at the unaccustomed uproar in the distance.

Hiero signaled for more speed, and they began this time really to run, though still avoiding the trail's center. It was a risk, but, Hiero thought, not much of one. All mental activity was enmeshed in the swirl of combat ahead of them, and he could pick up individuals more clearly with every step. The thoughts of frightened women and children were coming through now, as well as those of men who were not fighting and who were baffled by what was happening. The Unclean Masters of Neeyana had stayed pretty well hidden in the past, and the sudden surge of fighting men and Leemutes had come as a shock to a lot of traders and townsfolk who had never known— or preferred not to investigate—who actually ran the whole place. Now these neutrals or noncombatants were panicking, terrified by the fighting and running about trying to get out of the danger zone.

As they drew nearer and nearer, Hiero could pick out with his ears the screams of the unfortunate population whose world had suddenly been overturned. What he could not pick out were any thoughts of the Unclean Masters of Neeyana. He knew the reason was that they were shielded by their mechanisms. Any hope of learning anything from them of what went on was useless. He tried again to reach the attacking forces, whoever they were, but they too remained shrouded by their large, protective shield. He could feel the weight of them out there, but that was all.

Trying to keep watch on his own immediate way was growing wearisome, and he could not scan everything continually without exhausting himself. The physical drain of constant mental search was a very real one.

The roar of battle was now loud in the ears of his group.

As the forest drew to an end in front of them, they began to smell smoke, acrid and greasy. Veils of it were sifting through the last trees, and it grew constantly thicker, cutting off much of the sunlight and making the catfolk choke and sneeze. They were skulking and running through brush now, with Hiero in the lead, his sword in hand, his spear and shield slung on his back. Killing would be close work, but he hoped to escape without fighting at all. Through the shouts and yells ahead of them came the roaring of fire and another noise, the echo-crashing sounds he had caught earlier. At times these were regular, but at others seemed to be spaced irregularly. Mixed with the burning wood smoke was another unfamiliar smell, sharp and bitter, a reek of something he had never scented before.

Almost before they knew it, they were in the town itself. One moment found them in a sea of low bush, and the next they were in a narrow lane between rows of shabby huts, half-blanketed in the heavy smoke. The smell of filth and ordure was strong enough to contest with the burning wood.

B'uorgh hissed, and they all tensed as several shapes loomed out of the murk ahead. At the same time, a gust of wind, driven down the alley from the sea, revealed the two parties to each other.

Two of the great Man-rats, hung with weapons and carrying sacks filled with either loot or supplies, stood blinking in amazement at the blade of the man and the four scowling masks of the first Children of the Wind they had ever seen—or ever would see. Before the great ears could twitch or the greasy paws even loosen their hold on whatever they carried, they were dead, throats cut and naked-tailed bodies jerking on the grass in death agony. The incredible speed of his allies once again left Hiero gasping. Za'reekh and Ch'uirsh had moved so fast that they were back on guard, daggers ready for a fresh assault, even as the two loathsome Leemutes were still falling to earth!

Kill anyone armed, Hiero sent. *We must get on and try to find a place from which we can see. Look for something tall. There will be no trees, but these folks build tall huts, many times our height. There are too many minds here and too much excitement for me to listen with my own. We must use our eyes and ears instead.*

He was trying to remember what Gimp and Brother Aldo had told him long ago about Neeyana. Luchare, too, had been there, on her way to be sold as a slave. What had they told him? It was a very old town, so old that it might even have existed in some form before The Death. The Unclean were everywhere in the town, but usually hidden. And there were some old churches, decayed-looking, with no priests about. These were stone-built and had towers. Such towers would probably have an Unclean garrison, if only for purposes of observation. Still, something had to be tried. Everything was a risk in this smoky maze full of foul odors and the panic of the inhabitants.

Even as he weighed various chances, another of those explosive crashes came from ahead of him. Something heavy fell to the ground, making it shake beneath his feet. Farther off, he heard other booming noises. What could they be? He had to find some place from which he could see!

He glanced at the catfolk. They stood silently behind him, their ears laid back and their neck ruffs bristling. It must, he mused remotely, be terrifying to be brought from the clean forest air into this stench and murk, filled with horrid sounds and unknown dangers. But they were not flinching and were ready to fight. He found the trust heartening, though he wished, not for the first time, that he did not have the responsibility for them on his shoulders.

Slowly and carefully, they began to grope their way through the dirty clouds of smoke, testing each corner before they crossed it, straining every sense to locate any possible foe before they themselves were discovered. A particularly heavy wave of black fog engulfed them all, and Hiero signaled, though he was increasingly nervous of using telepathy. *Link hands with me and stay close. B'uorgh, you bring up the rear. Kill any not of us.*

The flat command made him regretful, but he could take no chances in this foul dark. The enemy had held Neeyana for too long, and their only hope was to remain unseen and unsuspected. He felt his way along a wooden fence of palings, now shutting out the multifarious cries, both in his mind and in his ears, trying only to locate some more substantial structure. He could feel the trembling of the hand, a delicate one, clasping his, and he tried to send strength down his arm to the

Speaker-to-be. M'reen had never anticipated all of this, or indeed any of it.

He halted in one moment as his left hand, outstretched, encountered something new. He was touching smooth, greasy stone, worn and slippery in a way that only age can create. He paused and he knew the others down the line were also halting, feeling his excitement and the hesitation.

None of the yells and cries were nearby, though the overall noise was a constant. The hot blanket of fumes and dirty vapor covered him and his friends, but what else might it cover? He tried to guess the hour and decided that it must be around mid-afternoon. How much time did that leave them and what were they to do with it? He shook involuntarily as one of the explosions shattered something he guessed was only a few streets away. The series of reverberations that had more or less gone on continuously while they advanced seemed to be dying off. The next one he heard was much farther off, probably in the direction of the waterfront.

He hand-signaled for a slow advance and, with the smoke stinging his half-opened eyes, felt his way farther along the stonework he had touched a minute back. For perhaps twenty feet, the wall remained unbroken and featureless as high up as he could reach, save for minute gaps in the aged mortar. The large stones held by this cement seemed irregular and not cut or beveled in any way.

A new wave of smoke blew down on them, and he choked and gagged, still creeping along the wall. Then he paused. He was tracing with his hand the edge of a massive doorpost, of heavy and polished wood. He stooped and made sure. It was not a window, but an open door. Blinking in the dirty haze, he listened both with his ears and with his mind.

✤ 9 ✤

WINDS OF CHANGE,
WINDS OF CHANCE

THERE WAS NO ONE NEARBY, UNLESS SHIELDED BY A MENTAL block or guard of some sort, as Hiero could tell with ease. He and the others were now in the lower room of some high building, almost certainly one of the abandoned churches that Luchare had described. There were minds, alien and inimical, below and above them, in the vaults and what must be the tower. But there did not seem to be more than three or four in either place. Making up his mind, the man began to feel his way through the gloom and smoke to where a faint gleam of light showed the beginning of a narrow stair. Behind him came the others, quivering with excitement.

I have to see, he sent. *B'uorgh, you stand guard at the bottom of this tower. If one or two come, slay them. If more, send a warning and follow us up.* He knew the big chief would probably resent being left, but would also have enough discipline to understand why the best warrior ought to stay as a rear guard.

With the others in his wake, sword at point, he began to climb the narrow steps, which wound upward in a tight spiral. The steps were cracked and greasy, as well as being worn with great age. The smoke was drawn up past their heads, and they had to fight to keep from coughing at each cautious step. They passed the first landing in silence and went on. Hiero could detect no sign of life on that floor, though a battered door yawned open. It grew lighter as they climbed, and the smoke thinned. Another apparently vacant floor was passed in silence, and Hiero sent a hand signal along to get ready. The roof lay

159

ahead, and daylight was visible through the last door. At his nod, they burst out onto the platform of the ancient spire, perhaps once the bell tower of the long-abandoned church. Now, however, it was a watchtower, and whatever the occupants had expected, it was not this sudden onslaught from the depths of the building.

There were four beings on the small square of the turret, and all had been gazing north to the waters of the Inland Sea, visible even through the smoke and haze which enveloped the lower parts of the town. The two Man-rats and one of the humans died, their throats cut before they could take in the fact that they were attacked. The fourth human fell limp as the iron edge of Hiero's left hand chopped at his neck below the base of his metal helmet. In seconds, the place was taken. Telling the two young males to watch the stunned man, Hiero strode to the wooden rail of the tower, which surmounted the ancient stones of an even older wall, and peered eagerly out. Below and before him lay an amazing sight.

He already knew that large portions of Neeyana were on fire, the aged wooden structures which made up the larger part of the town having the quality of tinder. The fires raged, whole blocks and streets spurting flame where wooden sidewalks passed the fire from house to house. Here and there, stone structures, probably older by far, resisted the heat and thrust up through the smoke. The wind was constantly shifting from east to west and back again, a light wind, but fluky and varying in force.

Down the narrow streets ran companies of Unclean troops, battling to reach the waterfront and being forced back by barriers of fire and by mobs of the civil populace, who seemed to have given in to complete panic and were struggling to get away in the opposite direction, to the south. There had obviously never been any plans for the defense of the place from a serious attack. The conceit of the Unclean Masters had not envisaged any such happening. Now they were having to improvise, with the usual results of such attempts. Appalled, the Metz saw a pack of Hairy Howlers hew their way with swords through a band of ragged humans who disputed a path with them, sending the bloodied survivors shrieking in renewed terror off into side streets and alleys. The cries and screams were nightmarish from all over the city.

It was toward the Inland Sea that Hiero's attention turned,

the rest being observed only in passing. The entire waterfront was under attack, and most of the ancient warehouses and crumbling docks were on fire, with only a wall of stone or some ruined jetty of the same material resisting the heat. But it was the water and what was on it that fascinated the man.

Five rectangular shapes lay out off the town, clearly visible through the veils of smoke. From their sloping sides belched fire at intervals as ports opened and closed. They had no sails, but carried squat twin funnels and one short mast at the stern. It was these masts and what flew upon them that brought Hiero's heart into his mouth. Out there, green upon white background, waved the Sword and the Cross of the Abbeys! The Metz Republic was at long last taking the war to the enemy!

His mind racing, Hiero noted the many anchored sailing vessels out beyond the five strange warships. This was no mere raid; this was an invasion fleet. He spared hardly a thought for the black muzzles whose projectiles were exploding in the town. There had to be a source of the continual crashing that he had heard in the last half hour. How the weapons operated was of small concern to him. They seemed larger variants of his long-lost thrower, the hand-carried rocket propeller which S'duna had taken from him in the North.

Vainly, his hands clenched against the railing, he tried to contact someone out in the fleet. It was useless. A powerfully held mind shield, as good as anything the Unclean had ever managed, kept all the ships under a mass shroud, one that his thoughts simply could not penetrate.

And he had knowledge that they needed out there, he knew something vital, concerning which they ought to be warned! He beat upon the railing in his despair.

A furry hand timidly touched his shoulder and brought him back with a rush to the personal situation. It was M'reen. *B'uorgh has come from his post. He says that many of the evil ones have come up from down below, under the earth, and then gone away outside. They did not see him. Unless more come now, we are alone in this place.* Behind her, the tall shape of the chief loomed through the thinning smoke.

Almost absently, Hiero noted that the wind was rising and also backing, blowing with increasing strength from the south, from the forest and out to sea. What to do now?

He looked out at the attacking fleet again. From the mind

talk he had caught the day before, he knew that there were at least two of the Unclean warships in the neighborhood, the metal-hulled craft driven by what he felt certain was the fury of the atom. And they had on their decks the dreaded gun which fired electric bolts, the weapon he called the lightning gun. If they appeared, could the Abbey fleet withstand them? The new ships, formidable though they were, appeared clumsy, like waddling turtles. He noticed that they were anchored in a line, bow to stern, and he shrewdly guessed that, although there was almost no sea running, they needed all the stability they could get in order to fire with any accuracy.

He turned and looked down at the prisoner, who was now squatting and rubbing his neck while he stared with frightened eyes at Hiero and the People of the Wind. He was a nasty-looking specimen, but he wore good clothes, and his boots and helmet were excellent in fit. Also, he was clean in his person. Around his neck hung a metal replica of the yellow spiral the Unclean Lords bore on their robes. He was an officer, then, and one of some rank in the enemy hierarchy. Hiero probed the man's mind and, not to his surprise, met blankness, an impenetrable barrier.

Strip him! he sent on the mind wave of the catfolk. In a moment, the keen claws had left the man's body bare to the waist. The sealed locket on the bluish metal chain contained the mechanical mind shield the Unclean used to protect their servants and allies. In another second, Hiero had whipped it off and thrown the device over the parapet. Now he addressed the man aloud, using *batwah*, the almost universal trade language.

"Speak the truth and only the truth and you may yet live. Lie, and I give you to my friends here." He saw the shudder as the other took in the avid, yellow eyes. "Where are the secret ships? How many of them are there? What strength of troops is in the town? Are there more on the way and how many? Where are your Masters and how many of them are here?" As he fired the rapid questions, hardly waiting for the answers, he listened to the now unguarded brain as well, a technique in which he had grown so practiced that his ease, compared with that of the previous year, was automatic. He could not *compel* his prisoner to do anything; that power was gone. But he could sense his thoughts.

The man was not a coward and he was indeed of some rank, the equivalent of a Metz regimental commander. His name was Ablom Gord, and he knew a great deal, all of it interesting. He tried to lie, but it made no difference to Hiero, though the Metz masked his face and never indicated when what his ears heard was not the truth.

It seemed that no more than two of the deadly gun ships were anywhere nearby, but those two had been summoned and were close at hand. The garrison of the town still was holding but might crack if and when the invasion took place and the Abbey warships were not successfully challenged. No lightning guns were in the town itself, only on the ships. The Unclean forces were rallying in great strength, having been summoned from far and wide; they were not mustering at Neeyana, but rather at a secret base many leagues to the east. More forces were coalescing in the north on the far side of the Inland Sea, and a mighty assault had been planned. But this sudden attack on Neeyana had been totally unexpected. No help could be summoned in time unless the ships with the lightning guns could alter the balance of forces.

Hiero stared coldly at the officer when he had learned all he thought useful. "You have lied to each question," he said finally. "You were warned." His signal to B'uorgh was sent so swiftly that the knife was in the man's throat before the mind could realize a death sentence had been passed. Hiero dismissed the matter. He had read enough in the fellow's past to sentence him to death a dozen times over, murder of helpless women being only one of the charges.

He stepped over the twitching body, realizing with distaste that his sandals were slippery with blood, and once more stared out at the Abbey war fleet, still engaged in softening up the waterfront with methodical, well-aimed fire. Behind him, the wind rose in increasing strength, ruffling his hair as it blew—steadily now and, aside from small gusts, always to the north, to the sea. The wind, he thought idly, now why was the wind on his mind? The enemy was undoubtedly coming fast; their grim, speedy ships, driven by silent motors in the sleek metal hulls, must even now be close upon the town.

Why on earth was the wind so much in the foreground of his thoughts? Then his thoughts clarified. *That* was the answer!

He wheeled and began to rap out orders, punctuating them

with an occasional question. In no more than a minute, so rapid was the mental interchange on the catfolk's mental band, the decision was made and the little party was groping its way down the stairs.

The lower part of the building still seemed silent and deserted. Smoke fumes swirled in through the ancient door. The shrieks and cries, the crackle of flames, and the roar of the bombs and shells outside, all came from a distance. The impetus of the attack, Hiero thought, seemed to have shifted a bit and was coming more from the west, as if the Metz fleet had moved in that direction. So much the better for his purpose.

As silently as so many ghosts, the five departed from the old building and darted off down the narrow street, all senses tensed to the uttermost. Hiero led, along with B'uorgh, for his human abilities were more needed here in this human-built maze than the more finely attuned nerves of his allies. Soon they came to a small square and shrank back against reeking walls as a mob of shouting people crossed in front of them. Its members seemed to be some of the bewildered and terrified human populace, running with no clear aim in view, and soon disappeared in the smoke off to the east. Hiero signaled, and the five ran swiftly across the square and vanished into the gloom of a smoldering building on the far side. They were heading, insofar as the man could tell, on a slight downward slant. If his judgment, backed by a view from the tower, was at all accurate, they would strike the water in a fairly short time. Once a running figure, shapeless in the murk, loomed up in front of them; but one sight of the five grim shapes, their size magnified by the poor light, was enough to send the runner shrieking away down a side alley.

We must be even more careful now, the Metz sent. *The main body of their troops will be down here near the water. We have to get through them and find a boat.*

M'reen answered. *The water is not far. I can smell it. Even through this dirty air and smoke, it smells clean.*

Suddenly, more quickly than the man had thought possible, they were there. They had been slinking down a narrow runway, lined with cracked brick underfoot, when it came abruptly to an end. Before them lay a tangle of ancient piers, some half-rotted and leaning drunkenly in the mud of the shore's edge, while others burned sluggishly, ignited either by the shells of the strange fleet or by chance-caught sparks. The wind still blew from behind the group's backs, and the wreaths of smoke wafted straight out before them to the open sea beyond.

Hiero scanned the scene, his eyes intent for one purpose. There were no Unclean about, at least not near. He could sense them on either side in strength, but none were close. He knew that if the catfolk had seen or sensed why, he would be told at once. He listened intently, but the gunfire was still off to the left, down toward the west. Here where he stood, due to some trick of acoustics, it was even quite quiet, and he could actually hear the lapping of tiny waves on the muddy foreshore at the foot of the street.

Then his roving gaze fixed on a small, pointed shape, half-hidden under one of the crumbling docks, moving gently to the action of the water. It was this slight movement that had caught his eye. He stared harder and again checked the immediate neighborhood for other movement. He could see nothing, yet instinct now began to warn him. There was another presence somewhere near, something watching!

It made no difference, he told himself. Time was too important for these vague fears. The decision had to be taken.

Wait here and keep watch on all sides, he sent. *If that thing out under the wood, that thing which sits on the water, is what we need, I will signal.* Without waiting for assent, he darted out into the open and sped across and down to the mud and the lapping, oily tide. In a second, he was over the side of the small boat and staring at its sole occupant—doubtless some local fisherman.

The man must have been trying to flee, for there were both oars and a net in the skiff. He was unarmed save for a belt knife and was clad only in a leather vest and a loincloth. Either in the act of fleeing or earlier, he had been shot, and the vanes of a crossbow quarrel thrust up from the center of his back. The oars were still bundled, and it looked to Hiero as if he had been carrying them to the boat when he had suddenly taken leave of life, one more unnumbered casualty of the war.

The Metz breathed a quick prayer, in case the man should have been honest and not one of the Unclean, then tipped the body over the side into the shallows. He turned and waved once, a beckoning gesture, then seated himself on the central thwart and began to cut the leather painter which held the boat to a cleat on one of the crumbling pilings. Seconds later, the other four were wading alongside and clambering aboard, to huddle excitedly on the bottom. In another instant, Hiero had the oars between the crude rowlocks and was easing the little craft out under the pilings toward the open sea.

Behind him, eyes glared in impotent rage from the narrow slit of a window set high on a ruined wall. A white hand fumbled with a neck chain of bluish metal; then, a decision taken, it dropped again. A hooded shape whirled and departed in haste on an urgent errand.

The little boat was about three times Hiero's length, high of prow and with a pointed stern. She rode the water sweetly as the Metz pulled hard away from the shore. The People of the Wind, nervous and yet stoic, crouched silently, two in the bow and two in front of the man and aft. All four were trembling with excitement and the newness of the experience, but they would have died rather than admit it. As the waves increased in strength, they simply laid back their ears and waited for whatever their new friend had to tell them.

Hiero was constantly checking the wind while calculating the course. His scheme was so filled with holes that he could only hope that it had a bare chance of succeeding. If only the wind would keep blowing from the south! Meanwhile, he watched over his shoulder for what the thinning smoke and reek of the burning town would reveal.

Ah! Sure enough, there was the Metz fleet! The five warships, looking more than ever like turtles or even the roofs of barns come adrift, were slowly steaming back to the east in his direction, firing as steadily as ever. If the offshore breeze obscured their targets, they gave no sign of it. Gaps in the smoke probably afforded them all the aiming points they needed. Farther out, the armada of sailing craft still moved sluggishly under light sail, waiting for a signal to close in. The offshore breeze held steady over the brown water.

Hiero rested on his oars and stared as hard as he could to the east, using his mind at its utmost, as well as his eyes. Was there something there? On the edge of his mind, that something came, then went, then came again and steadied. It was like a cloud, a moving shroud in his mind. He could detect no thoughts, nor did he need to do so. Once before, on the far side of the Inland Sea, he had felt this sensation. Ships were coming from the east, faster than anything driven by either sail or the engines of the new vessels of his country. The secret ships of the enemy were coming to the rescue of Neeyana, summoned by the devices of the Masters of the Unclean. The lightning guns were going to be opposed to the crude armor of the Metz warships.

Hiero had no hope in his own mind as to which would be the victor. The Metz ships were powerful and had taken Neeyana by surprise. But he did not for one moment think his people could stand up against the forces of the Unclean ships. That Abbot Demero and the Abbey Council were the source of the new war fleet, he never doubted. But he felt that, in the short time the Abbeys had had at their disposal, they could hardly have matched the strength and speed of the Unclean warships. Wonderful as it was to see a Metz battle squadron, those crude floating forts would be horribly outclassed by what was speeding from the east!

M'reen, he sent in haste, *get ready with your preparations. Hurry! The enemy comes! We must all lie down so that this craft appears empty. If our foes see nothing but a drifting skiff, they may pass before us to attack our friends.*

It was B'uorgh who answered. *She is working. And I can see our enemy. How fast they come!*

Hiero could see them now himself, two dots rushing at tremendous speed from down the coast to the east, growing larger by the minute. He almost wrung his hands. If only he could break the mental shield of his friends and tell them what was going on! He ducked below the gunwale with the others and tried to free his mind from worry. At the same time, he felt a sudden wave of fear come over him and secretly rejoiced. For M'reen's bag of hide was open and her hands were stirring, mixing, and blending. The fear was coming *back* from her, ignored by the cat people but acting on his human body chemistry! The Wind of Death was churning and drifting out over the open sea to their front. The veils of smoke from the burning port had something far more lethal than a throat irritant mixed in with their dark shroud.

Hiero stole a look to the west, then ducked back hastily. So far all was well. The Abbey fleet had formed a line well down the coast and was preparing to receive the Unclean forces. The ships were no longer firing at the town, and the sailing vessels had moved even farther down in order to take shelter behind them.

They come, B'uorgh sent. *Now we will see.*

Hiero shut his eyes and began to pray. He had done all he could, and only God could help now. Perhaps the Unclean wizards had learned long in the past how to nullify this awful weapon, back in the days when the catfolk had broken free and fled from their bondage of torture and enslavement.

As he prayed silently, he heard the sound he had been waiting for and dreading, the hissing crackle of the enemy weapon which had once struck him down—the lightning gun! Was it aimed at their little vessel? One blast could incinerate them in seconds. He could no longer restrain himself and peered over the side of the boat. So did the others, and all five beings watched the panorama of a sea battle in silent awe.

The Unclean ships, sharp-prowed and slender, had no tactics for pitched battle on anything like an equal basis. They had never had to learn any, since their mysterious craft so far outclassed any possible foe. As a result, they simply charged at the Metz fleet, bows on, the weapons on their foredecks firing as fast as they could. The two ships were quite close to each other, as if racing to be first for what they thought was the inevitable kill. They apparently never even noticed the drifting boat which floated on the oily sea a quarter of a mile to their south and well out of their path. And they were scoring hits. As the Metz priest had feared, the strange weapon on their bows, which somehow fired sheets of static electricity, outranged the crude cannon of the Metz fleet. Already one of the clumsy vessels was smoking from a great rent in its sloping hull, although it held its line along with the other four. None of the Abbey ships were firing now, and Hiero knew they were holding back until their outranged weapons could bear. He prayed again for the miracle he had tried so hard to conjure up, his eyes smarting both from the smoke and with unshed tears for the discipline that held his countrymen in their silent line.

And, as miracles sometimes do, especially when backed by courage and forethought, it happened.

The two slender Unclean war craft were well past the drifting boat, still pointing at the enemy fleet, when they seemed to go mad. Hiero suddenly saw one of them yaw wildly and head at full speed for its consort's unprotected flank. At the same time, the crackle of the lightning guns ceased abruptly, and the group in the boat could hear a screaming outcry come over the now silent waters. Black dots, which spilled and sprang from the metal hulls like demented fleas, showed where the crews of the stricken ships fled in sheer madness from their hitherto unconquered craft. And then came the final act. With no one— or perhaps a fright-driven lunatic—at the helm, the ship nearest the shore drove at full speed into the side of her racing neighbor, the sharp prow cutting like a gigantic plow, two-thirds of the way back from the peak.

There was first a small puff of smoke as the locked hulls drifted to a halt, then a blaze of white light which made the five cover their eyes. The roar of a tremendous explosion followed the light, and all ducked once more under the shelter of the gunwale. A whistling noise in the overcast air made them try to flatten themselves on the bottom even further. As they crouched in terror, splashes of water all around them sent a spray over their flinching bodies.

Fighting his panic, Hiero looked up and was in time to see the wave coming. He sprang to the central thwart and, in one motion, shipped the oars and turned the boat bows on to the wall of water sweeping down upon them. They rose high on the crest and rushed deep into the valley beyond, but the Metz had acted in the bare nick of time, and hardly a drop of water was taken in. The second and third waves were far smaller, and he had no trouble meeting them. Only then did he once more rest on his oars and wave the cat people up so that all could see the results of their work.

Where the Unclean ships had met in their final and horrific tangle, now a vast and greasy circle lay on the water, widening as the south wind sent the gentle waves to spread it yet farther out. Bits of wood and rubbish floated here and there, none of them large. Of life, there was no sign whatever. The grim vessels, which for so long had haunted the south shore of the Inland Sea, were totally gone. With them went their adept commanders of the Dark Brotherhood, their crews of ghastly mutants, and the human scum which served on them.

In the bow of Hiero's fishing boat, M'reen sat smiling, her leather bag on her lap, her furry ears cocked, and a broad and sharp-toothed smile on her expressive face. The Wind of Death had triumphed over the enemies of her race in a total victory, one on a scale of which she and her folk had never conceived. There would be songs around the hearth fires of her clan for countless generations over this! A keening purr of triumph rose from four lipless mouths, a wild rhythm of exhaltation, as the freest of the free rejoiced at the death of their sometime masters.

Hiero smiled as he watched the swelling throat muscles and the blazing eyes. He would have liked to join in, had his vocal chords been capable of so doing. He had already remembered to give thanks to his Deity in his own way, silently, but no less heartfelt. He had no illusions about their luck. They had been lucky indeed! The timing, the weapon, and the wind had all been just exactly right. One could not count on such things forever, or even more than once. And there was still a lot to be done. This was only the first skirmish of what promised to be a terrible war, one extending far into the future and over many thousands of leagues.

Reluctantly, he called the catfolk back from their paean of joy and brutally brought them to the present.

Friends, he sent, *the war is not over. We have much to do, and first we must meet my other comrades. This is what I have come so many weary paces out of the South to do.* He pointed with one bronzed hand at the Metz fleet, which was milling in some disorder, shaken by the totally unexpected end to the battle. *Sit quietly now, and I will row us out there. And pray to your wind gods my own folk don't turn their thunder weapons on us before I can tell them who we are!*

Actually, it was not that hard. The Metz warships were steaming slowly east once more, and an alert lookout spotted the little craft rowing toward them almost at once. The lead vessel slowed as Hiero and his party approached, the smoke from its twin stacks dying down as it did so. From a wheelhouse set forward, a group of figures emerged to gaze down at them. Noticing that several of the round muzzles set in the slanting hull were also pointing downward in their direction, Hiero shipped his oars and stood up, arms over his head. Then he lowered them and slowly began to cross himself with his right hand, moving it over his broad chest so that all could see his action clearly.

There was a moment of silence as he stood there and the fishing boat drifted closer. Then, over the narrowing gap, came a bull's bellow of a voice. "Look at that sword! Look at that dirty face! Look at that dung-eating grin! I told everyone they couldn't hang the worst priest and the most useless bum in the Metz Republic! He's alive!"

Hiero laughed with relief. "What are you doing on that hulk, you big moron? I didn't know they let you near water. You never bathed in your life and you're not smart enough to learn to swim!"

The big man smiled down at him with a weary benevolence. Per Edard Maluin was a head taller than Hiero and twice his weight. He had the thews of a bull morse and the chubby face of an innocent child, vastly enlarged. He was a veteran of the Frontier Guards, a murderous killer at need, and one of Hiero's best friends, having roomed with him in the Abbey Academy when they were only in their teens.

"Who are your friends, Shorty? And are you lucky! Did you see what we just dealt with? This ship, which I command, please note, and the others?"

Hiero took one oar and sculled over to the hull of the big vessel. Then he looked up, his face incredulous, at the small group above.

"*You* dealt with? You'd be so much garbage at the bottom of the sea, my friend, if it weren't for me and these four chums of mine. What do you think made the Unclean go crazy, then ram each other? The distant sight of your ugly face?"

Per Edard's eyes narrowed. Behind his broad forehead lurked a very good mind, and he was suddenly thinking hard. "So that was you, was it? I might have known. You always were the king of the dirty tricks league. And thank God for it! Now listen, come aboard quickly. We have a war to finish and we have to clean out that rats' nest. We have new mind shields and they're being held tight, so I can't talk to your pals. Come up on the bridge with me, and we'll get back to work."

In an instant, the five had leaped aboard, abandoning the little boat, and passed through a narrow entry port on the side of the sloping hull. Moments later, they stood, while Per Edard rapped out orders, peering through narrow slits at the smoke-covered town they had just left. And moments after that, the roar of the big cannon below and the trembling of the ship in response made them all wince in reaction. Between commands to the helmsmen, the gunners below, his signalmen, and many

others, Per Edard threw questions and snatches of talk over his
huge shoulders. He wore the leather breeches and shirt of the
Frontier Guards, but on his head was a leather band with a
short visor in front. Above the visor was an insigne the Metz
had never seen before, picked out in silver. Looking closely,
Hiero saw that it was a square-sailed ship, shown head-on, as
if coming at the viewer, and that behind it again, as a background, was a slanted anchor with a twist of rope around it.

"Oh, that? We all wear them. Demero found it in some old
book as usual. Lot of nonsense, I suppose, but the men like
it. The admiral is Colonel Berain from over on the Beesee
coast. His is *gold*, if you please. Lower ranks wear it in copper.
I'll try to get you one in lead. We're a *navy* now, Hiero." He
rambled on while all of them watched the shells burst in the
distant town. No answering fire of any kind was coming out.

"We had a hell of a time getting enough metal for the guns.
It's a bronze alloy from some old city, I guess. No, the hull's
not metal, just wood. But it's got thin plates of some ceramic
fitted over it. Damned good protection against most things,
though not those bloody electrics. I must admit, I think you
saved our necks there, my boy.

"The ships? Steer small, you copper-plated numbskulls!
Think this is a canoe? How can they aim below with you barging
around that way? Oh, yes, the ships. Well, Demero started
moving seamen from the Beesee area over to a lake northwest
of Namcush. A fair-sized lake, and the Dam People helped
dredge a big outlet. They're working with us now, you know.
Lot been happening since you went off gypsying down south."
He aimed an affectionate cuff at Hiero's head, which would
have stunned him if it had landed, then went back to bellowing
at the men who manned the twin steering wheels. In a moment
he was talking to Hiero again.

"None of this stuff is new. God alone knows where the
knowledge got dredged up from, but it was pretty complete.
All we had to do was ask a question and the answers came
quickly. The Abbey files, I suppose. They gave us everything.
How to build the damned things, how to build the engines.
They call them 'high-compression steam engines,' and we blew
up a couple before we got the hang of it. No one got killed,
though. The old ships, the ones we copied, were built the same
way, but with iron sheathing. We had no way of getting all

that iron, at least not fast. But we got the formula for this ceramic, like a pottery dish but twenty times as hard, and it works fine. Now that I think of it, I'm kind of glad we didn't have the iron. That lousy electric thing on those Unclean ships would have fried us all, maybe.

"Anyway, we got five of them built, the Dam People opened their sluices, and down the river to Namcush we came, early one morning, let's see, about three weeks ago. We towed two regiments in barges along behind and we had that town in one half hour. Not one ship got away. Not too many of the Unclean were there, but a lot of crooked traders, frontier scum, and some just plain pirates. We threw everyone into a prison and interrogated the hell out of all of them. We hanged the pirates and locked up all the ships of the others. No way the Unclean were going to get warned. Then we began to move down the coast to this place. We couldn't tow all those sailing ships, so we had to move fairly slowly for the others to keep up. And here we are. What's that, son?"

A teen-aged boy had appeared from aft and stood at the salute.

"Signal from the admiral, sir. Move slowly in toward the town and conform to his movements. He is going to pass the troops through our line and start them landing while we give any cover needed."

"Right. Cease fire and wait for commands below there." He straightened from the voice tube and for the first time stared hard at the Children of the Wind. "Your friends are going to have front-row seats, old buddy. One big tough, two young toughs, and a real cutie. Now, where did you find them? Never saw or heard of anything remotely like them, and I know more than most about Leemutes—sorry, aliens."

His admiration as his twinkling black eyes roved over M'reen's supple shape was so obvious that it transcended the barrier of species. The young priestess bridled.

"Down, boy," Hiero said. "The young lady you are leering at was solely in charge and responsible for ruining those two loads of Unclean, who otherwise would have happily blown your little toy boat here completely out of existence. Shall I turn her loose on you instead?"

Per Edard's eyes widened at this astounding comment, but

he knew Hiero too well to doubt a word of it. Instead, he bowed and addressed the four catfolk formally.

"I am honored to meet such brave warriors, the friends of my old companion. Please accept the thanks of all of us for your destruction of our mutual foes. You will receive more formal thanks later from our chiefs and wise ones. In the meantime, you are our honored guests and allies. Anything that we can do for you will be done at once. You have only to ask."

Hiero translated and waited to see who would answer. It was B'uorgh, which made sense. The big war chief was the senior, despite M'reen's rank in the Pride structure.

We thank you in turn. We have come far to help our friend Hiero and his people. We wish to be led to battle against those you call the Unclean. Our name for them is worse. May we soon talk to you with our minds in true friendship. Meanwhile, is there any way we can breathe clean air? These stinks from that town and this floating thing are choking us. We ask only if this is possible. If not, we can endure. We will eat and drink when you do, go where you go, fight when you fight, and, if necessary, die when you die.

As he translated the answer, Hiero could see that Edard was impressed in spite of himself.

"Please tell them, Hiero, that I'll get them on one of the outer picket ships as soon as I can. The air should be clean out on the sound, and those are sailing craft, so they won't have the engine-room coal dust and oil to contend with. We have plenty of lignite coal, but even I think it stinks. Right now I have to cover this landing. Here come the Guards going ashore."

While Hiero spoke again to his friends, they all watched as the Metz Frontier Guards sailed through the armored steamships and cautiously approached the rotting wharves in front of them. There was no talking now; all stood silent, waiting to see if there were any counterattack coming. Hiero tried to reach out with his mind and learned something new. The mind shield that the Abbeys were using to guard their war fleet blanketed his own powers as well. He could neither send nor receive on any mental band beyond the limits of the ship! He mentioned this to Per Maluin in a low voice.

"Yeah, that's right. Abbot Demero told me about you, Hiero. I sort of gathered you had become the grand champion of the world at this sort of thing in the last year or so. Well, we have a lot of people trying to do the same trick now ourselves. And, man, are they going to be glad to have you back! But that's by the by. When we got these shields for the fleet, the top people, which means the Council, of course, decided that we might just have one or two nasties in our own ranks. As a result, this thing clamps down on everyone, so no one has a chance to pass any little leaks which might get us killed in an emergency. Get it?"

Hiero nodded, and they returned to watching the disciplined ranks of the Abbey infantry disembark and scatter out through the smoke-laden streets toward the inner part of Neeyana. Aside from distant screams which came dimly to them through the haze and the crackle of fires burning nearby, there was no sound. No evidence of any enemy action, organized or otherwise, was apparent. A second sailing ship, a two-masted coaster like the first, appeared and unloaded troops. Officers, several of whom Hiero recognized, gave quiet orders on the foreshore and then followed their men inland. One ship after another disembarked its human cargo, until Hiero estimated that at least two full regiments, perhaps four thousand men, had gone ashore. He watched, somewhat jealously, as they passed. He had the rank of Major (Reserve) in the Scouts, the elite of all the Abbey forces; hence he found himself wishing—childishly, as he reminded himself—that he were going in with them. Part of this feeling, he knew, was simply the trained reaction of a professional soldier on seeing others going into battle. But he was wise enough to know that there was more to it than that. For more than a year now he had been alone, in the sense that none of his own people had been with him. He had journeyed thousands of leagues and found new friends, a mate, new rank, new everything. But all had been *new*, and what he really was feeling now was simple homesickness. As the bronzed files padded down the narrow gangplanks and vanished into the murk, he simply wanted to be one of them, to be a part of the master unit that he had been trained to serve—the hive, the swarm, the legion, the corps. His feeling was as old as mankind, and he had no way of knowing that a legionary of the Imperial Tenth, stuck at Vindobonum, watching his cohort cross the Danube to take on a swarm of Gothic horse, had felt the same sensation.

However, he was not simply a soldier. He was a priest. He made a silent orison of thanks to God and also silently confessed to pride and ingratitude for the many blessings he had received. He knew that the discontent which had welled up in his soul was unjust and based on pride. He had been blessed in many ways, far more than he deserved, and he admitted that he had less than no right to his feelings. But—oh, how he longed to be with those silent files!

His reverie was interrupted by a stiffening of all those on the bridge. Someone had entered by the rear companionway— in fact, several persons. But the man who came first riveted all eyes. He was not young and he was almost bald, a rare thing for a Metz. He might have been an old fifty or a young sixty and was clean-shaven. He wore no band and visor, but on his left breast was a badge with the fouled anchor and the sailing ship, only this time in gold. His iron face, seamed with scars, acknowledged Maluin's palm-up salute with a nod. He wore the same simple leather they all did, and a short hanger hung by his side. No one had any doubt that the Man had arrived. He turned quickly to Hiero and answered the salute with his own at once.

"Per Desteen? Congratulations on being here at all. Justus Berain, for my sins, the commander of this squadron. I have heard strange things about you—" He paused. "—and your friends here. Do I understand that the Unclean vermin destroyed themselves through your efforts? Let's have the story."

It took a while. After Hiero had formally introduced the Children of the Wind and all the mutual compliments were over, the admiral began to pick their brains. While he did so, messengers and couriers came and went, interrupting the interrogation at spasmodic intervals.

Hiero listened as they reported and formed his own opinion of what was going on. There seemed, from what he could gather, to be little fighting. The town had emptied itself in a very short time and in what appeared to have been a panic-stricken rout. The Abbey troops were all reporting in with no trouble. A few of the enemy Leemutes had shown fight and had been disposed of in short order. None of the Unclean wizards, the Masters of the Circles, had been glimpsed, but there were many corpses and hundreds of terrified civilians of both sexes. Some looting had been going on but was being put down with a firm hand.

"If I may suggest it, sir," Hiero said, "have the officers interrogate for headquarters locations and also personnel. This was a pretty big base, and they can't have had much time to destroy things. There aren't that many of the real top scum altogether, you know. They had to have lots of clerks and lower staff types. We could learn a lot. But they'll probably be underground, so for God's sake, tell our men to be careful if they go down to look."

Berain looked at him in silence for a moment. He was not used to junior officers who spoke quite so firmly. Hiero hardly noticed. He was the prince of D'alwah, and what he had been through in the last year made him the equal of anyone. Already he had turned away to look at the burning town. Per Maluin noticed and held his breath, waiting for an explosion. But Justus Berain was not the admiral for nothing. A slight smile touched the corners of the iron mouth; that was all.

"Quite right, Per Desteen. Should have thought of it myself. Are you in good enough shape to go ashore? I can give you a squad, and you might have a better idea where to look than most of us."

In minutes it was arranged, and Hiero eagerly led ashore, the four Children of the Wind padding behind him, ten Metz borderers and an NCO in turn following them. Led through the smoke by a young lieutenant, they were at the central square of Neeyana in no time, despite the smoke and confusion all about. Over a hundred prisoners were huddled under guard in the middle of the square. As soon as Hiero had identified himself, he began to look them over, both with his eyes and with his probing mind.

He suddenly pointed to one figure, a tall man who seemed to be trying to shield himself behind some others. *Get that one and strip him. He is trying to hide and he wears one of the metal things around his neck.*

Before the fascinated gaze of the Metz soldiers, the four catfolk fell upon the cringing shape and shredded its leather harness in seconds. One more of the blue-metaled pendants and its chain were handed to Hiero, who crushed the thing underfoot, his gaze fixed on the Unclean officer as he did so. He spoke in *batwah*.

"Tell me no lies, Master of the Second Level. You have one chance for life and one only. Where is the Central Vault? Where are the records kept? You have only a second between yourself and eternity."

The Unclean officer might have fought in open combat. He was evil but not a complete craven. But being suddenly assaulted by the awful catfolk, being stripped, and having his disguise and his shield removed in public—all this was too much. With a sob, he prostrated himself at the feet of Hiero.

"Mercy!" He embraced Hiero's sandals until the priest spurned him away.

"You shall have life as long as not one lie crosses your dirty lips. Answer my questions."

It was better than might have been hoped. Though no adept, the wretched man had been third in command of the city's military force and he knew much. With a rope around his neck, he led the squad, Hiero, and the catfolk to a small door, sunk in the side of a nearby stone tower. They had to force the lock. Then, as Hiero had expected, they found themselves at the top of a winding stair. Worn and slippery steps led down into darkness.

The party waited for a moment while torches were procured, and then, with the prisoner in the lead, they began to file downward, weapons held at the ready. Down wound the stairs and down. There were landings, but no doors issued off them. Down, until Hiero knew they were far below ground level. Now bluish fluors appeared, and they crushed out the smoking torches. They had emerged in a damp stone corridor which ran in both directions, off into shadowed distances. The dim blue light of the fluors, set in the ceiling at long intervals, revealed nothing. No one had to be told to keep silence. Hiero prodded the prisoner with his spear point. The gesture was enough, and the man turned to the left and marched numbly off. Silently except for an occasional clink of metal and the faint scrape of leather, the others followed.

They had come a long way and found nothing save emptiness before them when Hiero suddenly halted everyone by raising his left hand. His mind could touch something. With a grimace of disgust, he realized what it was. He led off again at a run, prodding the captive before him ruthlessly. They burst suddenly into a larger room, a great oval, around which were set many barred doors. And the doors were all open. From them came a stench of death and decay which made the entire party retch. One quick glance in each cell was enough. Men, women, even children—here were the choicest captives of the Unclean. All were chained and all were dead. The savage blows and sword cuts which had so recently killed them were in all probability the kindest death they could have asked for after their torment. Hiero had caught the last flicker of a dying brain back down the buried corridor.

"Fresh wounds, sir," the NCO said. "They must have just got it."

"Yes, and we'll follow. Look sharp, now. The tunnel goes straight out the other side. This scum here says that their main Council Chambers are just ahead, so—watch it!"

The few pale chiefs of the Unclean, no more than three in number, who had not been able to flee on the surface, had waited just a little too long to try the secret exit tunnels. Had they not paused in one last spasm of sadistic cruelty to slay the helpless captives in their chains, they might have gotten away. When Hiero and his pack burst into the great room at their heels, they had not yet opened the far door, which was hidden behind an arras. Instead, they were engaged in trying to destroy the great wire screen. Though its moving lights were all dark now, that nerve center of the Yellow Circle was an obsession with them, and they had not realized that a foe so deadly might follow them so soon. Their gray robes dabbled with the blood of their victims, they turned to fight. Their weapons were hardly raised when the Children of the Wind were upon them. Then three limp shapes lay in their own filthy gore, while Hiero looked about him and tried to imagine what he had found.

✤ 10 ✤

OF MUSTERINGS
IN THE NORTH

THE MOST REVEREND KULASE DEMERO, ABBOT SUPREME OF the Metz Republic and General-in-Chief of its armies, was a busy man. His lean, bronzed face was worn with care, and he slept little. His temper, never all that equable, was now tinder-dry, and woe betide any hapless subordinate who wasted his time.

At the moment, he was in council and he was having difficulties, both in keeping his temper and in understanding what he simply had to understand. Not for the first nor for the fiftieth time, he wished that Brother Aldo, the Elevener chief and his secret friend and ally for years, were present. The abbot had a fine mind, and so, no doubt, did this being before him, but one was human and the other was not! The abbot could use his mental powers and exchange thoughts as well as any man in the Republic. But only with men!

He sighed and once more tried to grasp what the other was telling him. Charoo, the chief engineer—for want of a better phrase—of the Dam People, was not all that easy to understand.

Charoo was as tall as the old human, even crouching on his haunches, and far vaster in bulk. His blunt, chisel-toothed head was keglike, and the small, short-furred ears were laid back tight against the long skull. He wore no clothes and needed none, being clothed in dark brown, rippling fur from his head to the base of the great, naked, paddle-shaped tail. He waved his clawed hands now, curiously delicate for the great bulk of his body, and his bright, beady eyes glittered as he tried once more to explain his thought to the man. A wave of pungent musk eddied from his body, and Demero managed to avoid coughing only with difficulty. The scent of castor filled the small room as it would have one of Charoo's own lodges out on a distant lake.

Cannot—indescribable—*make evil things go away if not*—unknown thought—improbable image—*water. Water people not*—negative something movement—*we must*—thought of a specific place—negative again—*cannot leave. Must be HERE*—positive thought now. Silence.

The great, mutated beavers had appeared like many other creatures, soon after The Death. Shy and unaggressive, they had steadily spread over the remote, northern lakes. Slowly, as they occasionally helped stranded hunters or returned lost infants, the people of the Metz learned to respect them, and a system of silent barter had existed in areas where the two cohabited for many years. No Metz would have dreamed of harming one of the Dam People, but they were not exactly friends, either. Each kept to its kind. Humans avoided their lakes out of courtesy, and the great rodents did not frequent the Metz towns. They traded timber and roots for knives, tools, and vegetables, but that was all. That they were highly intelligent was well known, though only recently had it been realized that they had a written language.

It was Abbot Demero, prompted by his Elevener friend, who had made the first overtures and had been well received, since the Brotherhood of the Eleventh Commandment had laid the groundwork. The Unclean had taken to raiding the Dam People in the recent past, and the great creatures had only two things the Dark Brotherhood and their allies wanted. Meat and fur! This made the Dam People natural allies of decent humanity, but the alliance was not easy. They were simply not warlike by nature, and it was very difficult to explain to them what was needed.

They had willingly helped dig the dams and channels to bring the new Republic fleet down to Namcush, but the abbot wanted much more. And he was not getting through. The hierarchical system of the Dam People was a mystery, for one thing. Charoo appeared to have authority of some kind, but how much authority was a question. Could he speak for many of his people or only for his own village?

Sighing mentally, the abbot leaned forward and prepared to try once more. He was interrupted by a low laugh from the door of his chamber and whirled in a rage, to blast the presumptuous fool who had dared to break in upon him. His fury turned to joy in an instant.

"Hiero!" He embraced the younger man heartily, patting him on the back over and over again. "I knew you were coming, but I had no idea it would be this quick. But listen. You can perhaps help me. I am having the greatest of difficulty in understanding what this worthy person wants to say. Do you suppose . . . ?" He stopped talking, for Hiero had freed himself and was standing before Charoo in utter silence. Then his hands began to move in certain complex gestures.

Charoo in turn began to move his own hands, and his round eyes were now sparkling even more brightly. In the silent room, the old man felt the pulse of thought, moving on an alien level and far faster than he could grasp. The four hands continued their strange movements; now they were touching and interweaving in a queer way as they did so, as if an invisible cat's cradle were being formed. For another moment this went on; then both stepped backward and stared at each other.

"Chirrup," the great beaver said. Dropping to all fours, he scuttled past the two men and out the half-open door. They heard his claws in the passage, and then he was gone into the night.

"Well," the abbot said at length. "I hope you got more out of that than I did. And how, may I ask, did you know what it was that *I* wanted to say?"

Hiero dropped into a chair and laughed. "Because, Reverend Sir, as soon as Maluin brought me here to Namcush, I started looking for you. And I have, I regret to add, been eavesdropping as I came to this house from well down the street."

"I see," his superior said slowly. "That means you got Berain to send you on ahead of the fleet in one of his precious warships. Not an easy man to persuade, Berain. And your powers really are quite extraordinary. I have been hearing things, my boy. I only hope you keep the fear of God in your heart. No man, no decent man and Christian soul, has ever had the mental strength you seem to have picked up, Hiero. You make me wonder. Do you realize what your mind would be, should it be allied to the power of evil?" He glared down at his former pupil.

Hiero met his gaze frankly. "You can hear my confession just as soon as you like, Most Reverend Father," he said flatly. "But first, wouldn't you like to know what Charoo and I said to each other?"

It was touch and go for a moment, and then the old man chuckled. He seated himself in another wooden chair and laughed, rubbing his eyes.

"Yes, you insolent, I would like to very much. I can deal with your sins later and I'm sure there were plenty of them in a year away. Tell me what that damned old water hog wanted, because I certainly couldn't grasp it."

"Well, first, they have a rather complex sign language to augment their mind speech. I was siphoning some of that out of his brain while we were talking on another level mentally. It's an odd band they think on, but not so odd as that of some other friends of mine you will meet presently. First, he wants to help, but is not sure how. His people are no good away from water, which is pretty obvious. What isn't so obvious, unfortunately, is how parochial they are. Except for the young males and shes in the spring of the year, they don't like being away from their own particular lake. They have a fantastic bond of affection for what might be called the home territory. I guess it's ancestral, but that's what he was trying to tell you. They have a council of sorts, and he has a lot of clout on it. They visit from village to village and from lake to lake, but— here's the catch—not for very long at a time. He was trying to tell you that they can't be counted on for any extended trips or journeys. They'd go crazy."

"I see. That is certainly worth knowing. It means if there is a big fight and we want them in on it, it had better be somehow staged near where they are in the first place or it's no go."

"Exactly," Hiero agreed. "And we'll have to think about that at length later. But just now, Father Abbot, I need some help. Is there any news of the South? Have you heard anything from Brother Aldo? No one in the fleet has heard of my wife, but you must have by this time. What news from the East? Have you heard anything—anything at all?"

Hiero had contained himself for a long time, but he was

close to the breaking point. Only by rigorously shutting Luchare from his mind totally by the exercise of mental discipline had he been able to hold himself in so long. Abbot Demero saw the agony on the younger face and wished himself anywhere but in the same room.

"I suppose you learned nothing from any prisoners you took?" he asked at length. It was an answer of sorts, but not what he wished he could say.

"Nothing," Hiero said in a dull voice, looking at the floor. "None but their adepts would have been likely to know, in any case. We saw only three of those, and they were taken in the act of murder and killed on the spot." The room seemed darker, though the small lamp had not dimmed.

"You deserve the truth," Demero admitted. "At least all the truth I have to give. Brother Aldo and I are far older friends than you imagine. For many years, unknown to the rest of the High Council of the Republic, I have been in contact with him. He has sought to warn me of the Unclean designs, and I have tried to spur his group to assume a more active part in our struggle. I sent messages to him when you first went south, and it was because of these that he was able to seek you out. Long ago, before your birth, he was of very high rank in your kingdom in the South.

"He brought back the books you found, and we have used them. It was only because of them that we were able to create and learn to use the computers. Without those, we could never have built the new ships so quickly, using and correlating knowledge from the old records. Those computers have saved us many months, and each day they save still more.

"But you want to hear of your princess. Aldo was here not too long ago. He had news of D'alwah—word that was passed over thousands of leagues. There is civil war. It is not good— such evil news that he left in the night to go south, where he could learn more."

The younger man turned away. Evil word from the South, so bad that Brother Aldo had left in haste! Yet Luchare had known of the rebellion. Her father had been alive, and she had been able to send the faithful hopper to Hiero. She was fore-warned. What could have happened? Whatever it was, he was helpless to do anything to aid her, lodged a thousand leagues and more to the north. There was nothing left but the soldier's creed: Endure!

His face was masklike as he turned once more to Demero. "I know you'll try to learn more and keep me informed, Father," he said. "I can't do anything to help D'alwah up here, except indirectly. Let's drop the subject. Have I told you we took one of the Unclean Council Chambers undamaged? They had a thing like a great metal screen, set with hundreds of tiny lights, but there was no power source. At least, none that we could find. I had it dismantled as best I could. I have a strange feeling about the thing. It ought to go to the top Abbey mind-psychs at once, but I also want you to put your top computer men on it. I think it may be a computer of some strange sort, but powered by mental energy, and so..."

Listening to the iron control in the flat tones, the abbot had to make an effort to compose his own face and to pay attention. Under the disciplined voice, he heard the terrible muted passion. Yet he could do nothing to help.

From an opening in the green forest wall, there came a great black beast. Klootz strode into a broad clearing, his heavy dewlap hanging under his mighty neck. In the center of the clearing, he raised his head and sniffed the breeze, seeking any news that the wind might bring either his broad nostrils or his mule's ears. His head bore only buds where the great antlers would come in the months ahead. He sniffed again, winnowing the airs of the great conifers and mighty oaks. Then, raising his head, he called, a far-echoing "Bah-oh." Three times the nasal bugle rang through the woods. He seemed to listen in silence for an answer, but if one came, it would not have been audible to human ears.

Farther away, at the remote edge of the call's carrying power, another animal abruptly checked his movement. Gorm stopped and sat up on his furry haunches, listening. His ears and nose twitched, and his eyes took on a look of mental strain. Then he grunted in satisfaction and set off in the direction of the bugling.

Klootz lowered his muzzle and suddenly lurched ponderously forward across the clearing and vanished into the woods, moving without a sound, his entry into the trees like that of a shadow—but a determined shadow.

* * *

The royal army of D'alwah was in retreat. What was left
of it was moving as rapidly as utter exhaustion would permit.
Many men and animals bore dreadful wounds. Every so often,
tired bodies simply collapsed, the energy to continue no longer
there. It was easy to lose the men and beasts that fell, for it
was night and none had the time or strength to help a neighbor.
The few baggage wains that remained were lagging badly,
though the kaws that pulled them were being goaded until blood
ran to keep them moving at all. The king was already far behind.
Many of the cavalry were without mounts, trudging dumbly
forward on foot. The surviving hoppers were limping and foot-
sore. It was the remnant of a beaten host, held together by
loyalty and discipline. But both were eroding fast.

Occasionally, the tired men glanced back toward the south,
where a red glare lighted the sky. D'alwah City was burning.
Many of the troops were natives of the city and had families
there. They closed their eyes and tried not to look, or even to
think of the horrors which must be going on behind them.

The Princess Royal of the kingdom rode in the van, her
hopper still surrounded by a clump of mounted troopers. At
her side, his right arm in a sling, Count Ghiftah Hamili com-
manded, his aquiline, dark face a mask of exhaustion. The
army had no goal except safety and a place to rest. They were
all, man and beast, utterly fought out. That there would be
pursuit in the morning, all were keenly aware.

They had fallen back into the city two days before, defeated
in the first battle, but still a strong and confident force. They
felt they could rest and hold the walls until the levies of east
and west, the marshmen and sailors of the coast and the Mu'
aman infantry of the great plains, came to join them. When that
happened, then they would sally out against the rebel duke and
his foul allies and cut him and them to pieces.

That was not the way it happened. What happened was
terrible. The conspiracy of beggars and street rabble they had
put down a week earlier had been the merest sham of an uprising, mounted only to catch them off guard. No sooner had
the city gates been shut than the *real* uprising started. The stone
barriers of the barred sewers and the access ports to the canals
were burst open in some cases, unlocked by treachery in others.
Out of the slimy waters erupted all the horrid life of the deeps,

the things D'alwah had guarded against for centuries. While fresh attacks from without assaulted the walls of the city, within it the army was faced with the terrified civil populace and hordes of great reptiles, ravenous for blood. Nor was this all. At intervals, strange, manlike shapes, hard to see and hideous when one did, were actually marshaling the onslaught of savage reptilian life and leading it in some fashion against the rear of the embattled troops.

As the reports came in, Luchare took counsel with her few remaining advisors. As best they could, they gave orders to fight their way to the northern gates. Some of the troops made it, but many stayed behind forever. When Luchare tried to assemble what was left outside the north walls, it was clear that the army had no more than a quarter of its original strength remaining, and that in frightful shape. There was no alternative except retreat—really flight. Duke Amibale and his friends, the Unclean and their allies, had been grossly underestimated. Unless she could rally the rest of the country quickly, the kingdom was lost to all intents and purposes.

As she rode in a daze through the steaming night of the South, Luchare tried to form coherent thoughts. She was so tired! None of them had had more than a catnap for over three days.

She wondered where Hiero was. Her faith that he was alive, she knew at times, might prove unreal. But they were so closely linked that she simply could not believe he was gone forever. Somewhere, somehow, he would come back to her. She had to keep on believing. As she slumped lower in the high-cantled saddle of her hopper, she never noticed that Count Hamili had taken the beast's reins from her limp fingers and transferred them to one of the guards. Numb with exhaustion, she allowed herself to be led on into the darkness.

Hiero awoke all of an instant. His narrow bed on the third floor of the new fort by the Namcush piers creaked as he sat up. Instinctively, he reached for his sword. What had wakened him? He peered at the open window, through which faint moonbeams glimmered. Listening, he heard the challenge of a sentry and the reply. The faint sound of lapping water came to him, along with other small noises of the night. There seemed to be nothing, but—he had learned to trust his instincts. Somewhere deep in his mind, a tiny warning bell had rung. Then, outside in the corridor, he heard the very faint scrape of movement, hardly more than a rustle of muted sound.

As noiseless as the night itself, he rose, sword in hand, and padded over to the door of the bedchamber, listening intently and probing with his mind as he did. Nothing, no mind, no feeling of one at all. But there had been the sound, and he knew that on the other side of the plank door was a presence! Something had stolen upon him. In this place of friends, there should be no such shielded thought!

His doubts were dramatically resolved. From deep in the wooden fort, far below his sleeping quarters, a horn sounded the alarm call, and the blast of the horn was echoed by others, all giving warning that some enemy was there.

At the same time, his door burst open with a crash, and a bulky form hurtled into the small room, arm overhead and a weapon glinting as it charged toward his now empty cot.

The assassin never had time to learn his mistake. Hiero's heavy, short sword, sweeping from behind and one side, struck the juncture of neck and shoulder with awful force. There was a single, choked grunt of agony as the razor-sharp edge went home, and a fountain of blood spurted in the dim light. Then the shape fell forward, struck dead on the spot by that one blow.

Hiero whirled to face the dark shape of the door, but the assailant had apparently been alone. He could detect no presence outside. Yet he remained crouching and ready until the light of torches and the sound of men came down the corridor. Only then did he step out and hail the patrol guards.

Ten minutes later, after the room was cleared of all but himself and the abbot, he was staring down at what had come in the night to slay him.

"Aldo mentioned them, I recall," Demero said. "I gather you had a previous encounter with one, out on the Inland Sea. A foul thing, even for a Leemute—and all of them are foul. What do you call it again?"

"A Glith. That was what Roke the pirate called it before we killed it and him." He stared down at the gray skull, earless and noseless, the fanged jaws agape in death and the mighty limbs, covered with fine scales, all asprawl. The thing wore the harness of a Metz soldier, but it could not have passed for a human in any kind of light. The heavy axe it had borne lay half under Hiero's bed.

"How did it get in here?" the old priest mused. "The alarm was given by one of those pendulum devices our scientists cooked up. I showed you one before you went off south, remember?"

"It may have been given, but it was way late," was the answer as Hiero knelt to examine the corpse further. Already a foul stench was in the room, despite the open window. "Look here. It wears the mind shield. I expected that. God knows what warned me. I guess I'm becoming attuned to the presence of the enemy somehow. But I had only a few seconds to spare."

He crushed the small box and crumpled the chain before going on. "What I'd really like to know is, if that shield was working—and it was—how did your pendulum thing work at all?"

"I don't think the scientists themselves altogether understand that device," Demero said. "The warning was late, as you say. Still, there *was* a warning. Perhaps it also works, though more slowly, on a level of emotion somehow. A pretty puzzle to set before the big brains when I get time to do so. But what *I* want to know is, how did this Glith pass the sentries at all?"

"I see what you mean. And I think I know the answer or can guess at it. Have the sentries examined as fast as you can by a psych-medic, one who knows the human brain. One of these things almost hypnotized me once. They have strong mesmeric powers. I'd be willing to bet that there is an unexplained lapse in the memory of some guard, maybe more than one. The damned brutes are probably bred for it. Anything else occur to you, Father?"

"Oh, yes. I'm not quite senile, not yet at any rate. It wanted *you*. It took a big risk to locate this chamber, son. And that means two things. I'll have to have the garrison mind-probed in depth. Though I think you may be right, and it could have got its information by mental compulsion. But I see further, and so do you. It came looking for you, so that means it was sent. The Unclean know you are here or at least suspect it. Others may have been sent to other places. The important thing is that they know you are alive, and that is something we hoped was not so. I wonder how?"

"I don't know. But only one thing makes sense. Someone

or some *thing* saw me in Neeyana. No other way it could have happened. They move fast, don't they?" Hiero's eyes slitted as he stared down at the repulsive corpse on the floor. "It makes me feel proud in a funny way. They certainly hate me."

The abbot smiled. "You were never very good at your classic studies, Hiero. Many, many thousands of years ago, far across the sea, there was a mighty king with a personal motto. Can't recall much about the man, whether he was good or bad. But I recall the motto. It ran, *Oderint dum Metuant*. Let them hate me so that they fear me, that is, in Latin. You see, my boy, there's the answer. As I told you yesterday, I worry about your powers. But you terrify the enemy. I think they would trade several regiments of our Guards if they could get you instead. I had hoped to use you as a secret weapon. Now I'll just settle for weapon, period. Do you have any ideas?"

"I think so," Hiero said slowly. "I think we have to keep them off balance. If you can spare me a few good men, the best of the bushrangers, I'll take my cats and go hunting. North of the Palood and east of the Otwah League boundary. Somewhere in there I think the enemy may be gathering. The way I see it is this: We dealt them a bad blow at Neeyana. We couldn't hold it, but we certainly wrecked it for them. We stole their records, broke up and brought back their Great Screen, sank two of their best ships, and killed three Masters of the Yellow Circle. Nothing like that ever happened to them before. If I'm right, we only have two main packs to worry about— the Blue, and that's S'duna, and the Red, both north of the Inland Sea. I think I know where S'duna's main base is—the isle of Manoon. Where the others are, I have no idea. But I think a hunting expedition is in order, something between a probe and a raid. I have never thought they had many of those ships, you know. Even with their powers, that much metal and technology must be very rare. I doubt if there are more than two or three left on the whole Inland Sea. Brother Aldo got one and my cats got two. I don't think there are that many left."

He began to pace the small room, and the older man watched and listened with veiled amusement as the younger continued to expound his plan.

"Surely some of the levies must be coming in from the Otwah League by now? They promised aid before I went south."

"They have a long way to travel, and the fact that the Unclean have hit them only lightly so far has made them cautious. They are afraid to strip themselves of troops. Also, remember that they are not quite the same as we, Hiero. They have a far higher proportion of the old white stock and they have other mixtures as well. We are homogeneous in population to a much greater extent. Not so many nerves to soothe, not so many little patches of local divergency that have to be kept feeling they are part of the whole. But they are coming. I have had word from their Council."

"Well," Hiero said, "tell them to stay well north of the sea, and I mean well north of the roads anywhere near the Palood. The less the enemy knows about them, the better.

"Anyway," he went on, "I ought to start as soon as possible. I want no more than six men and my furry friends from the South. We'll go on foot, not mounted, though the Children of the Wind could leave Klootz standing, I think." A look of pain crossed his face as he thought of his lost mount, but the emotion was suppressed as he continued. "On foot is better. We don't know that terrain well and I have no idea what we'll be getting into."

A heavy tread shook the corridor, and the tall shape of Per Edard Maluin loomed in the doorway. He was welcomed and the conversation resumed. It had not progressed very far when the newcomer interrupted loudly. "Hey there, hold up. Are you off again on some crazy trip, while I float around on that stink barge? Not on your life! Father Abbot, I appeal to you. This helpless shrimp needs protection. I resign from the navy here and now. I'm going along, that's what!" He stared defiantly at both of them.

Demero laughed quietly. "I don't know what Justus Berain will say, but I suppose I can quiet him down. It won't really be desertion if I have you seconded to special duties. I presume that you have an executive officer who can handle the ship?" It was an idle question. Maluin's noise and bulk had never disguised his keen mind. He would have had all his officers trained to a hair, and all three knew it.

Hiero was delighted. He knew his old friend's value. They had trodden many strange trails in the past. The thought of that stout arm and strong mind at his side was a real comfort. The old abbot also felt relieved. He had guessed at Hiero's loneliness and knew what the man must be feeling, with his wife's fate unknown and his mind torn with divergent emotions. A tried and true comrade could be a great help.

"I think Maluin has a good idea, Hiero. And though I don't want to pick your men for you, I have another one. There's a junior priest, just been made deacon, as a matter of fact, whom I'd like to send with you. He's here in the garrison, and I'd like to have him up. See what you make of him, and then I'll tell you why I think you should have him along."

The abbot called to a guard stationed in the passage. In a short time, a young man stood at salute in the doorway. He was no larger than Hiero and quite slender. He wore the standard garb of leather and, like all the others, a silver pendant of the Cross and the Sword on his breast. He was clean-shaven and seemed hardly out of his teens at first appearance, but Hiero was not fooled. The man's black eyes were dreaming and remote, as if he looked beyond things, rather than at them. Under the painted yellow leaf and the green caduceus on his forehead, they seemed to gaze far beyond the little, smoky room and out into vastness. Hiero felt a wave of power such as he had seldom encountered before, and not of his own kind, for that was primarily mental. This man's power came from the spirit. Once in a while the Church Universal threw up a great leader, a healer of souls; priest though he himself was, Hiero felt humbled in the presence of the youth who stood before them. If this priest lived, the church would have a prophet and a reformer such as had been rarely known, even in ages past. He radiated calm and inner power so strongly that it was almost an aura. Hiero knew without being told that he was a celibate. No earthly ties could ever bind such a spirit.

"This is Per Cart Sagenay, Hiero. Sit down, my son, and listen to what we have to tell you. You have heard of Per Desteen, who has done mighty works for us in the South. Per Maluin you also know. I have asked them, especially Per Desteen, to look you over. While we toil back here, building our strength for the onslaught of the enemy, Per Desteen will lead a scouting party to spy out the enemy strength. I wish them to say whether you should accompany them on their journey. I know that you, of all the sons of the church I have ever known, will obey any orders given you. But it is for Per Desteen to say whether I have chosen rightly."

Hiero had no hesitation at all. "Anyone you chose, Father, would be welcome. But I should like to hear from Per Sagenay's lips exactly what he himself thinks."

The young man inclined his head gracefully. His voice was soft and pleasant, but in no way weak. Indeed, it seemed to hum and ring in the room, even after the man had fallen silent. *An orator, too*, Hiero thought. *Well, that would follow.*

"Reverend Father, noble Pers of the church, I am not the world's greatest warrior. Such small gifts as God has given me lie rather with things of the spirit. I have a small talent for the Forty Symbols—"

Demero interrupted. "He sometimes can get *twelve* at a time. The Abbey schools have never produced anything like him!"

Hiero's only response to that was a mental "Wow!" Casting the Forty, the tiny, wooden, carved symbols, and trying to see the future with them was an art taught in all the Abbey senior classes. Hiero could get two or at most three and use those only uncertainly. He was about average. He had never heard of anyone who could cast and still make sense out of more than six. Any expedition which had this man as a member would be strong indeed and, he could not help feeling, blessed as well.

Giving the abbot a pained look, Per Sagenay continued. "I am greatly honored by this suggestion. If it be an order, I am more honored still, since I am young and without much experience of the world outside the Abbey walls. I can only wait upon your decision, sirs."

The decision was unanimous. They talked and discussed plans until the dawn came stealing through the narrow window, then separated for a much-needed rest. The scouting party would leave quietly and as unobtrusively as possible on the following evening.

S'duna was raging, but it was a cold rage, as everything about him was cold. "Namcush totally gone, not that it was ever entirely and completely ours. But we had no warning! The two secret ships which guarded the south sea—gone! Neeyana taken and sacked. Only two Brothers escaped of the five who were there. Do you realize, my friends, that S'ryath, the ruler of the Yellow Circle, is a fugitive in the wilderness, barely able even to communicate with us? We are almost cut off from

the South, the source of our strength! S'tarn and I, the Masters
of the Red and the Blue, we are alone to all intents and purposes. All of our strength now is here in the North."

The Blue Council of the Dark Brotherhood was silent. Then
one of them raised a pale hand. "Surely there is *some* good
news from the South, Elder Brother. The savages of D'alwah
have been broken. The starveling slut who calls herself a princess is destroyed. Our allies hold the kingdom under our rule,
do they not?"

S'duna withered him with a glance. In the cavernous chamber, before the great screen of lights and wires, his pupilless
gaze was baleful. "Oh, yes, my Brother of the Green, S'lorn,
has accomplished great works. He has the southern kingdom
under his yoke." The gelid eyes glowed with a light that came
from the Ultimate Pit. "And what of his profound assurance
about our deadliest enemy? What about Per Hiero Desteen, the
prince of D'alwah? The only being ever to escape from dead
Manoon? He lives, Brothers, he lives! So much for assurances
in the South!"

His voice sank to a hiss. "What wots it that the barbarian
kingdom of the South is felled? What does that mean for *us*,
here and now? It is our rule of the *North*, steadily over the
years increasing, spreading and ready to overwhelm the weak-
lings who call themselves the *true* church, that is threatened;
that is what is in deadly peril. The kingdom of D'alwah may
be destroyed. Their wretched king may be in our hands, the
slut, as you rightly call her, may be ruined. But what of us,
here in the North?"

With rising anger, he paced about the long oval table, a
smaller simulacrum of the table of the Great Council. At length
he paused and contained himself with an almost visible effort.
"In the last year, too many unlooked-for things we never expected have happened. Item, the Eleveners have openly come
out against us; only a fool would think they have no powers;
they have forsaken peace, as they call it, and are for the first
time in their stupid history on the other side, actively on the
other side. Consider that!"

The four shining heads, the four pallid, impassive faces,
moved with him as he went on. "And S'ryath saw *him* as he
fled the wreck of Neeyana. Whatever may be said, it was *he*
who destroyed those ships! I have heard reports from our spies

of the crude things the Metz have put on the waters. They could not have done so, I swear it. No, it was Per Desteen, who will hang on my torture racks before he dies slowly. Curse him! He himself is a mutation and does not even know it. How could he leave the distant South a drugged prisoner, helpless, utterly doomed, and then appear many hundreds of leagues to the north at exactly the right time? Perhaps those accursed Eleveners know something about this. One thing is certain—he had help and help that we know nothing about. There are currents working against us; I grow more sure of it daily. Something impalpable, something that lurks and pries and frustrates our plans in ways we cannot prevent. I shall root it or them out! Exterminate them!"

He ceased pacing and turned to face the others again. With another almost visible effort, he controlled his fury, and the faint flush over the pale cheekbones disappeared. He began to give orders, seek out information, and formulate plans. His colleagues leaned forward, their styluses ready, and proceeded to make notes as he spoke.

There were no horn calls, no salutes, and no ceremony as the patrol went forth from Namcush Fort. It was the cloudy dark just before the coming of dawn. Hiero wanted no eyes to spy out his leaving. He had bidden farewell to the Father Abbot in his chambers earlier, and that was sufficient. The little party left by a small postern, not by the main gate. Its members loped along the back alleys of the port, avoiding even the few Metz guard details until they came to the edge of the small town. Here they left the path entirely and at once plunged into the fringing bush which the inhabitants burned yearly to clear their garden patches. In less than a half hour, the last trace of civilization was behind them, and they were deep in the southern borders of the Taig, the mighty forest which spanned the continent, heading north.

Hiero led, his garb no different from that of the others, except that he no longer wore the painted leaf and caduceus, the looped snakes and rod, on his forehead.

"I'm no longer all Abbey, Father," he had said bluntly to Demero, who had noted its absence. "Now I fight for two realms. I hope you'll forgive me. It was you who sent me south. I *am* the prince of D'alwah! I cannot wear the badge of the northern armies any longer."

The old man had looked hard at him, then laid a gentle hand on his shoulder. "My son, you are still a priest, and that is what counts to God. I have no fears for your faith. And it is the work of the Faith to reclaim our brothers in every land. You still wear the Cross and the Sword and you got new insignia as soon as you went on our ships. You are still ours. If we share you with another land, the church can but approve. You are a missionary, Hiero. Wear what you will and take my blessings."

Musing on this conversation as he paced along under the great pines, Hiero wondered. *Was he still a priest?* He was certainly not the same priest. When he compared himself with Per Sagenay, he wondered if he were a priest at all. Even old Demero, much as Hiero loved and respected him, was more soldier and politician than saint or preacher.

Hiero sighed. Well, they all loved God, they all called themselves Christian, and that was about all one could say. The Lord presumably needed all kinds of help, even that of non-saints. He turned his thoughts aside and looked back at his command. He thought he might have a good one, man for man perhaps the best in the whole northern array.

Right behind him came Per Maluin, shield on his arm and his favorite weapon, one he preferred to any spear, over his brawny shoulders. This was a colossal billhook, one of the oldest weapons in the world, the peasants' tool of ancient, lost Europe and their last argument against the tyranny of their masters. On a curved axe handle, four feet long, was set a thin, brush-cutting, hooked blade like a deformed axehead. This tool, the ancestor of all later pole arms, was a dreadful implement in the hands of a master, and Per Edard was such. As Hiero looked back, the giant winked at him, his face alight with delight. A born woodsrunner, Maluin reveled in tasks such as this.

Behind him came B'uorgh and M'reen, and with them Per Sagenay. To Hiero's amazement, the quiet young priest and the catfolk had taken to one another at once. Moreover, Sagenay was learning, with amazing speed, to tune in on the odd wavelength the Children of the Wind used for mind speech. Already he could communicate better with them than anyone save Hiero. This would not have surprised Hiero in an Elevener, but the average Metz had little contact with alien minds, while the Eleventh Brotherhood was trained for it.

The younger man bore a longbow as well as a sword and dagger; he had said modestly that he had some skill with it.

The two young warriors of the cat people, Ch'uirsh and Za'reekh, were out on opposing flanks, out of sight but keeping mind touch.

In the rear came two more humans, but they were not priests, though they were legends along the border and far beyond. These were the twins, Reyn and Geor Mantan. Dark, lean men, identical in appearance, their age was unknown. Hiero guessed they might be in their fifties, but it was only a guess. Years before, they had come back to their small forest steading and found the mangled and tortured bodies of their wives and children in the ashes of their cabins. From then on, they had but one purpose, to seek out and slay the Unclean wherever they found them. Veterans of a hundred grim battles in the shadows of the woods, they spoke little but did much. Many thousands of lives had been saved by their sudden appearance, warning of a Leemute raid or ambush.

They did not serve the Church Universal or any other organized body. They appeared like shadows at intervals, always together, and got what supplies they needed, then vanished once more into the darkness, on the trail of their unending vengeance. They were known from the Otwah League to the Beesee coast, and none would deny them anything they sought in the way of food or help. They were, Hiero thought, like two grim hounds, silent and relentless. Abbot Demero had found them through some personal, arcane method and persuaded them not only to volunteer for this expedition but even to accept Hiero's orders, a feat that made Hiero, no soft citizen himself, wonder in amazement.

These two bore weapons of their own, used by almost no one else in the North, six-foot tubes of some strange, dark wood—blowguns which fired darts tipped with deadly poison, a secret brew of their own devising, said to slay on the instant. They carried the darts in slung pouches and also wore long knives and belt-axes, whose heads were tipped on one side with a long spike. Grim and fell they looked, like messengers of Fate in their stained leather. Hiero knew that woodsmen and hunters such as these were worth more than a host of ordinary men. Even the catfolk drew back as they passed to change positions, so dread was the light of their sunken eyes.

Down the long aisles of the great pines and spruces and between clumps of the sprawling palmettos, silent as ghosts, the little company flitted. As it went along, the dawn came pink in the east, and the chirping and warbling of countless birds began to greet the coming day. Tiny, dark figures, moving between the shaggy boles of the trees, never stopping, never keeping to a straight path, they were in view for but a brief instant—then they were gone, and it was as if they had never been.

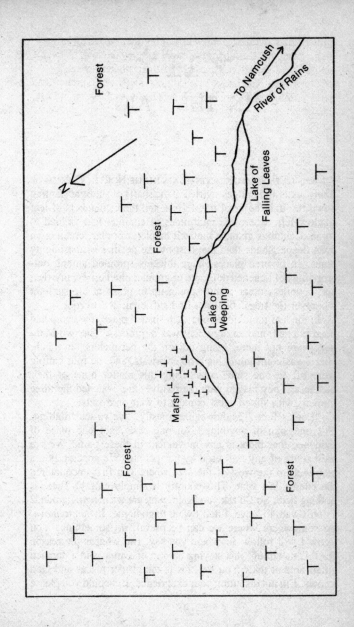

✤ 11 ✤

IN THE TAIG

IT WAS LATE SUMMER NOON AGAIN IN THE NORTH. CLOUDS OF tiny gnats and midges swirled in the shafts of sunlight slanting down through the great trees. Here and there, blankets of leaf shadow fell, where the multitudes of conifers had yielded to some deciduous giant, a mutated maple or poplar, creating an even deeper shade than that cast by the needles of the mighty pines. In favored places, huge thickets sprouted among outcroppings of lichened dolomite or granite; blueberries, myrtles, and countless other plants sprang up to grasp at the sunlight wherever the trees could not find sufficient soil to root.

In the leaf mold under one such shaded place, the camp had been pitched, and an argument was in process. The two Mantans were not there, being out on the perimeters on watch. Hiero was confronting his brother priests, and the four catfolk were off to one side, considering this matter none of their business. They played with their knives and watched the three humans with slitted eyes, content to wait on events.

"Look, Hiero," Maluin said earnestly, "we've seen nothing. Not one sign of anything. Not one trace, not one piece of evidence that there is any movement in these parts. We are well south of any trail used by our people. We apparently are also well to the west of the area where you first encountered the enemy last year. This country is simply empty! There is nothing here. So I'll ask you again, why are we hanging around? I don't want to leave, I don't want to go home. I want to *move*, go somewhere where we can be useful, *do* something. You know I will follow anywhere you say. But what is the reason for this dawdling, this staying here in one area, and a damned small area at that? You say this is the proper place, and God knows, I'm not disputing your experience. But could you please give me a reason! Per Sagenay feels the same way. Neither of us is new to the enemy or life up here. Why treat us as if we were new-joined recruits and dumb ones to boot?" He leaned back and lighted his short clay pipe again. He was the only one who smoked; as he held the spark lighter in his huge fist, he looked like the epitome of casual strength, relaxed and yet forceful. He watched Hiero narrowly over the pipe bowl, and Hiero had some trouble in meeting his eyes.

"I gather you feel the same, Per Sagenay?"

"No-oh," was the answer, given in equable tones. "Yet you have not asked me to try to read the symbols. This is one of my small talents, and while I will, as Per Maluin has been careful to point out, obey any and all instructions that you care to give us, still I am a little puzzled. No forelooking and no sign that some of the greatest foresters of the North can discern. But you feel that we should linger in this precise spot, as if we awaited something. Perhaps if you shared some of your thoughts with us, we might be able to help." The soft, clear voice fell silent, and, like Maluin, Sagenay lounged back on the bank of moss which shrouded the upthrust of rock behind them.

Hiero stood and stretched, then reseated himself. In the silence that followed, he seemed to be listening to the bird song which welled around them, his eyes for the nonce cast down. Finally he spoke.

"I could tell you all sorts of things, bring up the past, mention that I am a sensitive, and still tell you nothing. I'll be honest and say I simply don't *know* anything. We have been on the trail for almost three weeks. Two days ago, I felt—no other word for it—felt that this area we are in was crucial, that we ought to stay here. I can't tell you why. I don't know why. There is inimical life here somewhere; I feel it, I sense it, in some way I can't explain. There is also something else. Something is coming here. The catfolk don't see it, you two don't, nor do the Mantans, who excel all of us combined in woodcraft. But I do! We are at some sort of meeting place. I know it. For years, all of this area has been a blank to the Abbeys. We operate west of it and north of it. To the southeast lies the Palood and the Inland Sea. This angle is unknown. You know all that. I tell you, something is building here. I won't permit your talent, Per Sagenay, for one reason. The enemy has learned what I could do. We don't know what they can do, what they could have taught themselves in the past year. One of the things about the talent for forelooking that almost got me killed in the past is that it leaves one's own mind open. I won't have it! We are on the verge, the border, of some vast movement. Our business here is to probe it, not to let it know of us at all. I have sensed out and over a wide area. This forest about us is a blank indeed. A mental blank! No such thing should occur. Oh, the younger life, the Grokon, the deer, the hares, all are here. But they are muted, quiescent, and in far fewer numbers than they should be. Only the tiny, innocuous creatures—the birds, the mice, the insects—are in normal numbers." He leaned back and rested on one elbow. Then he added, "You will, I fear, have to take me on trust. Something is going to happen here, and we must wait for it."

It was Sagenay who finished the argument. "Per Desteen, you are the leader. All else is unimportant. Those who spread evil are all about us, and you are not only our commander but our chief warning signal. I have no more to say. Your thoughts are the only ones that matter."

The quiet voice left an empty space behind it. Maluin grunted several times and then waved one finger at Hiero in mock warning. He, too, settled back, and the three lay silent, staring over the ashes of their tiny fire. Yet all were alert, waiting for anything that would disturb the ether, any trace of trouble, any hint that they were not alone in the seemingly innocent depths of the great continent-wide wood.

All of them were travel-stained and travel-worn. They had marched a very long way north and east of Namcush to reach this unknown land. Not even the Mantans, veterans of a multitude of journeys in the untracked wilds, had ever roamed these parts. Their only guide now was the instinct of their leader.

Hiero had warned his comrades that they must always stay under the cloak of the trees. He remembered well that not too far to the east, he had first glimpsed and then contacted the flying device which lifted an enemy adept far aloft in the heavens. Since his reports, passed through Brother Aldo, had arrived at the central command post of the Abbeys, much thought and research had been devoted to his warning. As a result, he had some tentative information at his disposal. The thing he had seen was deemed to be an unpowered glider, a concept long lost but recorded in the central files. While its maneuverings in the air were nothing unknown in theory, no one had ever thought of a method of getting such a thing launched and up into the higher atmosphere. This was now being eagerly pursued, but as yet only the foe possessed the secret. And only Hiero had ever seen such a machine, which might mean that it was both rare and difficult to handle.

The afternoon waned. The four cat people groomed themselves and rested, and the men engaged in desultory talk. It was perhaps three hours until sundown, and still nothing disturbed the outward peace of the forest.

The interruption was sudden and silent. Reyn Mantan, his gaunt, swarthy face impassive, stood before them, looking as furtive and stealthy as some silent predator of the wood. His words, as always, were blunt and terse.

"I left Geor alone and circled camp in patrol at noon. I went east to have a scout, widen our range a little." No one commented that this was not exactly what his orders had been. The Mantan brothers took orders as they found them and interpreted them as they chose. They were proven allies, yet not soldiers, and their experience was too great and too valuable for them to be treated as if they needed constant discipline.

Now, brushing a bed of pine needles aside, Reyn crouched and drew a crude map with his dagger point.

"We're here, see? I went east and a bit north." He drew a wavy line. "Here is broken rock mixed with swamp. There's something in that area, hard to get at. Like a bad smell. I seen something like it once over to the coast." He meant the Beesee area bordering the great western ocean, far away over the mighty mountains, the Shinies.

"It moves around, something does, in there. I can feel it shifting. Maybe more than one thing. But it don't seem to come this way at all, only north and south, like it moves up and down in a line. Some kind of border, maybe, and some kind of guard. Want to go have a look?"

The others were on their feet now, and the catfolk had drawn closer, attracted by the excitement.

"What was the place on the coast like?" Maluin rapped. "Why do you think this is the same or at least similar?"

"Hard to tell. The place over west was more like a circle,

a blotch, but there's the same feel to it here. Like a stink you can't smell. Bad feeling. We didn't go into it then, me and Geor. Only a few Inyan camps in that area, and *they* didn't go nowhere near the place. Too scared. If we hadn't been in a hurry then, we might have tried. Up to you folks what you want done. I only tell what I seen."

Hiero thought hard. One of the greatest forest rangers of the North had found something inexplicable and was conveying his dislike of it. The man might not be a telepath of any kind, but his countless forays against the Unclean must have honed every sense he possessed to a razor's edge in the process. *Like a stink you can't smell!* What better way of describing some emanation of the enemy? Perhaps even a mental evil which the untutored but alert woodsrunner could only dimly detect. Hiero made up his mind quickly.

"Call your brother in and we'll march. Make it slow. Reyn, you lead out. No one use the mind touch at all!" He explained in a few thoughts to the Children of the Wind what he wanted, and they moved off in moments. All that had to be done was to don the light packs and adjust weapons more comfortably. This was a group which was never off guard or unready for an instant alert.

For an hour, they drifted like shadows of the wilderness through the forest giants. Reyn, soon joined by his brother Geor, stayed in front, and there were no flankers. The others were in a small, loose clump to the rear. Suddenly their guide checked and held up one arm. At Hiero's signal, they spread out and lay prone in the nearest cover. He positioned himself behind a huge, rotten tree stump and shut his eyes.

Ever so carefully, his mind began to reach out before them into the region which Reyn Mantan had described and which they could now see with their own eyes.

It was a type of country all of them had crossed before and was not uncommon in the North. Acid soil and low-lying ground surrounded outcrops of rotting stone, the latter often crowned with scrub. Broad patches of oily-looking, dark water glistened here and there in the light of the sun of late afternoon. Trees were few and those often dead and leafless, but many clumps of tall cattails and other reedy grasses obscured the view where the waters lay.

All of them noticed something else. The belt of marsh and

scrub was curiously silent. No waterfowl, such as herons, duck, or rail, called from the reeds, and only a slight wind sighed through them. The wind was from the north and, though gentle, made a faint, hissing rustle as it bent the tall stems. The group had come to a silent land.

Out and out, Hiero reached with his mind, concentrating on holding the most delicate touch possible, so that his mental probe would appear as no more than a feather in the wind—more of a caress than a stroke, more of a stray current of air than anything solid. As he did so, he scanned all the various wavelengths he had memorized in the past, shifting up and down from those of the lowest insects to those possessing the highest of intelligence. Out and out, infinitely slowly, holding the probe to a close range and concentrating only on the immediate area to their front.

Contact! He drew back at once and then carefully advanced again, his thought now targeted on a certain place. The contact moved; as the hunter had reported, that movement was neither toward them nor away, but following some invisible line which lay athwart their own course from east to west. He felt a sense of disgust, almost physical, and knew at once he had found the source of the "stink you can't smell."

He was not actually in touch with a mind, but rather with a presence, almost a shifting *id*, an emotional center of some foul kind. Whatever it was, its mind was guarded, but the guard was not that of the mechanical shields used by the Unclean upper ranks. This was natural to it and was perhaps a weapon against prey which might be mentally sensitive.

Still, an impression came through—a very ugly one. There was intense rage there, rage at some kind of control which the thing could not overcome. There was also malice and ferocity combined, cunning and deception, and above all—hunger! The feel of what he had sensed made Hiero wince. Not since his encounter with the vampire fungus he had named the House had he felt such avid desire for prey of some kind. This entity wanted to feed, to rend, to break and shatter, to shred some helpless life from its physical body and then to absorb it, bloodily and obscenely. It made the man think of an intelligent hyena in its self-absorption with death and the consequences of sating itself with the slain.

But it was not being allowed to do what it wished, and

therein lay the source of its rage. It had to stay within certain boundaries and it could not go where it wanted. Was it a barrier guardian of a strange and awful kind?

Hiero considered; while he did so, he used the lesser bands of small birds and insects to try to learn a little more about the area. The mixture of swamp and scrub-strewn rock and shale seemed to extend a very long way to the north and south. Probably trying to circle and bypass it would prove little and would take a lot of time. He was worried about time. The Republic's leaders needed hard information, and so far his group had not been able to provide any. At length his mind was made up, and he signaled the others to withdraw, back the way they had come. After fifteen minutes of marching, he gathered them around him in a circle and explained what he had found. He also sketched his plans for dealing with it and gave orders.

The three soldier-priests remained where they were, occasionally speaking in low tones. The catfolk and the two Mantan brothers had vanished in the wood to their rear, and there was nothing to do except watch the light wane in the west and listen with all of their senses.

"It is—or perhaps they are—hungry, ravenous," Hiero said. "I suspect this is some kind of Unclean boundary that holds them, or it, in place. I think the thing has eaten out the area and is not thinking too clearly, if it has a mind capable of thinking. The two brothers know all the game of the North better then any other living men. They can show B'uorgh and his cats what to drive when they find it. There's not much in the area, but there must be something; if there is, they'll get it."

After what seemed an interminable time, Hiero picked up the mental wave he sought and breathed a sigh of relief. "Hide yourselves. They've got something, and it's being chased this way. I just hope the trees don't check the Children too much. They are really plains hunters."

Concealing themselves, the other two waited tensely. Soon they also could hear the crashing of undergrowth and the beat of hooves in the distance. The frightened herbivore which Hiero had detected was indeed being herded in their direction. The Children of the Wind were not using the Wind of Death, but only their own speed, moving in a line, showing themselves where needed, stopping any gaps when the quarry tried to leave its line and check back. It was now panic-stricken, dreading both the hunters behind and the region it was being forced to enter in front. It did *not* want to go forward! Following the chase with his mind, Hiero marveled anew at the skill of the cat people as they headed the beast off again and again. Behind them, the two human hunters made the best speed they could, racing to try to keep up and be in at the climax.

Then the three priests saw it, bolting across a lane of sunlight under a clump of towering pines and into the shadows on the other side. They all knew the animal well—a great, striped buck, not unlike the extinct wapiti, the American elk of the lost ages, but with two-pronged antlers, now only soft stubs. Hiero suppressed his pity for the hapless prey. It was bait, and they rose as one man and followed on its slot, knowing the catfolk would wait for them on the border of the sinister marsh.

Panting, the two Mantans arrived in time to join them as they caught up with their furry allies. All crouched to listen and peer over the bog and brush tangle before them. The big deer had given up, and its tracks were plain in the mud before them where it had charged into the uncanny wilderness, the terror of those behind driving it to risk whatever lay in front.

Hiero listened with his mind. The onslaught of whatever lurked out there suddenly blended in his brain with an audible cry of agony as the killer struck. Now they could all hear the threshing uproar of the death throes; mingled with that was a new sound, a chuckling growl, vast and ominous, through which ran a purring note as well, a menacing evil to human audition. Even the proud felines laid back their ears at that noise.

All had their weapons ready, and the Mantans now had caught their breath. No further signal was needed. As one body, they all ran for the marsh, moving as silently as they could, leaping over patches of mud, avoiding the shallow pools, and utilizing the outcroppings of rock wherever possible. Ahead of them, the struggle had ceased, but the snarling was now re- placed by a new sound—the crunch and snap of mighty jaws, clearly audible through the hush of early evening.

The little band was very close. Suddenly the sounds ceased, and they knew they had been detected. They ran for their lives, hoping for a clear space in the mixture of mud, rock, and thicket, careless of what noise they made. As they ran, they spread out automatically. Almost simultaneously, they arrived at their target and abruptly halted at the sight before them.

The marsh opened here and formed a small swale, treeless and covered with some rank, brown grass, rooted in ankle-deep water. In the middle of this watery meadow lay the bloody, dismembered carcass of the stag, and over that reared its killer, glaring at them from mad eyes.

It vaguely resembled a colossal bear in general shape as it stood, swaying on columnar hind legs; but if the bear family had ever played any remote part in its ancestry, the horrid transmutation of the atom had long since changed the pattern out of resemblance. It was almost hairless, the leathery hide a dirty, mottled gray. The huge head was short-muzzled, and the naked ears were minute, lying flat against the skull. Long bunches of wiry bristle sprouted above and on either side of the gaping jaws, which were packed with monstrous, shearing teeth, blood-flecked and dripping. The bulging, reddish eyes glittered with insane fury, but there was also intelligence under the lowering brow. The proof of this lay in the torn-off club of broken wood, a man's height in length, which the thing gripped in one mighty paw; the forelimbs, though they bore great claws, carried these on crooked *hands*, five-fingered and with working thumbs!

In the brief second while the monster and the hunters took each other in, Hiero remembered the Abbey lessons of long ago. The notes had been few and those scanty indeed in detail, for those who glimpsed this horror of the Taig seldom lived to tell of it. This was the Were-bear, the grim night gaunt of the dark, known mostly by its ghastly after-trail, the haunter of the shades, the invisible death whom none could overcome. It lived by ambush and stealth; the ruins of some small cabin or the shredded remains of a hunting party, found long after the slaughter, were its usual traces. Fortunately, the deadly things were very rare and thought to be solitary in nature. All this flashed through Hiero's mind in the mere flicker of an instant as battle was joined.

Three missiles flashed across the air as one. The Mantans fired their blowguns at the same time that Sagenay loosed a slender arrow. The two small darts buried themselves in the bloody snout while the shaft from the longbow sank deep in the belly hide.

The horror screamed, a piercing shriek, high and yet mind-shattering in its sheer volume. Clutching the club and still erect, it shambled toward them, water and mud flying from the strides of the great, flat hind feet as it came. Its speed was deceptively fast. It was aiming straight for Per Edard Maluin, perhaps because he was the largest and at the center of their ragged line.

The Children of the Wind raced for the creature's flanks, two to a side, the shallow, splashing water hardly slowing their speed at all. Hiero saw M'reen swerve like lightning to avoid the stroke of the tree limb aimed at her. The next instant, all four were slashing at the brute's haunches with their long knives, drawing blood at every stroke, dipping and darting like hornets, as it checked itself and tried to deal with them.

The Mantans and Sagenay fired again, and once more the arrow sank deep and the darts feathered themselves in the frightful head. Hiero was close now and he hurled his heavy, crossbarred spear into the middle of the muddy, twisting paunch. The hoarse grunting of the Were-bear again rose in an awful coughing scream as the broad spearhead drank deep. He saw a rolling, crimson eye, distended with pain and fury, turn down at him and he ducked, splashing away in the sedge and liquid mud the fury had churned up. Another arrow drove into the center of the wild orb. *God, but Sagenay was a great archer! Would the damned thing never die?*

It towered up, dropping the useless club and clutching at its tormented face, to let out one last choking howl. Then it fell forward, splashing them all with a sea of water and filth, mingled with its own gore. It died. There was not even a twitch of rigor, just the vast corpse, prone in a wallow of muck and torn plant stems, while nine panting entities stood, weapons still poised, and looked at one another.

"You are an amazing shot, Per Sagenay," Hiero said to the younger man. "And you, too, gentlemen," he added, nodding to the Mantans. "I think that your venom slowed the brute down. It was more confused than I had been led to believe these monsters were supposed to be."

He sent his own message of praise to the Children of the

Wind, using their mental channel, and he could feel the pride in their response.

"I never got close enough," Maluin grumbled, lowering the billhook.

"It was aimed right at you when my friends halted it, you big oaf," Hiero said. "Another second and you would have had plenty to do. Now everyone be silent while I use mind search."

He was none too soon! Almost at once, the expression on his face and the tenseness of his body had all the others alerted, their weapons lifted anew.

A voice he had not heard for many months beat into his brain like a hammer on an anvil. *Watch out, Hiero! Another one comes fast from the north! We are following, but beware . . . !*

At the same time, the Metz caught the wave of black anger and killing rage which he had noted from the monstrous brute, only half an hour before. *Its mate!* He spun, cursing the dying light and facing to his left. The rest of his troop whirled also, and thus the second attack did not catch them totally off their guard.

The new menace burst from the screen of brush and charged, fangs agape, down upon them. It ran on its hind legs, and the vast, lumbering strides brought it on at a pace a racing hopper might have envied. Each of the giant arms bore a mighty burden. As the ghoul-thing came, it hurled a great rock from one of them with deadly aim.

Perhaps the onset of age had begun to stiffen B'uorgh's sinews; perhaps one of his lightning shifts, by plain bad luck, was in the wrong direction. The boulder—for it was nothing less—struck the catman chief with a sickening crunch and hurled him aside like a castoff doll, useless and discarded. M'reen's high scream of rage and sorrow rose above the triumphant bellow of the enemy.

Once more, one of Sagenay's bronze-tipped shafts sank home, though this time he struck an arm. The darts of the brothers Mantan hissed again; at this range, they could not miss. But their poison, so lethal to normal life, seemed to work very slowly on this alien flesh. Hiero had wrenched the spear from the corpse of his late foe and now stood erect upon the giant body itself, waiting to meet this fresh attack, trying to free his limbs of weariness in the seconds remaining before it closed. The gray light of dusk made the appearance of the demon hard to discern, and he knew that it was a creature of the shadows, the vague outline not the least of its weapons. Beside him, but lower down and braced for battle, his strong legs slightly bent, Maluin also awaited the onslaught, his fell weapon held two-handedly and cocked over his left shoulder. Then the monster was upon them, and they ceased to think.

The second rock the creature clutched was a long slab of granite; it did not hurl this, but used it like a club, as its mate had wielded the shattered tree limb. Hiero flung his spear but heard it ring on stone, even as the monster struck at him. He tried to duck, holding his shield high, but the grazing touch of the great rock swept him off his feet, left arm numbed to the shoulder, and pitched him down the side of the dead beast and into the marsh below.

Again he heard the bellow of triumph start; but as he tried to stagger erect and free his sword, he heard the awful cry rise to an impossible pitch of pain. On his feet once more, he saw what had happened.

As the second Were-bear stooped to crush Hiero's life away, Edard Maluin had seen his chance and leaped in. The huge billhook scythed down in a terrible stroke upon the left arm of the monster. The vast, deformed hand, severed at the wrist, flew away into the haze and murk, and a gout of blackish blood spouted and spat red through the evening air.

As the titan turned on Maluin, Hiero struck at its haunch with his heavy short sword, but his aim was off, and it seemed to him the stroke was slow and feeble. He tried to recover, noting almost absently that another of Sagenay's arrows had driven home in the gray hide. *It will kill us all before it dies*, a remote part of his mind decided. Half in a dream, he watched as the ghastly head turned back to him; he saw the yellow fangs, crusted with dried foam, as the monster moved forward and down to crush the pigmy who had defied it.

He was spun aside like a top and hurled yards away on his back, the sword flying out of his grip as he went. Helpless and with his eyes full of muddy liquid, he did not see what the others saw and thus missed the final event.

A great, black beast cut through the sedges with the speed of a pike darting through waterweed. Driven by a bulk not much less than that of the Were-bear and brushing Hiero aside in the process with its shoulder, the new arrival smashed into the enemy with the precision and force of a battering ram. The last, frantic bound carried two great, razor-edged feet smack into the space between the eyes of the northern horror. As they went home, the awful cracking noise cut off the gross snarling of the monster, ending its evil life instantly.

Frantically trying to get up on his feet, brush the mud from his eyes, and rejoin the battle, Hiero became conscious of a vast foreleg on which he seemed to be leaning. As he tried to deal with this most familiar but long-absent concept, an enormous tongue swept over his face and a wave of sweet breath enveloped his head. Then he knew!

"Klootz, you miserable, slab-sided piece of worthless dog meat! What do you mean by frightening me like that?" He pounded softly on the great barrel, his eyes shut to keep the ready tears locked within. How many thousand leagues had the great beast come, to home in on him and find him in the midst of a life-or-death struggle? He blinked at length and saw the long neck turn round and down again; once more the morse's tongue care-washed his face in a mighty swipe.

He wiped his eyes and managed to stagger away from his friend's side and stare about him. Maluin leaned on his bill a few yards off, covered with mud, but seemingly otherwise undamaged. He winked at Hiero, then began to brush himself and his weapon clean as best he could, whistling softly to himself. The Mantans and Sagenay were plucking their darts and arrows from the hides of the dead terrors, cleansing them in the marsh water and restoring them tidily to their quivers. Then Hiero saw the three young catfolk gathered around something silent in the sedges and he remembered that B'uorgh was dead. He was about to go to them when suddenly a very irritated voice burst into his mind, and he halted in his tracks, so that Klootz, who was following behind, almost ran over him.

Hiero, if all that mess is cleaned up, I would appreciate your telling your friends that I am not a target for all those things they shoot. Then I will be able to come out from behind this rock. As Hiero reeled with the realization of what and *whom* he was hearing, the mind voice went on, somehow conveying an acid tone. *Klootz didn't do it all, you know!*

Breathlessly, Hiero spoke. "All of you, listen. A new friend of ours is here. Don't shoot, for God's sake! He helped bring Klootz to us."

They all turned and looked with keen interest at the burly, rolling shape, coated in dark brown fur, which now emerged from a thicket to the north and ambled down their way. None looked with more interest than Hiero. It had been a long time since they had parted, far away in the South, after the destruction of both the House and the buried city of the ancients.

He saw that Gorm had changed and he wondered what changes the young bear saw in him. Gorm was perceptibly larger and also leaner, indeed almost drawn-looking. He had nowhere near the bulk he would attain someday—of that the Metz was sure—but he was a powerful animal now and he radiated a surety and inner strength which had not been there before.

The bear reached Hiero's side and rose on his hind legs until his small eyes were higher than the man's. His tongue barely touched Hiero's nose, and then he dropped back to all fours again and woofed gently. *A nice sort of thing you go about looking for, I must say*, his thought came. *Lucky that Klootz scented you somehow and told me. We've been trying to cross this area for days now, but we knew there were two of them and we couldn't risk it. You lost a friend over there, Hiero. Better go see what you can do. They need some comfort. Then we have to get out of here fast.*

Marveling at the speed and accuracy of Gorm's mental images, Hiero walked over to where the silent catfolk stood over the fallen chief. B'uorgh must have been killed instantly, for his whole rib cage was crushed. His fierce visage was unmarred, though, and he seemed to be smiling grimly, as if his death and indeed the whole universe were only one more bitter jest.

Hiero put his arm over M'reen's drooping shoulders and addressed the three on their own private wavelength.

He was a great warrior. He died as he would have wished, in the fight against our ancient foes, yours and mine. When you return to the Pride—and when I return also—we will sing a song for him that all will learn as cubs and remember as long as the Pride shall live. Now, let us put aside our grief. M'reen, you are the leader now. You will tell us what to do to send him to his rest. But we must hurry. He would not have wished us to delay on his account. The enemy is moving.

They lifted the body between them and bore it to dry land where, with all helping, they excavated a grave under a large stone. M'reen sang a short wailing song alone, and then Per Sagenay asked them if he might speak with his own God on behalf of the fallen warrior. Shyly, after a moment's talk among themselves, the catfolk agreed that this would be entirely fitting. *After all*, Ch'uirsh sent to Hiero, *we are far from the night winds over the southern plains. Your god up here can help send his spirit back down to our land, where it can finally rest.*

Hiero agreed solemnly that this was a perfectly sound piece of reasoning. *And, God*, he added silently, *You could do worse. He fell in Your battle, and I know You'll help*. He said a quiet prayer of his own, and the thing was done.

As they turned away from the lonely grave, Hiero became conscious that Gorm was growing impatient. He knew that the bear was not much of a deist and, indeed, considered all appeals to the Unknown as a waste of time. Agnosticism was not unheard of among humans, but, the man thought, it was a fresh puzzle for the Faith if it occurred among the newer breeds. He chuckled to himself, for he knew that he had a young priest in the group who would have to learn this for himself in a fairly brief time.

In a short while, they were all lounging in a circle around a tiny fire. Hiero had led them back along their previous trail and through the shrouded night for over an hour, until he deemed they were out of immediate danger and could take a rest. Outside the circle, Klootz stood silently, his vast, drooping nose flexing and sniffing, his mule ears twitching as he sought the scents and sounds carried by the wind. Already the buds of his antlers were two feet long. He looked thin, as did the bear, but he was obviously fit for anything, as the recent encounter had abundantly proved.

Gorm lay in the center, obviously enjoying the warmth of the fire, the light flickering on his thick, brown pelt. When he spoke, his speech in the minds of its recipients was so clear that all—even, to Hiero's intense surprise, the cat people—could understand him easily. Hiero threw a protective mind shield over the whole group with no trouble, observing with amusement that the stoic and impassive Mantan twins were frankly gaping for the first time in his experience and craning their necks to study first Gorm and then, in complete astonishment, each other. Maluin actually laughed, and a quiet smile stole over the face of Cart Sagenay.

First, I am but the forerunner of my people. The bears are coming, but it takes time. We do not live in tribes or villages, but in families. Thus, the incoming of all able to fight is not quick. The Elders have ordered it, and we are moving. We are not fast marchers and we must come far to the north and then swing south to join the human forces. We have to stay well away from the zones of the Unclean where I first met Hiero, lest we be detected and even stopped.

I was sent on ahead to carry the word to the Abbeys. As I journeyed, I heard a strange sound in the forest. He sent the mental image of a helpless fawn, calling for its mother. *It was this great lump of a weed eater, bawling his head off for Hiero. Fortunately, I remembered what he sounded like and was able to contact him. He is not as stupid as he looks and told me much.*

Here, Klootz snorted indignantly. Obviously, he too could understand at least some of the bear's sarcasm. Hiero looked on, his mind more at ease then it had been for a long time. While the bear paused, considering the next thought, a vagrant message entered Hiero's mind that was not from Gorm at all! *Lazy*—unknown concept—*carried on my back when tired*—unknown—*fight! Where (/)??? needed by HIM!* To his delight, Hiero realized that Klootz understood just what he was hearing and wanted his master to know it. The giant deer knew well what he was worth and was not about to be put down by his nimble-witted cohort.

Gorm continued, the silence broken only by the hiss of the little flames. Behind them, the forest wall reared up, dark and deep, a wall of black shadows. The stars blazed overhead through the gaps in the forest roof, icy-white in the night sky.

Here is what is important. I have learned, through the morse and from messengers from Brother Aldo, what has happened in the South, far away. The news is not good. We can do nothing about it, however. Our task is here. The enemy is on the march. They are moving as we sit here. They follow an arc, as do my folk, the bear people, from east to west and then south. But they move on an inner circle and have less far to go. They are no more than two easy marches behind us right now.

Maluin spoke. "Hiero, I can understand him, but I can't talk to him. How many are coming? What does he know of their battle order?"

The answer was not encouraging. *All! They bring every unit, every creature that can fight! We know many of their hidden forts and their buried places. We think they have left little but shes and young. If they be beaten, we can cleanse the North. If they are beaten! The Man-rats, the monkey-things you call the Hairy Howlers, the Devil-dogs, all will be with them. It is a great host. Can you match it?* His silence then hung, pregnant with doubt, in all of their minds.

What of machines? This was Hiero. *Have you any news of their powered ships? Any news of the lightning guns? Recall that thing that struck me down on the shore last year. And what of the sky? The flier that we saw long ago. Have any of those been seen and, if so, where and when?*

We have watched for all of those, Gorm sent. *The ship was seen once, but far to the east and some months back, not recently. We do not know how many they have. We ourselves cannot watch the sea and the islands. The Eleveners are trying, but we have no recent news. The flying thing has never been seen, save by us two on that one occasion. Perhaps they had only one and it was destroyed.* The bear's mental tone grew reflective. *The Elders feel that the sky is not to their liking, perhaps, or why do they not do more with it? Why not rear broods of evil fliers of some kind? No, they like night and stealth and burrowing in the dark more than the clear air and sun. They can fight in the blaze of day, but—it is not natural to such things. They are like those two Deaths-in-the-Dark whom you slew back there in the swamp. Ambush and the stroke from behind, the unseen terror of the lightless hours, the cruel and stealthy murder of the helpless, the old and the young— those are their chosen methods!*

I hope they cannot all be persuaded to fight like the enemies of God whom we just encountered! This was the limpid, clear mind of Cart Sagenay. Hiero guessed that it would take little training to make the young priest as good a mental linguist as he was. He saw Gorm look appraisingly at the younger man.

Those, I think, were allies, and unwilling ones at that. I consider that, if we had the time, Hiero, we would find some Unclean devices, like those things they block thoughts with that they wear around their necks. Maybe they buried some such devices to hold those creatures where they had to stay and keep watch. But we have no time for idle thoughts such as these. The enemy moves, and they are coming, direct and fast, for the main body of your forces. You know where those are. I do not. Too, there may be some good news, though vague and unclear. The Elders and the Eleveners, too, all feel the enemy is moving in haste, not along ordered lines. Something has upset them badly, and the thought is that they are striking out in reaction and not in the carefully planned way they would prefer. This may be encouraging, not so?

Hiero thought of the destruction of Neeyana and the two deadly ships and smiled. Yes, that *would* have upset the Unclean!

Gorm continued, addressing Hiero directly. *I think you and I can guess who leads them. There may be others in the command of their troops, but you and I know who hates and fears you the most, the mind that will never rest while you live . . .*

S'duna! Hiero stared into the orange glow of the dying fire. He could see the pale face and hairless skull of the Master of the Blue Circle, the pupilless eye-pits of evil. There might indeed be others in the high Councils of the enemy—Unclean adepts, mental wizards of dark arts, foes of all that was decent. But he knew Gorm was right. His greatest antagonist was coming with all the enormous power at his command. The Unclean had come out in the open at last, hoping to crush the Metz Republic in one brutal stroke before it could build its young strength. If the bear was right, they just could be making a mistake. Decades of raids, stealthy ambushes, plottings, and assassins in the night might not be the best preparation for open warfare. It was a cheering thought. Still, the other comment was right, too. Time was short.

Put out the fire and let's go, he sent. *We march southeast for the lakes. That's where we'll meet them. The Abbeys need to be told.*

And may God defend the right, was the thought of Per Sagenay.

✤ 12 ✤
BATTLE MORNING

THE MIST LAY COOL AND CURTAINED OVER THE LAKE. IT WAS the body of water, perhaps twenty miles in extent, that the Metz called the Lake of Weeping. Some women had died there long ago, supposedly of unrequited love. More important, Hiero thought, was the fact that the lake had a connection through the River of Rains with distant Namcush. The connection was by still another lake, this one called Falling Leaves, a long, slender lake. The Lake of Weeping was deep and shaped like a boomerang, the elbow pointing northeast, though the left arm, which faced almost due north, was the longer.

There were a few small islands in view, some mere stubs of rock and others crowned with trees, whose spires and branches pierced the shifting fogs over the dark water. There was movement out there, Hiero saw. Small craft rowed briskly from one islet to another. The rising mist, burned away by the sun's coming, revealed the dark shapes of several large sailing vessels. On a number of islands, smoke rose in the morning air. Activity, but not too much activity...

Hiero was sitting astride Klootz on the end of a low promontory which jutted into the Lake of Weeping almost at the angle of the elbow. It was a handy place to be, and he had picked it himself. He was the Commander of the Center under Demero, and the old man had brushed aside any complaints about seniority before they got started. "Who knows the enemy better than you do? No one. Who has encountered more of them than anyone else and still survived? Same answer. Justus Berain says he'll be glad to serve under you, anywhere, any time. Like to argue with *him*? I'm giving you Maluin and Sagenay as staff. The two Mantans won't serve under anyone else, insubordinate devils. The whole army has word of your cats, and they can serve as runners to carry written messages. Maluin has already got a bunch of juniors to handle routine. What's left? Nothing. Get to work, boy. I'm busy."

Now Hiero smiled wryly as he watched through his far-looker, the small telescope he carried clipped to his saddle. He could hear low voices among the group of young officers and NCOs behind him. He was finally beginning to realize that being a living legend was not an unmixed blessing. The awe in the eyes of the young men and women who served under him was annoying, but there was nothing he could do about it. He concentrated once more on the dispositions to his front. He had to use his eyes and those of others, for the Abbey machines had clamped an intense shield over the minds of all in the area. Presumably the Unclean had done the same for their own forces. Time would tell who possessed the most effective mental protection.

His scouting group had fled southwest at an incredible pace after Gorm had alerted them. They had actually cut off four days on their time going out, and they had been moving very fast indeed then. They needed every minute that they could get, and Hiero had driven them all unmercifully, using Klootz's broad back to carry those who were the most tired. This was usually Per Sagenay, whose young body was not as tough as the others' and who resented it but could only comply. But three days out from their front lines, Geor Mantan had sprained an ankle and, cursing horribly, had been made to ride as well. Otherwise they would have left him.

They had bought the Republic and its allies a week. In this struggle, that might be much. For the Otwah League's troops were still far off and already meeting some resistance as they came. Not all of S'duna's force had been sent west, and there was apparently a good deal wrong with security in the upper ranks of the League! *Just because I loathe S'duna's filthy guts, I shouldn't make the mistake of underrating his slimy brain*, Hiero thought to himself. *The bastard can think, and he knows enough to try and bleed off any help we might get, if he learns about it first. Let's hope there's some coming he doesn't know about.*

He looked down and saw a young lieutenant at salute. He eyed her approvingly. Save for the short leather skirt, her uniform was identical to his, and he knew his women could use their weapons and brains as well as or better than the men. Besides, she was pretty.

"Message from the Abbot-General, sir. Very hard fighting has started in the deep woods about twenty kilometers north and east. Our screens are giving back slowly, trying to see what's behind the enemy front. The morse troops have been ordered back because the country is too broken for them. He will keep you informed as he gets more data."

Hiero grinned down at the snapping black eyes, returned the salute and thanked her, then forgot her immediately.

It made sense to get the cavalry out. One or two might serve as couriers in the depths of the forest, but they couldn't maneuver as a unit. Demero had stripped the North to get those two mounted regiments, and they must not be wasted.

"Per Sagenay," he threw over his shoulder. "Bring me the map quadrant that shows the land opposite us and to the west, if you please."

Together, they examined it. It was bog and drowned land, but not deep in water, containing only shallow, slow-moving streams which kept it somewhat drained. There were few trees, but mostly grasses and rank growths of reed. The whole section eventually sprawled down to the low-lying shore of the lake they were on, over to their left and on the longer of the two arms of the V. The shore simply became the marsh, or vice versa, for a kilometer of total distance. A bad place to put troops, it seemed, but useful for the passive resistance it made, guarding a flank, like a broad, muddy moat. Now the question was, might this fact be too obvious to another keen mind?

Hiero spoke for a few minutes with Cart Sagenay, then sent the young priest back to his own group. He scrawled something on a small belt pad of reed paper and called M'reen over to his side. The sun had cleared the last of the dawn mist off the water now, and the blue sparkle against the green foliage was almost dazzling.

Take this to our old chief, the Wise One. Then hurry back. There will be much to do this day.

She was gone like her native wind, all eyes on the slender form until it vanished. Ch'uirsh and Za'reekh waited impatiently in the rear, ready for their own summons.

Edard Maluin strode over and patted Klootz absently. The

blade of his billhook tapped the ground as he balanced the huge weapon in his other hand like a wand.

"What do we know about the two flanks, Hiero? The left doesn't bother me too much. The arm of the lake there bends away from us and can be held pretty easily. The right, now, that's different. Falling Leaves Lake is not especially wide and it tapers into Bowstring Creek and the River of Rains. A long line to guard, all the way down to the Inland Sea."

"The Abbot knows it, you know it, and I know it. Pretty soon, if they don't already, the enemy will know it. We have four full regiments of Frontier Guards and two mixed regiments of militia whose women are as well trained as the men—not Guards standard, but pretty good. About seven thousand, if you count the auxiliaries, baggage, ammunition carriers, and so on. Two regiments of morse. A strong battalion of Scouts, now falling back in front of the Unclean. Certain aquatic allies, whose performance is still untested. Also what you both see and do not see out on the lake and similarly to east and west. Forget the League. They started too late and are well behind the enemy now. Maybe they'll get here in a week or so and maybe not. What they find when they do get here is something else. There *may* be other help closer to hand. I don't know; nobody knows. Gorm has gone to try and find out, but he'll have to go around the fighting and the enemy flanks to do it. All very problematical. And that, my friend, is *it*. We have nothing else, no reserve, except a small tactical one, taken from the above. This is our first *army*, just as what you served in was the first navy. We've never moved or fought on this scale before. No one in the North has—not the Unclean, either."

He shifted in his saddle and stared out over the water. Armies had fought in the South, if not here. He suppressed the wish for Luchare, leading a division of lancers on their hoppers, emerging from the southern wood to the rescue. *Might as well ask for a flight of angels.*

The morning wore on. Reports came in sporadically—estimates of Unclean strength and movements, losses of the Republic's forces, and whatever seemed of interest. One item was of great interest. Many, many light boats were being brought up. Some were large enough for ten men, others mere kayaks, but big enough for a single person. All the Unclean units seemed to have lots of them, and they were carried well to the fore.

"They must have a pretty good idea of where we are with all that stuff," he said to Per Sagenay. "Of course, the whole area is full of lakes and streams, but I think this was thought out more carefully. This is no baggage train, but something meant for quick assault. I want the information sent to Berain and the others at once. In fact, tell it to all units."

M'reen, who had long since returned, came up with her two warriors. The grim faces of the Mantans were just behind.

We can hear the fighting, Hiero. Can you not do so? These two, the men with the dark souls, they can hear it too. They told us with signs.

"That's right, Per," Reyn admitted. "Them cats caught it first, but just listen yourself now."

Hiero listened. There were calls from out on the lake, horns blowing, and the shuffle of moving feet behind him. Even a distant splash of oars from some guard boat came through. Then he caught it. It was a hum, a buzzing in the distance. He listened harder. Now he could pick out higher and lower tones like the shrills of far-off insects. There came a very faint series of thuds, no more than vibratory disturbances of the air. It was enough.

"Take charge, Edard," he said to Maluin. "Sagenay's your second or what you choose. Remember what I said. No movement until the crucial time. This is going to be a close one." He turned and looked speculatively at the twins, whose cold, set faces stared back.

"Can you two handle morses? If I can find any? Otherwise you'd be better off staying here."

Geor spoke for both. "We can. We've ridden double, too, case there's only one. Take us."

"All right. We're crossing the lake, down there on the left. I'll walk Klootz until we get aboard a boat." He signaled the catfolk to follow. He had no worries about their ability to keep up with mounted troops, and they would have been miserable away from him. He waved to the salutes of the staff and rode slowly down the twisting trail to the west, off the bluff and onto the path along the shore. The five others loped behind him.

In twenty minutes, they came to a tiny bay in which a small

rowing barge lay concealed. He led the big morse aboard, and the others clambered after. At a word to the NCO in charge, the ten long sweeps began to move the clumsy vessel out into the lake on a long slant, north and west, to where the marsh and the cleaner fluid of the deep water began to mingle.

All the while, the sounds of the battle had been growing in their ears. Clanging noises of metal came now, and the metallic, piercing sounds of enemy trumpets mixed with the sonorous Metz horns. Screams came as well, and chorused cheering. Hiero knew the orders had been sent and he knew the defense was thickening on orders as the Abbey forces drew near the Lake of Weeping. Yet the sounds of conflict were raging closer at a tremendous rate. The Unclean must be piling in all their strength, heedless of casualties, in order to make such speed. He cocked one eye at the bright sun and consulted his built-in mental clock. It was near eleven, and the timetable had not quite allowed for this burst of enemy speed. He watched the oarsmen strain at the great sweeps as they passed under the lee of a small island. They were three-quarters of the way across now and in plain view of the elbow of the lake, the curve of the northern shore stretching out of sight in both directions.

The din grew as he watched, and he saw the first Metz troops break from the forest and reach the long lines of boats drawn up on the shore. The skeleton crews who manned them began to help the wounded aboard. The movement was swift and disciplined, and he smiled. No panic here! As each boat pulled out, oar-propelled on this windless day, more men appeared and took their places in the next. He could see through the far-looker that no boat left the shore with an empty place or without orders.

Now he could begin to glimpse the fighting for himself. He saw a rank of veteran archers halt, fire a volley, then run easily back and turn for another. Men fell in their ranks as they fought, but the others closed up. As he watched intently, an eruption of the enemy burst from the forest wall, a small pack of the Plague Hounds, with Leemute riders screaming on their bony backs. These were Hairy Howlers, apelike brutes, brandishing clubs and axes and hurling long javelins with devilish aim. The hideous dog mutants were man-high at the shoulder and had naked hides, blotched and mottled in shades of orange and red.

Their ears drooped, and they had heavy jaws and gaping maws, filled with great teeth.

The archer troop slew more than half of them with one more volley, then dropped their bows as the survivors came on, unchecked. It was close-in fighting now, and the Plague Hounds raged in the Metz ranks, shaking men like so many jackstraws when they secured a grip. The Howlers fought like furies, seeking only to kill and not minding their own safety as they hacked and stabbed. Then it was suddenly over, and a sadly diminished troop fell back again from the heap of reeking corpses. They carried some wounded, but not many.

The battle was fierce all along the shore now, and many of the boats were not rowing, but lying off and giving covering fire. A sheet of arrows flew, and then another. The last Scouts of the defense were scrambling aboard, some having to fight as they did so. Now there were few left. The guard boats, with stocks of ready arrows, redoubled their fire. A pack of the great, scaly-tailed Man-rats, caught in one such blast, went down in heaps.

The boats pulled away from the shore. Many places were empty in these, Hiero noted sadly. The thin metal notes of the Unclean trumpets sounded over and over, and their creatures began to draw back to the shelter of the wood. As they vanished, the guard boats ceased their fire and began slowly to follow the rear of those who had passed on through. Now there was a widening gap and an empty shore, full of dead and wounded.

Hiero realized that his own craft was touching the mud of the shore, and he scrambled aboard Klootz and ran him over the blunt bow. The mud here was a man's thigh deep, but the big morse made nothing of it. His spreading hooves were designed for this element.

"Hold on to my stirrups," he told the Mantans. "You'll get a bit wet, but I can't help that. You would come!"

The cat people had been wet before this. They didn't like it, but it was no real problem. As they began to march inland through the tussocks of grass and the sloughs in which they grew, the warrior-priest looked back. The height given by his perch on the morse enabled him still to look down along the shore for some distance.

The Metz rear guard—what remained of it—was rowing away steadily, if slowly. A few other boats, not many, had come out from the chain of wooded islands and were helping the craft which either carried too many wounded or were hampered by lack of men to row. A couple of thin lines of soldiers were visible on the south shore. And a flag waved here and there, showing the green on white of the Republic.

But now the scene changed. The Unclean army, silent and intent once more, poured out of the trees on the north bank. This time they came prepared. Save for the officers, each man or Leemute carried either a small canoe or part of a larger one. Man-rats took to the water like the natural swimmers they were, needing no transportation and carrying their weapons. This, too, was a disciplined move and showed long hours spent in practice. Hiero glimpsed a group of sinuous, brown shapes slide into the lake and remembered the great water weasels he had fought long ago. The Uncleans were indeed using everything they had. Would it be enough?

His view of the battle scene faded, obscured by trees and distance. His little troops were moving deeper into the shallow waters and muck of the drowned land. There would be no help from using his mind. He had tried testing his ability continuously. The shields held by both the Unclean and the Abbeys were functioning too well for anything to break through. He could talk to his cat people at close range, but that was all.

Ahead, he glimpsed a line of black things moving and whipped up the far-looker. This was what he had come to find. Klootz lifted his dripping muzzle and bawled a greeting. In a few more moments, he had reached a mound rising out of the grass and water, and Hiero could greet his new troops.

The two regiments of morse and riders were in line, but loosely picketed. Hiero knew the two colonels, though both men were older. In fact, in the past he had even served under Colonel Saclare and been taught by Colonel Lejus at the Academy. They were typical Metz and could have passed for his own close relations; stocky, bronzed men in their forties riding with the ease of a lifetime in the saddle. With their aides behind, they reined up and saluted. Hiero acknowledged the salute and masked a feeling of some awkwardness.

Saclare disabused him promptly. "We are delighted to have you in charge. Lejus and I know your past training." One sardonic black eye drooped in what only those close by could have told was a wink. It was enough. All three broke into broad grins and gripped hands. Command was established and they were as one.

"Yes, I can find a couple of remounts, though we don't have many," Lejus said, staring at the Mantan twins with interest. "We all have heard of these two. Who hasn't? Thought they always fought alone, though. I expect you'll want to keep them with you. Heard of your cats, too, and what beauties they are. I gather they can look after themselves. But come along, sir. We're rigging something over there you might want to use. Saclare thought of it."

A little distance off on the mound, the place an ancient German would have called a *Feldherrnhügel*, or "general's observation hill," men and morses in harness were straining to raise a triangle of extremely long poles. As they locked into place, others lifted a long ladder and began with speed to lash down a rude platform. All the material had been precut and dragged through the wide marsh to this point.

Moments later, Hiero and the two colonels had a fresh view of the conflict and were glued to their far-lookers. They could see far along the northern shores, as well as across the Lake of Weeping, and they were barely in time to see another crux of the battle.

The Unclean troops, human and otherwise, still poured from the wood. At least a thousand boats, large and small, all of light weight, seemingly made of hide braced with wood stripping, were beating out in pursuit of the Metz rear guard. These, moving slowly, were still some distance from the southern bank and safety, though many seemed close. Hiero noted that those that *were* close seemed to contain the wounded, while those which were the most sluggish had none. *So far so good*, he thought, *but, God above, how many of the enemy were still pouring from the forest to the attack! And they still produced more and more boats!* The hideous, giant dogs were swimming out in packs also, some with Howler riders to guide the others. Most of the Howlers were in boats, but fresh swarms of the Man-rats still rushed from under the trees and flung themselves into the lake. The water weasels showed here and there as they dived and porpoised in the front of the van. When *would* the signal be given?

"Put these on, sir," Saclare said. He was holding a bundle of the laquered battle armor of the morse riders, surmounted

by a bronze, visored helmet. He and all the others were already
wearing theirs.

Hiero struggled absently with the cuirass, half-sleeves, and
greaves, not even noting that the two colonels were lacing them
on for him and that his helmet bore the white heron plume of
a general. His gaze was locked on the water. The main body
of the apparently endless Unclean horde was now at the level
of the larger islands, whose tree branches drooped over the
lake.

A sudden blare of echoing horn calls rang out over the cries
and yelps of the Unclean hordes. Branches fell into the lake,
and even some of the great trees were thrown down. Out from
their hidden island anchorages swept a flock of ships, the five
armored Metz steamboats in the van, belching clouds of smoke
as they charged the enemy. Justus Berain was not a man to be
hurried; he struck only when he felt the exact time had come!
The gun ports of the steamers had been widened and lowered,
allowing for point-blank fire. From the great muzzle-loaders
burst not solid shot, but masses of broken ceramic tile, mixed
with rock and metal scraps, causing instant havoc. Behind the
streamers came a fleet of stout rowing barges, wooden mantlets
and wicker screens protecting both the complement of archers
and the rowers. Volley-fired only by orders, sheets of arrows
swept over the enemy, adding to the carnage.

It was not all one-sided. Though blasted and torn, shredded
by the crude langrage, the blasting rubble of the war steamers,
and devastated by the arrow storm, the enemy fought back.
Their metallic trumpets signaled anew from the forest, and fresh
masses swept out and into the confusion on the waters.

Here and there in the swarming ranks of the foe, Hiero now
caught glimpses of gray-cloaked figures hurrying from one
point to the other. The Unclean adepts might be new to open
warfare, he realized, but they had come in strength and were
fast learners!

He tore his eyes away and looked down at what lay below
the observation platform. It made him feel easier. Unconcerned
by the uproar in the distance, just under four thousand troopers
of the Metz cavalry waited by their mighty steeds, all in four
broken lines, stretching across the marsh. The great lances were
planted in line, one at the head of each morse, with the troopers
lounging in place. The two Mantans, impassive as always,

waited patiently at the ladder foot; the three Children of the
Wind were beside them. Klootz stood, silent, next to the two
morses requisitioned for the hunters.

"Won't be much longer, gentlemen," he said to the two
colonels. "It looks good here. Downstream on the lower lake,
it may be something else. We only have one steamer, the
newest, there. But we have other surprises. We should know
shortly."

They all continued to watch the lake even as Hiero spoke.
As far away as they could see, until the angle of the lake cut
them off, the battle raged, the screams and cries of men and
beasts mingling under the veils of smoke with the roar of the
guns.

"By the Lord God, I think they are turning," Saclare muttered. "Even they have had enough. I thought they were never
going to stop coming out of the woods. But—look!"

They could all see it now, and Hiero sent a heartfelt prayer
up to Heaven. The frightful slaughter had turned back the
swimmers and the Unclean boats. The frail craft they had borne
so many leagues were no match for the keen arrows and the
great guns. The armored ships went where they would, spewing
destruction on all sides and grinding any smaller vessels under
their angled snouts. Repeatedly, the enemy swarms tried to
board and close in, only to be beaten back with heavy losses.
The arrow boats followed in the wake of the big five, and the
guard boats, which had fled so slowly to the other shore, wheeled
and re-entered the fight. Many others darted from the southern
shore to join them.

Here and there, some of the great mink mutants sprang
aboard a smaller boat or a load of Howlers tried to board. Man-
rats also tried the same tactic, but the wicker and plank screens
kept most of them out, and the others were quickly slaughtered.
The main body of Unclean human infantry was not one of great
watermen, and the horrible dogs were completely helpless.
There were so many bodies of all kinds floating on the waters
of the lake that it almost seemed that one could walk across
on them. The massed wreckage of the invasion boats made
larger lumps here and there in the sea of corpses.

The Unclean trumpets back on shore rose to a screaming
pitch, incessant and shrill. By boat and in the water, the enemy
fled for the northern banks. They had begun to do so even

before the signal to retreat had rung out. Beaten and demoralized, yet still in great numbers, they swam and paddled for their lives. Not one had come near to setting foot on the farther shore.

The war boats of the Republic moved in behind them, the terrible fire taking a continuous toll. Blasts from the guns swept the shore, and arrows flew through the smoke. Looking at the sun over the reeking clouds, Hiero realized that it was noon and that hardly an hour had passed since the enemy had launched its craft upon the lake. He wondered how the battle to the east was coming. The foe still mustered great strength and would fight hard if given a chance to rally. Would the interpretation of what came next be accurate?

"To your posts, gentlemen," he said quietly. "I want this tower struck at once. The enemy could see it if they came now."

They went down the long ladder like men possessed. In moments, the tower was disassembled and the three ranking officers were riding slowly along the lines. Saclare dropped off to command the right flank, and Hiero halted in the center; Lejus went on to take over the left. Listening hard, Hiero could hear a slackening of the gunfire from the lake. He could think of no reason for it but one—lack of targets of opportunity. Now only an occasional rumble came from the smoke bank in the southeast.

He turned to the catfolk, who stood waiting by his saddle. *I have a task of great danger for you,* he sent. *We must know if the enemy comes and how fast. Ch'uirsh, go to the left. Za'reekh, you go to the right. Try to reach me with your minds, but come back if you cannot. Do not be seen if you can possibly help it. Kill none unless it is death not to do otherwise. I seek knowledge, not bodies. Will you go? M'reen, you will go to my front, but not as far as the others. You can perhaps relay their thoughts.*

They did not even answer, but were gone like three marsh sprites, skimming grass clumps and knee-deep water as if they were not there.

"If this were dry ground, I'd send you two on a scout," he said to the twins. "But I don't want the enemy to see a single morse, and you can't move in this muck like those three." They nodded bleakly and settled themselves at rest in their saddles.

Waiting was not easy. Hiero tried to think about the future; when he found this too depressing, he narrowed it to the immediate future. He had two tasks before him, and they might come quickly, even together. *One—break the enemy flank to pieces. Come and be broken, damn you! Two—find and kill S'duna. You're out there, you filth, I know it. Too many of your dirty renegade humans, too many louse-bitten Leemutes. You threw everything you had into this one and you couldn't stay behind on Manoon, polluting the sun with your amusements this time!*

Behind his back, the long lines shifted and swayed. All the riders were mounted, simply waiting for a word. Where were the cats?

M'reen's thought came like lightning as he slapped at a cloud of hungry gnats and mosquitoes. *We are coming back! My males have found them! They come from the trees, many, many! Be warned!*

Hiero hand-signaled as previously arranged, and the ripple of readiness welled away from him in both directions along the ranks.

The Children of the Wind appeared in a clump, running and dodging like the racers they were. Missiles fell around them, but none hit.

The general bore no lance. His white plume dipped as he bent and drew the long, straight sword from its sheath on Klootz's saddle. The two Mantan brothers ranged up, one on each side, their slender war axes across their saddlebows. The front of the enemy appeared, Leemutes and humans completely intermingled.

Hiero raised his sword high in his gauntleted right hand, then drove it down, and they were off. *Come on, big boy*, he sent. *This is what it's all about!* Beside the three leading morses, the light pads of the cat people spurned the sedges.

Hiero's fist clenched inside the basket hilt of the cavalry saber as he held it straight forward like a spear. As Klootz gathered speed, his rider could hear the rising splash and thunder of the charging lines behind. He stole a glance to either side. *Good!* They had learned the orders!

The left wing, the northern line of the morse riders, was swinging slowly past him, never breaking ranks. The right wing was holding back, so that the line was beginning to show an arc. The left would strike first and then roll the enemy up, cutting them off at the edge of the swamp and driving them into the open, away from any cover.

Now there was no time to think at all, and he concentrated on what lay in front. The days and weeks of planning were over, and he was a killing machine and nothing more. Klootz bellowed with battle rage, and his kin answered from behind, a rolling, swelling roar which rumbled from one end of the line to the other.

The Unclean halted, milling in confusion. The Man-rats and the Plague Hounds, those that were left, had made little of the swamp, which hardly slowed them at all. But the men, though disciplined and deadly fighters on solid ground, were floundering, tripping over tussocks and slipping in the pools and mud. A great number of the Howlers were dismounted, and they liked this bog no better than their human allies. As the line of antlered heads and the glitter of the lance points and armor rose before them, many turned to flee. Others, of sterner stuff or with better officers, tried to form a line or at least a shield wall. The result was confusion! Order, counterorder—disorder!

From far left to far right, the terrible cavalry of the North charged home!

Hiero's sword point split the face of a giant Howler, and he withdrew it as Klootz lunged on. Every lance, seemingly, skewered one of the enemy, front or back, and then, butt lifted high, was withdrawn and leveled once more, seeking fresh prey.

It made no difference whether the Unclean fled or tried to stand. If the riders missed, their mighty steeds did the work, slashing and trampling, pounding the enemy underfoot with their giant hooves, seizing them in their teeth and shaking them off like bits of tattered bark until they fell away, mangled and lifeless.

A monstrous Hound, jaws agape, sprang at Hiero's bridle hand. Without thinking, he dropped the reins and raised the unbreakable shield, the gift of his strangest friend, to dash the brute aside. A long-handled hatchet swept past his side, and Reyn Mantan's blow split the creature's skull.

The impetus of the charge was slowing, but not very much. As all the riders angled to the right, never stopping or allowing the Unclean to form and make a stand, the edge of the deep woods loomed up in front. It was hard fighting now, for the compressed masses of the broken foe were trying desperately to reach that shelter. Enemy crossbowmen and javelin throwers, human and otherwise, shot and hurled their missiles from the trees in a last effort to hold the mounted men back from their quarry. Saddles were being emptied, but the mutated giant moose were no scared beasts when bereft of their riders! They fought on with empty saddles, keeping the lines intact, as they had been taught. If one of the gallant animals fell, the others, with men in the saddle or not, closed the line and kept on to the attack. The extreme left took the heaviest losses, but narrowed in without letup, herding the squalling Leemutes and their fragmented masters out and away from the refuge of the trees.

Hiero was unscathed so far, but his right arm was growing very tired. The beloved creature who bore him bled from a dozen light wounds, of which Klootz took no note at all. His eyes were red with blood lust and he felt no pain. Reyn Mantan and M'reen, her long knife bloody, watched Hiero's left while the two male cats and Geor Mantan protected his right. The Mantans had produced light oval shields of laminated bark from some pack or other and deftly deflected the missiles of any sort which menaced their leader.

Hiero never noticed, intent only on coldly killing anything that stood before him. He struck and stabbed, hacked and slew, with no compunction at all. Here was the enemy at last, where he could be reached! Here was revenge for the empty months, the loss of his mate, the treachery, and the pain! Death to them! Kill them all in their vileness, until the decent earth was empty of them forever!

It took a strong hand on his bridle to check his pace and a strong voice to penetrate the madness of battle. His lifted sword dropped, and he finally realized that a friend was trying to get his attention. Breathing in great gulps, he saw that Klootz had stopped and was trembling with the aftershock of the mélée. Hiero managed to break the fog in his brain and rest, though it was an awful wrench.

"Stop fighting, General! Look, we've beaten them. Maybe a quarter got into the woods, no more than that, sir. Look at what is happening now!"

Almost against his will, the Metz turned his head. It was Colonel Lejus who had reined him up. Hiero stared at where the man was pointing, half in disbelief.

The Unclean, beaten back and decimated on the waters of the Lake of Weeping, had been rallied, once they were back on shore and behind the screen of the forest. They were still a hideous and mighty host, and their leaders had turned them into the apparently empty marsh on their right. Here they were supposed to sweep around the defenses of the Republic, turn the long arm of the lake, and strike in the rear of their hated foe.

What had happened was just a little bit different. The wise old Abbot-General and Hiero himself had led the Unclean to conceive of this maneuver, and were waiting with the only cavalry in all the world's history that could fight in a swamp even better than on dry land! The result lay before Hiero's sight and was hard to take in, even though he had helped plan it.

Cut off from their rallying places in the woods, harried and shocked by the lances of the morse riders, what remained of the Unclean who had assaulted the marsh was being driven in a grim battle toward the waters of the lake. Stumbling, lurching, and screaming as it was ridden down, the ragged and broken crowd was herded toward the waters. The lines of morse and men had no gaps. The Republic had lost perhaps an eighth of its mounted force, but what remained was more than sufficient. A thin line guarded their backs, but no fresh eruption came from the silent trees to the east.

Out on the waters lay the final death. Silent and watchful, the five steamships waited. Extending their line out of sight, the arrow barges also waited. The late noon sun beat down from overhead on total destruction. Horns blew, and the Metz mounted troops halted and dressed ranks, tightening their formations. They now were a shallow half-moon; within its crescent, the Unclean, a shrieking mob of foul men and foul brutes, were driven inexorably to the place where the shifting foothold of the marsh became no foothold at all.

His lids half-lowered against the glare, Hiero watched, well content. The orders were "No Quarter." What the enemy would have done in its place was well known. This at least was a clean death. For long years, the attempt of normal and reviving humanity, who wished only to live in peace and happiness, had been frustrated and constricted by these creatures who had been spawned by the Ultimate Dark. This was their reward. They had embraced the Darkness, and that to which they had given their souls was now upon them. Under the high, golden glow of the sun, let them perish. Forever!

The horns of the mounted men of the Republic sounded the charge for the last time. Lances in place, the crescent went in for the kill. It was slaughter. Pierced and ground underfoot in the marsh, the Unclean died if they took to the water. Should any manage to escape by diving under the line of waiting ships, a second and even more alert line of smaller craft waited for them. There were no survivors. Nor were there meant to be any.

Hiero had turned away when the end became inevitable. He looked now both around him and also at the line of morse riders who watched their backs and fronted the green wall of the forest.

He remembered to return his long sword to the saddle sheath. Both of his colonels were now beside him and looking at him in a way he found disconcerting. *Why should they look at me this way? These men both taught me!* At his stirrup, M'reen tied a piece of rag around the forearm of Za'reekh, while Ch'uirsh tried to scrape mud off his pelt. They looked at him the same way. The brothers Mantan, apparently unharmed, sat their mounts in their usual stolid fashion at the rear, but their eyes were also aglow!

I did nothing, he told himself. *A little planning, but it was mostly Kulase Demero. Maybe I helped a little. But I didn't earn this adulation!* He fell back on prayer, looking off into the distance.

Father, preserve the least of Thy servants from the dreadful sin of pride! Besides, he added in a lower key, *I really don't deserve it!*

God, or someone deputizing, brought a most welcome interruption. A mud-spattered morse rider pulled up beside them and handed a dispatch to Saclare. He wasted no time in tearing it apart.

"Hah! What is left of those scum is fighting for its life in the forest. They are being driven—driven, mark you—back on our lines! Your plans, sir, are working beyond all belief. I congratulate you. Who else would have had troops that no one knew about waiting to pounce, once they were beaten back? Do you realize, General, we have won *everywhere*?" His native emotion took over. "By the blood of Christ, Hiero, there are none of them left. We have blotted them out!" He withdrew at once, conscious of a gaffe. "Your pardon, General. I forgot myself in the excitement."

"Troops that no one knew about," Hiero said in low tones, almost to himself. "We met the main attack here, but what of the lower lake and the eastern rivers down to Namcush? What of them, Colonel?"

"I have dispatches, sir." This was a young man, one of Saclare's mounted aides. Hiero noted that the boy had one arm in a sling. He had been to the wars.

"Let's hear it, lad." The Metz hated to see that glow in the boy's eyes. How many had died for the cause this morning?

"Sir, the lower crossings were hurled back completely. Our ships and the Dam People stopped every attempt to pass. We had one big warship there. It was enough. The Dam People killed the rest. The enemy sent no more than a light wing in that direction."

"So none crossed. Good news." Hiero was physically exhausted, but the second task was unfinished. The Unclean mind shields ought to have been either taken or dispersed. Then where was *S'duna*?

He brought himself back to what the young officer had said. The Dam People! How many of Charoo's young males and females had died? The lower lake and the upper reaches of the outflow rivers had cost lives. Which kittens would not see their father or mother come back to the lodge? He wept inwardly, then swept the feeling aside.

Something else, something more important, had been told to him! "Troops no one knew about." Least of all himself! But he could guess.

"Colonels! Parade the troops!" His voice blared, and he could see the faces wince as he yelled. He tried to become calmer. "Great new allies are coming from the north. I want them received with all courtesy, all honors. The Unclean scum are driven into the water. I want *all* the troops available in line to receive our guests."

Funny, the Unclean mind shields were gone, totally gone. He would have thought S'duna would have guarded himself.

No, there was nothing of the kind. It was nice to know Gorm was coming, though. Even nicer to feel that emptiness in the rear!

The Metz lances, many still bloody, dipped in salute as three figures came out of the forest and advanced in Hiero's direction. M'reen knelt, her furry arms outthrust, and her two males followed suit. The Children of the Wind had never done this for Hiero, but he didn't blame them.

Gorm was barely visible behind the other two presences. Huge and ambling, the two emissaries of the bear people who led were larger even than ancient Kodiak or Kamchatkan brown bears. Only the high foreheads and the longer, more egg-shaped skulls behind the small, furry ears might have set them apart. Their ambling, rolling gait carried them through the muck of the swamp at an amazing pace.

The leader—there was no mistaking his importance—reared up on his hind legs at Klootz's side. Absently, Hiero noted that the morse showed not the slightest sign of disturbance at the titanic proximity. A rank scent came from his silver fur. *I have no name*, the huge creature sent. *At least until I see more of you men-things. The men you call the Eleventh Brothers brought us to war, those creatures of peace. What is peace? Being let alone. Yet we came to fight, and I think not mistakenly.*

His fellow Brobdingnagian had simply lain down in a wallow and was rolling. Hiero carefully avoided looking at the smallest of the trio. The Metz cavalry still stood at salute, lances raised.

I gather, the ponderous but powerful mind which lowered down at him went on, *that these mentalities are standing thus to do us honor? Such is not necessary. You are the one who took our little cousin to the South. We are in your debt. Your march coincides with that of the Great Dens. What we can bring to the mutual contest, that we shall. Produce the gift, little one.*

Gorm moved forward. Around his neck and slung over his back had been a sack of some bark derivative. Now he spilled out the contents.

The two shining skins, the two bald pates, the two hating faces, rolled through the surface of the wet grass to Klootz's feet. One was unknown, but the other could never be forgotten.

Obviously torn roughly from the torso, S'duna's head lay before Hiero, the lips drawn back in the agony of death.

The leader of the bear people was still sending. *We thought such vermin should be removed from the world. And we owed you a debt. These are the leaders you sought, Red and Blue. Their Circles are both destroyed. We think you had much to do with that, and our young and unlicked cub agrees. Someday he may attain wisdom. That is up to him and to you.* The enormous head swiveled down to stare at him again. *You are flighty by our standards. Never mind. You may be the first of your kind to find enlightenment.*

When Hiero could concentrate next, the two great bodies were vanishing into the woods. He looked down, and Gorm was still there.

They said I could stay, the young bear sent. *This is not over. Hiero, where is Luchare?*

The unexpected question cut through all Hiero's fatigue, crumbling the barriers he had forced himself to erect. His brain seemed to gather itself, then to launch a single, explosive thought.

Luchare!

EPILOGUE

UNDER HER, LUCHARE FELT THE EXHAUSTED HOPPER STUM-
ble and come to a halt, unable to continue. For a moment,
she sat there numbly, before forcing herself to dismount. Her
legs were shaking with fatigue, and she had to lean against the
heaving sides of the beast for support. Vaguely, she was aware
that one of the three men of her guard was offering help. She
shook him off and stood there, trying to gather her energy to
survey her surroundings.

Three men—only three now! How long had it been since the
count took the others and turned back to protect her rear? Time
was a jumble of confusion in her head. How long since they had
turned into the forest, trying to lose themselves in its vastness?
And to what end? What had all the weeks of endless flight gained
them?

She forced her mind back to the present and looked about.
Before her, the little trail they had been following came to an end,
and the colossal trees of the forest gave way to a moss-floored
clearing. The day must be ending, with the sun already far down
in the west; but after the dimness under the great trees, the light
from the open sky seemed glaringly bright. She stared about her,
suddenly conscious of a curious sense of familiarity. It was as if
she had been here before in some other, far happier life.

She saw that the weary men were trying to make camp for the
night, gathering moss for their beds and wood to build a fire.
Supper, she knew, would be what remained of yesterday's kill.
One man was working with flint and steel to kindle a small mound
of twigs. Under him, the ground was blackened with evidence
of some previous campfire. Again, familiarity tugged at her mind.

As she stood there, a feeling of something wrong grew in
her. Then she realized that the forest had become strangely
silent. Even the cries and chattering of the birds were stilled.
She strained her ears to listen and her senses to reach out . . .

Luchare!

Faintly, at the very edge of her awareness, the call came through to her, demanding the answer that welled up in her mind. Then it was gone.

Night had fallen hours before, but torchlight showed a bustle of activity around the dock where the warship lay. Inside the captain's cabin, a single candle revealed two white-bearded men sitting at a small table. They looked up as the door opened to admit a younger man.

"They said I'd find you here, Father Abbot," Hiero began. Then he stopped, and a surprised smile crossed his face as Brother Aldo rose to greet him.

"I've been hearing about your winning the battle," the Elevener said. "Too bad I was just too late to witness it. Hiero, you look as if you need a week of sleep!"

"Later. I don't have time now," Hiero told him.

Demero indicated a third chair. "Sit down, my boy. Aldo has returned with news from the South—terrible news, but I swore you should have the truth. D'alwah City is lost, the army has been totally beaten. Luchare and the king fled, nobody knows where. And no one knows whether she lives..."

"She's alive," Hiero stated. "And I'm pretty sure I know where."

"She is near enough for you to contact?" Aldo's voice was filled with doubt.

Hiero shook his head slowly. "No, she's impossibly far away. Yet for one instant, I *know* I made contact with her mind. That's why I've come here to find you, Father Demero— to ask your permission to leave and go south to find her. Klootz, Gorm, and the cat people will come with me. And a few others have volunteered. They also ask permission."

"How far south will you go?" Aldo asked, before Demero had a chance to reply. "After you find your Luchare—if you do, as I pray you will—are you willing to go on to where only a man of your proven ability to defy the Unclean can go? Will you go far south of D'alwah into the reeking jungles where Amibale's accursed witch of a mother took that young traitor and Unclean ally to learn his evil? Because it is there, from the slender bits of evidence we have, that my Brotherhood and I believe the evil source of the Unclean may lie."

Hiero considered, remembering that Solitaire had also warned of a great and evil mind far to the south. But there was only one possible decision. "If I have permission, I will go."

"Very well." Abbot Demero stood up, as if the meeting were ended. "You shall have permission—but only after I see you tucked firmly in bed and about to get the sleep you need."

"There isn't time!" Hiero protested. "The trip around the Inland Sea may take too long, even if we have nothing but good luck—which seems improbable. We should leave at once."

Aldo began chuckling, and the abbot was smiling as he laid one arm around Hiero's shoulder.

"My boy," Demero asked, "did you really think I wouldn't know what was going on when you went around making preparations? Or did you think it an idle whim of mine to refuel this ship and load it with supplies for you?" He snorted with mock indignation. "Hiero, ships can be used for better purposes than destruction. Now give me the names of your volunteers, in case I missed one. Then we'll put you to bed in a cabin here. When you awake, you and your band will already be well on the way to your princess."

The princess was lying on a bed of moss, far to the southeast, but she was not asleep. There was too much on her mind.

Hiero was alive and well and free! All the doubts that had come to haunt her were gone, erased by the certainty of her brief contact with his mind. He would come for her. And she would be here, waiting for him.

She let her eyes rove about the clearing, now lighted by the nearly full moon above. She knew it now—this place where they had all camped on the long road south, just before they met the strange women who lived in these giant trees. She listened to the silence of the forest, remembering that the same silence had first heralded the coming of Vilah-ree and the others. They would remember her and provide a haven of safety for her and for the three men—most certainly for the men!—in their tree nests.

She turned on her side, smiling. And finally, she slept.

GLOSSARY

Abbeys, the: Theocratic structure of the Kandan Confederacy, comprising the Metz Republic in the west and the Otwah League in the east. Each Abbey has a military-political infrastructure, and the Abbey Council functions much as the House of Lords in eighteenth-century England, with all science and religion also as its prerogatives.

Batwah: Trade *Lingua franca*; an artificial language used throughout the areas bordering the Inland Sea, and well beyond in some places.

Buffer: Giant bovines, probably mutated bison, which migrate in vast herds through the western Kandan regions on an annual basis.

Chespek: Small kingdom on the Lantik Sea, often allied to D'alwah and equally often at war with its immediate neighbor.

Children of the Night Wind: An intelligent, bipedal species of mutated, man-sized feline; runners of unbelievable speed. Bred by the Unclean for warfare, they managed to escape their masters and establish themselves in a far country. Proud and volatile, they are in *no* sense Leemutes.

Circles: Administrative areas, named by color, of the Unclean and its Masters of the Dark Brotherhood. Hiero passed through three, the Red, Blue, and Yellow, as he went south and east. Until his journey, their existence was unknown.

D'alwah: Largest and most developed of the east coast states on the Lantik Sea. A kingdom, organized as a benevolent despotism, but where commoners have few rights. A debased branch of the Universal Church exists.

Dam People: Aquatic rodents of human intelligence and more than human bulk, who live on artificial lakes in the Metz Republic, under terms of mutual toleration; probably mutated beaver.

Dark Brotherhood: Their own name for the Masters of the Unclean. The fact that they use the word "dark" indicates that they sought universal conquest and, more important, gloried in it and realized that they were, in fact, basically evil. Modern Satanism, in its real sense, is a parallel. (See Circles; Unclean.)

Davids: Similar to the Mu'amans in that they follow a quite different monotheism from that taught by the church and one which they claim to be far older. Found in D'alwah, Chespek, and perhaps elsewhere, they occupy positions in all levels of society. (See Mu'amans.)

Death, The: The atomic and biologic blight which destroyed the major population centers and most of humanity some thousand years in the past. Still a name of dread and ultimate menace in Hiero's day. "All evil came with The Death" is a proverb.

Deserts of The Death: Patches of ancient atomic blight where there is little or no water and scant or no vegetation. Yet life exists in these horrible places, though most of it is inimical and strange, bred from hard radiation and a ferocious struggle to survive. Some of the Deserts are hundreds of square miles in size and, in Hiero's day, are avoided like The Death itself. They are rare in Kanda, but many exist in the South. Blue, radioactive glows mark the worst of them at night.

Eleveners: The Brotherhood of the Eleventh Commandment. ("Thou shalt not destroy the Earth nor the life thereon.") A group of social scientists who banded together after The Death to preserve human culture, love for all life, and knowledge thereof. This group permeates all human societal life and, though opposing violence, battles the Unclean, often in hidden ways.

Forty Symbols: The tiny wooden signs that a trained priest-exorcist carries on his person. By putting himself (or herself; there are priestesses of great power) in a trance state, the priest can forelook, or to some extent see the future, using the symbols.

Frontier Guards: The army or embodied forces of the Metz Republic. The Otwah League has a similar group. There are sixteen legions, self-contained units, in the Metz Republic. They are under, *not* the Republic's orders, but those of the Abbey Council, which, in turn, reports to the Lower House (Assembly) on its decisions, which are always approved. Priests usually lead and direct the Frontier Guards.

Glith: A recent form of Leemute, possibly bred from a reptile by the Unclean. A humanoid, scaled and very strong physically, utterly the slave of the Dark Masters.

Grokon: Giant descendants of our present-day hogs, which roam the northern forests. They are much-sought-for as meat but are very dangerous to hunt, being clever and the size of extant oxen when adult.

Hairy Howlers: One of the commonest and most dangerous varieties of Leemute. They are great, fur-covered, tailless primates, highly intelligent and used as soldiery by the Unclean. They hate all humans, save their Dark Masters. They resemble huge, upright baboons as much as anything.

Death Hart: A monster found, though rarely, in the southern Deserts of The Death. The ancestry of this foul mutation is unknown, but it is carnivorous and bears both claws and horns.

Hoppers: Giant marsupials, closely resembling the kangaroo of the present, save for greater size. They were no doubt bred from mutated survivors of The Death. They are the riding animals of D'alwah and adjacent areas.

Inland Sea, the: The great freshwater sea formed by the ancient merger of the Great Lakes and covering roughly an area of all their present outermost boundaries. Many islands exist, and much of the Inland Sea is uncharted. Ruins of ancient cities dot the shores, and much commerce, interrupted by piracy, moves on the waters.

Kanda: The area of the ancient Dominion of Canada has kept its old name, almost unchanged, though much of it is unknown in Hiero's day, save for the central parts of the Metz Republic and the Otwah League, in west and east, respectively.

Kandan Universal Church: The state religion of the Metz Republic and the Otwah League. An amalgam of most current Christian beliefs, with a strong core of traditional Roman Catholicism, though there has been no contact with Rome for millennia. Celibacy is long gone, as are many other beliefs and attitudes held by the ancient churches. A related sect, though much corrupted and debased, is the state religion of the east coast kingdoms and states, such as D'alwah.

Kaw: A beast of burden used south of the Inland Sea, both for agriculture and raising, as is the Korean ox of today. A large bovine, probably an almost unaltered member of some ancient stock of domestic cattle.

Killman: A highly trained warrior of the Metz Republic, who has taken intensive training, much of it psychological, in warfare and the use of all known weapons. Killmen are officers of the Frontier Guards automatically, but also rangers of the forest and special agents of the Abbey hierarchy. Hiero is unusual, though not exceptional, in also being a priest and exorcist. This combination of talents is highly approved but rare.

Lantik Sea, the: The Atlantic Ocean, though with a much-altered western shoreline. No records exist of any trans-Atlantic contacts for over three thousand years.

Leemute: A word meaning an animal, or other nonhuman creature of human intelligence, which serves the Unclean. Gorm, the bear, would never be described as a Leemute, nor would the Dam People. The word is a corruption of the phrase "lethal mutation," meaning an animal which cannot survive to replicate under natural conditions, but its meaning is now altered to mean "inimical to normal humanity," and even normal life of all kinds. New varieties (such as the frog creatures Hiero found) are continually appearing as discoveries spread. Not all such new finds are Leemutes, however.

Lowan: A species of incredibly large, flightless water birds, fish eaters and divers, which are found in remote areas of the Inland Sea. Though very shy, Lowan have few enemies, since an adult can reach eighty feet in length, with weight in proportion. They are uncommon, and thought by many to be a legend.

Lucinoge: An Abbey drug, used to enhance the spiritual powers of its adepts and priests, especially when they are seeking mind contact. Also a relaxant and, in small amounts, sleep-inducing.

Manoon (the Dead Isle): A rocky island in the north-central Inland Sea, the place of Hiero's captivity. One of the main headquarters of the Dark Brotherhood's Blue Circle.

Man-rats: Giant, man-sized rodents of high intelligence, a ferocious type of Leemute, much used as warriors by the Unclean. Probably mutated *Rattus norvegicus*, which they resemble in all but brains and bulk.

Metz: The dominant race of Kanda. A corruption of the ancient word *Metis*, a term used for a racial stock of mixed Caucasian and Amerindian strains. The Spanish word *mestizo* has the same root and means the same thing. The Metz survived The Death in an undue proportion to other races, mainly due to rural isolation and the fact that they existed in small, somewhat isolated groups, in more remote areas. Atomic and bacteriological blights thus slew relatively few. The Otwah League Metz tend to be lighter in color, due to more Caucasian genes.

Morse: The basic riding and plow animal (though only scrub stock is used for the latter) of the Metz Republic, which first bred them, and, to a lesser degree, of the Otwah League. A very large and intelligent variety of the present-day moose, the largest member of the deer family. (Moose have been tamed for riding and carriage pulling in modern Scandinavia, though not often.)

Mu'amans: Non-Christian, non-church-linked followers of a separate form of monotheism. Apparently confined to the kingdom of D'alwah; in the main, stockbreeders, who live on the western plains of the kingdom. (See Davids.)

Namcush: Port on the western border of the Inland Sea. Much trade passes through it, but it is full of rogues as well, slavers and pirates seeking a place to dispose of loot. Both the Abbeys and the Unclean use it to spy on one another.

Neeyana: The largest port in the southeastern area of the Inland Sea. Though legitimate trade passes through it, the Unclean actually rule, through a merchants' council dominated by their appointees. In fact, the main headquarters of the Yellow Circle of the Dark Brotherhood is buried *under* the town. No one untouched by evil lingers in Neeyana. (Possibly a corruption of "Indiana.")

Otwah League: The eastern sister state of the Metz Republic. The League, which takes its name from ancient Ottawa, is smaller than the Republic, from which it is separated by a vast expanse of wild land and Taig, through which run few roads. But close contact is maintained as well as possible, and the Abbeys are a unified structure in both, serving the League government in the same capacity as in the Republic.

Palood, the: Greatest of all the northern marshes, the Palood stretches for hundreds of miles along the northern edge of the Inland Sea. It is avoided even by the Unclean, and many strange forms of life not found elsewhere exist in its trackless vastnesses. Terrible fevers often wrack those who venture in, and its boundaries are largely uncharted.

Per: Corruption of "Father." Title of respect for a priest of the Kandan Universal Church.

Poros: Monstrous, four-tusked herbivore of the great southern forest, perhaps twenty feet tall at the shoulder. Its ancestry is unknown.

Snakeheads: Giant, omnivorous reptiles, found in small herds in the depths of the southern forests. Primarily eaters of soft herbage and fruit, they will also devour carrion and anything else slow enough to be caught. Something very like a bipedal dinosaur, though bred from some smaller reptile of the pre-Death days.

Snapper: Seemingly the living snapping turtle, grown to the size of a small car. A universal pest of any large body of water, being ferocious and almost invulnerable.

Taig, the: The great coniferous forest of Kanda, not too unlike that of today, but containing many more deciduous trees and even a few palms. The trees run larger on the average than those of today, though nowhere near the size of those in the far South.

Unclean, the: A general term meaning the Dark Brotherhood and all its servants and allies, as well as other life which seeks, through intelligent direction, to destroy normal humanity and to subvert natural law for evil purposes.

Were-bears: A little-known variety of Leemute. Not truly a bear at all, but a sort of grisly, night-prowling monster, short-furred and possessed of strange mental powers by which it lures victims to their doom. The things have been glimpsed only once or twice. Though of the Unclean, they seem to be allies rather than servants. Their origin is unknown. Fortunately, they seem rare.

ABOUT THE AUTHOR

Sterling E. Lanier, born in 1927, graduated from Harvard in 1951. When he was an editor at Chilton in the '60s he published Frank Herbert's *Dune*, which went on to become one of the greatest sf bestsellers of all time. Lanier was trained as an anthropologist-archeologist. He is also a well-known sculptor whose work is on exhibit in several museums, including the Smithsonian. He lives in Maryland.